THE RECLUSE HEIR

A DARK ROMANIAN MAFIA ROMANCE

MONIQUE MOREAU

MEET MONIQUE!

Join Monique's Newsletter (and receive goodies and release information)
https://bit.ly/SteamyReadNewsletter

Join Monique's FB reader's group
Possessive Alpha Reads

Like her Facebook Page
https://bit.ly/MoniqueMoreaufb

Follow her on Instagram
https://bit.ly/MoniqueMoreauIG

Follow her on Book Bub
http://bit.ly/MoniqueBookBub

Learn all about Monique's books
MoniqueMoreau.com

AUTHOR'S NOTE

A quick note about the Romanian mafia, or *mafie*. After doing quite a bit of research on the subject, I can honestly say that there isn't a plethora of information. I've let my imagination run wild and taken liberties by inventing rules and societal norms I have not found any proof of in the real world, in either Romanian culture or Romanian *mafie* culture. For example, Romanians do not have clans, they have families, but I have created them for the purposes of this *mafie* world.

I've also given certain Romanian words special meaning within this unique world. I've introduced the Lupu clan, the main Romanian *mafie* family, whose center of power is in "Little Bucharest," a name I've coined for the Romanian community in Sunnyside, Queens, New York City.

The surname Lupu does in fact mean "the wolf" in Romanian, but I created the Lupu tat, a wolf baring its teeth, that is required of all members of the Lupu *mafie* clan.

And with that, I'll leave you to enjoy Luca and Cat's story!

Monique

PROLOGUE

*V*irginity is power, *dragă mea. One of our great powers as women. Do not be careless with it.*

My mother's words rang in my head while I sat through the droning lecture in my senior history class, causing heat to crawl up my nape. The sounds of clacking on keyboards and riffling through books sifted through the classroom. I tore a few sheets of paper from my notebook and used them to fan myself.

"Ms. Popescu?"

My head snapped up; my gaze fixed on my history teacher, who'd approached my desk without me noticing. His frowning visage pinned me to the back of my seat.

Clearing my throat, I stammered, "Y-yes, Mr. Holland."

"And exactly how did the Reagan administration's massive military spending program, the largest in US history, impact the Soviet economy, pray tell, Ms. Popescu?"

Shoot. This is what happened when my mind wandered. What was once a rare occurrence happened much too often lately. Of course, it would come as no surprise to anyone who knew what my life was really like.

Although I'd worked my butt off to graduate at the top of my class in this exclusive boarding school, none of it mattered because I wasn't going on to college like every other kid in my school.

No, instead, I was getting married to a man I barely knew.

Nicu. The youngest, and most vicious, son of the Lupu clan. Ugh.

My mother already sent me a pic of my engagement ring, along with posting it on her social media. Yes, so help me God, my mother was on Insta.

The ring was truly atrocious. Huge. Sparkly. *Tacky.* My family had a rep for not being classy. *His* family was known for their refinement, so there could only be one reason for picking the ring he did. To taunt me. To show the world that the Lupu clan was powerful and rich *and* to flaunt the fact that they now owned me. Me and my virginity. We were nothing more than expensive possessions, like that horrid ring.

"I'm waiting, Ms. Popesc*u*," Mr. Holland said, dragging out the *ou* sound of my last name as if it were an ugly thing. The classroom was so quiet that I could hear the branches of the tree outside scratching against the windowpane as it swayed in the wind.

"I'm sorry, Mr. Holland. I got distracted and didn't…"

My eyes darted to my side. My best friend, Jewel, shot her hand up. Yet again, trying to save me, but Mr. Holland wasn't having any of it.

"Ms. Popescu, Reagan's massive spending program was one of the pivotal factors that led to the final downfall of the Soviet Union. *That* is the answer, and it behooves you to pay closer attention in this class if you wish to continue your sparkling educational career. More importantly, to become an educated citizen of the world, because that is the real goal behind an education at Roman Academy."

"Yes, Mr. Holland. I'll try to do better," I muttered, heat creeping up my neck and flushing my face.

"I should hope you do more than *try*, Ms. Popesc*u*," he replied tersely.

"Yes, sir," I whispered, slouching down in my seat, eyes glued to my desk.

He was right, of course. Mr. Holland wasn't being rude on purpose. He believed in the worthiness of history and the importance of a stellar education. Normally, I agreed with him. Being called out in front of the class was so humiliating precisely because I was one of his favorites. I was a model student. A teacher's pet. It came from my heart, not from the pressure to please my parents, like so many students here. My parents couldn't care less. My father hadn't even completed high school. He was running the streets of Bucharest by the time he was in his teens, hustling to feed his mother and siblings, selling drugs or anything he could get his hands on. These were the suppertime stories I grew up listening to, not about fraternity hazing rituals at an Ivy League college.

I did well academically because being the best was the only kind of positive feedback I got, and negative attention wasn't an option for a *mafie* girl like me. While some of my classmates rebelled, I came from a world where you didn't bring unwanted notice to you or your family. Yet, despite my love for school, the impending doom of my wedding had blunted my drive to learn.

Bending my head down and pretending to focus on whatever was on the screen of my laptop, I let out a weary sigh. The only silver lining of going back to New York City after I graduated was that Jewel had gotten accepted to

Barnard College, the women's college, so she'd be in the city as well.

It would be painful to watch her go off to classes while I rotted away in a lonely apartment with my new husband, but, at least, we'd be in the same city. Besides living vicariously through her, I harbored a secret hope that once I settled into the marriage with Nicu, I could convince him to let me take a couple of classes with Jewel.

My eyes darted briefly to Jewel. She caught my look, her expression softening with pity. The Popescu pride should have burned at the sympathy on her face, but it didn't even penetrate the cloud of sadness enveloping me. She knew how determined I had once been to be the perfect student and how now I was...lost. What was the point of it all now that I wouldn't join the rest of my graduating class off to college next year? Of course, I always knew I was destined to marry a *mafie* made man, but I hadn't expected to be thrust into an engagement quite this soon.

Despite the guilt of being away from my family, I should be grateful for this opportunity, this slice of heaven that I was afforded. No other *mafie* girl got a chance like this. They stayed at home, to ensure they were virgins when they got engaged after graduation. It took witnessing my father, the head of my clan no less, killing a man in front of me at the ripe old age of twelve for that to happen.

A shudder racked through me as the memory flittered into my mind. I'd been on my way to the kitchen in the middle of the night to grab a glass of water when I'd heard strange sounds and bumps beneath me. Half asleep and confused, I'd crept down the steps to the basement.

Glancing around a corner, I had arrived just in time for the main attraction. Frozen in place, I'd watched as he choked the life out of a man, his face in a twisted grimace of pleasure and pain.

Hearing my sharp inhalation, his head had whipped toward me. With a curse, he'd snapped at me sharply to *go back upstairs.* My heart stuttered at the murder in his eyes.

Taking advantage of my father's distraction, the man tore out of his grip and lunged toward me. I shrieked as I dodged his clawing fingers. In a flash, my father tackled him to the ground. Knee on his victim's chest, my father choked him. Gasping and gurgling, his eyes bulged open, and his face turned an unnatural shade of red.

Tearing my gaze away, I spun around and bolted up the stairs. Diving under the covers, I huddled in my bed in a fetal position. Much later, he came to my room and apologized. "None of that was meant for your eyes, and I promise it won't happen again," he said in the same heavy accent that was usually a source of comfort to me.

I'd been too freaked out to say much of anything, but I couldn't help the full-body shudder that racked my body. My tongue lay thick in my mouth, unable to move. *No biggie, Dad. I now know, without a shadow of a doubt, that you're a cold-blooded killer.* Of course, I had known what my father and brother did for a living but had been spared the violent reality up to that point. I had worshipped my dad. Scratch that; I had worshipped them both. Still did.

That night, I hadn't slept. The following night, I'd fallen into an exhausted stupor, but with it came the nightmares.

Nightmares where I shrieked so loudly that I'd wake up the entire house. My mother was upset, my father worried. It had caused a rift with my mother; she blamed me for allowing this to happen. Only months of endless nightmares and my father's persuasion convinced her to forgive me. Soon after, my father decided that a change of scenery was the best solution, and I had been sent to boarding school.

It was only supposed to be for a year, but then I met Jewel, a New Yorker like me, and one year turned into two. Now six years later, I was in the last semester of my senior year.

The bell rang.

"That's all for today," Mr. Holland said with a dismissive wave of his hand. The class broke into movement as students slapped their notebooks or laptops shut and gathered their stuff. In the midst of all the noise, I slowly turned to Jewel.

"It's okay, Cat. It's okay," she said in a soothing tone, patting my forearm in reassurance.

I was the good girl. The good student. Sure, I had a mouth on me, but I strove to be number one in everything I did. Who knew where it came from, this overachieving gene? Cristo certainly hadn't inherited it. Whereas his entire life revolved around our *mafie* family, I didn't want to limit myself to being a wife and mother. I may have known better than to yearn for a career, but I dreamed of continuing my education. At the very least, I wanted to make it through college.

"Come on," she coaxed, as she helped me collect my things. "You'll be late for your next class."

My shoulders drooped. "What does it matter, Jewel? Seriously, with my current GPA, I could flunk out of every one of my classes and still graduate. It's not like it matters what my GPA is anyway. I'm not moving on up," I replied as I dragged myself to my feet.

"Hush now, stop that. It matters a whole lot because you're one of the smartest people here, and you busted your butt to become valedictorian. Don't let what's going to happen in the future get to you," she said guardedly, not wanting to mention my engagement out loud. "Don't let anyone undermine the work you've put in these past four years, Cat. You can still graduate valedictorian. You know you'll regret it if you don't."

With a pained groan, I meekly followed her out into the hallway. She was right. I may not be able to get the image of that engagement ring out of my head, but I had long ago set a goal for myself to be the best. To graduate and give that stupid speech that only valedictorians give. No one besides Jewel and my guidance counselor knew I wasn't going on to college. My best friend told everyone that we were going to attend Barnard College together.

The valedictorian graduation speech was my last hurrah before I went under lockdown as a trophy wife-slash-arm candy-slash-breeding heifer. I had no choice in my future. There was no way I'd disappoint my mother, bring shame down on the family name, and turn my back on my community. Not only would it be a tragedy to give up after working so hard but focusing on academics had saved me once before. I had to believe that it would do the trick again.

God, please let me be right.

1

Cristo opened the front door and swept his hand out for me to enter my childhood home. Stepping inside, I inhaled the scent of polished wood and too many carpets. I tapped my black graduation cap with its little golden tassel against my thigh as I glanced up at the stairs. Childhood memories flooded me of waiting for my father to return late at night. I would leave my bedroom door open, and the instant I heard the front lock unbolt, I'd rush out of my room and skip down the stairs to stand at the bottom so the first thing he saw when he stepped across the threshold was my face.

Cristo ruffled my hair as he passed me. Shaking off my memories, I followed him with my eyes as he hauled my luggage upstairs.

"Do you need help?" I called out, even though I knew he would dismiss my offer. He was old school like that.

Cristo waved me away, so I slipped off my shoes and took a right from the foyer into the living room. My gaze coasted over the heavy, dark wood furniture, the intricately designed rugs covering the floor, and the traditional red-and-white embroidery scattered around, from the runner on the coffee table to several of the pillows piled high on the couch and armchairs. The warm late-spring air breezed through the open windows. The only thing missing from making the place an exact replica of a traditional Romanian home was a stove fireplace decorated in ceramic tiles.

I spied the little shrine in the far corner of the Eastern wall of the house, holding an Orthodox icon, which I knew was Saint Parascheva, grandmother's favorite. The votive candle, which she lit every morning, illuminated the gold leaf of the small wooden painting. A surge of nostalgia welled up inside me. Along with guilt. Guilt and worry. Guilt for not being around this past year as my mother fought leukemia. Cristo and *Bunică*, my grandmother, took care of her, and the toll it had taken on them showed in the small dust bunny that rolled past my bare foot.

Worry because Cristo confided in me that the family was having money problems. With the Americans evacuating Afghanistan, certain warlords that my father partnered with to smuggle raw opium and ephedrine out of the country were being replaced by the Taliban. The drop in income, on top of the medical bills coming in for my mother's treatment, had led to a cash shortage. Guilt swooped in again at the thought of my hefty boarding school tuition since my parents refused to pull me out my senior year.

I had to make it up to them somehow, and that started with linking our family with the Lupu clan. For now, Mama was in remission, but leukemia was a sneaky disease, and the very thought that she might not be with us at some point drove me into near panic mode. I'd be the dutiful daughter if it killed me—and marrying Nicu just might.

But how could I deny her anything? I'd already disappointed her when I caught my father killing someone and the mess that had created. More than anyone in the family, she was concerned about our image, and I knew she had been worried about my prospects. *Mafie* girls did not move away from home and go to boarding school. This marriage took a huge weight off her shoulders, and the engagement-wedding whirlwind gave her something exciting to focus on.

This homey townhouse had been the center of my world, a sanctuary until the fateful night that had changed everything. Unlike other girls my age who were getting ready to leave home, I was determined to take an active role in my family. Leaving at such a young age, I had missed out on so much, and I was determined to make it up to them.

I plopped down on the couch, my fingertips grazing the new material. Had they gotten this reupholstered since the winter? Cristo waltzed in and sat down heavily beside me. I grabbed his hand and gave it a squeeze. He felt like he'd failed in his duty to protect me. After my father called me at school to tell me about my engagement, Cristo FaceTimed me. He had fought with my father to give me more time, arguing that I was too young. But, as he'd painfully confessed, their hands were tied.

In our video chat, his jaw was tight and his teeth clenched as he gave me the verdict of my future. I expected to be engaged, but I thought I might get away with a year or two of college with Jewel. Of all the Lupu men, my brother hated Nicu the most. With his temper, I worried he'd do something rash. We were on the phone for hours. Holed up in one of the few private bathrooms in the girl's dorm so no one would overhear us, I talked him off the ledge from starting a war with the Lupu clan. That's when he divulged the whole story. He and my father had tried to trick the Lupu *şef*, or boss. It had backfired, big time. Not only was I going to marry a man I hardly knew, but everyone in his family would hate me.

The kitchen door swished as it swung open, and I heard the hurried pitter-patter of my mother and *Bunică*. Sweeping in behind them was the delicious apple and cinnamon scent of her favorite pastry, *plăcintă cu mere,* that I was certain she'd prepared specially for my arrival.

Throwing their hands in the air and clapping, they exclaimed, "Cătălina! Cat, you're home!"

Bunică's thin arms wrapped around me, cocooning me in warmth and love that I missed, the scent of apples and sugar floating off her. When I was a toddler, and again when the nightmares had invaded my nights, *Bunică* had insisted that a cot be moved into my bedroom so that she could watch over me as I slept. It was such a *bunică* thing to do. Standing up, she hustled back into the kitchen, probably to bring her *plăcinte*.

Meanwhile, my mother shoved Cristo out of the way. He grumbled something about being disposable but gave up his seat for my mother, who wrapped her arms around me.

"We're so glad to have you back home for good, sweetie," she crooned.

"Sadly, I'm not here for long," I reminded her, giving her a pout. How unfair was it that, just as I was coming home, I'd soon have to leave?

She tutted, rocking me back and forth in her bony arms. She'd lost a lot of weight this past year with the chemo.

"But you're here for now, and we'll make the best of it. After your wedding, you'll be in Manhattan, which isn't far compared to Massachusetts. I don't know what that uppity Lupu woman is thinking, letting her sons live in those penthouses in the middle of busy midtown when there are nice quiet townhouses just up the block."

My mother tried her best not to complain, but we both knew that the Lupu clan made their own rules. They were known for their modernism and love of culture. Nicu's father had bought the four penthouse apartments in the two towers of the Time Warner Building off Columbus Circle before construction had even begun. From what I heard, their *şef*, Alex, lived with his wife in one apartment, while his *consilier*, Tatum, occupied the other penthouse in that tower. Nicu and his older brother, Luca, lived in the two penthouses in the opposite tower. That would soon be my home.

"Get your father," my mother ordered Cristo, fluttering a hand at him to hurry up. I caught his eye and gave him an apologetic look.

He leaned over our mother and clapped my knee with his big hand, shaking it lightly. "I'm glad you're back for good, little sis."

My mother nudged his shoulder and pointed to the foyer, where the stairs going down to my father's office were located. He let out a long, suffering sigh as he heaved himself up.

"Oh, please, she spoils you rotten," I jested.

That was their way, to banter and complain about each other. I had missed that, too. The joking and playful teasing. The laughter that always rang somewhere in the house.

"How was the train ride? Too crowded? With all the baggage you had to bring home, you should've let your brother pick you up," she complained.

I shook my head. "It's almost four hours each way, and that's without traffic. It's too much for Cristo."

"He could've driven up, stayed overnight in a hotel, and brought you back the next day," she insisted.

"Mom, I'm not a little girl. He's done it so many times

over the years," I reiterated, as I had over the phone half a dozen times this past week alone. "It's too much and completely unnecessary."

"Nothing is too much for you. Your brother hates to drop you off, but he loves to pick you up."

And pick up the girls, when he's at my school, I thought to myself. Whenever he visited, the girls in my dorm would make fools of themselves drooling over him. It was gross. He had brown wavy hair, whereas I was a blonde, but we shared the same brown eyes. The difference was in our build. Where I was slim, except for in the hips and butt, he was big and tall. I knew he didn't touch jailbait but still...hearing about him hooking up with one of the girls I went to school with was too skeevy to bear.

The only one I would've tolerated was Jewel, but she was horrified when I told her about some of our archaic traditions. After that, she swore that she'd have nothing to do with Romanian *mafie* types. No matter how many times my brother flirted with her, nothing was worth the risk of curtailing her freedom by force-tying herself to a man. After witnessing the serious lack of romance in my engagement, who could blame her? She was a romantic, and there was nothing romantic about marrying a guy who hated you on principle.

My father's heavy tread came up the stairs from his basement office. I was on my feet and flinging myself at him by the time he reached the opening to the living room.

His strong arms wrapped around me and held me tight. "My Cat. How's my *fiica frumos*, my beautiful daughter?"

I buried my face into his button-down shirt, inhaling his cologne. It smelled of safety and home. He worked long hours, insisting that he should be involved in the daily workings of his clan. I already didn't have enough time with him. I sniffed. Soon, I'd have even less. Once I was a married woman, and part of a rival clan no less, I'd rarely get to spend alone time with him. It was sporadic enough when we lived under the same roof.

"It's good to be home," I choked out.

My family hadn't come to my graduation. I hadn't told them that I was valedictorian because it didn't hold any significance for them. The long car ride would've been too much for my mother. Cristo would've come if I had asked him, but it seemed pointless to drag him away when it was always so busy here. Even though they'd never understand what education meant to me, that didn't mean I loved them any less for it.

His eyes bled regret. "I know you had hoped to stay with us longer. I blame myself for this. If we didn't need this contract with the Lupu bastards to bring in revenue, I would've considered breaking it, but my hands were tied."

I appreciated the sentiment, but I knew how crucial this marriage was. *Mafie* marriages were powerful contracts between families that usually included financial arrangements. At first, Cristo was supposed to marry the Lupu *mafie* princess, but she ran off. Although the bride might have absconded, the marriage had to go forward. I replaced Cristo, and Luca, the second son of the Lupu clan, was supposed to take his sister's place.

He refused to play along.

Even though it wasn't personal, that rejection stung a little. My father always wanted the *şef*, Alex, to become my husband. As a punishment for his attempt to trick Alex, I was given to Nicu. He had the worst reputation of any made man in our circles.

"At least Mama is thrilled," I joked. I loved her, but her near obsession with the status of our clan was legendary.

He snorted. "There's that."

I covered his hand with mine. "You know I'd do anything to make your lives easier. Anything."

His eyes dipped down, attempting to cover his shame for not being able to shield me from the harsh demands of our world. He cleared his throat.

"How was the train ride? You know your brother could've picked you up?" he asked in a gentle reprimand.

Dashing a rogue tear from the corner of my eye, I replied, "I know, I know. But with a shipment coming into Jersey two nights ago, I knew he'd be tired. I'm fine taking the train. There's a gang of us who go together, some going as far south as Washington, D.C., so I always have someone to sit with."

He'd heard this numerous times, so he simply nodded. He didn't have bodyguards on me while I was at school, or on the ride there and back, but that would change now that I was home. New York City was home, but it was also where our greatest enemies lived.

As if hearing my thoughts, he mused, "I'll get Simu to arrange a soldier to be on call for when you go out."

Simu.

Oh, Simu.

I swallowed around my tight throat and nodded.

Simu was Cristo's best friend and my father's *consilier*. It didn't get more complicated than that, considering how protective my brother was of me. Simu might have come from a famed aristocratic Romanian family, the Cantacuzino, but my father had pulled him off the streets of Bucharest.

Simu was like a brother to me until I came home for winter break two years ago. Suddenly, it was as if I'd seen him for the first time. When he'd stopped by to chat with my father, he'd done a double take. His eyes had raked down my body in a way that made me feel all tingly.

I'd caught him watching me, time and time again. At church during the Christmas Eve service. At the café where Cristo hung out. At the warehouse when I'd stopped by to drop something off for my father. Every time, he'd pause to take a good, long look at me. Last summer, we'd shared a few kisses. They were...sweet, which was a surprise considering his reputation as a bad boy. My father never broached the subject of Simu with me, so when I was told Nicu was to be my husband, I knew our little flirtation was over with.

LATER, as we sat down for dinner, Simu came by to talk to my father. This time, his eyes didn't linger. His lips didn't either when he bent down to kiss me on the cheeks. If anything, he avoided my gaze. My heart sank a little. He was acting as if I'd betrayed him.

Late that evening, I was about to take the stairs up as Simu rounded the corner and made a full stop. My foot paused on the step. Hand tightening around the banister, I sent him a withering look.

His gaze flicked away.

"Jesus, Simu. Are you going to punish me just because I'm engaged to be married?" I hissed. "You know it's my duty to this clan, right? God, you're such a hypocrite."

I was miffed. He had no right to be upset with me. He knew the rules. Hell, he helped enforce them. I may not be a believer in arranged marriages but refusing would be the equivalent of spitting on my family. My father had shed blood, sweat, and tears for this family. Then there was my mother, who'd sat across the dinner table, happy and smiling for once. Not to mention that I'd become a pariah if I turned my back on our traditions. I could never escape my duty, and I resented the way he was treating me.

He stalked up to me, backing me up against the wooden banister. Gripping my forearms, he trembled as he gritted out, "Is that what you think? What do you take me for?"

"What else can I think?" I sneered. "You won't even look at me."

Shaking me a little, he growled. "I'm not mad at you. I know you're the innocent victim here, but it's tearing me up inside. You were supposed to be mine. Your father practically promised you to me and—" He shook his head and cut himself off before he said too much. He didn't think I knew what had gone down between the Lupu family and mine.

"Cristo told me that their trick blew up in their faces and this was the consequence."

"Yes," he seethed between clenched teeth. "I can't stand the idea of that Lupu fucker touching you with his filthy hands. You're a Popescu *princess*. You're beautiful and pure and deserve so much more, but I'm powerless. I can't do anything to help you or fix this, and it's fucking killing me."

I blinked. Okay, that was not what I had expected.

My shoulders drooped, and I went limp in his hold. He clutched me to his chest. My face was smothered in the starchy cotton of his dress shirt.

"You already do so much for us, Simu," I murmured into his chest.

"I'm only doing my job," he replied.

That was a serious understatement. Cristo had confided that Simu had been instrumental in keeping our clan afloat during our current money problems. Simu's uncle was the *consilier* of the Hagi clan, a rich and powerful clan on the West Coast. Simu convinced his uncle to advance my father money to keep our enterprises functioning while he scrambled to create new alliances in Afghanistan. It was a risky high-wire act, but none of it would've been possible if Simu hadn't vouched for my father.

His grip tightened around me. "Fuck, Cat. I want to find a way…"

I shook my head, my cheek rubbing against the harsh cotton. Planting my palms on his chest, I pushed myself off him.

"You know as well as I that there's nothing you can do," I asserted. "My father needs this of me, and my mother is so happy. You saw her at dinner. She had more energy tonight than she's had since she got sick. I can't take that away from her."

"So, you're willing to sacrifice your happiness for her? For them?" he asked, his tone laced in bitterness.

Of course, I was. Only, he wasn't what I was sacrificing. Abandoning my chance to go to college was the real sacrifice. The thought triggered the same old sinking feeling in my stomach.

"As if I have a choice in the matter," I scoffed.

"At one time, I was your choice."

"That's not fair. I never had a choice. If I had been lucky, then yes, I would've married you, but it was never in my hands."

"Your father's a fool," he snarled.

"Hey," I snapped. "Don't you dare call him names. Do you think he's thrilled about this? Cristo is beside himself. You know the long-standing competition between him and Nicu. He feels he's failed me, and it's eating him up inside." Not to mention that, at times, I coasted on the edge of feeling like I was drowning.

He cast his head down and rubbed the back of his neck sheepishly. "Sorry, Cat. You know I didn't mean that."

I rested my hand on the center of his chest and sighed. "I know, I know. If he almost promised me to you, that's a hard thing to swallow."

"More like unbearable," he groused. "How can you be so resigned to it?"

How? Only a man could ask such a ridiculous question. As a man, and one that held a powerful position, he had more freedom to choose. I was resigned because I had no agency in this matter. He didn't wake up in the morning to the depressing reality that I would be taken from my family, that I wouldn't continue my education, that I'd be tied for life to a stranger who hated me.

"It's never been fair, but I grew up knowing that I didn't have the final say. I could make suggestions, and my father would try to accommodate me, until he couldn't. As the daughter of Nelu Popescu, I'm too valuable to marry whomever I want. A marriage is political in nature. Mine more than most."

"I'm not giving up, Cat."

My eyes flared in surprise, my heart doing a *thump-thump* in my chest. I did not need Simu causing trouble. It was hard enough pushing myself to do what was necessary.

Taking a step back, I replied, "I don't even know what to say to that, but you know I will always follow my father's wishes."

His jaw clenched. "Then I'll just have to change his mind."

Of course, I'd prefer Simu to Nicu any day. I knew Simu. I already loved him, and given half a chance, could fall in love with him, but what he was suggesting was a pipe dream.

Letting a little twinge of exasperation show on my face, I reminded him, "The engagement is a few weeks away."

"I'm aware," he drawled out. "It's not a done deal until you're in front of a priest. I'm the one who loves you, not him. That Lupu scum doesn't want this any more than you do, so there's that."

I swallowed down the hurt that bubbled up at his harsh comment. Our world *was* harsh, and I had to remind myself that he hadn't said anything untrue. First Luca rejected me. Then Nicu accepted, but with hatred in his heart. The hurdles I faced were almost too much. I took a deep breath around the band of tension constricting my lungs.

I patted his chest, my hand smoothing down his shirt before dropping away. I took a couple of steps up the stairs, placing us eye to eye, and gazed into his face, trying to read what he was planning. He returned my gaze with a stoic one of his own, revealing nothing. Suddenly weary after a day of traveling, returning home, and now this, I let my questions go. I didn't have the energy for it. I'd already put my family through enough, and I wouldn't add to their burden by entertaining an alternative.

"Just...don't do anything foolish, Simu. The cards are stacked against us, and I don't want you to get hurt. With Mom the way she is, I couldn't stand it if anything happened to you."

He broke our stare, his eyes fixed on the wooden banister to my side.

"Promise me," I demanded. "Don't do anything that will get you killed or start a war."

His gaze flicked toward me and darted away again. With a belabored sigh, he nodded once. "Yeah, okay. But anything less than that is fair game."

Stubborn man.

I should've pushed for an oath of some kind, but I wasn't sure I'd get more. The pride of an aristocrat underlined his deep hatred and rivalry with the Lupu men. Something he and Cristo had in common. It was a surprise that he was a member of our clan. The Lupu, with the royal blood in their lineage, would have been the obvious choice, but Simu had joined us. It spoke to the fact that he had his own mind, and I always admired that quality about him.

Still, what he was contemplating was risky, and we already lived in a dangerous world. Honestly, the less I knew, the better. I'd learned that lesson the hard way. The one time I found out more than I should, I ended up leaving my family for six years.

Backing off, I threw my hands up. "Fine, do what you must."

Bringing my cheek to his, I gave him a kiss on one cheek and then the other and bid him a good night. Taking two steps at a time, I fled up the staircase without a backward glance.

2

The meeting was going about as well as could be expected, considering how long my brothers and I were in the same room together. Since Alex, the *şef* of our family, married my little sister's best friend, Nina, he'd gotten territorial over his apartment, so we now convened in my apartment, since I rarely used it for my own personal use.

Was it possible to feel like an orphan in the bosom of a large family? I could testify that the answer was a resounding yes. I loved my family, but that didn't mean they understood me. Alex, who was two years older than I was, knew the most, but even he didn't know half of it.

Luca this, Luca that. Luca, Luca, Luca. Every fucking day, my name thundered through the house as the Lupu patriarch tracked me down to punish me over some minor infraction. Call it pride, but I never revealed the extent to which my father tortured me.

Which is why I fucking *loved* seeing my half brother, Sebastian. His very existence made my fucking day. It was a "fuck you" to my brothers, a reminder of the colossal stain on our dead father's otherwise pristine reputation. A mistake that he hid from us for years: his second family. Not only did he have a side piece, but he'd impregnated her twice, bringing forth Sebastian and my half sister, Emma. Christ, but that guy was a narcissistic bastard, and the truth had finally come to light. It was hardest on my youngest brother, Nicu, who worshipped him. *God only knows why.* It was a continual source of tension between us.

On the agenda was Nicu's impending engagement party. Alex wanted me to host it at my country estate in Westchester. Normally, I kept my private life separate from family and business, but I was willing to make an exception this one time. It seemed like the right thing to do since I was the reason for his looming marriage.

I doubted I'd ever marry. I got my base needs taken care of by whichever woman was available. Made sure all parties walked away satisfied and then moved on. I didn't fuck the same woman twice because that created expectations I had no intention of fulfilling. If I ever did marry, I'd sure as hell never marry a *mafie* woman. When you married a *mafie* girl, you married for life. Divorce was forever off the table. End of discussion.

I refused to be the sacrificial lamb for clan and family. Even though I was technically the next one in line to get married, I figured it was good form to accept Alex's request. I had warded off my big brother's pressure, from his cajoling to his threats, and had won. I could be magnanimous by opening up my home to the brother who'd caved in on my behalf, even if I judged him for it.

Palms out, I lifted my hands and gave my consent. "Hey, as long as it's not me, I don't care."

Tension in the room shot up. Alex narrowed his eyes at me. Nicu shot me a vicious scowl.

It wasn't necessarily the most diplomatic thing to say, but I resented Nicu for kowtowing to Alex's demands. Perhaps I shouldn't hold a grudge, considering I refused to marry the Popescu girl, but I couldn't help myself. Nicu toed the line like a little bitch, happy for any scraps of approval from Alex. Despite the serious darkness deep within him and a rep for being violent, when it came to the family, he was as docile as a sheep.

And I would never, *ever* be a sheep. Unless I was proudly toting the label of black sheep. I didn't have anything against marriage per se, I just wasn't interested in it for its own sake, which was about all a *mafie* marriage would ever be. No doubt the ever-present baggage of the past was behind my decision, but it wasn't the only reason. *Mafie* girls, for the most part, were superficial and…sheeplike. The very antithesis of me.

Tatum, always the peacemaker, cut through the tension. "This doesn't have to be a fight—"

Nicu and I were long overdue for a fistfight, but I was willing to let it lie until another day…if he was.

"Doesn't it though? Isn't there always a fight?" I asked with a sardonic raise of one eyebrow.

Unlike Nicu, I didn't stand down. I didn't do whatever I was told like some mindless idiot. I questioned. I argued. I fought, if necessary. I certainly got beatings from my father more times than I could count. Each one only served to harden my resolve. That's what the man could never understand. He always thought that the next punishment would break me. Instead, it reinforced my determination.

Tatum replied, "There's nothing to argue about. Your house is the biggest. Considering you rejected the girl, it's the least you could do."

"*Et tu, Brute?*" I teased.

Tatum was the closest I would ever call a man a friend. He knew more about my childhood than my own brothers. I was toying with him; he wasn't really throwing me under the bus. If anything, he was usually my ally since Nicu always backed Alex. Whereas I rarely missed an opportunity to challenge my șef.

He rolled his eyes at me. "Stop acting like the victim. If anything, it's Nicu we should pity, but look at him. No complaints from him."

That's because he's a sheep, and he doesn't give a shit whom he marries.

"Hey, at least I heard she's hot. A blonde no less," I rumbled out.

"And feisty. She is a Popescu, after all," piped up Tatum.

"Thrilling news, Tatum," Nicu replied dryly. "As if a virgin will have a clue how to satisfy me."

Nicu then turned to me with a raised brow. "Thanks for trying to pimp her on me, but you're the one into blondes, not me. Which underscores that you should have stepped up to marry her."

I sent him a droll look. "We've already established that hell will freeze over before that happens."

Guilt nipped at my heels. I was well aware that I was being difficult. It was in my nature to be a contrarian, but Tatum was right. It wouldn't kill me to open my house for Nicu's party. It was my safe place, but nothing they could do there could sully it. I wouldn't let them.

I bought the estate in Westchester, north of the city, to escape. While they went home to Sunnyside, Queens every weekend, I drove my Bugatti in the opposite direction.

I hated cities in general, but Queens was a shit borough, through and through, especially the tight *mafie* community of Little Bucharest. Just hearing the subway rattling above ground on Queens Boulevard made my back teeth grind. The second I had enough money in hand, I chose a fancy suburban neighborhood and snatched up a wooded estate with a long-ass driveway. I sought out the isolation and quiet for a reason. Namely, to get away from the city and my family.

"Fucking fine. My house it is, then. But swear to God, you better not get into a shoot-out in there or I will be mighty pissed."

"Yeah, yeah, we'll keep your precious house spotless, okay? Jesus, Luca, it's an engagement party," Alex said. "It's a celebration. There won't be a bloodbath."

I gave him a baleful look. It wasn't too long ago that Nelu had tried to con Alex into marrying the Popescu girl, and they'd been at each other's throats.

"Whatever, I said everything would be all right. I have no intention of getting into an argument with Nelu or Cristo," Alex stated. "I have a honeymoon to go on and I want to peacefully start my new life with Nina without drama. I can't afford a war, at the moment."

"Since everyone will be congregating, it's an opportune time to invite other business associates from abroad. Nothing screams more 'innocent' than your baby brother's engagement party," quipped Tatum.

"Agreed," replied Alex. "Anyone with an iota of sense would know that engagements aren't a big deal for Romanians, but it will create a perfect cover."

"Since the DEA knows next to nothing about our traditions, we can take advantage of it. I'd like to meet Nelu's Afghan contacts face-to-face," said Alex.

"Then we'll need serious protection. And don't think for a moment they're staying at my place," I snapped.

"Of course not," replied Tatum smoothly. "I'm certain

there are hotels nearby. We'll book the most extravagant one."

Alex turned to me and gave me a hard look. "Nelu and his family are staying at your place. That's nonnegotiable. He won't be able to deny us and it will put him at a disadvantage to be in our territory. We'll need at least three days to get in the number of meetings I've deemed necessary. Of course, we'll have to fortify the locks to make sure everyone is safe. Add more guards." Snooping wouldn't be a problem since any valuable information was encrypted and stored in a bulletproof server farm, owned by an eccentric cybercriminal who lived in an underground bunker in Germany. It took all kinds to make a criminal network viable and thriving.

Alex turned to address my half brother, "Sebastian, you and Emma can return to the city if you'd like. I want you to stay close to her during this time. How is she handling the shift?"

"You mean since you put a guard on her?" Sebastian asked with a sardonic tilt of his mouth. He was a cool motherfucker. It was a miracle that he'd turned out so normal. Apparently, our father had doted on them. He hadn't thought Sebastian would enter the family business. If he had, I bet their childhood would've been vastly different. Was I resentful of how he treated them compared to me? Not one bit. I'd have to have yearned for his approval and love for that to happen.

Since Alex welcomed our half siblings into the fold, their lives had changed. The transition had been more difficult for Emma since she'd grown up as a freewheeling American girl for the first twenty-two years of her life. Now, not so much. Those were the breaks, though. Once she became a pawn that could be used by our enemies, it was our duty to protect her to the utmost.

Alex replied, "That is exactly what I mean. I heard that she got the drop on them a few times."

"Meh, you know..." Sebastian answered.

We all turned, waiting for him to finish, like the idiots we were. She obviously didn't like it, but we had next to no idea how it affected her. We'd been raised in our world, with its strict rules, our entire life. We'd met her, sure. Spent time with her. But Sebastian was the one we saw on a daily basis. Hell, we discovered that we barely knew our own sister, Tasa, when she ran out on her engagement to Cristo. Here we thought she had accepted her lot in life as a *mafie* princess. That backfired on us. Turned out, she wasn't as biddable as we thought. Turned out she was deeply resentful of the domineering way Alex had treated her for her entire life. Turned out she ran off and got hitched to a former Bratva prince turned biker and got knocked up by him. Turned out we knew jack shit about what her life was like.

Seeing our blank stares, he sighed and muttered, "Not great. She's not handling it well. Luckily, she's reserved and likes to spend most of her time at home or in her lab with her research, but even having a guard outside her office at work did not go down well. She'll adjust. She needs time."

"It's been a couple months," Alex said matter-of-factly, as if that amount of time, in and of itself, would suffice. Despite what happened with Tasa, Alex's wife, Nina, had taken to the life like a fish in water.

"She's not like Nina, Alex," I explained. "She didn't grow up next door to us and have Tasa as a best friend practically her entire life. Nina knew what she was getting into. Anyway, most women are not like Nina. Not so...pliant."

A grin spread over Alex's face. I had to look away at the expression of lust mixed with pride over his new wife.

"Christ, Alex, we see what you're thinking. Mind reeling it in?" Nicu griped.

He sobered and shook his head. "I seriously doubt you know what I'm thinking," he trailed off with a glassy-eyed look.

After pining for each other for years, they'd finally hooked up. Granted, he was more insufferable than usual those few weeks after he'd fucked up and broke it off with her. Not that it was entirely his fault. I never envied Alex his position as head of our clan. His life wasn't his own.

Right after Tasa ran off, Nelu wanted Alex to take her place and marry his daughter to save the trade agreement that underpinned the marriage contract; that alone was a powerful enough reason. Alex would've normally had no issue with it, but for the fact that he'd fallen for Nina. So, he tried to force me to take his place, and I categorically refused him. There was no doubt I loved my family, was loyal to it. But blind loyalty didn't work for me. Our father broke me of that nasty little habit. I was as loyal as I could be, considering what that fucker had put me through.

Did I feel guilty for not taking Alex's place?

Not really. Especially since part of his motivation was to deliver on our father's dream to reconcile with the Popescu family. In his place, would I have sacrificed the love of my life to fulfill our father's dream and reconcile with those Popescu dogs? Hell, no.

But all that was water under the bridge.

"Anyway, Tasa's coming. It will be her first time back home since she left. I don't think Mama can handle having her *and* her baby daddy under her roof. Not until they're married, at least. It's better if they stay over at my place," I said. Tasa was already nervous about coming back, and I'd go out on a limb to smooth the way for her and Mama.

"God knows, you have the room," Nicu replied snidely.

Always a thorn in my side, that one.

"Don't act like you care. You love the city."

"True that," he retorted. The man wouldn't be caught dead off the dirty city streets. The one and only time he visited me, he fidgeted the entire time, desperate to get back to where the action was. And action and speed were always the endgame for my little brother. He was an adrenaline junkie, racing bikes and cars. Hell, the madman even piloted planes for the thrill of it.

Alex turned to me. "Thank you, Luca."

I nodded, suppressing a chuckle. This thank you on the part of the *Lupul* was clearly Nina's doing. She was "working" on Alex's interpersonal communication skills, or so she told me last Sunday, during dinner at Mama's house. A tradition I only attended for my mother's sake.

"What the hell do you do all day alone in that big, empty house?" Nicu asked.

"I do what I do," I answered evasively. I wasn't about to tell them that I mostly took care of my flowers in my garden. I wasn't going to tell them that, while I had a little army of gardeners at my fingertips, I stripped off my T-shirt, grabbed a handful of tools, got down on my hands and knees and pulled weeds to relax. These fuckers would eat me alive, but gardening was one of the few activities that gave me peace.

"You're doing it again," he called me out. "Avoiding the answer."

"I'm alone is what I do. I'm a motherfucking loner, and I like peace and quiet. Besides work, I play video games, I stream, and read. Work in the garden, work out in my gym, and take swims in my huge-ass swimming pool." I shrugged.

"No, I don't have a family holed up in there or a woman tied to my bedpost in an underground dungeon. Don't worry, I'm not a mass murderer."

With a perplexed expression on his face, he asked, "Don't you get lonely? Bored? You're not that old yet."

My brother never did understand me. He was a mama's boy and stayed close to our family home.

"Not in the least. I work hard, and I'm at the club every weekend, checking on things. Going to Westchester, I'm away from the noise and bustle of the city. It's the closest to being at peace. No one's watching over my shoulder. I don't answer to anyone or contend with bullshit. I'm not neighborly, so I don't have anyone stopping by. No one knows my name when I walk down the street. And that's how I like it. Anonymous and fucking free. It's the exact opposite of growing up at home."

At home, I'd constantly get reprimanded and smacked around.

Alex's eyes darted away in shame. I sighed. Our father, whom everyone called Tata except me, kept what he did to me a secret. If he was too obvious, then Alex would've been forced to take sides, and the honorable protector in him would've had to defend me. Alex's problem was that, until recently, he worshipped our father and, in his drive to be perfect, strove to match him.

Me, on the other hand? At a young age, I learned that when a powerful, respected man chose to divert from the path of righteousness, people forgave him his indiscretions. Our family was an organization. Duty, sacrifice, and the chain of command were essential to making our little world tick. Since we lived in the shadows, in the underbelly of the rest of the world, everyone had to follow the rules. It was the underpinning that held everything together. In a strict world like ours, where my father's word was law, my personality became a thorn in his side.

Eyeing Alex critically, I always wondered how much he knew exactly. We'd never spoken about it and I was too prideful to divulge the extent of the abuse I had undergone. Shaking my head, I figured he'd known enough. While I could forgive him for not protecting me, I struggled with his idolization of my father. Which was why the discovery of his great betrayal was a godsend. Alex had been ready to sacrifice his happiness with Nina to fulfill his duty of marrying a *mafie* girl. But for once in his life, my oldest brother granted himself the reprieve of not being perfect, turned away from what he considered his duty, and married the love of his life.

Changing the subject and moving our meeting along so I could get the hell out of the city and return to my oasis in Westchester, I said, "So...let's talk L.A. Now that the setup in Chicago is going well, I think we should focus on L.A. What about meeting with the ruling clan there, the Hagi clan? They're a small outfit."

Alex's gaze swung toward me and hardened. "Oh, hell no. Don't even think about it, Luca. I'm guessing you want to move out of New York. Get that idea out of your head right now for no other reason than it would break Mama's heart."

"She'll be fine," I assured impatiently. "I'm the one traveling there every other week. I know the operation better than anyone."

"Even if I gave you the position of underboss, don't think you could keep it while being unmarried," he argued.

I dropped back into my seat on one of the two white couches facing each other in my spacious living room. Picking up the Turkish coffee on the large coffee table between the couches, I mused that Nina's so-called "work in progress" was purely a surface-level thing. Not that I was surprised. You didn't become *şef* by being soft. While I had worked my ass off to open a base in Chicago and tentatively put feelers out for Los Angeles, I hadn't agreed to marry the Popescu girl, and this was my payback.

Well fuck. I stared out the large floor-to-ceiling windows overlooking Central Park as disappointment clawed at my chest. While I made it work in New York as best I could, my dream was to move away somewhere new. I'd be more of my own boss and get to make a mark. Once we opened up an outfit in Cali, I was hoping to pivot there.

"And when do you think that's something you can entertain?" I was pushing. I knew I was, but I had to fight for what I wanted. No one was going to hand it to me on a silver platter. Not me and not in this family.

"When I deem that it's the best decision for the family," he replied matter-of-factly. Family always came first, and until I showed him that I learned my lesson on sacrifice, I was stuck in this noisy, crowded metropolis. I gazed out the penthouse window into the bright blue New York sky. It reminded me of the blue ocean of Laguna Beach. I was transported back to the first time I'd visited. The feel of the warm, soft breeze coming off the water. The pristine golden sand sifting between my toes as I looked out on the crashing waves, surfers skating over the tops like large birds in flight.

I would've bought a place at the beach in the Hamptons instead of in a suburban neighborhood in Westchester, but I grew up hearing stories of my mother going to Constanța, the beach resort on the shores of the Black Sea, every summer. If I'd bought a place at the beach, my family would come crashing in on the weekends and throughout the summer months. The beach is where I dreamed of having a place, but my family intruding on my private alone time had to be avoided at all costs. A regular old American family might rent a place. That wasn't how it worked with my family. An open-door policy was an unspoken assumption. A shudder ran through me at that thought. It was bad enough that I shared a floor with Nicu, while Alex was one tower over in the same building.

Alex's eyes on me turned brittle. "You know I don't like to get into your business, but it won't happen before you're married."

After mentioning it for the third time, I couldn't ignore it anymore. My gaze zeroed in on him. "You're serious?"

He held up his hand. "It's not the first time I've mentioned it and I don't do anything without a purpose. But to clear up any misunderstanding, yes, I'm damn serious. You need to mature and demonstrate that I can trust you. That you're not going to negate every request I make of you like an unruly adolescent, especially if you're living away from me and in charge of your own territory. Prove to me that you're willing to do what needs to be done, regardless of how you feel about it or whether you *feel* like it," he ended in air quotes.

I rose to my feet and thundered, "Prove myself to you? *Prove* myself?" My tone dropped to a dangerous level. "Haven't I proven myself?" He knew exactly what I was referring to.

"Settle down, Luca," Tatum interjected, grabbing my wrist, and tugging me down.

Guilt flickered over Alex's face before it settled into firm, determined lines. "If you want to have your own territory, you need to be married. Your men won't take you seriously if you haven't settled down. At least an engagement before you leave. That's about as much leeway I could give you."

"He's right, Luca," parroted Tatum. "At your age, a man should be married. He'll be considered more mature, and therefore, more trustworthy. Our soldiers would need to have complete faith in you."

My hands trembled slightly from the energy it took to hold back the desire to pummel my brother. While his request might seem reasonable, I instinctually rebelled against any kind of imposition or condition made on me. I balled my hands into fists to get a grip on my fury. This reminded me so much of my father's ultimatums that I'd challenged, which led to subsequent punishments. It took me a few moments to talk myself off the ledge. Inhaling sharply through my nostrils, I woodenly sat back down and took a sip of my coffee.

I couldn't say anything for fear of what would come out of my mouth. Clenching my jaws tightly, I focused on my breathing. I had a goal in mind, and I always achieved my goals. My father's punishment had given me practice in endurance for the long game. I had no intention of getting married for this, but until I came up with an alternative plan, I'd keep my mouth shut. There was a time to fight and a time to plot. A fight was brewing, but until then, I'd begin with plotting.

3

I had to escape the suffocating pressure of being dragged around by my mother, who prodded me to smile wider and laugh quieter in order to seem more ladylike. Pfft, as if any of that would help my case. It didn't matter what I said or how I acted. The man, or rather stranger, who was my fiancé, was as stuck as me with our engagement.

My mother was relishing every moment of the charade, especially since the Lupu clan was paying for the entire engagement party weekend. Considering our financial problems, I tried talking her out of a big wedding, but she said it was a matter of Popescu pride. I didn't see what pride had to do with it. If we couldn't afford it, we couldn't afford it. My father was already in debt, and the idea of adding to it to pay for my wedding seemed insane. While my mother was ecstatic, I was trying to manage Cristo, who slunk in the background, growling and snapping at anyone who passed by.

Meanwhile, Simu was working hard behind the scenes

with my dad. Getting nowhere, he too, was acting like a grouch. I had too much on my plate to deal with him and was relieved that he had to return to the city in the evening.

My mother got embroiled in a deep conversation with another *mafie* matriarch, and seeing my chance, I held my breath and inched away slowly until I melted into the crowd. When I was far enough away, engulfed in the large, bustling reception room, I scooped up a champagne flute from a passing waiter, took a deep swallow, and slipped out the nearest open French doors onto a patio.

Guzzling down half the glass, I felt the bubbly blend with the acid roiling in my stomach. Not the best combination, but screw it. I followed the wraparound patio around the corner of the house and pressed my spine against the rounded, ancient-looking stones protruding from the wall. The back of my head thumped lightly on the wall as I closed my eyes and expelled a long sigh.

"Needed an escape, huh?"

A gasp slipped past my lips as my eyes popped open wide. My head spun in the direction of the intruder. My gaze landed on a man, half a dozen feet away from me. Leaning a shoulder against the stone wall, a cigarette dangled from his full, sculpted lips. I gaped at his face. God, what a face. His expression confirmed that he was a devil. Wasn't every man here? But damn if his features didn't give him the look of an angel.

How unfair.

A spring breeze blew blond curls off a face that might as well have been carved out of marble. All the angles were hard, from his strong, wide forehead to his high cheekbones to the jut of his jawbone. But his eyes were what paralyzed me, rooting me to my spot. Bright silver and hard, but with a faint trace of mischief in them. Staring at him was an experience in and of itself. An unusual mixture of the desire to scream and laugh hysterically warred inside me.

"Uhhh..." I trailed off. Caught off guard by his cruel beauty, my brain hiccupped. "I-I didn't see you there."

A feral smirk curled the edges of his lips upward as his eyes slowly made their way down my body. Heat singed every inch he touched with his eyes. It took every ounce of pride I had not to fidget under his blatant perusal. Sheesh, at least he found me attractive, which was more than I could say for my fiancé. The thought burned a hole in my gut. Normally, I didn't seek the approval of others, but it was a doozy to experience Nicu's eyes gloss over me like I didn't even exist.

Nothing like that could be said of this man.

"Hmm, apparently not. Who are you running from, beautiful? Or were you also escaping the general bullshit of this absurd party?" he asked, his voice doused in mockery.

I cleared my throat.

"General bullshit," I croaked out.

He nodded knowingly, as if we shared a mutual secret. As if we were co-conspirators of some kind. Good God, I wish I could conspire with him. Preferably between the sheets. I didn't really mean that, of course. It was my unbridled libido talking. But that's what happened when a woman of eighteen, who had never been touched, was faced with such raw, sensual beauty.

Between the arrogance that oozed from him and the fact that I didn't recognize him, he was most definitely a Lupu. Lupu men were dangerous, and this one had to be the most perilous of them all. There was a wild, rough energy that rolled off him in waves, even though he hadn't moved a muscle. He reminded me of a caged feline.

Powerful. Untamed. Unsafe.

The smartest move I could make was to leave his presence, but then my eyes dipped to the cigarette in his hand.

I stammered out, "D-do you have another one of those?"

Alcohol. Nicotine. Anything to help me get through this ludicrous farce of an engagement party. If it wasn't for the fact that it was my duty, that I wanted to make my family proud, and that my mother was having the time of her life, I'd never have put up with this ridiculous situation.

His eyes slid over my face critically. "Are you even legal?" he asked, tipping his chin toward the glass that I gripped. His lips turned up into a half smile and a deadly dimple popped out on his left cheek.

"Yes and no," I teased.

His eyebrows drew down. "What the hell does that mean?" he ground out.

Jeez, no patience, this one.

"I'm eighteen," I clarified.

He nodded sagely. Instead of giving me a cigarette of my own, he passed me his own, butt facing me. I glanced down, searching for the imprint of those full lips on the filter. Finding nothing, I snatched it and took a drag. The burn exploded in my lungs, giving me a little head rush, but I savored it.

"You're not going to tell on me, are you?" I threw him one of my toss-away flirty smiles.

His eyes turned hard. Clearly, it didn't melt him. He snorted. "No. I'm the last one to tattle."

I didn't know exactly what he meant by that, but as long as I had a moment to regroup before I returned to my mother, I was good.

"You must be a Popescu," he said neutrally.

"Obviously," I said before taking another drag. "And you must be a Lupu."

He gave a bark of disbelief at the snark in my tone.

"A little attitude. I like it."

Those last three words coming out of his mouth did something to my tummy. It was like a swarm of butterflies had suddenly found refuge in there. Damn, with that edginess and rough tone, he was too sexy by half.

A few curls of sandy blond hair flopped over his forehead, and I itched to reach out and sweep them out of the way. I always had a thing for blonds, a rare unicorn among dark-haired, olive-skinned Romanians, like Nicu.

"A little," I agreed, giving him a real grin this time, with a shrug of one bare shoulder. My dress was pretty revealing, with a plunging neckline from my spaghetti straps. I cupped my elbows to warm myself in the still-cool weather of the late spring day. While not far north of the city, being away from the incubation of the concrete jungle dropped the temperature by a few degrees.

Searching for something else to say, I observed, "It's pretty here. Different from the usual *mafie* parties, always on some fancy rooftop or, even worse, a blinged-out reception hall." My gaze absorbed the garden, with its swaths of tulips in brilliant colors. There was a marble fountain of a woman, water pouring out of the urn she was holding.

"You're the pretty one," he commented, his voice dripping with dark promises. His gaze coasted over me, and there was a snap, crackle, and pop on every inch of skin he pored over. *Holy hell.* Suddenly, I was burning up.

"Ahh...a player. I should've known," I replied with a sardonic shake of my head.

"How would you know?" he scoffed. "You're barely an adult."

Delectable heat turned to hot shame. Okay, that was uncalled for. Grinding my teeth together, I took a turn at patently looking *him* over. Two could play this game, and oh, was I going to take advantage of my one and only chance to look. Tease him with my overtly sexual gaze. It might be my engagement party, but screw that, this man was taunting me. Besides, I was no delusional miss who thought my engagement and marriage had anything to do with love. I was a pawn, and my marriage was a contract. Nothing more. Nothing less. So, while I had a teensy bit of freedom, I'd snatch it up.

And he was nothing like the immature teenage boys from school that left me unimpressed and uninspired. This Lupu was a full-grown male. Biting into my bottom lip, I took in his broad shoulders and defined chest, obvious beneath his jacket and tie, down to his tapered waist and fitted slacks. This one was a lady-killer. He exuded a combination of sensuality and dominance that would bring women to their knees.

"For a little girl, you have a dangerous way of looking at a man. Could get you in trouble," he murmured low, the gray in his eyes turning darker and more turbulent as he moved closer. Close enough for me to catch the musky scent of him, with a hint of bergamot.

That and the way he called me "little girl" shot lust down my middle and settled in between my thighs. I may have felt something when I'd kissed Simu, but what this man made me feel was in a whole other category of heat.

It could go no further than this moment, but I enjoyed the flirting, even with the edginess he threw into the mix. I chuckled, dismissing his comment. "I seriously doubt that."

My fiancé had barely looked my way since I arrived, over an hour and a half ago. And I was watching his behavior closely. I got nothing. *Nada. Nichts.* You couldn't feign that level of disinterest. Again, I knew this wasn't love. *But couldn't lust at least make an appearance?* Boys at school hit on me. Simu liked me. Hell, he could've at least glanced my way. I wasn't ugly. In fact, people had commented on my looks in the past. I'd been called pretty.

But clearly not by my fiancé. Maybe he had a side girl, like Cristo had. Or maybe he was at the bottom of the totem pole and didn't have the clout to reject me.

This one, on the other hand...I checked him out beneath my lashes and caught him staring at me again. This one was...something else. He took out another cigarette from a gold cigarette holder and lit it with a Zippo that he'd extracted from his jacket pocket. There was interest in his eyes. Deep interest. And I loved being the center of his attention. I felt like a butterfly coming out of a chrysalis and stretching its wings for the first time.

His hand moved, picked a strand of hair that had flown across my face, and rubbed it between his fingers. My tummy swooped. The gesture felt proprietary. The cigarette I was holding had burnt down to the butt. Mesmerized by him, I dropped it to the ground. He crushed it beneath his heel.

"It's quiet here. So different from the city," I said, to cut through the heavy tension between us. I'd never felt this with a man before.

"It's my hideaway," he divulged, continuing to caress my hair.

"I love flowers," I confided on a gentle sigh. His hand paused on my hair for a moment. There was an emotion in his eyes that I couldn't interpret, him being a stranger and all. If I wasn't mistaken, there was warmth in his gaze, along with a glint of pride.

Breaking our connection, he looked across the explosion of blooming flowers. Why would a man like him want to hide out? Men who looked like him were meant to rule in nightclubs, getting to choose the pick of the litter of women that inevitably flocked them. And yet, at the same time, I completely related. Boarding school was a hideout for me. It offered me an escape from the parts of my family and the *mafie* world that I hated, necessary evil that they were. I just assumed that only women, who were locked away most of their lives, were desperate to break away.

Before I could ponder this enigma or the man behind it further, I caught a flash of red.

My cousin, Dina, turned the corner and I pulled away from him. He held on for an instant before letting go just as Dina noticed me. Letting out a huff, she gave him a brief nod of respect before chastising me, "Your mother's been looking for you everywhere. God, you can be such a pain sometimes."

"I haven't been gone for more than ten minutes. I needed a break."

Her eyes softened as she came to me and pulled me into a hug. "I know, I know. The whole situation is maddening, but this is our lot in life. We have to make do, sweetie," she said as she wrapped her fingers around my upper arm and dragged me off the wall like I was a child. Ugh. My head snapped to him when I heard a low growl, but I must have imagined it because his face was a mask of nonchalance.

"Come on, things could be worse," she muttered.

His eyes were narrowed on Dina's hold around my arm, and my heart soared. As we passed him, he brought his hand up and broke her contact on me. She drew back, rattled, but he ignored her, his eyes on me now.

"Could they?" I replied as I nodded a thanks to him before following her. Glancing over my shoulder, I gave the sexy Lupu a little wink and downed the rest of my champagne before Dina poked me in the side to get moving.

4

I slumped against the side of my house and huffed out a laugh. Fuck, she winked at me. That girl was as hot as they came. I watched her sway her nice round ass as she was prodded forward by her relative. So far, I had done everything in my power to avoid the circus playing out in my living room. Numb with boredom, I'd slipped out for a smoke. I rarely smoked anymore but today called for it.

She hadn't lied when she said she was eighteen. Her wide brown eyes swirled with an intoxicating mixture of innocence and intrigue. Her peach and nectarine fragrance, riding toward me on a slight breeze, was sweeter than the scent of the spring flowers in my garden. And her pink bow-shaped lips turned up in a smile that made my heart stop for longer than was healthy.

Then there was her smoking body. Although on the slim side, she had tits that could fill my palms and flared hips to hold on to. But most importantly, there was that sly irreverence. I was a sucker for irreverence, being the king of it myself. It was even scarcer in my ultra-serious *mafie* community than it was in the outside world. She was a rare gem, indeed.

For an eighteen-year-old, there was something knowing in her eyes. I could tell that she'd seen her share of stuff. She knew what a farce, what an absurd piece of theater was being played out in there, and she was as disgusted by it as I was. Disgusted enough that she ducked out on her mother, and I knew what a tight leash they kept the princesses on at such events. An engagement party wasn't only about the so-called lucky couple. It doubled as a meat market to show off their girls to potential suitors.

I pulled out another cigarette and lit it. Her sassiness spoke to me as well. I felt that spark in my chest. Her smile twisted something in me. I'd never felt anything like this with a woman, especially one I'd barely interacted with.

There was also the fact that she was a blonde. Always had a thing for blondes. Hers wasn't the peroxide kind either. I had picked out at least three different shades of gold in the lock of hair I held between my fingers. There was really only one way to find out if she was a true blonde, and hell, I'd be the first in line for the privilege to peel the panties down those slim thighs. And while I was down on my knees in the name of investigative research, I'd take advantage of the opportunity to give it a little lick. Get myself a little taste of her. If it was anything like her scent, I'd be in paradise.

To that end, I stubbed the cigarette out and slipped through the French doors into my living room. Stripped of furniture to make enough room for the throngs that had come to acknowledge this bullshit union between two strangers, the place looked like a reception room. There were small high tables everywhere, with ridiculous bouquets of flowers on them, where people could deposit their drinks as waiters flitted about with trays of hors d'oeuvres.

I stretched my neck, surveying the large space for that honey-blonde head.

Ahh, found her.

Pushing through the crowd, I almost reached her when Alex approached the gorgeous girl. I screeched to a halt when he gave her a kiss on each cheek before placing his hand on her forearm and wrapping it around his elbow.

What in the ever-loving fuck...?

With his other hand, he waved Nicu over.

No.

No, no, no.

It couldn't be.

She was the fiancée. *She* was the Popescu *mafie* puppet.

Fuck.

A *ping ping ping* broke through the loud hum of conversation as my mother tapped a crystal glass with a fork.

"Welcome, everyone! Thank you for coming so far out of the city to our little reception. It's nothing fancy, but we wanted to introduce the wonderful new couple to our friends and family. Welcome Cătălina to the Lupu family!"

My mother lifted her glass in a toast.

"Cat," she corrected softly. My mother didn't hear her, but I heard her soft, melodious voice.

Cat.

She certainly resembled a pussycat, with her luxurious mane of glossy light hair. I wanted to stroke her like I would the back of a ginger cat, from ears to tail. I'd stroke more than that if I had any say in the matter. She was as blonde as a Norse, calling either to the German or Slavic blood in her. She was the most beautiful creature I'd ever set eyes on. I wasn't a stranger to beautiful women, but no one compared to her. A flame of jealousy blazed in my chest. I smothered it immediately.

"*Noroc!*" my mother toasted, wrapping her arm around Cat's shoulders.

Raising their glasses in the air, everyone repeated, "*Noroc!*"

Her cheeks turned pink, her eyes shooting everywhere but to Nicu, who was staring at her with cold disinterest. Her eyes ping-ponged until they landed on me. And there they stayed, making my chest burn with pride.

Her eyes widened, as if she'd been caught out. And she had been.

"Luca," my name was called. Alex gestured to me to join the rest of the family. I moved forward slowly, my eyes on hers. Keeping her roped to me.

The girl's eyes bulged, her lush lips parting. I could almost hear the gasp she made in my eardrums. In my chest. In my fucking soul.

"Luca," he called me again as I approached, planting a hand on my shoulder. "Let me introduce you to your new sister-in-law, Cat."

At least he'd gotten her name right.

Turning to Cat, he said, "This is Luca, our middle brother. Tasa, Nicu's twin, will arrive tomorrow." Peering over the crowd, he added, "Sebastian and Emma are here somewhere. Luca, can you stay here with Cat while I find them?"

Alex pushed through the crowd, looking for our half siblings, and despite being in the middle of a crowd, we were left alone.

Crossing my arms over my chest, I glared down at her. "So, you're the bride-to-be. You could've mentioned that when we met earlier."

"I didn't know who you were!" she exclaimed in a harsh whisper, her eyes darting right and left. And truth be told, she should be afraid. She'd been flirting with me, dammit. It was a bad look for her. I didn't give a shit, of course, but she didn't know that.

"I swear," she continued, "I never..." she waved her hand, at a loss for words to describe what had transpired between us. Nothing of consequence on the outside, yet something *had* passed between us. Sheer horror was stamped on her face, and the urge to alleviate her panic gripped me.

"I know you're a good girl," I said calmly, because I couldn't let her walk away worried for her reputation.

Yes, it was a slip. The teasing and the way she made eyes at me. But deep down, I knew innocence when I saw it. This girl was it. She was most definitely a virgin. Any other option was unfathomable, but more than that, she was without artifice.

"So you flirted with me a little. It's not a big deal," I said casually, my eyes carefully assessing whether we could be overheard.

"Oh...yeah, oh, okay...thanks," she stammered out.

My gaze shot to hers. There was relief and...was that hurt? Fuck. For no clear reason that I could fathom, her tender little feelings mattered to me. Like the odds of being struck by lightning, I was struck with the desire to soothe this girl. She would be trapped in a loveless marriage, and if I knew Nicu, he hadn't batted an eye in her direction. He didn't care to know anything about her after what Nelu and Cristo tried to pull on us. She was a means to an end and nothing more.

But when we were alone in my garden, there'd been a spark. I felt it. So did she and, being emotionally unattached to him, she followed it like the innocent young teenager she was.

Again, her innocence struck me. I'd never had a thing for it before but sensing that she was untouched by the violence and darkness that dominated my life seemed like a near miracle. It was a shame really because Nicu would never forgive her for her father's scheming. She'd be a hole to fuck and breed. Nothing more. My jaw tightened at the thought of my brother touching her. An ugly feeling of jealousy that I'd never felt before slithered in my chest.

"I know I'm irresistible, so, yeah, I get it," I teased lightly. "What can I say? My allure is overwhelming." I gave a dramatic sigh. "It's my cross to bear."

She puffed out a laugh and took the lifeline I threw her. Uncurling her wringing hands, she straightened her spine and threw her shoulders back.

"Oh my God, I can't believe you just said that, but okay, sure it is," she joked. "That's exactly how it went down."

I grinned.

She grinned back.

Goddamn, it was like being hit by a pure ray of golden sunshine right in the solar plexus. My breath stuttered in my lungs.

For the first time in my entire twenty-seven years, I was jealous of one of my brothers because I wanted this woman. And the irony? I'd had my chance and rejected her. Karma was a fucking bitch.

At that moment, Alex broke through the crowd, with Sebastian and Emma at his back. As he introduced them, I stepped back and melted into the crowd. Sebastian, who looked almost identical to the rest of us Lupu brothers, with our height and frame, took her small, delicate hand in his. Emma looked the least like a Lupu with a head of strawberry blonde curls that ended at her chin. She was petite and curvy. And nerdy as all hell. She was a riot, in fact, and I liked her best of all. We could talk shop since she was an AI researcher and I was into anything digital.

Although I stepped away, I was unwilling to leave the vicinity, so I stopped to congratulate Nicu with a clap on the shoulder. He gave me a look of unadulterated boredom. Nicu was most comfortable in a barefisted street fight, or maybe a cage fight. Either way, it was someplace rough and dirty, not a pretty engagement party in a lux suburban mansion like mine.

A rush of anger, mixed with being offended on Cat's behalf, surged through me. "Your fiancée is beautiful. You lucked out, you know that, right?"

"Y'think? I don't have a thing for blondes like you do," he mused, tilting his head as he inspected her critically, like she was an insect mounted in a display case. "Plus, she was your responsibility first." My eyes narrowed at his unnecessary dig as he motioned for a waiter, swiped a shot of țuică, and threw it down his throat. When was he going to let go of his conviction that she was mine and start seeing her as his responsibility? He was going to marry her after all, not me. That realization slapped me hard across the face, yet again.

I glared at him. How he did not take one look at her and want her was a mystery. *The girl's a beauty.* I couldn't recall the last time I'd seen someone so stunning. I shook my head. He was fucking insane. Although, I was the idiot who agreed to host the Popescus for this extended weekend. What the hell had I been thinking? Oh yeah, that Tasa and her man were coming, and it would be easier for everyone if they didn't stay in my mother's house. She still hadn't completely forgiven Tasa for running away from her engagement to Cristo to marry another guy. This extended weekend-long engagement party was also an opportunity for Alex and Nelu to discuss business and meet Nelu's partners from Afghanistan.

But the woman drew me like a moth to a flame. Even now, standing beside my brother, her *fiancé*, I had trouble keeping my eyes off her. I could struggle through the entire long-ass weekend, but what about the rest of my life? I couldn't go on lusting after my brother's wife. It didn't matter that they cared nothing for each other. If I knew Nicu, that wouldn't change anytime soon, if ever. I was more determined than ever to get away from New York. Laguna Beach was where I wanted to be anyway, even if our presence there would never be as strong and impressive as New York and Chicago in the future. To hell with it. My sanity and peace of mind were more important than the size of my territory and reach of my power. I'd have to try to catch Alex alone at some point and work on convincing him to let me go. It was my only option. As for the marriage condition he'd imposed, I was going to pretend I didn't hear it and try to wear him down.

5

I was roaming around the empty garden, flitting from place to place, burying my nose in flowers, and inhaling the deep scent of the different varieties planted throughout the lavish space. I pressed my nose into a drooping, heavy bloom and inhaled. Early morning dew tickled my nose. A camellia. I recognized it from boarding school. Their bushy pink blossoms were so potent and lush, they were unmistakable.

I took a seat on a stone bench under a cascade of lavender-colored wisteria that dripped from the arbor above me, shielding me from the strong sun. I appreciated the shade since I had a little hangover from the night before. The weight of having to pretend to be the blushing fiancée was straining. Then, there was meeting Luca, and the blunder I committed in flirting with him. Which is what led me to drink one too many glasses of champagne, leaving me with the added problem of a headache. Taking in a deep breath, I raised my face to the soft breeze, listening to the tinkling of the fountain and luxuriating in the peace and quiet. We were here for the entire weekend, which I thought was an exaggeration, but my mother was more animated than I'd seen her in a year. My father, Simu, and my brother were conducting business with the Lupu men, so I didn't have much say in the matter.

After a while, I returned inside and continued my aimless wandering. Having found out that this was Luca's place, I was curious about the house and what it said about him. The place wasn't a simple plot of land. It was more like an estate. The front half was a forest of trees, with a long road cutting through from the tall, spiked iron front gate to the semicircular driveway in front of the mansion. The white facade had eight groupings of double Doric columns that extended past the second floor, which was dotted with French doors, to the gabled roof. It felt like a mash-up of a Southern plantation and a French chateau, ostentatious without being tacky.

Since I entered through the front entrance, I took the large sweeping stairway in the foyer to the upstairs, pausing at the landing dividing the floor into two wings. The wing where my family was staying to my left—the guest wing. And to my right was the family wing, which was off-limits. I heard my parents rousing behind the door nearest to me. Not wanting to simply go back to my room until everyone was awake, and not able to explore the other wing, I returned downstairs.

The first floor was decorated with simple, clean lines in white and different shades of light gray with pops of color. Modern, but not sleek. It was...comfortable. I sailed through the sprawling living room, which had been returned to its normal arrangement with groupings of furniture. It was simple and elegant but also surprisingly comfortable look-ing. I shied away from the clusters of women settled in the various couches and armchairs gossiping and checked out the other rooms. There was a formal dining room in deep reds with the beginnings of breakfast being laid out, a comfy family room in dark blues, and a library, which was the only room that was heavy on dark wood, like libraries should be.

I passed the kitchen, where a cohort of employees was busy finishing serving breakfast, and spotted a narrow set of steps going to the basement. Slipping down the stairs, I coasted through a large room with an enormous screen, past a few empty bedrooms, and into an exercise room. An open sliding door looked out onto a deck, where I caught sight of bright blue water that could only be a pool and more flowers.

Curious, I was silently moving farther into the room to get a better look when I noticed that the door of the bathroom was slightly ajar. I heard the sounds of a shower going, and as I crept past, I paused and froze in my spot. There were earbuds, a phone, and an expensive watch laying on a bench near the bathroom. My mouth instantly went dry. I recognized that watch from yesterday. I swallowed around the lump lodged in my parched throat. A rush in my eardrums competed with the pulsating jets of the shower. Would I risk it? Would I nudge the door open and satisfy my curiosity about who was on the other side? In the shower, naked?

My fingers twitched by my side as I battled with myself. I squeezed my eyes shut, willing myself to walk away. *Just walk away, Cat. Walk away!* But I couldn't. I took a step closer. Then another. Still battling myself, I leaned in closer, placing my ear closer to the tiny opening of the door. I heard a low moan followed by a grunt. Those sounds went straight to my clit, like it had been zapped by an electric prod. Seriously, it was such an immediate and powerful reaction, I stumbled back a step. My heart skipped a few beats, my hands flexing at my sides. The noises I heard sounded remarkably like the ones in a porn clip Jewel showed me one time to demonstrate how to blow a guy.

Biting my bottom lip hard, curiosity and lust got the upper hand, and I lost the battle. In an explosion of movement, I shoved the door open. It bounced against the wall and smacked me in the side, but I stood stock-still in shock, my eyes glued to the vision before me.

Dear. God.

Past the glass of the shower was Luca. One large hand braced on the tiled wall in front of him, his other hand was wrapped around the thick trunk of his veiny cock. Hanging between his muscular thighs were heavy testicles, and for some reason, that was as sexy as the hand moving intently over the rigid length of his shaft. I'd never seen a penis in real life and this was one hell of an introduction. Heat flushed my cheeks as wetness pooled between my legs.

I started panting as he slapped the stone-colored wall and groaned.

That. Sound.

Oh, man, I was close to hyperventilating from the surge of lust volleying through my veins.

"It's not polite to walk into a man's bathroom," a growly voice intoned.

I jumped out of my skin and yelped, but my eyes were stuck on Luca and his huge cock. I snapped my mouth shut. My panting must have given me away.

I stuttered, "I-I wasn't... I mean, I didn't..."

His piercing gray eyes snapped to mine. "Didn't what? Didn't mean to stray? Didn't mean to watch?"

Amusement seeped through the harsh tone of his voice. I should've spun around and run off. I should've gasped and backed out. I should've done anything but stand there like an idiot, watching hungrily like a starved beggar, but I was powerless to move. I couldn't move an inch. I couldn't tear my eyes away from him if I wanted to. Hell, I could barely breathe. Did I mention he was still jacking off in front of me? That he hadn't stopped for an instant, hissing through his teeth when he treated his cock to a particularly rough hand? The man was bold; I'd give him that.

But then again, so was I.

He moaned again, a sound that wound its way through my body once again. My nipples stiffened. I pressed my thighs together, trying to create a little friction.

"Beautiful," he warned. "You shouldn't watch."

"You're right, I shouldn't," I rasped out, but there was no stopping me. This was the hottest, filthiest thing I'd ever witnessed, and I needed to see it to the end. His molded ass cheeks, tight and flexing with each thrust into his big, clenched hand, showcased concave indentations on the sides with two perfect dents. Oh, and did I mention the tats on his hand and fingers? There was a beautiful, intricate rose in the center with different symbols on each finger.

"Maybe you should stop," I counseled, marveling that my voice came out somewhat even.

He barked out an incredulous laugh. "With those beautiful brown eyes on me, gorgeous? Not a chance. I don't claim to be a good man."

I didn't bother to respond because there wasn't much else to say. Here we were: him jacking off and me watching.

"You're a curious kitten, aren't you?" he asked, his voice hoarse as his hand gripped harder and went faster until it was a blur. The crown was getting darker, and his shaft seemed to elongate and maybe stiffen. In the sauna-like heat of the shower, one floor separating us from the regular world whirling around above, we were trapped in our own dreamland. Time slowed; every movement he made was loaded with deliberation and intensity.

Secreted away and cocooned in this sheltered realm, I moved closer to get a better look. Since I was long past the moment of leaving, I intended to squeeze every sexy drop out of this experience. Bringing my bottom lip between my teeth, I licked it repeatedly. Then I gave the top lip the same treatment.

"Keep doing that to your lips, baby girl. You watching makes me want to fuck myself raw," he muttered, his glittering silvery eyes blazing into me and then returning to his cock. My own fingers twitched to touch myself.

"Oh, fuck it," I muttered as I dragged my skirt up and plunged my fingers down my panties.

His nostrils flared.

"Christ." Lower jaw slackening, he ordered, "Let me see it. Let me see that slippery wet pussy. Come on, let me see that good-girl virgin pussy."

I was so far gone that I instinctively followed his command and yanked my panties down to midthigh, turning to give him a good view of my fingers rubbing my clit and pushing in between my slick lips. He was right when he called me good. Until now, I didn't do crazy. But I was so far gone that I didn't care. The despair of my upcoming marriage coupled with an insane attraction to a man who couldn't be more off-limits, I'd fallen off the deep end. But, at this moment, I was powerless to turn away from him. I had single-mindedly determined to see this to its conclusion.

My first live penis, and what a specimen it was. His entire body was drool-worthy, with his ridged abs and the large slabs of muscles that were his thighs. The water plastered his dark golden hair to his skull, coloring it a few shades darker.

His glittering eyes were riveted to me. Having stayed a virgin this long in life, I was a pro at masturbation, and my fingers went faster and faster. The rhythmic sound of his hand slapping his cock pushed me over, and I came with a cry of surprise.

Stumbling, my back hit the wall of the bathroom. Hips jerking, my vision blacked out as a strong climax tore through me. When I finally came down and regained my sight, he'd already come. Head thrown back, his thick neck stretched taut. His hand slowed its pace, and I only got to see the last few spurts of his seed, joining what he'd splattered on the shower wall. Dammit. I frowned in disappointment.

Suddenly, shame slammed down on me. The impact of what I had done shuddered through me like an earthquake. I just got off on crazy-hot almost sex with my soon-to-be brother-in-law. What the hell? My stomach roiled. I clutched my belly. He was right that I was a good girl. I didn't do things like this. He had a twisted power over me that made me lose control.

"Oh my God, oh my God," I rambled to myself.

I shuddered once, yanking my hand away Panicking, I batted my skirt down with shaking hands, spun around, and ran out of there like the devil was on my heels.

MOTHER*FUCKER*. I was a sick bastard. Seriously, I always knew something was wrong with me, but now there wasn't a shred of doubt that I was out of my goddamn mind. I masturbated in front of my kid brother's fiancée and goaded her to do the same. And holy fuck, the way she looked when she was coming. Jesus, it was a thing of beauty. I'd *never* get that image out of my mind.

Slamming the shower off, I grabbed a towel and roughly dried myself off. Conflicting emotions tore through me like an avalanche. On one hand, that had to be the hottest non-sex *and* sex I'd ever had, hands down. Christ Almighty, they should fucking handcuff me, beat me to a bloody pulp, and throw me in a dungeon to rot for eternity.

Nothing could take away the image of her lovely slim thighs pressed together, underneath her skirt rucked up to her waist. The elastic band of her panties left a red mark halfway down her thighs as she opened them to get better access to that sweet pussy. And seeing her sweet, bare pussy? So pink and wet. The way her eyes sparkled as she stared at me, riveted. And when she came, it was a sight to behold. The way her gorgeous face twisted in ecstasy. She obviously knew her way around her own body, which was hot as fuck.

Cat might be a virgin, but she was no blushing, hesitant prude. As inexperienced as she was with sex, she was already a sultry creature. She was as curious as she was sensual and knew how to seek her own pleasure. That combination would be explosive in bed. She was too inquis-itive for her own good, but under my tutelage, I'd harness that fiery curiosity into something even more beautiful than it already was. With the right touch, she'd flower into a deadly siren.

Her shocked expression told me it was the first time she'd ever seen a cock. And this was from someone who had chances to experiment, coming from a co-ed boarding school. What were her parents thinking putting her in a school with boys? It testified to how obedient and disci-plined she was. I shuttered my eyes, letting out a low groan as I gripped my burgeoning cock. Fuck, what I could do with all that sweet obedience under my power.

Afterward, the way her cheeks flushed and the droopy drowsiness of her eyes before she snapped back to reality was adorable. But by God, she had a beautiful pussy.

A pussy not meant for you, I reminded myself.

But, even with that, nothing, and I mean *nothing*, could rip the vision of her orgasm away from me. It was *mine*.

Mine.

The vision was, but she wasn't. She was most definitely *not* mine. Fuck. Every fiber in my being thundered at me to run after her, tackle her to the floor, and fuck her into oblivion. Which I could *not* do. Absolutely not. *What the hell are you thinking?* It must be the aftereffect of one of the hardest climaxes of my life. That was the only logical explanation for the drive raging inside me to run her down.

Nicu. She belongs to Nicu, not me.

My hands clenched so hard that I was sure my blunt nails drew blood. I threw on a pair of sweatpants and yanked on a clean T-shirt from the pile that the maid left downstairs for me, since I always took a shower down here after taking a swim or working out.

Not only was she irreverent, but Cat was bold. Strong. A virgin like her, watching me rub one off. Instead of screaming at the top of her lungs and running away, she moved closer so she could get a better look. When I ordered her to let me see her pussy, she instantly did as she was told. She simply shoved her panties down and showed me the most perfect cunt I'd ever laid eyes on. A breath shuddered out of me. Watching her touch herself made for one hell of an erotic vision. Christ, the way her mouth dropped open as she came. The little mewling sounds she made. It was a damn privilege to witness her undoing.

And now I lived with the knowledge of what Nicu's future wife looked like when she came.

And she was not mine. *Fuck me, because she could've been.* If I hadn't categorically rejected her, without getting a glimpse, I'd be her goddamn fiancé. In three months' time, I would've been the one balls deep in that pretty, *tight* pussy. Instead, I had outright denied Alex when he ordered me to marry her. I fought him tooth and nail for weeks until Nelu tricked him into accepting Cat himself. Thank fuck he'd investigated the situation and eventually figured out that it was all a ruse.

Once the cat was out of the bag and Alex was off the hook, he came back to me to marry Cat *again*. Which I refused *again*. I had been given *one more chance*, yet still managed to fuck it up.

And now?

Now, I'd never get to that untouched pussy. I was so fucked. If I hadn't been a contrarian, automatically rejecting whatever Alex asked of me, this weekend would be my engagement party. *Mine.*

I dragged my fingers through my hair, grasping the ends and tugging.

No.

There was something extraordinary between us, an underlying energy that I'd never felt with another person before, much less a woman. This level of intimacy was unprecedented in my life.

And I wasn't about to let it go.

Something had to be done. I couldn't allow it to end like this. Although I had no idea what I was going to do, I would go to her. Not now. Not with a house full of people. But I'd figure out a way to see her alone soon. *And do what?*

I had no fucking idea.

6

After coming hard and not able to do anything but helplessly watch Cat flee like the devil was at her heels, the rest of my day was exhausting. The house was full of pampered women, with manicurists and a variety of other beauticians coming in and out, that I had to monitor for security reasons. Meanwhile, the men were holed up in the library for meetings, taking the necessary breaks for eating, drinking, and to watch a soccer game.

It was past midnight by the time I nodded to the guard in the hallway as he patrolled the house. On the landing of the stairway separating the two wings of my home, I paused. When the guard turned the corner, I ducked into the wing that held the rooms occupied by the Popescu family. I should never have dared step onto their side of the house, but I knew I wouldn't fall asleep after what happened that morning.

Palming the master key in my hand, I decided to visit Cat and just...feel her for a moment. Sit in her presence and breathe her in. Maybe that would help guide my next steps.

It was obvious that I was grasping for excuses to see her, but that awareness didn't deter me one bit.

Unlocking the door, I slipped quietly into her dark bedroom. In the center of the room was a canopied bed, with burgundy velvet curtains tied to the tall wooden posts. Peacefully asleep, her long lashes fanned across her cheeks, blonde like her hair, eyes moving beneath her lids. Her lush lips curved up in a small, mysterious smile, reminding me of the Mona Lisa.

Her full breasts strained against the pink silk of her nightgown, shadows of her nipples evident against the thin, light-colored material. I salivated at the thought of bending down and sucking them into my mouth, making them nice and wet. Maybe swiping my tongue over the wet material, rubbing until her nipples went stiff. I'd slip my hand beneath the single sheet and tickle her little clit until she woke up moaning into my mouth.

She made a movement, throwing off the sheet and flinging her hand over her head. My eyes greedily drank in her flat stomach. Fuck, she was gorgeous. Her leg bent and slid upward, pulling the silk of her nightie and exposing a beautiful slim thigh. My cock went rock hard. All the while, the scent of fresh nectarine blossoms drifted over me. I could only imagine what she tasted like.

Glaring down, I stared at the slight gap between her thighs. My fingers twitched, and I had to stop myself from helping her silk nightie farther up her leg to show me that sweet, innocent pussy again. Fuck, I was a bastard. Thank God, I'd never pretended to be anything else. Otherwise, I'd take the prize for being a hypocrite.

Mumbling, her brows drew together before they smoothed over and she tossed her head to the side, away from me. What a restless sleeper. That didn't surprise me, for some reason. As strong as she was, there was a fragile innocence about her. If she were wrapped in my arms, I'd keep her still through the night.

My fingertips coasted down her cheek.

So soft.

Her arm flung out, and she made a distressed sound like some evil interloper had crashed into her dream. Her shoulders swished from side to side as if trying to shrug off the unpleasantness. A keening sound, pitiful really, came from her parted lips, getting louder and louder by the second.

Worried someone might hear her and try to enter, I laid down and wrapped her into my arms. Her intoxicating peach blossom scent wrapped around me. It was like lying in a fresh meadow in the middle of a hot summer night under a cascade of shooting stars.

Turning into my chest, she nuzzled the cotton of my T-shirt. I felt it grow damp beneath her cheek. She was crying. Having a father and brother like hers would make anyone cry, but what the hell? She was a protected princess. A jewel. She shouldn't be weeping in her sleep.

Suddenly, a rage took hold of me, choking me. What the fuck had they done to her? Why hadn't they done a better job of protecting her? It was their duty to take care of her, coddle her, and make sure none of their nonsense encroached on her life. One of the few traditions I supported was protecting our women.

Something niggled in the hidden recesses of my mind. Whatever was giving her nightmares was the reason they'd sent her off to boarding school. Cat was the only *mafie* girl I'd ever heard of being sent away to school, that's how unusual it was. Maybe I was conflating two unrelated occurrences, but my gut told me something was off. And I followed my gut. It was one of the first lessons of any *mafie* made man. If I had to take a guess, I'd say something happened to her, and they sent her away to either help her or hide their fuck up.

Petting her hair gently, I racked my brain, trying to recall how old she'd been when she'd left for that fancy school in Massachusetts. I shushed and hummed to her until her heartbreaking crying tapered off and she snuggled into my arms. Drawing her knees into her chest, she huddled into me as if seeking comfort from a thunderstorm. I caressed her cheek with my knuckles until she settled down into quiet, normal sleep. My chest swelled with pride at her response to my ministrations.

I couldn't leave her. At least, not yet. My lips brushed the crown of her head. The gentle pressure of her lithe body nestled against mine humbled me. For the first time in the longest time, I had a purpose that extended beyond myself and my family. Watching over her made sense. Something clicked inside me, and for the first time, I felt like I belonged. Snuggled together in the cocoon of her bed, where she and I were all that existed, felt right. Her warm breath fluttered over my skin. I soaked in the richness of these feelings.

The night would pass too quickly, and with it, the spell would be broken. I'd stay for a while and creep away like a thief before she woke up. A strain of sadness quivered inside me at the realization that I couldn't share this with her. That she'd never consciously experience this time with me. She belonged to Nicu and the only moments I'd have with her alone, holding her close, would be stolen ones like these. And even they would have to end once she was married.

I SMELLED something spicy and warm. Speaking of warm, one whole side of my body was as blazing hot as a furnace. I shuddered at the cold front on my back and nuzzled deeper into the warmth of my pillow.

My *hard* pillow.

My fingers flexed against white cotton and again...I felt hardness. Soft cotton snagged over a hard surface beneath my cheek.

My eyes fluttered open and I stared into this strange white cotton. My head ticked up and my vision was filled with the beautiful, cruel face I recognized so well. *Luca?* I must be dreaming. This was a dream. I stared at dark blond eyelashes casting shadows that sloped over the hard angle of his tanned cheekbone.

A puff of breath ghosted over my forehead and I blinked. This was no dream; I was awake and Luca was in my bed.

Lifting onto my elbow, I shook my brain fog and found myself curled into Luca's side. Good grief, he took up space. His broad chest heaved once and his shoulders stretched the wrinkled cotton of his shirt. Now I knew why the front of my body was so hot. He gave off some serious heat.

And that spicy male scent...I bit into my lip. His chest lifted and fell rhythmically beneath my splayed hand, my fingers digging into the soft cotton.

Okay, okay.

I took in a bracing breath.

Think.

My head snapped left and right.

The room was empty. The door was closed. Dim light filtered through a part in the curtains. No noises came from the hallway, so it must still be early. What the hell was he doing in my room? In my bed?

Panicking, I quickly rucked up my nightie and peered between my thighs.

No blood. No reddened skin.

My gaze inspected the sheets where I was lying.

Pristine.

I blew out a long breath.

Okay, I'm still a virgin.

Spinning my head around the room, I forced myself to focus. I had no idea how or why he was here, but the most important issue was getting him gone. Fast. As long as he was out of here before anyone found him, this situation was salvageable. Otherwise...I shuddered. My father would murder him in this bed, and I'd have another traumatic incident to deal with. Oh, and the little fact that Luca, second son of the Lupu clan, would be dead. Slaughtered by my father. World War Three would be triggered. The streets of Queens would run red with rivers of blood.

Staring down at the hard planes of his chest, I noticed that his T-shirt had ridden up, exposing his tiered abs. A slim trail of dusky blond snaked down between the ridged muscles, and the vision of him jacking off flashed in front of me. That memory dragged my gaze down to the stiff column of his morning wood. Oh, God. I twisted my head to the side and swallowed audibly.

Shaking his shoulder, I hissed out in a low, harsh whisper, "Luca, Luca, wake up."

Luca's big body jerked.

His eyes fluttered open.

"Fuck," he muttered, ruffling his hair with his fingers. His sleepy eyes blinked a few times until they came into focus. Yikes, but was he sexy. I didn't know what men looked like when they woke up, but there was a moment of vulnerability when he resembled a little boy. It was downright dangerous. I couldn't lounge back and admire him like I had the right to have him in my bed, but if I did...*yum*.

Instead, I had to get him the hell out of here, pronto.

"What are you doing here?" I rushed out in a whisper.

"We didn't do anything," he assured me, his hand covering mine. The weight and warmth of it was delicious and my lashes fluttered in response.

Shaking it off before I did something stupid, I huffed out, "Duh, I know. I already checked."

His lopsided smirk slid in place. "You checked? Like you checked to see if that silky pussy was still intact? Fuck, wish I had seen that."

In a gruff just-woke-up voice that had my nipples pebbling, he teased, "What, you don't trust me?"

Crossing my arms to hide the evidence of my arousal, I glared at him. "Why should I?"

His gaze slid down my body, pausing at my arms as if he had X-ray vision and could see the hard peaks that I was so desperate to hide. Forehead furrowed in concentration, his eyes continued down my body in a possessive stare that left me trembling with the urge to spread myself for his perusal. "Maybe you shouldn't."

A shudder rolled through me, and I jerked away from him. "What are you even doing here?"

His eyes shot away from me, embarrassment crossing his face. My pulse accelerated. What happened that made him shy away from me? Breathing in, I focused on keeping myself calm. I didn't remember anything, but I'd had too much to drink again last night. *Whatever happened between us, I can handle it.*

"I was patrolling the hallways and heard you crying loudly. You're marrying my dickhead brother, but...even so, you sounded in pain. I happened to have the master key on me, so I checked to see if you were okay." He shut his eyes, as if recalling what he walked into last night. "You were in distress. I didn't think you'd want everyone to hear you and come knocking, so I laid down on top of the covers and... held you." He cleared his throat. "You settled down right away. I meant to leave, but I guess I fell asleep."

I felt the color drain from my face. Oh. My. God. My nightmares were back. They had gone away while I was away at boarding school. At least, my roommate never complained and she would've if they'd woken her up. They hadn't returned when I came home. Perhaps the stress of my depressing marriage had triggered their revival.

I averted my gaze in shame. There was no way I was going to explain to Luca why I was crying in my sleep so loudly that he'd been driven to enter my bedroom in the middle of the night. At least he'd been kind enough to comfort me. But now? Now there was no explaining away the fact that we'd shared a bed the entire night.

"What happened, Cat?" he asked, watching me carefully. Not with pity, thank goodness.

I shifted nervously under his scrutiny.

His jaw tightened. "Did someone hurt you? Your father or brother?"

My eyes got wide.

"What? No, of course not!" I knew my clan had a reputation for being ruthless, but my family would never hurt me. "That would never ever happen. My family loves me and treats me like gold. I'm their princess."

The anger flashing in his eyes and the tension in his expression triggered a thunderbolt of heat through my body. He stared at me for a long moment, as if debating something. Finally, he must have decided to trust my word. I let out a sigh of relief. If he was protective enough to comfort me in my sleep, I didn't want to consider what he would do if he hadn't believed me. He looked like he was about to tear down the walls of the house. As scary as he appeared in that moment, I felt a well of pride at how defensive he was on my behalf. I'd never been on the receiving end of that kind of sentiment from anyone other than my father, Cristo, and Simu. I wasn't a member of his clan, yet he was already protective of me. That left me light-headed and giddy.

"So, what was it? Did someone hurt you at school?" His fingers curled into fists. "I'll go up there myself and tear the fucker limb from limb."

"No, no, nothing like that," I insisted, twitching my nose in nervousness. Oh, God, I was going to have to tell him so he didn't think something god-awful happened to me. I mean, it did, but not directly to me.

Inhaling deeply, I peeked at his solemn face.

"It was an accident," I started with that caveat to lessen the impact of my confession. "I witnessed my father choke a man."

Fury lined his face. I flinched at his expression and quickly lifted my hands, palms out, in a pleading gesture. "I was in the wrong place at the wrong time. It was no one's fault. It just happened, but it...rattled me, and I've had nightmares ever since. Well, not at school. For some reason, I don't have them at school. Maybe because I know that I'm far away from all of this."

"You slept well last night," he said, his voice dropping. His finger reached out and caressed my kneecap in small comforting circles that made me want to keel over in a swoon. "Once I pulled you close to me, you calmed down immediately."

"Right," I said, heat creeping up my neck and flagging my cheeks. Shifting my leg away from his touch, I checked my phone charging on the night table. "It's after six. My *bunică* is up by now. I have no idea how you're going to get out of here without getting caught."

He sat up. Scratching his abdomen, his fingers raised his shirt up, exposing those ripples of firm muscles that made me gulp. My own fingers itched to touch, to explore. I pulled in a harsh breath. *Restrain yourself.* Yeah, I had to get him out of here before I did something irresponsible. Something more irresponsible than what I had done yesterday.

He caught my eye. Grabbing my fidgeting hand, he held it tightly as if to comfort me and assured me, "Hey, it's going to be okay. I'll get out of here and no one will be the wiser."

I cocked my head, listening for sounds. I heard nothing, but that could change in an instant, and then how would I hide this huge male specimen in this room. There weren't any closets, only an old-style wardrobe that he'd never fit in. I leaned over and checked beneath my bed. Not enough room for him to hide underneath. Why did he have to be so enormous? I would've definitely fit under the bed. This was a disaster.

"Even if you get out of here without anyone spotting you, no one can ever find out that you were with me alone. Promise me, Luca."

His sober eyes bored into mine. "I promise. I'm not trying to fuck up your life," he swore as he released my hand and hopped out of bed. Striding to my window, he peeked out from behind the curtain. I couldn't help admiring the broadness of his shoulders or how his back tapered down into a narrow waist.

With his back to me, he said, "The guards are on duty circle every fifteen minutes. I'll wait until I see one and then go over the balcony and make my way down to the bottom."

"That's like a lot of distance down there. You'll fall."

His head swerved in my direction and he gave me a devastatingly boyish grin. "I won't fall. I was a gymnast in my teens."

Of course, he was. God, could he be any more perfect? Really, it was sickening. Nothing was more catnippy to a Romanian girl than a gymnast. My eyes slid down his tall frame, pausing on the definition of his triceps, and I didn't doubt his skills for a second. The man was built. I shook off the lust, firmly reprimanding myself. I couldn't have him, and I needed to keep that in mind.

How was I going to manage once I was married to Nicu and we were forced to be in the same room? It was sure to happen. Both their penthouses were on the same floor. The very penthouse where I would be living, day in, day out. Oh, God, what if we were stuck in the elevator together? His huge body crowding me up against a wall, hoisting me into his arms and spreading me wide. Me, writhing against his hard cock, legs dangling over his firm ass. I mentally smacked myself. *Get a grip, Cat, and focus.* First things first. I had to get out of this situation or there would be no marriage, no living next to him. And when I did live near him, I'd have to avoid him like the plague because I wasn't a cheater.

He popped the French doors open and focused on what was going on outside. I slipped out of bed and stood beside him. Although I couldn't see much past his wide shoulders, I did get off on his spicy scent and the warmth emanating from his body.

Five minutes later, he whispered, "Okay, the guard just passed."

Pushing the door wide enough for him to exit, he swung his leg over the little metal balcony, and expertly scaled down the stone wall of his house with ease and jumped down without a hitch. I watched the whole thing, stunned. Once on solid ground, he glanced up and winked at me before jogging off. I followed his progress until he rounded the corner and was gone.

I pressed my back against the wooden frame of the door. Holy fuck.

What in the world just happened?

7

After creeping out of Cat's bedroom, I worked out to burn off the extra energy I was storing from having a hard dick after sleeping next to her luscious body. I showered, grabbed food from the buffet laid out in the dining room, and sought cover in the library to brood in peace. The bright morning sun streamed through the open French doors leading out into the garden, lighting the dark leather furniture and shelves of books that lined one wall.

Waking up in Cat's bed, with her sexy little body beside me was something else. Her arousal didn't escape my notice when she crossed her arms over her chest to hide her peaked nipples. Her deep brown eyes were heavy-lidded with lust, her pouty lips red from gnawing them. The potent desire between us was a palpable thing. Still, I was impressed that she didn't jump out of bed screaming when she woke up beside me.

Then again, I shouldn't have been surprised. The girl had a spine of steel. I suppose one had no choice, growing up in her family. When she'd told me that her father had been so sloppy as to murder some fucker in her presence, I almost blew a gasket. Violence was endemic in our society, but there was a time and place for torture and death. Which meant that he'd brought one of his quarries home. What kind of father was so careless? My blood started pounding hard just thinking about it.

I'd never reacted to a woman like I did to Cat, even when I was young and the desire to fuck rode me hard. But this one...this one was special. That undeniable fact made her dangerous. Ravenous didn't begin to describe how I felt. I wanted to gorge myself on her. I couldn't stop thinking about her, which was why I was hiding out in the library, avoiding her at all costs.

While I was eating, Alex strolled into the library with a chessboard under his arm. He sat down, propped his smartphone up against a green-shaded lamp on the huge desk, turned it on to Twitch, and moved the pieces as he followed along with an online game. He was the perfectionist in the family, constantly working on his moves. I watched for a while, and then we started a game together. Later, Nicu strolled in and took a seat nearby, poking at his cell phone while throwing a glance at our game every once in a while.

That was how Mama found us.

"I have two things I'd like to discuss with you, Alex," she began as she took a seat on the oxblood leather couch closest to him, taking my attention away from my wayward thoughts of Cat.

Carefully placing the knight down on the board, he turned to her and said, "What's up?"

"I think we need to have Tasa's wedding first," she began. Her reunion with Tasa had been dramatic, to say the least, but they had made up. "With the baby coming, it would be wrong for Nicu to be married first. You'll have to make Nelu understand."

Alex's brows gathered. "How long do you intend for the Popescus to wait?"

"It's only fair that it will take three months, like for Nicu's wedding. Tasa would like to have her marriage at the Orthodox church in Manhattan. Afterward, it will take months to prepare a wedding that will make the right statement for Nicu."

"Fair enough," he replied with a nod. "I'll speak to Nelu. It won't be easy, especially since he will not want to concede for Tasa's sake."

"I think I have something that could make it go down easier," replied my mother.

"Which is?" Alex prodded.

"I was talking to Cat and her mother yesterday...and she mentioned that she'd like to take summer classes at Barnard College. You know, the women's college on the Upper West Side? I have to say that it speaks well of her that she wants to continue educating herself. Apparently, she went to a prestigious prep school and took her studies seriously. Perhaps you can use that as leverage. Make it seem like a concession. Insist that it is a point of honor for us to take care of her protection since she's Nicu's fiancée." She gave a little shrug. "Just an idea. I haven't really thought it through."

Alex placed his elbows on the end of the desk, steepling his fingers together as he reflected on her suggestion.

"Hmm, I could work with that. What kind of classes will she be taking?" he asked.

"Something about Anthropology and Feminism."

Nicu rolled his eyes. "Feminism?"

My eyebrows lifted. Huh, I didn't know much about this girl, but I was intrigued. She was smart and into academics.

Alex and I took to our studies like fish to water, whereas Nicu struggled to finish his B.A.

"Maybe she wants to major in Gender Studies," I taunted.

"Oh, please," he grumbled, returning to his phone.

Mama gave Nicu a withering look, and emphasized, "Like I said, it speaks well of her. She's obviously invested and isn't wasting her summer going to parties or clubs. She seems like a serious girl. She'll be good for you, Nicu. Get you to settle down."

Nicu snorted.

Mama narrowed her eyes on me and jabbed a finger at me. "And you. You'd do well to find yourself such a fine girl. Popescu or not, she's a woman of quality. Not only is she sweet-natured, but she's clearly lively and intelligent."

Yeah, that wasn't the only thing about her that was lively. Her nipples poking out of the silk nightie she was wearing were pretty damn lively as well. Given half a chance, I'd *live* between her tits.

"Don't worry about me. You have your hands full trying to convince Nicu that she can rise above her status as a Popescu," I retorted. "I'd be willing to give her a chance, but he hates them with a passion and doesn't see anything beyond her last name."

"I'm a little worried about that, Nicu. You make no effort whatsoever to get to know her. Any time I try to bring you two together, you go out of your way to snub her." Her eyebrows knitted in worry. "She's noticed, and I see her retreating into her shell around you."

"Don't push him, Mama," Alex advised. "That's not going to help the situation. They have to find their own way to live together. If you start butting in now, it will only take them longer to find their footing in the marriage."

"But if you told Nicu that he should drive her to school and back, they'll be forced to spend time together and he'll warm up to her. She really is a lovely girl."

Oh, I could attest to that. And the idea of my brother in the car with Cat for several hours a week was making the hairs on my nape prick up in alarm. Which made no sense because soon they'd be married and spending a lot more time together. I shook my head.

"Mama, what did I just say? It could as easily backfire if you push," chastised Alex.

"You got that right," Nicu griped under his breath, eyes glued to his phone.

"Plus," Alex continued, "there's no way Nelu will allow them to be alone, traveling back and forth for weeks, just prior to the wedding. It's not appropriate. If we don't find someone to protect her from the upper echelons of our clan, he'll insist that Cristo or Simu drive her."

Simu?

I hated that bastard more than I hated Cristo, and that was saying something. The rivalry between Simu and me started with a woman. Of course, it did. Nothing could be more stereo-typically *mafie*. I'd fucked one of his women. She'd come into *our* nightclub and hit on me hard. I simply took what she was offering. How was I to know she was his? Afterward, the girl went around comparing the two of us in bed. I came out on top.

Only in a small, insular world like ours could a woman's big mouth start something. It triggered an insane rivalry that lasted for years. We stole each other's loot and poached each other's women. Truth be told, I didn't really have women, but it didn't stop Simu from trying to hook up with anyone I'd fucked.

It hit a high point when, one day, I mocked Simu. Told

him that his father was laughing his ass off seeing how far down the gutter his son's Cantacuzino ass had fallen. Granted, it wasn't my finest moment, talking trash about a man's dead father, but he was constantly provoking me, and I had put him in his place. Aristocratic family or not, he was as dirty as we were.

To my point, I'd caught the way he looked at Cat this weekend. He was half in love with her. No one else might have noticed how his beady little eyes constantly settled on Cat, but I sure as hell did, and I didn't like it one bit. The idea that he lusted after her made me want to tear him apart with my bare hands. She was practically a married woman! I was legit losing my mind considering what a hypocritical thing that was for me, of all people, to say. Nonetheless, there was a crucial difference between him and me. I was, and always would be, a Lupu. I'd never hurt my brother or disgrace my family. I wouldn't put it past Simu to go after Cat for the sole purpose of spitting on our name or trying to increase his clout with Nelu.

If he couldn't curtail his base instincts in a room full of people, what would stop him if he was alone with her for hours? Oh, hell no. That was not happening. Not under my watch.

"Make Luca do it," Nicu pronounced.

"What?" I huffed out, although my heart rate accelerated at the thought.

Alex's head snapped to Nicu. He jabbed a thumb in my direction as he asked, "Him?"

Irritation flared. Granted, I rarely volunteered, especially for something as inconsequential as babysitting duty, but Alex didn't have to act so stunned.

"Yes, him," Nicu replied languidly.

"I don't think so..." I said. As tempting as it was, it wasn't a good idea.

Nicu's gaze bored into me, a calculating expression on his face. My skin felt itchy under his scrutiny. As much as I wanted it, being around Cat would be torture.

"Seriously, I have better things to do," I muttered.

Staring at me with a serious look, he demanded, "Step the fuck up, man."

"Fuck you," I snarled, glaring at him. We had a staring contest for a long minute.

"Are you going to let Simu do it?" he taunted. "Because that's the alternative if you bail out, yet again."

Fuck, that cinched it. I tapped out first, breaking our stare.

"Fine," I bit out. "Just to be clear, I'm doing this to prove to Alex how flexible I can be." Hopefully, being forced to undergo this test would help my case regarding Cali.

Nicu inclined his head in agreement.

"It's not necessary," Alex responded. "I have other less pointless jobs for you that won't waste so much of your time. I can find a soldier who can easily do this."

Over my fucking dead body. For some reason, I refused to explore, I didn't like the idea of a soldier spending hours a day with her in my place. Anyway, a soldier wasn't high up enough to replace Simu.

"She's not pointless, she's our responsibility and we take care of our responsibilities," I ground out. "Family duty is nonnegotiable." Heard the phrase enough times in my life that it was tattooed on my brain. "She's engaged to a Lupu, and within a couple months, she'll be one of us. Until then, I'll personally make sure she's protected. It's our duty and we don't skimp when it comes to duty.

"Anyway, the more time she spends with our family, the

easier it will be for her. I'm sure they've filled her head with lies that we're violent brutes. She probably grew up listening to horrific bedtime stories about us. This way, she'll get to know us and we'll become human to her," I finished.

My forehead furrowed. I wasn't bullshitting. It had dawned on me that it mattered what Cat thought of us. Earlier this morning, I'd sworn to stay as far away from her as possible. I'd holed up in the library with that express purpose in mind. Despite my best efforts, here I was, lost in her once again. What was it about this girl that reeled me in, time and time again?

Before Alex could reply, Mama stood up as if everything was resolved. "Very good, then I'll leave it to you boys to make it work."

"If you offer Luca, Nelu can't refuse without insulting us," Nicu suggested.

"You're positive you want to bother with this?" Alex confirmed, one eyebrow raised. I still bristled at his question.

"I'm stepping up," I gritted out.

He threw up his hand in surrender. "Alright, good. It's settled."

IT WAS ANYTHING BUT SETTLED.

Instead, it had turned into a pissing match between Simu and me.

The Popescu and Lupu men had been in the library for hours. After going through the points of contention regarding the contract between the Popescu and Lupu clans regarding trafficking Afghani ephedrine from Nelu's suppliers through our transport routes into Europe, Alex brought up waiting on Nicu and Cat's wedding. Things were going at a steady clip until my brother offered me as the person to drive Cat to her classes.

Nelu seemed to be fine with the idea until Simu whispered into his ear.

Giving a short nod of his head, Nelu cleared his throat and carefully stated, "I'm not sure your brother is the right candidate for this job."

Stiffening, my eyebrows shot up to my forehead.

"Excuse me?" I replied in a dangerously low tone. If he thought I'd tolerate an underhanded insult from him or anyone from his family, he was in for the surprise of his life. "What in the fuck is that supposed to mean?"

"It means what it sounds like," answered Simu, his eyes burning into me with unfiltered hatred. I blatantly stared him down.

Ditto, motherfucker, ditto. The hatred was fully mutual.

I pushed forward until I was at the edge of my chair, about to launch an attack, when Alex put a staying hand on my forearm. Showing disrespect in front of our rivals was the only thing stopping me from shrugging him off.

"Please explain, Simu, and I suggest you choose your words carefully," prompted Alex.

Yeah, motherfucker, be really careful. Swear to God, I couldn't remember the last time I had such an overwhelming urge to clock the guy in his ugly-ass face.

Taking his time, he leaned back in his armchair, crossed one leg over the other, and folded his arms over his chest. I sent him a narrow-eyed glare. If he thought holding our attention captive would change the end result, the fucker had another thing coming.

"Luca has a reputation of being...unbiddable. He's not

one to follow rules. Therefore, I'm not sure he's the best person for this delicate job."

I snorted. "What the hell is delicate about driving a woman to her class, guarding her, and then driving her back? She's not a porcelain doll or made of spun glass. She's not going to break in my presence. Why don't you tell us what you really want?"

Simu's face hardened. "See? That just shows how little respect you have for our women—"

"What? Because I don't treat them like fragile objects? Because I treat them like human beings with minds of their own, somehow this connotes a *lack* of respect to you, you fucking barbarian?"

Realizing that I'd outed him as a misogynist, he tried another argument. "She'll be better off being protected by one of her own. Until the marriage, her last name is Popescu. It's our responsibility to protect her."

The heat from the sun coming through the windows doubled the fire burning in my belly.

"Actually, it's not that cut and dried. She's engaged to my little brother and we have already started working together under the contract running parallel to the marriage contract. We have already begun merging our family businesses together. We didn't wait until Cat's name was legally changed to begin working together," observed Alex.

Remaining silent, Nelu sat back in his chair and watched our interactions as if surveying a ball being volleyed back and forth in a tennis match.

Simu waved a dismissive hand. "That's work. This is about family."

"They're intricately connected," Alex replied bluntly. "You cannot separate one from the other. Therefore, it is completely within our rights to become involved in Cat's protection."

"She's safer with us," Simu snapped.

I flew to my feet, looming over him and thundered, "That's a fucking insult."

Nelu stood up, putting a hand on my shoulder, which I shrugged off before backing down.

Raising his hands in supplication, he began with a conciliatory little chuckle before saying, "Settle down, boys. I'm glad to see that my only daughter is so important that you're fighting over her. She'll be a great asset to your family. It's impressive that you already see her worth and consider her one of your own. That is a compliment to her upbringing." His hand landed on Simu's shoulder. "But we are still attached to her and worry about her comfort. She'll be more at ease with one of our family."

"But she *is* one of us and it's about time she began to get to know us," I insisted. "The groom should have a say in this as well. Nicu, what say you? Give us your final word."

Nicu hadn't said a word during this entire discussion, observing everyone closely, likely trying to interpret everyone's motivations. Thank Christ I had the excuse of doing this as a test of my newfound flexibility, but there was no way I was backing out now. Simu's opposition had turned this into a point of honor.

I held my breath as I waited for his response.

Nicu's incisive gaze narrowed on Simu for a long moment before turning to me. Clasping the arms of my chair, I shut down my expression and maintained a mask of disinterest, but I had no idea what he really saw. Our relationship wasn't as complicated as the one between Alex and me, but I'd never call it easy. We spent much of our time throwing digs at each other. I resented him for worshipping our bastard of a father and kowtowing to Alex's every demand. He was irritated that I didn't toe the line and lived to needle me. I didn't resent either of them for my radically different upbringing. It wasn't their fault. Nor had I ever been jealous of them.

Until now.

And I didn't know what to do with that information, so I buried it down deep.

Even though Nicu and I weren't close, we were brothers. I'd never hurt him. He didn't care a whit about Cat, so I wasn't worried about his feelings, but his pride was another thing. Cat was off-limits for that reason alone.

Finally, after what seemed like an interminable amount of time, he said, "She's going to be *my* wife. Her protection is *my* discretion. Regardless of how unbiddable he may seem, I trust my brother."

Thatta boy. There's the old Lupu loyalty.

Turning to Simu, he spat out, "Honestly, Simu, your opinion means nothing to me while my brother's does. As payment for your insult to his character, I insist it be Luca. Your lack of subtlety has only forced my hand. Let that be a lesson to you in the way you speak to us in the future."

Take that, you fucker.

There were few times when my family outright pleased me, but this show of allegiance had to have topped the list.

Whether I wanted it or not, rain or fucking shine, Cat was mine. A car ride from Queens to the Upper West Side could take at least an hour, each way. I had the enviable task of figuring out what the hell I was going to do with that bounty of time. And how I was going to keep my hands off her.

8

I was in the living room, waiting for Luca to pick me up and drive me to my first summer school class, a course on Culture, Society, and Catastrophe. Despite the shock of learning that Luca would be my chauffeur and guard, I was excited for the chance to study disasters through an anthropologic lens. Ever since I'd taken an elective in Anthropology as a junior, I'd been enthralled by the subject. Not only that, but Jewel was also taking this course.

Jewel was living on campus since her father was still doing time in an upstate federal penitentiary, and her mother had flown off to Monaco. This class was the perfect opportunity to spend time with her. Now I only had to see if Luca would let me have lunch with her. He was a busy man, so I wasn't sure he had the time to spare.

The summer was going far better than could be expected. The marriage had been pushed off until the fall for Tasa's wedding, which I was thrilled about. I wouldn't have to abandon my summer classes to go on a honeymoon, I'd live at home longer, and it gave us more time to scrounge up the money for this over-the-top wedding. Cristo was on my side about tempering the wedding expenses, but my parents were adamant about maintaining appearances.

My mother was still disappointed, but I consoled her by reminding her that she now had more than six measly weeks to host a wedding for several hundred people. I also promised to become more involved, which I had been avoiding like the plague up till now. I'd actively pushed away any thoughts of trying on a wedding dress, and I cringed at the thought of going with her to taste test the wedding meal, but I'd suck it up to please her. She was still weak after finishing her last round of chemo and I was willing to do anything to bring light into her eyes.

I was still getting over my surprise that Luca would be ferrying me back and forth to school. When I asked my father why Nicu wasn't driving me, he answered that it wasn't appropriate. He added that Nicu supported the decision. Cristo cursed under his breath and Simu looked like he was about to murder someone. And that was just about a car ride. Neither of them knew a fraction of what had transpired between Luca and me. A shiver shot down my spine at the thought that either of them would find out that Luca slept in my bed an entire night. God forbid they ever found out about what transpired in the bathroom. I couldn't even think about Luca jacking off without heat shooting in my core and my cheeks turning red.

Clasping my hands together, I leaned into the bay window overlooking our street as a sleek black Lamborghini SUV pulled up to our home. My tummy flip-flopped. He hadn't even gotten out of the car and already nerves exploded inside me. I didn't know how I was going to handle being alone with him. Since he was soon to be my brother-in-law and nothing could ever happen between us, I had to look at this time together as an opportunity to channel my feelings for him into friendship and platonic respect. Any other option would be emotional suicide.

Luca stepped out of his car and buttoned his fitted jacket over his tapered torso as he took the steps up to the front door. The man was devastatingly handsome. Compared to his tall, suited frame, I felt decidedly young in a casual summer dress. His sandy blond hair was groomed and under control, not like the time he woke up in my bed, with his wavy locks in a riot. He smoothed his hand down his patterned royal-blue tie, his long fingers gliding over the silk, the red of his rose tattoo contrasting sharply with the impeccable tie. God, what I'd do to have him caress me like he did his tie. I bit down on my bottom lip, forcing myself to stay in place as the doorbell rang.

I wanted to jump up and rush to open the door, but he had to get past one of my parents or Cristo first. Waiting with bated breath, I heard the heavy clop of two men coming up from the basement. My eyebrows lifted as I spotted Simu behind my father. Simu's pout reflected his foul mood. He reached the front door first. This was about to get brutal, for sure. From what I could recall, he and Luca had issues going back years, something about insulting his father. Men could be so juvenile sometimes. Considering what they did for a living, I marveled at how bent out of shape they could get over verbal insults.

From my seat at the bay window in the living room, I watched as Luca entered and greeted them. Compared to Luca, my father suddenly looked diminutive. Luca was at least a couple of inches over six feet, and with his broad shoulders, he towered over my father. After shaking his hand, my father stepped to the side and waved Luca in. Simu stayed glued in his spot, trying to intimidate Luca with a ferocious scowl. Ha! There was little chance of that working.

Luca didn't bother extending his hand for a handshake. He passed Simu with a nod and a smirk on his face. When his gaze landed on me, thank God, my father couldn't see his expression. Luca's eyes flared hot, the silver giving way to a dark gray. My insides vibrated and I was left short of breath. How a color as cold as silver-gray could express such heat was a mystery to me, but there was no denying the path of fire he left in his wake as his gaze swiftly traveled down my body. I wasn't wearing anything sexy or even particularly revealing, but it was like he had X-ray vision because I felt undressed by him. I'd seen lust on men's faces before, especially Simu, but I had never had such a forceful and immediate reaction to it.

I desperately hoped that my bra covered my nipples, which had hardened instantly. I couldn't cross my arms without giving myself away to him, and possibly Simu, so I hunched forward in the hope of hiding my arousal.

Schooling his expression, Luca approached me coolly. When he bent down and kissed me on the cheeks, his spicy cologne, mixed with his underlying musk, enveloped me in a swoony feeling. The instant I felt the rough bristles of his jaw scrape my cheek, my skin crackled. My simple dress suddenly felt too tight and constricting.

Quickly stepping back, he asked, "Ready?"

His eyes dipped briefly to the swell of my breasts, exposed to him from his position standing so close to me. Shifting in place, I nodded and grabbed my backpack with my laptop.

"I'll have to stop by the college bookstore afterward to buy my books," I blurted out.

"Not a problem. I brought my laptop with me so I can

work while you're in class. We'll stop by the bookstore after class."

My father carefully watched our interaction from the foyer. Simu, right behind him, was throwing daggers at Luca's back.

At the door, Luca said, "I should have her back around two or three, depending on the traffic."

"Two or three?" spat out Simu. "It's not going to take that long."

Luca raised an eyebrow at Simu's tone. "I thought we could have lunch and get to know each other."

"Lunch?!" Simu's face screwed up into a rageful grimace.

He opened his mouth to say something, but I cut in and said, "Jewel is taking the class, as well. I'll invite her to join us. I was planning on asking Luca anyway."

Darting a pleading glance at Luca, I asked, "If you don't mind hanging out with two silly teenagers instead of just one?"

He gave a shrug as he twisted the knob and pulled the heavy wooden door open. "Sure, not a problem."

I kissed my father and Simu on the cheeks, although Simu possessively clamped a hand on my arm.

As I walked past Luca, he said, "Do you have a light sweater or something? The air conditioning in these classrooms is always high. I've taken enough summer classes to know."

Simu let out a low growl behind me.

I paused, looked up at Luca's serious expression, and was battered with another wave of heat and lust. Flustered by his concern, I reached into the closet and pulled out a light jacket. Clasping it tightly to my chest, I said goodbye and skipped down the steps to the car.

Luca spoke to my father for another few beats before

clicking the doors open with his fob. Perhaps I should have waited for him to be a gentleman and open the car door for me. His Romanian upbringing would have prompted him to, but I needed to be out from under Simu's eagle-eyed stare.

Slipping into the seat, I slammed the door shut. I threw my head against the headrest and let out an exasperated sigh. The leather seat felt cool against my heated skin.

Luca slipped into the driver's seat, shut the door, and sealed us in the silence of his car. His big hands wrapped around the steering wheel. The little tricolor Italian flag blinked at me from the base of the steering wheel as he twirled it around to back out of the parking. On the hub of the wheel, the large black and gold Lamborghini emblem of a raging bull was proudly displayed. That seemed like an apt totem animal for Luca. Even the black and gold of the logo, denoting power and luxury while staying simple and bold, was a perfect fit.

Once he'd driven far down the street, he let out a brilliantly vibrant laugh. I'd never heard him laugh before. The sound echoed through me, shaking me to my core. His facial features shifted in a way that left me breathless. I'd seen his light eyes flash with humor before, but I'd never seen his generous mouth spread into such an incredible smile. Crinkles emerged at the corners of his eyes and the dimple on his cheek made its rare appearance.

"Why are you laughing?" I asked.

"Because Simu was about to blow a gasket at the thought of you and me lunching together," he answered with another chuckle.

"He's protective of me. That's not so unusual," I explained.

He gave me a side-glance. "He's more than protective.

He's downright rabid. What's the deal between the two of you anyway?"

I fiddled with the flirty hem of my light-blue silk dress.

"Nothing," I lied.

I cringed, hearing my voice go high.

He gave another little smirk. "Okay, now you have to tell me," he ordered. "I can tell you're lying, so you've piqued my curiosity."

I remained silent.

"Come on, beautiful," he coaxed. "You can tell me. Remember, I'm not a tattler."

His gentle teasing was so alluring. I don't know what came over me, but I found myself saying, "My father practically promised me to him before whatever craziness happened with Alex. I'm so embarrassed to say this, but we even...kissed a few times last summer."

Everything I'd felt for Simu, including those kisses, seemed silly after what I had shared with Luca. And I wasn't even discussing the physical aspects, although my physical desire for him was intense. It was the intimacy between us after what happened in the bathroom and when we talked, alone in my bed, the morning after he'd consoled me in my sleep.

In a flash, his entire body transformed, going from civilized to beast-like in the blink of an eye. He coiled over the steering wheel like a large feline about to strike.

His tone was low and hard when he commanded, "Repeat that?"

Flustered, I stammered out, "Nothing happened. I mean, I'm a dutiful daughter, but we thought we would get married, so it didn't seem wrong...at the time. Once I was engaged, everything stopped. A—and it's not like Nicu would care anyway..."

"I care," he exploded.

I jolted, back flattened to the seat. The shock of his confession blasted through me, leaving me scrambling to keep up with this new development. Close behind it, tendrils of fuzzy warmth seeped into my very bones. *He cares.*

He was breathing heavily through his nostrils.

"It doesn't fucking matter what Nicu thinks. You don't know Simu like I do. He's an animal. He could've taken advantage of you. He could've *hurt* you." He emphasized the hurt like it was a personal offense to him.

"He would never. You don't know him like I do. Simu is my brother's best friend and my father's *consilier*. He'd never cross that line."

"He already has," Luca spat out. "You have no idea what he's capable of. If he respected you so much, if he was your brother's best friend and your father's right-hand man, then he shouldn't have touched you before your wedding day, in *any* manner."

Luca's reaction sent a frisson of excitement and fear down my spine. At that moment, he seemed more dangerous than Simu.

In a hushed voice, I said, "But you've touched me."

"That's completely different," he snapped.

"Is it?"

"Goddammit, yes."

"How?" I persisted.

His face contorted in confusion and I saw the conflict within him. Not wanting to push him away with my questioning, I changed the subject. "You're not going to tell anyone, are you?"

"If I haven't revealed anything that's happened between us, what makes you think I'd divulge this secret. Fuck, I don't want to start a fight over something like this, but make no mistake, Cat, that doesn't mean it wasn't a major transgression."

"We didn't spend enough time alone for anything else to happen between us," I explained, trying to justify myself. What Luca thought of me mattered. A lot.

He let out a snort of derision. "I know you're innocent, but how can you think that? You and I had enough time and space to do a lot more in a house filled with our entire families. Christ."

I released a shuddering breath. "I shouldn't have told you."

He made a sharp turn of a corner, and the wheels screeched. "You should tell me everything. Every damn thing. Fuck, the idea of that man's tongue in your mouth makes me want to punch something. Was that your first kiss?"

I cast my eyes down to my lap. My bottom lip pushed out, I answered softly, "No."

"And have you gone any further?" he interrogated me.

I shook my head, strands of hair fell down the sides of my face, hiding me.

"Words, Cat. I want to hear the words out of that bewitching mouth of yours. And you better tell me the truth," he bit out.

"I've never done more. My first kiss was a boy in sixth grade the year before I went to boarding school. Nothing ever happened in school. It was co-ed, but we were watched carefully. I could have if I wanted to but, honestly, I wasn't interested. I had my schoolwork and Jewel. More than that, I'm a good girl to the core. And if I haven't behaved that way with you, I lay the blame at your feet."

It was the truth. Luca was different. He pulled things out of me that I would never have considered with anyone else.

He sighed deeply. His hand clapped my knee and I inhaled sharply at the electricity in that touch. He was so intense; being with him was like being in the eye of a tornado.

"I know you are, baby girl, I know you are. I take full responsibility. This isn't on you, but last year, you were what, seventeen? A grown-ass man should've done better by an underage girl. I would've never allowed anything to happen between us if you weren't legal."

The easy way *baby girl* came out of his mouth shifted something inside me.

"I mean, I'll be spending more time with you alone than I ever have with Simu, and you're more dangerous to me than he ever was..." I confessed in a quiet voice, my eyes glued to the dashboard in front of me. I swallowed hard, my throat suddenly dry after my bold admission.

He squeezed my knee, causing my inner core to clench in response, before returning his hand to the steering wheel.

"And you can't imagine what a temptation you are, Cat. With your sexy little body, your big bright eyes, and your sweet, soft voice. Plus that spine of steel I see glimpses of when you make a confession like the one you just did. That you want me is a damn gift I don't deserve." He shook his head. "You have no fucking idea what I want to do to you... but I'm a Lupu and there's a marriage contract on the table." He moved the gearshift with his strong hand. "It doesn't matter what we want."

Dual emotions clashed inside me. Elation that his admission matched mine, but despair at his last statement. And to think he'd had a chance to be with me and had thrown it away. We had never met so I knew it wasn't personal, but it still left a sting. My throat closed completely. I don't know what I expected to come of my declaration. While Luca hadn't made me feel stupid, my confession had been pointless. *What were you thinking?*

There was nothing we could do to stop the wheels that had been put into motion. *Nothing.* While Nicu didn't seem interested in me, I couldn't be tossed around from brother to brother like an object. There'd been enough of that already. Anything further would be a bold-faced insult to the Popescus. Not to mention, Cristo would fly into a rage. And Simu would have a legitimate reason to murder Luca.

And yet, this man called to my soul like no one else. Besides his deadly allure, there was a raw honesty and authenticity about him that I'd never encountered before. People were always posing, gaslighting, or outright lying to one another in *mafie* circles. Aching with the pain of unshed tears, I nodded numbly and turned my head toward the window, watching the teeming city streets glide past me.

He was right. As intense as this unnamed thing was between us, nothing could ever come of it.

9

Fucking hell, this discussion with Cat topped the charts in terms of raw agony. It was fucking killing me. The light in her bright eyes dimmed and turned glassy with unshed tears. I had done that to her. If it would help, I'd rip my beating heart out of my chest and hand it to her to crush under her dainty little shoe. At least I had the wherewithal to admit that our powerful attraction was mutual. I could never let her walk away thinking that I didn't want her. That would've been a travesty and an outright lie.

I tapped on my horn at a pedestrian jaywalking diagonally across the street, tugging his dog behind him. Fuck, I hated this city. Especially in the summer. In Manhattan, the buildings practically touched the sky, blocking the sun's rays even in the middle of the day. People swarmed everywhere, the noise was constant and the traffic brutal. There was no space, no greenery. The stifled, cramped trees with cement or grates plastered over their roots didn't count in my book. The miserable place—dirty, noisy, and oppressive—left me with a headache.

Instead of spending the entire summer in L.A., I'd spent the last two weeks there. Working nonstop. I got as much done as possible and cleared my schedule so that I could be back to shuttle Cat to her class and back home. Things were heating up in L.A. The small *mafie* family that no one had paid attention to took issue with us for encroaching on what they perceived as their property, but what we equally regarded as free, unmarked territory. I'd met the *şef* of the Hagi clan. Although small, I could attest that they were a feisty bunch. Feisty was best treated with kid gloves. For now.

If an issue came up out West, I'd take the red-eye and be back before Cat's next class because no one was taking my place. Over my dead body would Simu *ever* drive her. That fucker had to be kept in check. Knowing that he pressed his lips against hers made me to want to smash my fist through the windshield. This had nothing to do with our rivalry. This was all Cat. I wanted each and every one of her kisses and touches.

After she told me about those innocent kisses he'd stolen, swear to God, I was about to turn the car around and tear that man to shreds. Fucking poacher. I didn't give a shit that they thought they were promised to each other. Fuck that. He shouldn't have touched her. Period. The only reason I didn't go beat his ass was because I wouldn't have gotten away with it without breaking her confidence. But his time would come.

For the first time, I learned what it felt like to be possessive, and...I gave zero fucks about it. To keep hold of my sanity, I'd soon have to extract an oath from her to stay away him. One day, I'd get my revenge. The reason? Because he'd touched what was mine.

Stop.

She's not yours.

Try telling my heart and my dick.

I was living through hell, but I didn't give a rat's ass. I was prepared to suffer any amount of pain to be around her. To check her out in that sweet little dress, with the hem riding up her thighs. Or the way her bare shoulders gleamed in the light coming in through the windows. Her enticing floral peach scent alone had my cock in a chokehold.

It was excruciating, and yet...I couldn't get enough.

A tense silence had descended between us. Not knowing what to say, but unable to take the silence any longer, I burst out, "Well, I'm sure you've heard about my father and his enormous faux pas."

Cat turned to face me with a blank look.

"You know..." I made a little waving motion with one hand as if that could somehow hurry along her memory and we could get past the humiliating acknowledgment that my father was a cheating son of a bitch who should've had his balls cut off. *Christ, am I a glutton for punishment or what?*

A frown marred her smooth forehead and she pursed her lips in an expression of concentration that was cute as fuck.

Shaking her head, she said, "No, I don't think I have. I haven't been around much these last six years, and my best friend is from school. I try to keep to myself and avoid the other Romanian girls from the neighborhood, because honestly, they can be catty."

I stared at her like she'd sprouted two heads. A Romanian *mafie* girl who wasn't on top of the latest scandal? A Romanian *mafie* princess who wasn't absorbed in our world of intrigue? If I wasn't such a good judge of character, I'd have thought she was pulling my leg. I knew for certain that Cat was the furthest thing from manipulative as a person could get.

"How did Alex introduce Sebastian and Emma to you?" I asked curiously.

"As your brother and sister," she replied straightaway.

"Didn't you find it strange that he introduced you to an additional set of siblings?" I prompted.

That adorable expression of concentration returned.

"Now that you mention it, there's only ever been the four of you. Alex, you, Nicu, and Tasa. It was so hectic that weekend, I guess I hadn't noticed."

"Yeah, well, they're our siblings by another mother," I replied, blowing out a breath.

"You don't like them?" she queried.

"Sebastian's a stand-up guy, and Emma is funny and sweet, although she shares the same stubborn streak that Tasa has. It's my father's betrayal of my mother that I can't forgive."

She gave a little sound, half snort, half huff. "I'm baffled when we pretend to be better than we are. We create this honor code to make it seem like we're virtuous, but considering what our families do to survive, I can't see how you're surprised by his behavior. You and I both know that it's by far one of the milder things your father has done."

"While I appreciate you calling out the fake bullshit, it's rare that anyone notices, much less says anything about it. I would know better than anyone how deep hypocrisy can run in a family, but I still believe in loyalty. We're supposed to treat family better than the way we treat people on the outside," I ground out. "At least, in principle."

"And how often are we able to keep up that pretense?" she scoffed.

"For such a pretty, young thing, you're quite jaded. And

to top it off, you're a woman. It's not like you've engaged in any of the unsavory activities we men are routinely forced to partake in."

"I've witnessed them," she replied softly. "And that was bad enough."

Fuck, how did I forget? Impulsively, I reached out and squeezed her hand. "I'm sorry, beautiful. You should've never seen that."

She shook her head slightly. "No worries. I suppose, you're right. I am jaded. Seeing the father you've admired your entire life kill a man in cold blood can do that. And I don't even have cause to complain. My father and brother treat me well, and I've seen many fathers over the years. Not all of them can leave what they do during the day at the door. My father's ability to compartmentalize is impressive, but I operate under the assumption that it's the exception, not the rule. How can a man not let violence bleed into other aspects of his life?"

Her observation hit a little too close to home. My father did let it bleed in. He confined his abuse to me, but with me, it was no holds barred. Hell, he used methods on me that he'd used on men he'd tortured.

Impulsive. Contrarian. Reckless. The words came out in a staccato rhythm between the thwacks of his belt against my back, the buckle catching the flesh of my ribs and tearing into it. I absorbed each of his insults into my fucking soul and swore to never release them. I would become all that he accused me of and more. Not only would I not try to change. I would make sure *never* to change. What he hated most, I would preserve and nurture.

"We're supposed to be able to separate them. To protect you from the ugliness."

"I understand where that impulse comes from, but every

single member of a clan is implicated. Having the veil ripped off did me good. It made me stronger," she replied. "I don't live in a protected little bubble like so many other *mafie* girls. It also changed my life for the better. I was able to go to a prestigious school. My loneliness forced me to focus on academics. I would've become a pampered, spoiled *mafie* princess if I had stayed in Queens."

She paused, her forehead creasing in concentration. "My father tried to shield me, but sometimes, bad things happen. Especially in our world. At least it was an accident. He hadn't failed me on purpose, like some men. Some take their entitlement too far or exploit their power to do whatever they want, regardless of who they hurt. Like your father did by cheating on your mother."

"Not only cheated on her. He maintained an entirely separate family for decades," I clarified.

She pulled back; her eyes flared wide. "Oh, that *is* bad."

She really hadn't heard the whole sordid story of how my father kept a separate household with an American woman. Apparently, he'd had photos of us children scattered around the house when Sebastian and Emma were growing up. How fucking twisted was that?

"If only it stopped there, I would've considered myself lucky," I huffed out. "He was a bastard, through and through."

I snapped my mouth shut before I gave away any more.

Shit, I'd gone too far.

I made a disgusted sound from the back of my throat. Should I go on? Should I reveal what he was really like? I'd never spoken about it with anyone but Tatum, and only because he'd found me, bound and gagged in a closet, in a dog crate no less, when he and Alex were playing a game of hide-and-seek. That was when he began inviting me over for sleepovers at his house and we created our own independent friendship, despite our two-year age difference. Even knowing that he pitied me, he was one of the few people I allowed in. It was a sign of how lonely and desperate I was at that time.

My father ingrained in me a culture of silence, to protect my siblings. I didn't have to protect Cat, but I'd just finished spouting off that it was our duty to protect our women from the brutality of our world. On the other hand, she herself said that she was strong. I had seen glimpses of that steel in her spine. It was part of what attracted me to her.

Always so perceptive, Cat's head snapped toward me.

Eyes narrowed, she demanded, "What is it?"

Her eyes glided over the tension in my facial muscles down to my clenched jaw. "Tell me, Luca. *Tell me.* I know you want to protect me from the ugliness, but I don't break easily." Her voice dropped. "I can handle whatever your secret is. I want to know, and I promise that you can trust me."

Fuck, that little speech hobbled me. How could I deny her?

The quiet hum in the tight confines of the car resembled a confessional of sorts. We were in a small, hushed space, with little noise outside the occasional honk penetrating our bubble. Although we didn't know each other well, we had shared intense private moments, creating a shared sense of security and intimacy. Perhaps it was the way she'd been so brave and honest with me earlier. Either way, I had the urge to speak of what he'd done to me. To speak my truth.

"You'll find Nicu and Alex have a very different view of my father than I do," I began. She pivoted her body toward me in anticipation, her full attention on me.

Clutching the steering wheel tightly, I focused ahead and continued, "Rebellion wasn't tolerated with my father, but as my mother told it, I'd been a rebel right out of the womb. I always chafed against rules and regulations. My disobedience provoked him, and he allowed himself a free hand. Over time, I embraced the label and went out of my way to antagonize him."

"Allowed a free hand? What does that mean exactly?" Cat asked me, concern lining her sweet face.

I gave a little shrug. "Means that when he was pissed off about something, he came home and beat the hell out of me."

She remained silent.

"I provoked him with my behavior—"

"Don't," she cut me off abruptly, eyes flashing in anger.

I shook my head. "Don't what?"

"Don't say it's your fault or lay the blame on yourself in any way. You were a child. His son. He was an adult. His job was to take care of you, not hurt you or take advantage of you because you were smaller and weaker than he was. You do know that, right?"

No one had ever said that to me. Not even Tatum, who mostly sat and listened, which had been a gift in and of itself. But what Cat said to me? Removing me from the equation and laying the responsibility squarely on my father's shoulders was mind-bending. It left me a little light-headed. I had spent years attempting to understand his behavior, justifying it to try to make sense of what I had lived through.

In a single moment, she'd summarized the years of relentless torture and simultaneously judged him for it. It wasn't your fault, is what I heard. It was on him. He was the adult, the father. I was the child, the helpless one, and he'd taken advantage of that inequity. I already knew Cat was smart and perceptive, but she became my savior in that moment. By being there for me, by succinctly stripping away the excuses for his behavior, she'd gifted me with the freedom that eluded me for years. I'd never be able to repay her, and that only bound me to her more securely.

"I know it now," I replied.

The car rolled to a stop at a red light at the corner of the college. To our left was the towering crenellated black entrance gate framing Barnard Hall, a three-level red brick building with Corinthian columns.

As we waited for the light to change, she asked, "What did he do to you, Luca?"

She wanted the details, and I was powerless to keep them from her, even if it shamed me to admit to having once been so weak. But if I could be weak with anyone, it was with her.

"He was into punishment and humiliation. He tried to break my spirit. There were the usual beatings and whippings, but he would also gag me and throw me into a dog crate for hours, things like that," I replied with a thick swallow around the constriction of my throat. It was hard getting the words out.

I pressed my foot on the accelerator, rolling past the light when a man sprinted across the middle of the street. Braking hard, the car lurched and Cat slammed hard against her seatbelt, gasping harshly.

"The fuck," I shouted, my arm crossing over her chest. Honking, I scowled at the foolish student who'd weaved in between passing cars.

"Are you okay, baby?" I queried, worry clogging my chest.

Hand on her chest, she said, "Yeah, I'm fine. Thank God, you have good reflexes and braked in time. We would've definitely hit him." Peering over at the young man laughing with the crowd of friends he'd joined, she shook her head. "What the hell?"

Driving on, I turned into the nearest street, searching for parking. Eventually, I found a spot on Riverside Drive.

Her hand touched my forearm. My eyes shifted to her. Holding my gaze, she swallowed and said, "I can't begin to imagine what you've been through, and I know you only scraped the surface. God, Luca, you're a survivor and I'm awed by your endurance. I already thought you were incredible, but now...to know what I know, it humbles me."

Her praise left me speechless. My gaze roved over her face, riveted. There was only one thing I wanted to do and so I did it. My lips ghosted over hers slowly. She released a little sigh of delight. I took that as an invitation. My hand slipped beneath her thick hair and clasped her nape, bringing her in closer. Our mouths opened to each other and I dipped in for my first taste of this gorgeous creature. Goddamn, the flavor of sweet peaches and nectarines exploded on my tongue. I groaned, delving in deeper. Fuck, I hadn't intended to taste her, but I was vulnerable, and her praise cut me at the knees.

Her fingers clung to my shirt, her tits pressing against my chest with the most delicious pressure. My hand slid down her side to palm her ass. Aww hell, I had to stop before it went any further. I had to.

I took another slow swipe of her mouth and forced myself to pull away before we reached the point of no return because there was a fair chance that her cherry would get popped in the back seat of my car. She nipped my bottom lip before I broke away completely and it took every ounce of control not to haul her back for more.

We were both panting, our breaths mingling together.

I leaned over her and shoved her door open.

"Out," I warned.

One leg out of the car, she turned to me and asked, "Are you sure you want to keep your fancy car parked on the street? Why don't we drive it to a lot?"

The little minx was baiting me.

"Parking lots are for wimps. But, more to the point, if I stay any longer, there's a good chance we're going to do a hell of a lot more than kiss."

I heard a gasp behind me as I swung my door open. Facing away from her, I smirked. "Come on, you'll be late."

We entered onto the college campus through the front gate we'd passed earlier. A collection of stately red brick buildings encircled a lawn sprinkled with groups of students. I stopped one and asked for directions to the building where Cat's class was situated. She was practically bobbing up and down in excitement as we strolled through the campus.

Walking beside me down a path around a pristine lawn in front of the right building, Cat's shoulders slumped.

"What is it?" I asked, immediately on the alert.

"My best friend from school, Jewel, will be starting here in the fall. In fact, she's living on campus for the summer. I wanted to join her, but my parents didn't see the point of me starting college when I'm getting married. I hope Nicu won't mind if I take a class or two," she replied, darting a worried look my way.

"You like studying," I noted.

"Yeah, I was valedictorian after all," she confided forlornly.

My eyebrows rose. Valedictorian of that prestigious prep school? "Impressive."

Her eyes brightened. She liked my compliment but then she gave a self-deprecating little shrug. "Yeah, well. My family isn't like yours. They're not really into academics, and they wouldn't think it's something worth paying for."

"I'm sure Nicu will be supportive, even if he wasn't enthusiastic about his studies. Nothing but graduating cum laude was considered acceptable. Alex had to leave his pre-law program at Columbia University when my father was killed, but he insisted we finish our education with honors. I completed an MBA in Corporate Finance."

She looked at me hopefully, "Yeah?"

"You should definitely go to college, Cat. Our family will do everything to help you. We can stop by the Admissions Office after lunch and find out the requirements and dead-lines, and you should check out other colleges in the city and apply to them as well," I suggested.

"The application deadline has long passed," she grumbled.

I gave a little snort. "Exceptions can be made. You'd be surprised what money can do to facilitate these kinds of things."

A gorgeous smile spread over her cupid's bow lips. She was stunning. I'd be willing to do anything to bring that smile to her face. "You really think so?"

"I know so," I said as we reached the ivy-covered building and I propped open the door for her. After convincing the guard at the front desk that I was her brother, all the while ignoring her dramatic eye roll at my lie, I followed her down the wide, high-ceilinged hall to her classroom. Waving her in, I ducked into the nearest empty room and dropped my briefcase on the wooden desk that the professors used. Pulling out my laptop and secure portable Wi-Fi router, I set it up and got to work on the cryptocurrency scheme, playing with one of the most market-capped crypto after bitcoin.

One good thing about playing guard with Cat was that I could work uninterrupted for several hours. Realizing that she'd have a break at some point, I squeezed into the hard plastic seat of a small student desk facing the open door, positioning myself so that I'd spot her if she left.

There was no denying I was taking this assignment above and beyond the call of duty, considering she was simply sitting in a classroom the entire time. She wasn't exactly engaging in a high-risk activity in a dangerous area. Everything about her called to my possessive side, in a way I'd never experienced before. It was uncharacteristic of me to be so attentive to another person. Attentive to work? Yes. To my duties? Sure. To another human being, and a woman at that? Highly unusual.

Regardless of the madness that had clearly taken hold of me, there was no denying that I *ached* to be in her presence. I had foolishly judged her before ever meeting her. I assumed that she was a vapid, spoiled *mafie* princess. Wrong. The distance she kept from the gossiping misses and her dedication to hard work and education shattered those misconceptions. Not only that, but it was her dedication that made her seem so...Lupu-like, so very *un*-Popescu.

Via this arranged marriage, I assumed that Nelu was planting her as a spy. Wrong again. It was obvious from the moment I met her that she was an innocent. That innocence, combined with her thoughtful introspection, drew me in like a moth to a flame. Forget the fact that I wanted her writhing underneath me or riding my cock, I enjoyed conversing with her, watching her lively mind respond to my questions or challenge me. Hell, I simply liked being around her. The bottomless pit of loneliness, that I never fully shook, vanished in her presence.

Everything I never knew I wanted in a woman was

dangled in front of me with Cat. Being with her taunted me with intimacy that I could never have. Once she married my brother, I'd be driven into further isolation, forcing a greater wedge between Nicu and me because I wouldn't be strong enough to stand by, watching her at his side. The worst of it was that while I had the chance to be around her before she married, and I'd be forced to move halfway across the country to stay away from her, I'd indulge as much as possible.

Propping my elbow on the tiny desk, I pinched the space between my eyebrows.

I was so fucked.

10

Over a month had passed with Luca ferrying me back and forth to my summer class. In contrast, I hadn't spent any time with Nicu. It was as if, once our wedding had been postponed, I'd ceased to matter to him. Out of sight, out of mind. It almost seemed as if he was avoiding me. I didn't run into him at any *mafie* parties or get-togethers, not at the Romanian butcher, pastry shop, or the various cafés where people routinely gathered. Once the wedding was back on his radar, I figured he'd have to contend with me again.

Meanwhile, I was getting more and more attached to Luca. The way he confided in me about his father, the kiss afterward, and then his confident support of my quest to go to college had shifted something in me. Every day we spent together, my heart cracked open a little more. Not only did I admire his grit, but his irreverence and stubborn determination to maintain his independence, despite the demands of his family, inspired me.

With only one week left of classes, I didn't know what I would do without him. We spent quite a lot of time together between the car ride each way, the time it took to circle around the same blocks until we found parking, taking my class breaks with him, and sharing lunch together.

We'd shared some ridiculous situations, like when he saw a car behind us pulling out of a parking space halfway up a one-way street. Leaning over me, he threw the car door open and told me to get out and hold the parking spot where the car pulled out. I ran to it, waiting as the steam coming off the black asphalt seeped through my sandals. Luca drove to the corner of the street to let the car pass and then threw his car in reverse and illegally backed up until he was adjacent to me. Waving me onto the sidewalk, he expertly parked into the tightest space possible. I really didn't think he'd make it, but the man was a pro.

He was an expert at more than just driving and parking. He was an expert at deep existential conversations and silly teasing. He was an expert at long pauses when the heat between us blazed like a bonfire as his silver-gray eyes raked down my body. He was an expert at lingering hooded gazes and inadvertent touches that left me feeling achy and itchy. Luca was a detriment to my peace of mind.

I finally broke down and asked Jewel to buy me a vibrator online and have it delivered to her dorm room. There was no way I could have it come to my house. My grandmother didn't care who the box was addressed to. If it was dropped on her stoop, it was public family property. But I couldn't go on much longer with my right hand and I was in desperate need of relief.

Currently, I was lounging on Jewel's bed in her dorm room. I'd convinced my mother to let me sleep over, and although Cristo grumbled about leaving me there, he was finally convinced that it was safe enough after Jewel explained to him the on-campus safety protocol. A security guard at the main entrance scrutinized everyone that entered. It was a woman's college, I reiterated to Cristo as often as possible. My brother still had his doubts, but I swore to him that we'd stay on campus and eat dinner at the cafeteria. I felt a little guilty since I didn't intend to follow through on my promise.

It was summer in the city. I could hear cars passing below Jewel's open window, along with the hum of people talking as they walked by, punctuated by the occasional laugh or scream. Jewel's roommate, Sofia, was a beautiful dark-skinned Dominican girl who'd grown up a mile away in East Harlem. She was already gone for the weekend, but she'd kindly let me sleep in her bed for the night. Through Jewel's door, I'd hear the occasional shriek as the other girls in the hall flitted from room to room to get opinions on their outfits as they prepared for a summer Saturday night out. It made me nostalgic for boarding school, especially knowing I'd never experience it again while girls my age would begin the adventure of living on their own.

I was propped up against the wall on Jewel's bed. Besides the two beds, chests of drawers, desks and chairs, the room was decorated in posters. On Sofia's side, it was plastered with various singers that I didn't recognize, something having to do with reggaeton. On Jewel's side was a poster, right above my head, of Frida Kahlo, and facing me was another of *Nanas*, the female figures of the sculptor, Niki de Saint Phalle.

With her large hazel eyes and long wavy brown hair, Jewel could pass for Romanian, even though she was blue-blooded American, through and through. Maybe I was subconsciously drawn to her because of her looks, missing my family as I did when we first encountered each other at school at the age of twelve. There was also the fact that she was a city girl like me. Even though she grew up on Park Avenue and I grew up in a modest house in an outer borough, those distinctions faded when one was far away from home, in New England. Her Romanianesque beauty was certainly the reason Cristo checked her out. I hadn't missed his interested looks, but no woman was less suited to being a *mafie* wife than my best friend.

Dropping a plain, unlabeled box on my lap, my friend said with a smirk, "Here's my gift to you. Hopefully, it will give you the relief you need. I know you asked for something simple, but I did a little research and got you the best. It has clitoral stimulation and penetration, just in case."

My cheeks heated up as I mumbled out a thanks. Jewel not only wanted to be an avant-garde artist, but she was also a serious feminist. Having been sexually active going on two years now, she was my go-to person, so I appreciated whatever she had gotten me.

"So, how's it going with the brooding Romanian hottie?" she asked as she stretched across the bed. I pulled up my knees to give her more space.

I gave a deep shrug. "It's horrible and wonderful at the same time. One week left and then my time with him will be over. He's so intense and—"

"Looks at you like he's going to eat you whole?" she finished for me.

I did a double take. "I don't know about that...it could be one-sided."

"Did you forget that I had lunch with the both of you. Sheesh, I could cut the sexual tension with a knife."

"He's my fiancé's *bro-ther*," I emphasized.

"Yeah, so? Sure, it's inconvenient, but you can't force who you're attracted to. Better make a bold move now, before your window of opportunity is closed forever."

"Window of opportunity? Pfft, it's more than a little inconvenient. It's downright impossible," I grumbled.

"Oh, please, it's so not impossible. If, as a society, we've learned to separate Siamese twins, this is a walk in the park."

I burst out in laughter. "Okay, I'm pretty sure that doesn't make any sense. What do Siamese twins have to do with anything?"

She waved away my question as inconsequential. "Cat, it's not like you aren't a person. You have a brain. You're not simply a vehicle for your family's ambitions." Her gaze turned serious. "What about what you want? Doesn't that matter in the least?"

Wasn't that the million-dollar question?

"I'm starting to really, *really* like him, and that scares me."

She huffed, "Doesn't sound half as scary as marrying a guy you know you don't really, *really* like. And since when are you a coward?"

My chest burned with pride that Jewel saw me as such a strong woman, but my life was complicated.

"It's not that simple. In my culture, arranged marriages are customary. Even if I don't care for it, it's what's expected of me. My mother would be crushed if this wedding was called off. Even if I did turn Nicu away, who says that Luca would want me? He had his chance. He had the right of first refusal, and he turned me down as a bride."

Jewel snorted. "I'm sure that was before he met you. A traditional guy like him...if he found a *mafie* girl he half liked and wanted a lot, he'd marry her. Especially if it was the only way he could fuck her."

"If she was *mafie*, and he had sex with a virgin out of

wedlock, he'd be forced to marry her. That's what the blood bond is for," I divulged.

"The blood *whaa*?" she asked, turning onto her side, and propping her head in her hand, her attention completely on me.

I shifted in my seat, suddenly feeling self-conscious. While I had told Jewel that I was Romanian early on in our friendship, it took me years to trust her with the more sensitive information about my family. If her father hadn't been incarcerated for a Ponzi scheme that went bust, I would've never told her at all. But her father lost everything and was still in jail. It was only because of her mother's independent trust fund that she and her mom were financially secure. Everything else had to be liquidated. They lived in these cavernous Park Avenue family apartments that both she and her mother hated. It had been a painful time, and the central reason her mother sent her off to boarding school.

Despite having told her about my family, I kept things very vague. And I hadn't confided about my engagement until Jewel threatened to go to the school psychologist because my grades were slipping. It was her alarm that finally made me break. Jewel came from a world so different from mine, and while I knew she'd never judge me, I was embarrassed.

Fidgeting enough that she had to lay a calming hand on my knee, I peered at her and said, "It's really barbaric, I'm warning you now." I took a deep breath. "Blood is how bonds are formed between people inside a clan. Men are inducted in a ceremony where they cut themselves and make a blood oath. For women, a blood bond is formed when she loses her virginity. *That's* why it's so important that a woman remain a virgin until marriage."

A look of horror quickly passed over her face before she

snuffed it out. "So, what happens if a woman loses her virginity before marriage? Is she killed or something to avenge the stain on her family's reputation?"

"No," I replied with a laugh. "If she had sex with a *mafie* guy, then she has to marry him. No exceptions. If he's not *mafie*, then it depends. Is he close to a family? Does he know about the blood bond? Obviously, if it's some random American bro she hooks up with in a bar bathroom, then no, no one's going to force him into marriage. But the more he's associated with us, the more he's expected to conform to the rules. God knows, men are constantly warning each other to protect themselves and the women. If a man is caught checking out a Romanian girl, his friend will tell him right away that he can't tap that unless he wants to put a ring on it. That usually shuts them down immediately. There's strict protocol around marriage, and girls live very confined, protected lives."

Jewel turned over and flopped on her tummy, processing what she'd learned.

"Very interesting," she mused in a cryptic tone.

A prickle started on the back of my neck.

Uh-oh.

Jewel's face spun toward me, a determined look on her face.

"What?" I asked. "Why are you looking at me like that?"

"*Becaaause*, all you have to do to get out of your marriage is get Luca to blood bond with you," she exclaimed, jolting upright on her bed.

"What? No, I couldn't do that!"

A notch developed between her brows. "Why not? It's simple. You seduce him, he pops your cherry, and *voila!* You're married to the guy you're crushing on. It's a perfect solution."

My heart began pounding against my ribcage. That was quite inspired of Jewel, I had to admit. The idea that I could have Luca...it was...incredible. But...things weren't as simple as she made them out to be. Or were they? God, this tilted my world on its axis.

I shook my head. "No, no, it's not a solution *at all*. My family will be disappointed—"

"Why? You said your mother would be disappointed if the wedding was called off. It won't be, you'll just be marrying a different guy. The *right* guy. Your family had already picked him as the first choice, so why should they care that you managed to marry the guy they wanted," she elaborated.

"Actually, their first choice was the oldest son and şef of the Lupu family, Alex, but he fell in love with an outsider. Luca was the runner up."

"But Nicu was the last choice, so they'll be *happy* you moved on up. Isn't it a better sign of prestige or something like that?" she queried, tucking her luxurious dark hair behind her ear as she tilted her head to the side.

Hope unfurled in my chest.

Huh, what she suggested was scary but logical. My mother would have her wedding and I know my father would prefer Luca. He'd never said anything outright, but I could tell that he was peeved that I was marrying the youngest son. Unlike Simu, Cristo's hatred was concentrated on Nicu, whom he always claimed was the cockiest of the Lupu men. *Mafie* custom dictated that after Alex was off the market, Luca should get married before Nicu. While Luca clearly didn't care, people grumbled about the break in tradition, so this solution might be welcomed by his clan.

Yet, a blood bond was nothing to sneeze at.

"But Luca didn't want to marry me," I insisted.

"He'd never met you, though. You were away at school with me, and you'd never been introduced to him whenever you were home, right? Anyway, he knows you now and he wants you. There's no doubt in my mind about that," she argued. "And that's what counts, not what happened in the past."

"It would be a scandal," I countered.

"Scandal shmandal. Sometimes you have to break a few eggs to make an omelet. Do you want to eat an omelet or do you want to marry a rotten egg?" she asked, one eyebrow raised, her mouth wobbly from holding back a laugh.

"Okay, again, not making sense!" I cried, throwing my hands up.

She laughed. "You know what I'm saying, Cat. You'll still marry a *mafie* man. Sheesh, you'll be marrying in the same family, only with someone better. You'll fulfill your obligation to your family, but more importantly, you'll be doing what's right for you. What's wrong with that? Why not give it a chance if you can have your cake and eat it, too? You already told me that Nicu doesn't pay any attention to you. Why tie yourself to a man who isn't even interested in getting to know his fiancée when you can marry a man you care for and you know cares for you? I don't even understand why you're hesitating," she said, looking at me perplexed. "It's a no-brainer."

Oh, that logical brain of hers. It got me every time, and even more so when it aligned with my own desire. Hope fluttered in my chest, joining the jangling of my nerves. *Nerves is right, because this plan will require nerves of steel.* But now that the solution slapped me in the face, I couldn't turn away from it. That would show me to be a coward, and I was a Popescu, dammit. We went after what we wanted. That's how we clawed our way up to become the second most powerful family in New York City. A Popescu would never shy away from a challenge, and I'd call on that Popescu pluck. Would I be able to seduce Luca? Good question. There was only one way to find out. Luckily, I had a pretty good idea where to go to find him on a Saturday night.

I turned to Jewel and declared, "Let's do it."

11

I was upstairs in the VIP section, silently nursing a drink with Nicu beside me at our club, The Lounge. Downstairs, black leather and purple lighting was the predominant theme. Strobe lights and booming music hit you when you stepped through the door. There was a long bar on either end of the huge space in front of a backdrop of flashing purple lights. The club was best known for the rotating DJ booth in the center, with dancers in skintight neon leotards on platforms of various heights scattered throughout the dance floor.

Upstairs, the mood shifted in favor of decadence. The black leather theme continued, but it was interspersed with scarlet-red velvet instead of flashing purple lights. Beneath striking black crystal chandeliers throwing off dark sparkles were groupings of black leather and red velvet chaise lounges, couches, and low tables made of black wood. The black and scarlet motif was picked up in the velour faux-relief floral pattern of the wallpaper.

Pretty classy if I said so myself. Downstairs was for the masses to twerk and grind against each other, while upstairs was for lounging and hanging out. At the long black wooden bar, stools of the same shade of red as the couches were occupied by one willowy-thin model after another. The only difference between them was the color of their skin or the style of their hair. But not one of them held a candle to Cat.

Apparently, I thought dryly, every woman I laid eyes on failed in comparison to my little brother's fiancée.

My brothers and I were on club duty most weekends, silently monitoring our realm as various people came up to us to pay homage or talk business. We were like princes of a fiefdom. The men respected us and the women were at our beck and call. Facing the entrance, I leaned back into the booth when my head snapped up. Vladimir, the bouncer, was unhooking the black velvet rope for Cat and her side-kick Jewel to enter.

The first thing I noticed was the bright shade of red lipstick covering her bow-shaped mouth. I was glued to her mouth for one long beat before I remembered to breathe. My eyes wandered down her frame and my body tightened. The tight, black dress might have ended at her knees, but when she turned around, it was backless, leaving little to the imagination. The jutting of her hips alone made my cock weep in my boxer briefs. She looked like she was out looking for a good time. My hands curled into fists.

Bad girlie.

What in the fuck was she doing here? She shouldn't be in a place like this, and for good reason. My gaze snapped left and right, eyeing the various men who'd become aware of their presence and were blatantly checking them out.

Oh, hell no.

Nicu leaned into me and asked, "Who the hell is that?"

My forehead wrinkled as I mocked, "Who? Your soon-to-be wife?"

Tense, he leaned forward, gnashing his teeth. "No, the chick with her."

Seriously? He had a drop-dead gorgeous fiancée and the first thing he asked about was her boring little American friend?

"That's her best friend, Jewel. Don't you dare think about tapping that, you sick fuck," I threatened. *Like I should be talking, but whatever.*

He reared back, realizing how blatant he was, and heaved out, "Of course not."

Of course not, my ass. No one expected Nicu to be faithful, and Cat was too bright not to know better, but still. Nicu had shown such a lack of interest in her that he didn't even know that Jewel was her bestie. It was a damn shame because Cat was incredible. She was intelligent and driven, yet sensitive and loyal. Oh, and hot as fuck. She deserved a man who was attentive to her every need, but once they were married, she'd be bound for life to my idiot brother. I loved him, but he was delusional for not realizing what a lucky fucker he was. I shuddered in my suit. Once they were married, once she'd spilled blood for him, any fantasies I harbored about her would be dead in the water. I bared my teeth at the thought as Cat sauntered toward us with her friend.

"Hey, Nicu. Luca," she greeted in a soft tone, her eyes mostly on me.

"Hey Cat," responded Nicu as we both simply stared at them. The energy was taut. At least on my end it was. The slit of her slinky dress went high up on her thigh, showing off her slim leg. I saw a flash of a satin band around the top. Was that a garter? Oh, fuck me, just *fuck me.*

"Who's your friend?" asked Nicu, eyeing her in a way that was borderline obscene it was so ravenous.

"Nicu, this is Jewel. Jewel, Nicu," she introduced, slipping into the seat beside me. For the love of all that was holy, she better not—*fuck*, she was touching me. Her hand landed on my lap. For fuck's sake, as if life didn't hate me enough already. The unique fragrance of nectarine, peach, and spring blossoms poured over me, making my stiff cock even harder.

"What the hell are you doing here, Cat?" I gritted out.

Her long eyelashes fluttered in surprise. I'd never used a hard tone with her before. But what was she thinking, coming here, dressed like a sexy vixen, her hair falling in waves around her bare shoulders? Pointed nipples poked through the thin double layer of her gossamer dress. Was she expecting that to cover her? If so, Versace wasn't doing a good job of it. Fucking hell, if she wanted to show off her body, she should do it for me alone. Yeah, and I got how out of line my possessiveness was, but I didn't care.

I pushed Cat off the banquette of the booth and to her feet, followed her out, and said to Jewel, "Why don't you sit down, order a *non*alcoholic drink, and get to know Nicu?"

My eyes dipped down the length of Cat's spine in her backless dress.

Wrapping my fingers around her delicate upper arm, I said to Nicu, "I have something to discuss with Cat. We'll be right back."

Eyes on Jewel, Nicu nodded to me absentmindedly. Lifting my chin in the direction I wanted us to go, I tugged Cat across the floor and turned into the quieter hall leading to the employee bathroom and break room.

Pressing her back to the wall, I slapped my palms on either side of her head and crowded her.

Dropping my head until my face was inches away from hers, I snapped, "How the hell did you get in here?"

Considering only people over twenty-one were allowed

in, I already had a pretty good idea, but I wanted to hear it straight from her mouth.

"Vlad," she replied simply. "I spoke to him in Romanian and told him my name."

Of course, she did.

"And downstairs?" I growled through clenched teeth. "They don't speak Romanian down there."

She opened the little silver clasp of her clutch and pulled out an ID.

I snapped it up and inspected it closely in the dim lighting.

A fake.

"Jewel and I flashed those and got a couple drinks," she confessed flippantly. I swear, the urge to turn her over on my lap and give her a spanking was riding me *hard*. "We danced between ourselves until we drank enough to get a buzz since we had no idea if you guys would let us drink once we got upstairs," she volunteered without prompting, blinking her wide eyes up at me oh-so-fucking innocently.

Innocent, my ass. Every word out of her mouth made my stomach twist into tighter knots. I knew they weren't careful down there. We ran a business, not a day care center, and keeping little girls out was not on the agenda. The idea of a random douche pawing her on the dance floor clouded my vision with red sparks of fury. Clearly, someone fell down on the job if she wasn't being watched.

"How did you get out of your house? Where's Cristo? He could show up here any moment, you know."

"He doesn't know I'm here. He thinks I'm staying over in Jewel's dorm room. I convinced him that it would be safe. They have guards at the front gate, patrolling the campus grounds, and at the entrance of her dorm. I also promised to be good."

"If this is what you call being good—"

"*Aaand*," she interrupted me. "I happen to know that Cristo is going to a party with his new girlfriend. I seriously doubt he would appreciate being called in to pick me up after the week he's had."

"You don't know your brother very well if you think him coming here to irritate me and Nicu would put a damper on his night."

An indentation appeared between her brows. Shaking my head, I dragged my gaze down to her breasts that were lifting and rising in harsh breaths. "And what the fuck are you wearing?"

She gave me a little pout, flouncing the flimsy strips of gossamer barely covering her chest. "What, this little ole dress? You don't like it?"

This girl was trying to kill me. She'd been born with the primary objective to kill me, and she was nearly succeeding.

My hand reached up, clenched midway, but then kept moving against my will and circled the column of her throat. "I like it too much. Problem is, so does every other male in the vicinity, and considering the mood I'm in, they'll be thrown out on their asses if they keep staring at your tits."

Her eyes flared wide. After a little lick, her tiny white teeth sank into her lush bottom lip, making me groan.

What was she doing to me, with her bedroom eyes, her sexy dress, and her sultry voice? Yeah, that was a rhetorical question if ever there was one. If I didn't know better, I'd think this little girl was making a move on me. God, I'd give anything to have that to be true. *I must want it because I'm conjuring this out of nowhere.* Knowing I was losing my mind, I dropped my hand and took a step back.

A flare of distress passed over her face.

Suddenly, her hand shot out and grabbed my tie. Gripping it tightly, she stopped my movement backward. We stood suspended for a long moment, both staring down at her slim fingers crushing silk.

She tugged once. What did she want?

My torso leaned forward, desperate to follow her prompt.

Her eyes glinted with purpose.

She tugged again. Okay, that one answered my question.

Me, she wanted me.

Her scent wrapped around me like I wanted her lips wrapped around my cock, pulling me *in, in, in.*

"Don't play with me," I warned, breathing heavily. My brother was right outside, in the main room. Anyone could walk around the corner and find us in this compromising position. I should pull away, but my will was in shambles. Seconds away from cracking, it was imperative that I left before I did something irrevocable.

"I'm taunted to do bad," I confessed. "I mean, I *really* want to lean into the bad."

She pushed herself off the wall, raised up on her tiptoes, and pressed her lips against mine.

Mother*fuck*—

My brain stalled.

My control snapped.

I grasped the front of her dress, dragging her up to me while my other hand wrapped around the base of her head, keeping her in place. Slanting my mouth over hers, my tongue pushed past her lips. She tasted of rose water and sugar rolled into one. My tongue lashed inside, like a roving marauder, seeking to taste every inch. She opened up to me like my good little girl, meeting my assault with a strike of her own.

Letting go of her, my hand snaked down and grasped her ass cheek. I moaned into her mouth as I took hold of the supple flesh. It felt fucking divine and so damn right. I palmed the slit of her dress, yanked it away, and placed my hand on her hot skin.

I was touching her skin, and holy fuck, nothing felt better. My fingers dug into her bouncy ass, my middle finger curving inward and so damn close to her back entrance. The heat of it was burning the tip of my finger.

There was a roar from a crowd outside, breaking into my trance. *Fuck.* We were practically in public with my little brother around the corner. I tore her mouth apart one more time before pulling off her.

Glaring at her, I gave her tight ass a sharp slap. "No more going out alone."

Her eyes flashed. She nipped at my chin.

This woman was twisting my insides, but she had to learn who was boss.

I gave her another smack, this time a touch harder.

She let out a sharp gasp.

"Do you hear me? Answer me," I demanded, nostrils flaring. "No more dresses like this." We had bigger problems than her damn dress, but I clung to the one thing I could control.

She gave a short nod, followed by a small whimper that almost buckled my knees.

Christ, I'm trying to do right. Everything inside me screamed to wrap my arms around her. And then pound into her against the wall and make her mine. Make her mine. *Make her mine.* The words pounded into my brain like the staccato rhythm of drums at the start of a battle. Once they entered my consciousness, there was no beating them back. They took hold like amped-up, mutant plants in fertile soil, like Jack and the Beanstalk on steroids.

Fuck it. I swooped back down and captured her mouth again, taking and using it as if it was my own personal toy to mouth fuck.

She melted against me, feeding off the succor I provided. Pushing her chest out, she rubbed her high little tits into me. I slammed her into the wall, the wallpaper rasping against my knuckles as I ground into her. This girl undid me like no other. My cock was as hard as stone, and she scraped her belly against it, moaning into my mouth. That luscious sound reverberated down my body to my balls. I was about to spill like a damn teenager just from dry humping her.

I needed this woman under me like I needed my next breath, and I sure as hell wasn't going any further here. All hell would break loose if we were caught before I finished what I intended to do.

"We're leaving," I snarled.

"W-what?" she whispered, blinking up at me, the haze of lust dissipating as she focused on what I had said.

"We're leaving. You're coming with me," I pronounced.

"What about Jewel and..." she hesitated and swallowed, probably scared to say his name out loud.

"Nicu? Fuck him. You're coming with me, Cat. This is happening," I declared.

My hands still on her, I turned her around and pressed her back to my front, nestling my pike-hard cock right between her ass cheeks and said, "Go out there and tell Jewel that you're leaving while I talk to my brother."

She twisted her head over her shoulder, wide eyes searching mine. "Do you mean w-what I think you mean?"

"The blood bond? Fuck yes, I do, woman. You're mine," I rasped. I'd never spoken truer words. Despite the lust coursing through my veins and guilt pounding inside my head, an inexplicable peace permeated my soul. I was clear-headed and the path in front of me was illuminated like flares on a runway. I always assumed marriage wasn't for me, but I had seized on something that was as awe-inspiring as it was frightening. And that thing was...hope.

Hope.

Insane as it was, I let it flare in my chest, growing brighter by the moment. Turning Cat around, I placed the flat of my hand on the center of her back and propelled her forward. This was fucking happening.

We returned to the booth, and she immediately asked Jewel to go to the bathroom with her.

Leaning against the banquette, I addressed Nicu, "Cat doesn't feel well. I'm taking her home. Do you mind watching over her friend and driving her back to her place when she's ready to leave?"

Avoiding my gaze, he cleared his throat and said, "Yeah, sure. I can do that."

I rolled my eyes. He was clearly smitten with Jewel. Even though I was gunning to fuck his girl, I was suddenly irritated. "Don't you want to know what's wrong with your fiancée?"

His eyes darted to mine and then away again.

"No," he retorted with a stubborn tilt of his chin. "She's the enemy. I don't trust her, and you know me. Once I make up my mind about someone, I don't change it. I'm not like you, making decisions based on my fucking emotions. I was ordered to marry her, so I'm doing what I was told. Nothing more, nothing less. I didn't make that decision freely, and while it may not be her fault, it's her family's fault. That's the way it is. Anyway, she's not my type." His eyes drifted toward

Jewel, where they stayed. "Since the beginning, she was more yours than mine."

What the hell did he mean by that? I was too focused on Cat and what I was about to do to concentrate on Nicu's strange comment.

As pissed off as I was at the way he treated Cat, his declaration sealed the deal. I was taking her from him. He didn't deserve her. He'd make her miserable. Cat was marrying him out of duty, but she didn't know him like I did. He would break her and I was going to save her from that fate. If it meant that I'd have to marry her, so be it. That was the natural consequence to a blood bond anyway.

He turned toward me, his expression crafty. "You seem to have developed quite a rapport with her. Ironic, isn't it?"

My eyes snapped to his. "What the hell do you mean by that?"

"Only that it was your responsibility to marry her first. I was a stopgap measure to save the contract, but we all know those Popescu dogs preferred you."

Distracted, I caught sight of Cat winding her way between the couches with Jewel behind her. The low cut of her dress exposed the dimples right above her ass cheeks. *Goddammit!* How had I not noticed how much that dress exposed of her back? Every cell in my body strained to cover her with my jacket. I saw red. My mind emptied of all thoughts but one. Carry out the blood bond.

"Whatever, I don't have time for this shit. Just make sure you get Jewel home safe," I commanded and stalked off as I yanked my jacket down my arms. "You can do that much, can't you?"

Meeting her halfway to the exit, I grabbed her elbow and tossed my jacket over her shoulders. Mumbling a good night to Jewel, I crowded Cat into the stairway leading downstairs.

As we waited for the car, I wrapped her into my arms and pulled her into my chest. She nuzzled into the base of my throat, gliding her nose up and down in a way that was tipping me right into a place of insatiable greed. My other hand fell to her ass, squeezing her firm bottom in public, as I muttered out complaints about her backless dress. I should've kept my hands off her, at least until we were alone, but I was done fighting with myself. After weeks of dancing around each other, innocent and accidental touches here and there, I had direct access to her and I wasn't about to let go.

She trembled slightly in my hold.

I bent my head down, snuggling her close to me. "You okay?"

"I-I'm scared," she replied.

"Shhh, I'm going to take care of you, Cat. You know I wouldn't touch you unless I'd make good on it."

"I know," she paused a beat, "but maybe we should go to your brother and my parents first."

I dropped a kiss on the crown of her head. "You're such a good girl, and I love that about you. I love that you want to do what's right and know how to follow orders. That's critical to being my partner, but you also have your own mind and a spine. Those are going to come in handy. It takes guts to do what we're about to do. Once it's done, no one will be able to argue against us, no matter how angry or disappointed they might be with us," I explained.

"The blood bond," she stated simply.

"Yes," I breathed out. "It's the only way."

She nodded into my chest. I caressed her long tresses. Grabbing them, I tilted her head back until her eyes were on me. "Trust me, beautiful. There's no way I'm going to let anyone hurt you, understand?"

Licking her dry lips, she nodded. That was all the consent I needed.

A sleek black Ferrari rolled up on the curb where we were standing. She tilted her head to the side, inspecting my car.

"Only Italian for me. Like my suits," I clarified.

"Such arrogance," she replied with a huff.

I gave her a shrug as I caught the keys the valet tossed in my direction.

"We can afford it," I affirmed, "so why not enjoy it? And don't worry, I have every intention of pampering you as well," I teased as I opened the passenger door.

Her body stiffened as she slipped into the seat. She locked eyes on me. "I don't need your wealth," she replied.

My brows furrowed at the edginess in her tone. My joke had touched a nerve. I knew the Popescus were proud, and sensitive about their status, but it would be my duty to provide for her, and I'd take it seriously. Leaning down, I pressed a kiss against her temple.

"Good to know. Anything else we need to clear out of the way?" I asked lightly.

Forehead crinkling adorably, her mouth pursed in a cute bow and she shook her head solemnly.

In a tone brooking no argument, I finished, "Then let's do this."

12

My first taste of him had my head swimming. The way our tongues danced together was a revelation. A whole new world opened up to me, like those novels I read in school of walking through a closet or falling down a rabbit hole. Surely, I was living in an alternate reality. Everything was upside down and topsy-turvy.

What we were planning to do was insane, but Luca was right. It was the only way. After what happened in the club, it wouldn't be fair to marry Nicu. I'd gone too far. Touched another man, kissed him, let him grab my butt and smack it. The last one had a possessive edge to it that I liked more than I'd ever admit aloud.

As much as my family might get upset, I'd been given the chance to follow my own path while doing right by them. My hands shook from nerves at the thought of losing my virginity. Sitting beside Luca in the tight confines of his car, I inhaled the familiar fragrance of his cologne with the scent of fine wool from his jacket, and the quivery feeling settled.

I'd been with Luca in a car before, of course, but this time was different. The small, sleek Ferrari fit the kind of ride we were taking. It was luxurious to the point of being sensual, like him. We sped through the city streets and suddenly veered into the entrance of an underground parking lot.

"Where are we going?" I asked, a little alarmed.

"We're going to the penthouse. I can't wait the forty minutes it will take to get to Westchester. Anyway, it's better here. I'll leave the door unlocked so that Alex can discover us in the morning."

"What do you mean by *discover us*?" I squeaked out.

His fingers curled over my bare knee. "Courage, baby, courage. Alex is supposed to come over tomorrow morning to go over business. It's perfect. Once he sees us, the deed will be done."

"Oh, God," I stammered out, my nerves rushing back. My breath came out, shorter and shorter.

He pulled into a space, pulled on the brake, and turned toward me. "Calm down, everything's going to be okay." After pushing his seat back, he unclasped my seatbelt and dragged me onto his lap. Immediately, his warmth seeped into me and my trembling abated.

Pushing his jacket off my shoulders, he murmured, "Like I said, I love that you're rule abiding, and I have plans for you to abide by my own set of rules soon, beautiful. I've had a lot of experience doing the opposite of what I'm told, but you don't. It's normal that you're nervous, but you have to trust me, okay?"

"Y-yeah," I stuttered. Firming my voice, I replied, "Yes, yes, of course, I do. I wouldn't be here if I didn't trust you."

"I won't let you down, but you have to be brave tonight. Tomorrow, you have to be brave again and let Alex catch us.

Don't worry about his reaction. He won't hurt you, and I'll take care of him. But tonight, you have to open your beautiful thighs for me, relax, and let me in." He cooed into my hair, "It's going to hurt when I pop that tight cherry of yours but, afterward, the pain will go away and I'll make you feel so good."

"Okay," I said. My heart melted. He wasn't saying anything I didn't know, but his need to reassure me was adorable.

He kissed the tip of my nose, then dipped his head and grazed his lips over mine. Once, then twice. It was a tight fit in the car, but I loved that all boundaries were obliterated. I moaned and opened for more. Sweeping his tongue inside, he took my mouth until I forgot everything but him. His hand caressed my breast a few times before cupping it tenderly. He did this thing with his finger, swiping it over my nipple with the perfect amount of pressure until I was squirming in his lap.

Breaking our kiss, he groaned into the crook of my neck and peppered kisses up the side of my throat before pulling back. Closing his eyes, his head thumped against the leather seat. "Let's get out of here before I end up taking you in my car."

A nervous giggle slipped out. His eyes popped open, the silver-gray under his hooded lids twisted something hot and bothered in my belly.

"Fuck...that sound. You don't know what you do to me."

Shaking his head, he shut off the engine and threw the door open. We took an elevator that went straight up to the top floor. We must be in the Time Warner building, where the infamous Lupu penthouses were. Everyone knew that Alex's father had bought the top floor of both towers. Alex and his wife, Nina, lived in one penthouse and Tatum lived in the other one. Nicu and Luca occupied the two pent-houses in the second tower.

The elevator doors slid open, and I anxiously peeked out before scurrying out to follow Luca. Logically, I knew Nicu was either still at The Lounge with Jewel or driving her home, but misguided guilt settled in my chest. Nicu didn't care for me; he was about as attached to our engagement as I was. But I felt like I was betraying him. I took a long bracing breath. Again, I had to trust Luca. In the long run, what we were doing was best for Nicu as well. Now he'd be free to find someone he cared about. If I didn't know how much contempt Jewel had for *mafie* men, I'd selfishly hope that they'd hook up.

Swinging the unlocked door open, Luca gestured for me to enter as the lights turned on automatically. Happy to get out of the hallway, I hurried inside and inhaled sharply. Whew, this place could be a spread in *Architectural Digest* or some fancy interior design magazine.

I wandered deeper into his apartment. Various shades of white dominated the room. Two identical long white leather couches faced each other with a white marble coffee table situated between them. Stepping onto a rug that had a modern, diamond-shaped pattern of white and an icy blue, I dropped my black clutch on the table. Facing me was an enormous fireplace made of black marble with white vein-ing. The black was picked up in the base of the lamps dispersed around the large room.

The place was pristine, if a little cold and impersonal compared to his home in the country. The only touches of humanity were huge vases of white lilies and blue and white delphiniums on the mantle of the fireplace, the coffee table, and the pedestals on either side of the fireplace. And were those cherry blossoms? Yup, only Luca would find a place that forced cherry blossoms. As ridiculous as it sounded, the man had a thing for flowers. Besides the multiple gardens he had, I noticed the care that had been given to the bouquets of flowers scattered around his house in Westchester during my engagement weekend.

"It's very...modern," I faltered in my description as I turned to face him. My eyes widened at the two walls of floor-to-ceiling windows overlooking a sea of lights glittering in the inky black night sky.

"Different from my other home," he mused. "I don't spend much time here outside of work. I have my office here and we use it as our go-to conference room for business meetings."

Walking toward the windows, I noted, "The view is amazing."

He walked behind me, wrapped an arm around my middle and pulled me into the cove of his warm chest. His heat seeped into me, the warmth but also the intimacy of his gesture melting me in this sterile environment.

We both looked down into the gleaming lights of the city spread out below us.

"Once the buildings were done, my father said it had been worth the investment for the view alone. He was so proud of having gotten in early and locked down all the penthouses for the Lupu clan. Maybe that's one of the reasons I never took to this place. That, and the fact that I hate the city," he confided.

"I'm not a huge fan of cities, either. Might be the six years I spent on a posh prep-school campus in New England. Although Jewel hated being away from the bustle of New York. She missed the noise of the traffic. It took her months to learn to fall asleep."

"Do you think you'll be happy in my other home?"

"Of course. I'm already in love with your garden, and your pool." My voice dropped as I finished, "And your shower downstairs." And just like that, the air between us shifted. I felt his muscles tighten behind me, like a predator on the alert. And I was his prey.

Burrowing into the side of my neck, he murmured, "Is that right? You can't imagine how much I wanted you that day. Truth is, I wanted to touch you the moment I laid eyes on you, creeping around the corner to escape that suffocating party. But downstairs, the spirit you showed, the courage of watching me...and then when you lifted your skirt and thrust your hand down your innocent white panties..." He groaned into my skin, the hot breath and vibration of that sexy sound making its way down my spine.

His hand slid up my torso and cupped my breast, thrumming my nipple to a hard point. "You're a good girl, but you can be such a bad girl at the same time. Christ, it was one of the hottest things I'd ever seen."

Bending slightly, he hooked his arm beneath my knees and swooped me up in the air. I let out a squeak as I grabbed hold of his solid neck. Giving me a long, scrutinizing look, his eyes roamed over my face from my eyes to my nose and mouth, and back up again.

"I'll make it good for you, Cat. Ready?" he asked, his deep tone had a fistful of gravel in it.

Touched by his concern, I swallowed hard. I'd preserved my virginity much longer than many of my peers, that was for sure. Although I'd done it for my family, I was surprised to realize that I was feeling a little sentimental. I was glad that my first time would be with Luca and not a husband that I didn't choose. It was a moment of empowerment to take the clout behind this prized virginity and wield it like a weapon to forge my own path.

"I'm on the pill if that makes a difference as to what we do."

His head dropped back on his shoulders and he let out a low moan that had me wiggling in place. "It makes a hell of a difference. I'm going to get my big cock in you bare, baby girl. You think you can handle that?"

Heat shot through my core. God, his dirty talk. I didn't finish nodding before he was moving, gliding swiftly over the marble floor, down a hallway. Passing one door, he pushed open the next door with his shoulder and brought me into a large master bedroom. It contrasted starkly with the white of the living room.

Here, everything was dark, various shades of midnight blue with accents of azure and cobalt. The centerpiece was a huge, canopied bed with large swaths of patterned blue damask that were gathered at each intricately carved wooden post. It gave off the air of a throne. A very dramatic location for the deflowering of a virgin, I thought as he placed me on my feet right beside the bed.

My nerves returned at the sight of the huge bed and the fact that we were on the verge of the big moment. What if I didn't do it right? What if I didn't satisfy him? I felt his erection rub against my belly as I pressed against him. I'd seen him jerk off, so I already knew he was massive. What if it didn't fit? I shook my head. No, that was impossible. They all fit in eventually. Didn't they? But what about with virgins?

Concentrating all my attention on his tie, I fiddled with it as I confessed, "I don't really know what to do…"

A long breath blew out from his sculptured lips.

His hands smoothed down the sides of my body, settling on my waist. "It's normal, beautiful, but I'm not going to rip into you right out of the gate."

A wave of relief tumbled over me and my shoulders

slumped forward in relief. His hand cupped my cheek gently.

"First, I'm going to prep you with my tongue and my fingers. Make you come and scream my name until you're primed and begging for my cock."

"Oh," I replied, heat flashing through me.

He chuckled, bringing his lips to mine and simply leaving them there for a bit, as if to acclimate me to his touch before he made his next move. "All you have to do is follow my lead."

I gazed up at him from beneath my lashes. "And you're sure that you'll...get off? Even with a virgin?"

He dropped his face into the crook of my neck and laughed. "I'm sure. Baby, you're going to be so tight and wet that getting off won't be my problem. Holding back until *you* get off will be the real challenge."

Scorching heat flushed my cheeks and coursed down my throat. His filthy mouth morphed my nervousness into a thrill that ran down my spine. His thumb found my nipple and thrummed it in the most distracting fashion.

"Beautiful, I'm dedicated to your pleasure. I'm going to learn every single inch of you and mold this pussy until it flutters with anticipation every time you set eyes on me." His hand pressed between my legs, a finger tapped my clit and my body jolted against him. "This sweet little body will know whose fat cock makes it come. And I will satisfy you. Each. And. Every. Time." A shudder racked through me. I pushed into his hand, seeking more. *More.* I needed more.

SHE SHOOK IN MY ARMS, but the way she writhed her hot pussy against my hand, I figured she'd turned the corner on her nerves. When I dropped her to her feet, her eyes bounced around my bedroom like I'd thrown her into a BDSM dungeon. It was to be expected. Cat was giving up her virginity and it wasn't our wedding night. But, courageous girl that she was, she was willing to break that sacred rule and plunge into unknown territory. For us. For me.

With closed-mouth kisses, I caressed my lips over hers, putting her in charge of the pace. I wasn't going to maul her like a beast. No, I had every intention of relishing her and making her go mindless with pleasure. From the way she thrust her hips and ground her mound against my palm, she was on the right path. The chemistry between us was already explosive, so I shouldn't have been surprised. Here she was, a nervous virgin, but already she began following her instincts.

I was so damn proud of her.

Once she opened to me, I brushed my tongue inside, stroking leisurely until her fingers curled into my shirt. She'd already loosened my tie, so I finished the job as she whimpered in frustration. I took our kiss deeper and she responded in kind. Dragging the straps of her dress down, I peeled it off her body. My fingers made contact with hot skin. So smooth and silky. I found a beaded nipple and flicked it. She jerked against me with a throaty moan and then pressed closer.

Goddamn. So responsive.

Losing a little patience, I fisted her hair, crushing the satiny locks in my big hand. So absorbed in our kiss, she didn't balk at my rougher touch. I slipped under the hem of her dress and palmed her ass. Twisting the string of her thong between her ass cheeks, I yanked it, released, and yanked again to give her pussy a little friction. Hips bumped against me, her back arching in response.

Pushing down on the dress gathered at her waist, she wiggled her lithe frame until it fell in a pool at her feet. My gaze scoured her gorgeous body. Braless, her high tits and peaked nipples made my mouth go dry. My eyes skittered to the black garter belt hugging her thighs down to the delicate black fishnet stockings encasing her slender legs. A triangle of black satin covered her tightly sealed pussy.

A surge of ownership flooded me, leaving me shattered and almost trembling with anticipation. No man would ever touch her pussy, but me. I had no clue how hot that idea would make me. Yeah, I was a savage, but I didn't care.

Suddenly ravenous, I tore at my shirt, renting the buttons off in one fell swoop, scattering them across the floor. After stripping off my clothes, I flipped the duvet down and laid back on my bed.

Patting the space beside me, I said, "Come here, I need to taste that cunt. Leave the tights on and straddle my face. I'm going to lick every delicious pink inch of you."

Cat's eyes were wide, fear and excitement warring for dominance. A little fear never hurt anyone. It would only add to the adrenaline coursing through her veins. Taking her panties off, she stood for another moment, stalled by nerves again.

Watching her battle them, lift her chin stubbornly, and choose me over fear, filled my ears with a roar of triumph. My hands trembled with anticipation. Her momentary pause heightened the preciousness of the gift she was bestowing on me. Fuck, I was a lucky bastard. This beautiful girl had turned to *me* to deflower her.

Breath rattled from my chest when I caught sight of that tight, almost-bare pussy until she covered it with her hand.

"Move your hand," I demanded roughly, swiping at it. "Never keep me from what's mine, understood?"

Lust flared in her eyes as she nodded.

Her hand slipped off, giving me a full-frontal view of the prettiest little puss I'd ever seen. The patch of blonde hair told me she was a natural, as I had suspected. It screamed *untouched.* An idea popped into my head and I asked Cat to hand me my tie. Her eyes bulged, but she bent down and handed it to me.

I placed it carefully by my side and prompted, "Come on, brave girl, let me tongue fuck that sweet, innocent pussy."

"Really?" she breathed out, but her chest rose and fell faster, signaling her anticipation. Crawling up the bed to me, her tits swung from side to side, tight nipples begging for my mouth. Gingerly, she placed her knees on either side of my waist, looking at me for approval.

Oh, I approved alright.

Every fucking inch of her was magnificent, and it was all mine. Taking hold of her hips, I leaned in and lathed her nipples, sucking them into my mouth, leaving one a bright pink to administer the same treatment to the other.

Patting my chest, I directed her to move higher. I slid down and there she was in all her naked glory, suspended right above me. Her thighs quivered on either side of my head. She was so close that I could smell her sugary musk, leaving me salivating for a taste.

Parting her glistening lower lips, I said, "Right here. This is the opening to paradise, Cat, and I'll never forget that you gave it to me first. But know this, no man will ever lick or fuck this pussy but me. Let it be known, from this day forward, that you are mine. As I am yours."

I pushed one finger inside and holy fuck, but it was tight. Tight and slippery. My gaze flicked up to her face, scrutinizing every reaction. Her mouth popped open on a groan.

Good girl.

"I promise to hold and cherish and fuck you into oblivion every day of your life. For better or worse, for richer or poorer, through sickness and health, I will be there. Give me your hand."

With the tie, I bound our hands together at the wrists. In Orthodox weddings, the priest bound the hands of the groom and bride together to symbolize their union through the happy and difficult times, similar to American wedding vows. If you told me a month ago that I would be in bed, binding myself to a woman for life, I would've lodged a bullet in your skull for the perceived insult. Yet here I was. Absolute certainty permeated every cell of my body. This was right. This was perfect, and it was due to Cat.

Surprise crossed her face.

"Are you serious?" she asked. "You don't have to do this. I trust you..."

"I'm not a priest, but you deserve to have it done right, and this is as close to married as we can get right now. Bring your pussy down on my face," I commanded.

The instant it was in reach of my tongue, I dragged the stiff muscle over her lower lips, stabbing inside, moaning at her taste. Sucking her clit between my lips, I locked eyes on hers just in time to see them glaze over, lost in lust.

"Oh my—" her next words were cut off by a choked scream. Her hand slapped the headboard above my head as her entire body shuddered. Grasping her buttocks, I brought her further down until all my senses were devoted to her pussy. Growling as if possessed, I delved in to teach her my ways. By the end of the night, her pussy would be trained to clench when I entered the room.

"Such a good little cunt you've kept nice and tight for

me. I'm going to eat it and stretch it and make it bloody just for me. Now grind down on me, baby," I instructed her.

Her breathing hiccupped, her clawing fingers searched for purchase, tearing my hair by its roots, but nothing would push me off my game. Her wild scratching goaded me on. I humped the air with my hips, the tip of my cock bumping into her lower back and ricocheting to my balls. Stroking my tongue in and out of her, she writhed above me and I had to hold her in place, laving and licking to my heart's content.

She broke abruptly, screeching out my name, "Luca, *Luca, LUCA!*"

I was stunned by how fast she came but relished the taste of her orgasm on my tongue. When she was over the peak of her climax, I tilted her off me and onto her back. She lay sprawled out, head swinging from side to side. Our hands bound together the whole time, I slowly spread her pussy open, glistening with come and saliva.

She was as ready as she'd ever be. I worked my cock inside her about an inch. Fuck, the sight of her pussy lips stretching over my girth was almost too much. Clenching my teeth, I bore down another inch, and I continued to press my advantage when her virgin flesh decided to suction around my shaft like an airless vacuum. Resisting my intrusion. Attempting to keep me out. I kept going until I was halfway in but had to pause to regain my control because the drive to pound into her whipped through me.

Pinned beneath me, Cat had tensed. "You won't fit," she whined.

"Trust me, I will," I assured her. I caressed a few strands of her hair stuck to her forehead. "Don't worry, baby girl, it takes time and practice to mold you to fit my cock, but I'll take care of you."

Bending over, I kissed her thoroughly until she turned

pliant once more. A rush of wetness eased my way and I resumed my efforts, withdrawing and easing in until I was fully sheathed.

She whimpered against my mouth. I hushed her and praised her, "You feel so good, beautiful. So slick and small and *tight*. Such a snug virgin hole you've kept for me. The pain will subside and soon you'll be taking my cock like a pro."

My filthy talk worked because she circled her hips, tentatively at first, but soon, she was flexing to meet my thrusts. Her little pussy sucked my dick on all sides, leaving me delirious. Christ, I'd hit the pussy jackpot. I had to steal my little brother's fiancée, but it was worth any fallout. I'd take whatever punishment was meted out because I'd never regret this.

"Feel that, baby girl?" I thrust hard, balls slapping against her ass. "We are bound as one. You're mine and I'm yours."

Rutting into her, I knew I wouldn't last much longer. She felt too good, too slippery and tight. I jiggled my thumb on her clit and moved my cock inside until her gasp let me know I'd hit the right spot. Strumming that little pearl, I elongated my strokes. Her tender flesh undulated around my cock. Every muscle in my body screamed for me to take her rough, and just when I was about to lose the battle, she was coming again. Screaming out my name, her cunt throbbed and squeezed impossibly tight. Her little feet were latched to my lower back, heels digging into me. Nails streaked down my back, leaving trails of blood. Another gush of wetness and I was a goner.

I fucked her like I was mating her, like I was meant to breed her.

It was official.

Cat was mine.

Baring my teeth, I pummeled into her. Her inner muscles contracted, milking me, drawing the come out of me. I might be a dirty talker, but I was never a screamer. Until now. I boomed out a beast-like sound, more growl than anything else.

Headboard smashing against the wall, hips smacking, flesh squelching, I was dragged into an undertow of liquid heat. The cells of my body exploded, separated, and joined again to form another being.

I was reborn.

When I came back into my body, I found myself collapsed over Cat, who was moaning hoarsely beneath me. Lifting off her on shaky arms, I blinked down in disbelief. Her hooded eyes languidly met mine, cheeks flagged red, forehead beaded with perspiration.

My heart expanded. It was about to explode with this overwhelming feeling.

Holy fuck, was this love? I wouldn't know, having never felt it before.

Shaking my head, I stuffed it down. It was too soon, too sudden.

Yet...it felt true.

Clearing my throat, I asked, "You okay?"

"Yeah," she croaked out. "That didn't hurt too much. You kissed me through the worst of it and then after... just...wow."

I pulled out, my cock streaked in red. The sight made me want to beat my chest like a barbarian because nothing blared out "CLAIMED" more than that. Yeah, I got that I was sick. Perhaps I should have cleaned us up, but my muscles felt like lead, and I couldn't have separated myself from her if I tried. She curled into me, satiated and purring like a cat. That settled it: I wasn't moving an inch. A chuckle bubbled up from my chest. This girl would be my undoing, for sure.

I wrapped my arm around her and pulled her closer.

Part one of our plan was a success.

Tonight was ours alone. Tomorrow, we had to face Alex.

Knowing him as well as I did, that was easier said than done.

13

I woke up slowly. It was hard to come back to consciousness, cocooned in strong arms and enveloped by a sensual musk that worked to drag me back into oblivion. My eyelids fluttered closed a few times before I managed to prop them open. Spooning me from behind, Luca held me like he was afraid I'd escape. His deep breath coasted down the side of my neck and shoulder to tickle my nipple into a pucker.

Shifting my legs, I felt a twinge between my thighs, but I'd been lucky because losing my virginity hadn't been as painful as I'd feared. The way Jewel described it had been borderline scary and had added to my nerves last night. Maybe the difference was Luca. What he did between my legs put anything I'd tried on myself to shame. My heart was bursting with the knowledge that he'd gone to great lengths to make sure that I was ready to take him. Even in my inexperience, I knew he was big. Like *big*, big. *As they say, it's not only the size but what you do with it.*

Gazing over my shoulder, my heart melted. Like the time I'd woken to find him in my bed, I was struck at how peaceful he looked. For a man nine years older than I was, he resembled a sleepy little boy. His usually well-managed hair was tousled, a few locks falling over his forehead. The lines around his mouth vanished, and his full, sculpted lips parted, his breath puffing out onto my bare skin. He was stunning. Simply stunning. Raw possessiveness shot through me at the thought of any other woman having had the privilege of seeing him like this. The force of it left me almost winded.

Oh, God. It was almost like I'd fallen for him. For some reason, the realization scared me more than losing my virginity out of wedlock. My eyes fell on the tie laying abandoned on the side of the bed. A wave of tenderness swelled in me, stemming the tide of fear. Knowing how hard it was for me to defy my family and our traditions, he'd bound our hands together, like during a marriage ceremony, enforcing the blood bond between us.

Luca was incredible. A man of such a strong will, such determination. It was in the way he marched to the beat of his own drum, knocking down any obstacles in his path to live his best life. Luca was one of the most authentic people I'd met, and that was unusual in our insular *mafie* world, where there was lots of striving and intrigue. Knowing what he'd been through with his father made me protective of him. His brothers loved him, but he needed someone who had his back, and only his. I'd be that person.

Turning gently in his embrace, I brushed away the sandy locks on his forehead and traced the strong line of his brow. I could barely believe that he was mine.

His mouth twitched.

His cheek flexed.

Stirring awake, his eyes flickered open and focused on me.

With a voice full of gravel, he said, "That's the second time you got the drop on me and woke up first."

I snuggled closer into his warm, bare chest, his coarse hair tickling my breasts. "It just shows you're comfortable around me. Maybe I'm more motivated to be the first."

Eyebrow raised, he queried, "Oh yeah? Why would that be?"

"To watch you while you sleep," I answered, unabashed.

He ruffled his hair self-consciously, saying gruffly, "Can't imagine why you'd want to do that."

"You're at peace," I intoned.

His eyes softened. He cupped my bare shoulder, caressing. "Hmm, I could say the same about you. You're relaxed and...soft."

We stayed there, eyes on one another, just...feeling each other. His fingers glided down my arm and dipped underneath the sheet to settle on my hip.

"You sore?"

My chest tightened at his concern, but my clit throbbed, desire pooling between my thighs.

"Not too much," I replied in a rasp. At the sound of my voice, his eyes turned sharp. Predatory. With a handful of my ass, he brought me into him and I felt the length of his cock against my belly.

Blinking up, I confided a fantasy I had. "I want to please you like you did to me yesterday."

He choked and swallowed hard. "Like before we had sex when I licked your pussy? Like that?"

"Yes, I want your cock in my mouth." Suddenly embarrassed by my forwardness, I ducked my head. "Sorry, I didn't mean to say that."

"Shhh," he hushed me. "*Never* be sorry for anything you do or say when we're together. You can do no wrong." He placed a finger beneath my chin and tilted my head up. When I finally gathered the courage to meet his heated gaze, he said in a low voice, "Never doubt for an instant that I'd *fucking* love to have my cock in your mouth."

Without breaking eye contact, he flung the sheet off. My gaze broke to get a good look at him. Last night, it was dark and I was still a little tipsy on alcohol and a lot too drunk on Luca to really focus on his manhood. This was the perfect opportunity and I got an eyeful. Of course, I'd already seen everything when I'd caught him jacking off in the shower. But that had been a "look, don't touch" situation, plus I was busy getting myself off at the time.

Here, I had the chance to focus solely on him. God, I was already into his cock. The way it stood up so straight and proud, with a thick vein snaking down the underside. There had to be at least nine inches, but really, who was counting? I knew what it felt like moving inside me, and my pussy clenched involuntarily as if from muscle memory. The way he'd fucked me had been that memorable.

Kneeling, with my legs tucked beneath me, I wrapped my hand around his shaft, velvet smoothness wrapped over steel, and pumped slowly. Luca bent his leg up and languidly let it fall open. The defined planes of his pecs, covered in curly light hair, gave way to the ridged edges of his six-pack, down to a flat abdomen, with a little trail of hair leading to his thick cock. His posture would make a perfect centerfold.

"That's right, beautiful, this is your playground," he said with a pump of his hips into my hand. "So, go play."

Moving up from the root to the crown, I instinctually squeezed the tip.

A hiss came through his parted lips, followed by, "Fuck."

Pre-come spurted in my hand and, wanting to get a taste, I bent over and took a lick.

Another choked growl emboldened me to circle the entire crown with my tongue. Salty and musky, it tasted as good as I'd expected. This was a radically different experience from last night. Here, I was in control. It was a heady experience, having this strong, bold man growling and snarling under my touch.

I got into the rhythm of stroking him with my hand while suctioning as much as I could with my mouth. My head bobbed up and down until his hands took hold of my hair. Held in the position he wanted, he began to use my mouth. *Guess playtime's over.* Luca was taking over and it was just as thrilling. I jimmied my thighs open and teased my clit as he took me further down his cock.

"Relax your throat," he rasped out.

I nodded in understanding and tried to follow his instruction, but it was harder than I thought.

"Breathe through your nose," he instructed.

It took a few tries to get the hang of it. Eventually, I relaxed enough that he could work his way down my throat while I hollowed out my cheeks. My jaw ached, but the discomfort was worth it. Glancing up, I was shocked by the expression on his face. His eyes were at half-mast, and his teeth were clamped down on his bottom lip. He looked almost undone. Now this, I could get addicted to.

I swallowed, constricting my throat muscles around the crown of his swelling cock. He loosed his hold on my hair and dropped his head in surrender. Raw guttural sounds spilled from his mouth. Sheesh, my new goal in life was eliciting those little noises every chance I got.

"Fuck, those are savage moves you've got," he confessed.

"I'm going to be wrapped around your finger with that wet mouth and pussy."

I preened with pride. Despite my inexperience, he was clearly enjoying himself. I hummed around his cock and he jerked in response. My chest expanded. The control my itty-bitty mouth had over him was empowering. I did it again. My hair was instantly curled around his fist. With a firm grip, he took over, thrusting in and out, taking what he wanted. Teeth back on his bottom lip, he made a keening sound as if begging himself to keep a hold on his control. I stretched my neck, opening up my throat. The crown hit the back. I heard a growl, followed by a curse and a choked, "It's too *good*." Luca's big body shuddered once, and then he was climaxing. After that, everything happened fast. He was coming in my mouth, but then he abruptly pulled out. A spray of come spewed across my chin, throat, and breasts. My hands flew up in surprise.

Breathing hard, he fell back against the headboard. His hooded silver eyes took in his seed dripping off the pointed tips of my nipples. I was almost disappointed that I didn't get a chance to swallow, so I slid a finger through his come and sucked it dry.

Enthralled, his jaw dropped open.

"Holy fuck," he heaved out. "So dirty. How did I get so lucky?" After a moment to recuperate, he swung his legs over the side of the bed, got on his feet, and held out his hand. "Come on, let's take a shower and clean you off."

I scrambled off the bed, eager at the chance to shower with him, and stumbled when he next said, "And I want to lick that sugar pussy again."

～

AFTER THE SHOWER, where he'd done exactly what he'd promised, he wrapped me in a fluffy bathrobe. It fell midcalf on me, which told me that it was his. As he tied the belt around me, my stomach let out a growl. I pressed the heel of my hand over my tummy, staring up at him with bright pink cheeks.

Chuckling, he said, "I see I have to replenish your energy after last night and this morning."

Padding back into his bedroom, he donned a pair of sweatpants that did nothing to hide his bulge. Knowing what I knew of his skills, his walking around shirtless was distracting as hell. Taking my hand, he led me into the kitchen, which continued the white-on-white theme of the foyer and living room.

Across the long counter, there was a small table beside a floor-to-ceiling window that looked out onto Columbus Circle below. Slipping into a seat, I gazed down at the cars and buses. They resembled miniature toys from this height, zipping around a granite and marble monument in the center of the congested traffic circle.

Assuming Luca couldn't cook, I offered, "Would you like me to make something?"

He gave me a withering look. "I can cook. My *bunică* made sure to teach us how to fend for ourselves, so I will be doing the cooking. What would *you* like to eat?"

"Anything," I replied simply to give him as many options as possible. I didn't want to suggest something that he had no idea of how to cook. He might *say* he knew how to cook, but I knew Romanian men, and the chances of a *mafie* prince like him cooking anything beyond a boiled egg were slim to none.

He leaned his hip against the counter and crossed his arms over his bare chest, a peeved expression on his face.

Even annoyed, he looked so hot. I just wanted to lick my way across his pecs and down his abs.

"What. Do. You. Want?" he emphasized slowly.

Figuring it was best to go with something simple, I suggested, "Eggs. Any way you like. I don't have a preference."

"Oh, ye of little faith. You don't think I can cook. I can see it in your eyes," he accused as he opened the fridge and bent over, giving me a prime view of his perfect ass. God, that was so unfair.

Pulling out a carton of eggs, milk, an onion, a bell pepper, ham, and sausage, he said, "I'm going to make *omletă țărănească*. You know what that is, I assume."

"Of course, I know what that is. It's a peasant omelet," I replied with a touch of scorn. Who did he think he was talking to?

"Yeah, well, you need the calories after the workout I gave you...and for what's coming later," he replied with an arched brow.

The first part made my insides turn into molten heat. The second part had me quivering on the inside. Pressure was building, what with the fear of what was coming with our families. I had never crossed a line on purpose. Certainly not one of this magnitude, that was for sure. I cringed at the thought of my parents' reactions, and especially Cristo's. God only knew what he would do. I just prayed he held on to his temper.

Then, there was Alex. He hadn't been given the honorary title of the *Lupul* for nothing. Not only was he physically imposing, but he was cunning. He'd outwitted my father and brother more than once. The man could not be underestimated, and our blood bond would live or die on his word. I blew out a ragged breath.

Not used to sitting around in a kitchen and too nervous to relax and do nothing, I offered, "Should I make some coffee?"

"Sure," he replied. Pointing to various cupboards, he called out where the *ibric*, coffee, and sugar were located. After asking him how much sugar he liked in his coffee, I got to work and soon had the coffee foaming in the long-handled copper pot. It felt intimate to be enveloped in Luca's spicy scent from his bathrobe, making Turkish coffee while he prepped an omelet beside me. It was so very domestic. A feeling of giddiness hit me, and a smile spread over my lips.

Soon, this would be our life.

Since the engagement party, I tried to imagine my life with Nicu and came up empty. Not really knowing him, and having spent no time with him, I had nothing to go on. Besides a handful of dutiful texts that he sent here and there, his goal seemed to maintain distance between us. He was as much a blank slate as the day my mother told me of my engagement. While my ego had been a bit bruised by his blatant neglect, I was now grateful for it. By actively avoiding me, I could move forward in my new life with Luca, unencumbered by dreams, thoughts, or memories of another man.

I gave Luca a stealthy side-glance as he stood beside me. *This* man would be my husband. *This* would be my life. I almost let loose a foolish little giggle. Unbelievable. Only a few weeks ago, I resigned myself to a loveless marriage. Now I was feeling as close to blissful as I'd ever felt in my life. I'd felt pride over my grades at school and I'd felt comfort at my parents' home, but I'd never felt this sense of completion, of...joy. And it was all due to this man.

Breaking into my thoughts, Luca said something, which

I only caught the tail end of, "...Romanian summers that I learned to cook." He frowned as he efficiently chopped half an onion. "But that ended when I was thirteen."

"Why did you stop going when you were thirteen?" I asked. I loved that I could ask him any question that popped into my head. I stopped asking questions of Tata and Cristo, who tried to shield me from anything unpleasant about our lives after "the incident."

But Luca saw me as an adult and as his equal. Another thing I loved about him. Frowning into the cutting board of onions, he said, "My father, Alex, and I were ambushed driving back from *Bunică*'s hometown to Bucharest. A Roma gang launched a surprise attack in the middle of nowhere. We brought a few down, but then my father was shot. Thinking they'd killed him, they scattered like roaches. He waved us out of the car, commanding Alex and me to hunt them down. I still remember his warnings to not come back until they were all dead. It took us hours, tracking them down one by one in a birch forest. We killed them all except for the last one, whom we kept alive to torture."

Luca's eyes were glazed over as if he'd been returned to that day in his mind and my heart broke for him again. This man had been through so much. First, he survived an abusive father. Then there was the violence that came from his position as the son of a *şef*. I knew a little bit of how that violence could eat away at you. Long after it was over, it lingered at the edges of my consciousness. What effect did it have on him? An urge to protect him surged through me. I wanted to take care of him somehow.

I touched his shoulder, and he jerked back into the present.

"That's horrible, Luca," I said softly, not knowing what I could say that wouldn't sound trite or stupid.

He flashed me a small smile—to comfort me, I knew—but I wasn't having it.

"No, that's really terrible. It was an awful thing for your father to do. You and Alex were only kids. And you could've been hurt or killed."

That last realization shot a blast of frigid cold through my chest.

"We were trained. We already knew how to handle a gun. Part of our trip to Romania was hunting in the mountains. While I hated the way my father treated me, I understood his motivation that day. If we didn't get them right then and there, we might never have found them. That was unacceptable. We had to eliminate them, and what better statement than having two boys hunt down and eliminate an existential threat? It made for a great story. Once we got back to Bucharest, it spread like wildfire."

I swallowed. "I don't want that to happen to our sons, Luca. If we have sons."

"We will have sons, Cat. And they will follow in my footsteps. You know this." He lifted his hand, caressing my cheek with his knuckles. "I promise to protect them so that they never fall into such an unfortunate situation at such a young age, but they will need to be prepared. It's for their own safety. For all of our safety. Weakness has no place in this world," he ended softly.

He was right, of course. I knew that, but I couldn't face it right now. Stifling a small whimper, I rushed out, "I don't want to have children right away. You're older than me by what...eight, nine years? I know that I'm expected to pop them out right away, but I want to go to college."

At the very least, I could push this problem back a few years. If I accomplished one of my goals, then maybe I wouldn't feel so powerless. Choosing Luca as my husband through the blood bond was definitely a step in the right direction, but I wasn't done. Not nearly close to done. This discussion itself was jumping the gun. It was based on the premise that we got away with the blood bond, a fight that hadn't even begun yet.

Cracking the eggs, one by one, on the edge of a large porcelain bowl, he said, "There's no rush. I'm sure that Nina and Alex will be starting soon. Nina wants a big family, so that should stave off my mother for a time. But after you graduate, I'd like us to start." His hand slipped down to cup my belly. "I can't wait to see you ripe with our child."

I puffed out a laugh. "You did not just say that," I teased, but his warm hand on my belly elicited a yearning to feel a baby kicking inside me. I was stunned. Placing my hand over his, I squeezed. He made me feel things I'd never felt before.

He threw me a wide grin. "What can I say? I'm a possessive bastard." He arched an eyebrow. "During the last month, I was snarling under my breath the entire time, thinking of you and Nicu together. You didn't know that already, *Pisoi*? These past few weeks together have been both heaven and hell for me, wrapped into one."

"You did not call me *Kitty*," I said in the most outraged tone I could summon, although I was secretly touched. Nicknames were a sign of how he felt about me.

He dropped a kiss on my lips. "I did. Because you purr like a kitten after I've licked your pussy or fucked you good."

I let out a scandalized gasp, but in reality, I was thrilled. Being coveted by this man had warmth bubbling inside my chest and spreading throughout my body.

Swatting his arm, I said, "How could you?"

"I could, I did, and I will again. So, your only choice is whether you prefer I call you *Pisoi* or Kitty."

"Kitty," I rasped out. His decadent whiskey tone as he spoke my new nickname was as good as foreplay.

"Fuck, don't look at me like that, Kitty, or I'll never finish this omelet. Alex could come in at any moment and I want you fed before the battle begins," he warned, grabbing my hip and dragging me against him so I could feel his stiff cock.

"Why aren't you more nervous, knowing what's coming?" I asked.

"Because I'm used to being the maverick and stirring up trouble." Gazing down on me with regret, he tapped my nose. "But you're not and I wish I could protect you from it. I'll be able to handle Alex but, at some point, you'll be on your own with your family. You'll have no choice but to be strong."

"I know," I replied with a gulp, my stomach churning at the thought.

His hold tightened around me. "It's going to be tough. How are you feeling, baby?"

"Anxious. Scared. I've never defied my parents before." I lifted my chin and met his gaze head-on. "But I chose this. I chose you. There's no going back."

"You're right about that," he murmured low as he nuzzled my throat. I took a moment to relish his arousal, breathing in deeply as I rubbed my abdomen back and forth before gently pushing myself off him.

"Back to work," I warned as I moved away to open the cupboards in search of the Turkish coffee cups. After pouring the coffee, I set the white fine bone china cup on a saucer within reach of his hand.

He stopped in the middle of whisking eggs to give it a taste.

His eyebrows rose.

"Delicious," he noted. I glowed at his compliment. I retrieved silverware and cut a few slices from a loaf of bread I found in a breadbox as he finished the omelet and portioned it out onto plates.

"For someone who doesn't live here, you're certainly well-stocked," I noted.

He shrugged. "I'm down here practically every day for work, since my brothers and I basically use this place as an office. A babushka comes in daily. She does the groceries and cooks a few times a week since I don't always have time to prepare meals." His hand holding the coffee paused midway as he realized, "Now that you'll be here, I'll look into renting out an office on one of the floors below."

We dug into our meal. I opened my mouth, about to compliment Luca on the omelet when the front door opened and a voice called out, "Honey, I'm home!"

14

Like clockwork. Alex entered my apartment on time.

"Hey, what's up?" he asked as he sauntered into the kitchen. I smirked at the irritation in his tone. My door and Nicu's were never closed since we were the only two who shared the floor and the elevator was special access only. I saw Cat's lovely nose twitch as Alex's feet halted behind me.

"Cat?" he said. After a beat, he continued, "Are you alright? What are you doing here?"

Turning around to face him, I waited as Alex processed the sight of me with my shirt off and Cat, her hair a mess from last night, in my robe. I'd made sure she wore something of mine as a statement, although I did like knowing my scent covered her.

Laced in danger, his eyes jumped from me to her to me again. Alex's voice dropped. "What in the fuck is going on?"

Casually taking a sip of my coffee, I declared, "Congratulate your new sister-in-law, *frate*, Cat and I are getting married."

"Explain yourself and make it fast. You always call me brother when you fuck up," he spat out, his green eyes darkening as they narrowed on me.

I gave a long, audible exhale. Granted, I was used to getting flak from him, but shit could escalate rapidly between us, and I wanted to spare Cat any of Alex's unfettered commentary. He was pissed off enough that he wouldn't hold back much longer. Leaning over, I planted a kiss on Cat's forehead and whispered in her ear for her to leave us and to shut the door of the bedroom behind her. Eyes flared wide with trepidation, she stood up and cradled her plate to her chest. After a little swat to her plump ass, I got to my feet and followed her far enough to make sure she disappeared down the hall.

Once I heard the door click closed, I stalked toward the kitchen and rounded on him, "Watch your fucking mouth around her."

Sitting at the table, his brows hit his forehead. His expression told me exactly what he was thinking—since when did I care about women or how they felt? The question was branded on his face.

"She's eighteen years old. She's got a good reputation. She's a damn virgin, for fuck's sake. You took advantage of her," he proclaimed, his voice hard.

"She's not a virgin anymore." I sat down heavily beside him, making a scoffing noise in the back of my throat. "Right, like Nina was only twenty when she ambushed you into popping her cherry and forging a blood bond. Don't insult them by underestimating how willful they can be."

A low growl emanated from him.

Now it was my turn to apologize. Raising my hands in retreat, I said, "Hey, no disrespect to Nina. I'm trying to explain that Nina and Cat may be young, but they have brains. Hearts. They make informed decisions, regardless of their age or experience level. Nina knew she wanted you and went to great lengths to lock you down. Cat knows who she wants to be with, and I can assure you, it's not Nicu."

Pinching the bridge of his nose, he squeezed his eyes shut like he was in physical pain.

"Why, why, *why*? And why now? Just when we have Nelu where we want him, you have to choose this moment to fuck up our advantage? You know how conniving he is. After years of strife, we finally have the upper hand. Christ man, I gave up on you ever marrying, and now this—" He thrust his hand out. "You had your chance. I cajoled, I begged, I fucking pressured you to take her, and you rejected her. You do realize that, right?"

"Hey, just because I didn't bend to your will doesn't mean I'm incapable of caring for someone," I snapped.

"Sure about that? You rejected her, Luca," he emphasized. His words triggered a little tsunami of remorse in my chest. Guilt wasn't an emotion that I had much experience with, but I felt it, nonetheless.

"It's not that simple," I replied. He could blame me all he wanted, but I didn't even know her then. *Yeah, okay, lay the blame on me.* Anything to spare Cat.

In an exasperated tone, Alex went on, "We had an ugly-ass fight that dragged on for weeks. *Weeks.* Through it all, you held strong. I thought you said that you didn't trust her, that you could never trust a Popescu, that they were planting her as a spy to undermine us. God knows, that's what Nicu still thinks."

"That was before I met her. Before I got to know her," I ground out. "I wasn't going to get bullied into a *mafie* marriage, so, yes, that was partially why I rejected her. If I had met her, things might've been different. As for not trusting her because she's a Popescu..." I waved my hand dismissively. "Knowing her as I do now, she could never be underhanded like that. Betrayal is not in her nature. She's the one pure, untouched thing that's come out of that mongrel clan. She's a goddamn miracle, but there it is."

"Well, too fucking bad," he retorted, his eyes snapping dangerously.

What a double standard.

"Don't act as if you pushed me to marry her for my own good," I scoffed. "It was your duty as şef, but you tried shirking your responsibility off on me so that you could marry Nina. You didn't hesitate sacrificing me for your happiness."

Rising slowly to his full height, he snarled, "Don't you fucking dare lecture me on responsibility. I fucking live and breathe the Lupu clan. I've sacrificed far more than you have for this family."

I rose swiftly to meet him, the chair screeched against the tiles behind me. We eyed each other like a showdown in a spaghetti Western. We'd fought for years, but there was a shift in me. Maybe it was talking to Cat about my father that loosened my tongue, or maybe it was me stepping up to fight for her, for us. Whatever the reason, I was prepared to bring up the unmentionable.

My tone was controlled, but deadly. "Bullshit, I sacrificed in ways that you will know nothing about. I have scars you know nothing about. *Nothing.* And thank fuck for that, Alex. Yes, you've sacrificed, but the fundamental difference between us is that your sacrifices came of your own free will. I sure as hell can't say the same, and maybe that's why every demand or, yes, every request on top of those endless years of sacrifice seems like one too many for me."

His gaze shot away from me, shame and regret stark on

his face. Again, I wondered exactly how much Alex knew, but another part of me didn't care. Keeping Cat took precedence over my lifelong code of silence.

"No, don't look away from me. You were ready to go toe-to-toe with me until I dragged out the one secret we never talk about. Only then are you consumed by guilt. Why do I need to remind you, huh? Oh, right, because *you didn't live through what I lived through*. You can afford to forget. And I rarely bring it up because I don't want to go there, but I'm doing it now. That's how important this is to me."

"Fuck," he muttered under his breath, eyes shooting to the ground.

My shoulders dropped a little. "I'm not playing the victim card. I despise reliving the past, but it rears its ugly head when I'm asked to put myself aside for the needs of the family. My childhood was consumed by the drive to remain silent to protect the cohesion of our family, to protect his absolute authority, to protect your sensibility and the twins' sensibilities. Once the bastard died, I was done. Do you know what level of self-control it took to go to his funeral? Watching everyone weep over a man who was a monster? I rejoiced in his death. I was drunk from relief. I wanted to throw a party—"

"Enough," he interjected with a slash of his hand.

"See, you can't bear to listen to me even now. How could you handle listening to the details of what he did to me? You've never asked me what happened. Not once."

His eyes flew up to mine. "It's true. I didn't want to know, but I also knew you wouldn't tell me." He paused for an instant. He always paused before asking me something he didn't want the answer to. "Will you...will you tell me now?"

I huffed out a weary laugh. In moments like this, I admired my big brother. I was reminded of why I loved him, despite the perpetual distance between us. He never backed down from a challenge, no matter how difficult, how painful. That's what made him not only a boss, but the *Lupul*, a title bestowed on only the most impressive of Lupu șefs. While he might know the broad strokes of what went down between my father and me, he didn't know the particulars.

Could I tell him about how our beloved *pater* ordered me to strip and lie down in the downstairs bathroom tub? A tub filled halfway with water so when he whipped me with a telephone wire, the blood, the proof of his cruelty, swirled down the drain, leaving nothing behind but my scars. Scars my father knew I'd take great lengths to hide. Scars that were now faint, barely noticeable lines. But what about the scars those sessions left on my fucking soul? Yeah, telling Alex was never going to happen.

"No, I won't. It's my burden and I won't share it," I replied. "What good would it do to tell you? It would only tear you up inside. Divide your loyalty. And, let's be honest, you psychologically *need* to admire our father, if not outright love him, to effectively lead this family. I know what it's like to live with hatred and distrust in my heart, and I don't want that for you. Your job is difficult enough as it is. As the second oldest, my duty is to make it as easy as possible for you to rule, and that hasn't changed. Do you remember that time in Romania, hunting down the Roma assassins who shot at us?"

"Of course, I remember," he grunted.

"In the silence of that birch forest, we had to work as a team to track them down. We were united. That was the only way we could succeed in picking them off. If we hadn't worked as one unit, we would've been slaughtered out there." I clapped a hand over his shoulder and squeezed hard. "That birch forest is a metaphor for our world, Alex. We still work as one, yet we each carry our own burden. I've been labeled as the contrarian, the difficult one. I know what Nicu thinks of me. I hear the whispers behind my back. The recluse, the rebel, they call me, but only I know the truth of how much I carry, and trust me, it's more equal than you think."

With a heavy sigh, Alex fell into the chair, slumping over the table. "Be honest, how much does this have to do with Nicu? From the looks of it, once your little brother had her, you went after her."

It might seem like a rational conclusion, and one that was sure to come up again in our vicious gossiping circles. Luca, the jealous older brother, snatching away his younger brother's fiancée, whom he loved so much. Yeah, right. It might sound logical, but the accusation felt like a slap in the face. I did my best to take it in stride.

Pulling my chair toward the table, I carefully took a seat and laid my cards out on the table. "What I have with Cat has nothing to do with Nicu. Don't for an instant think this is about jealousy. I may be many things. Impatient, rough, unruly. But jealous is not one of them. You know damn well that I've never been envious of either you or Nicu. Sure, I hate the way Nicu behaves like a spoiled brat hero-worshipping his father figure, but that has nothing to do with this situation."

Rubbing my knuckles against the scruff of my jaw, I added, "If he cared for her, if he'd shown a sliver of interest in her, hell...if he looked at her like he wanted her, then I would've backed off. It would've killed me, but I would've done it. Instead, last night he lusted after her best friend in front of her, blatantly disrespecting her. He doesn't care for her. At all. But I do." I smacked my hand to my chest. "I fucking care for her. I *will* be a good husband to her. I blood bonded with the full intent of making her mine. No one's taking her away from me. Not even you."

By the time I finished my speech, my chest heaved with emotion. The muscles around my throat were strained, but to hell with it. For the first time, I was speaking my truth. I was willing to suffer through feeling exposed. I'd go out on a limb for Cat, but also because I had to make him understand. It was the only way to win him over.

"If it wasn't to get back at me or Nicu, or to simply make my life harder, then tell me why? Of all the women you could have, why did you have to go after her?"

I gave a humorless chuckle. I understood his confusion. His frustration. But my brother hadn't seen me and Cat together or he wouldn't ask such a ridiculous question. Why, he asked. A better question was how could I not? She was pure gold. Precious and untainted. When a man like me found someone like Cat, he had no choice but to grab and hold on for dear life. It was the closest to clean as I'd ever get.

"I'm not a good man. None of us are, but the difference between us is that Tata took that chance away from me early in life. For her, though, I want to try. Do you remember when we were boys, we'd challenge each other to stare straight into the sun? We knew that it was too bright. Too strong. Mama would scold us that it could blind us, but we'd try anyway. That's what being with Cat is like. It makes me want to reach high."

His face went slack with shock.

Fucking finally.

He got it.

"I don't have words," he replied.

"Believe me when I say that I didn't *intend* to fall for her,"

I explained. "The baggage I carry was one of the reasons I figured I'd never marry, although by no means the only one. If daddy dearest failed to beat the stubbornness out of me, you certainly wouldn't have succeeded in pressuring me into a traditional marriage. Perhaps I took one too many beatings for *the sake of the family* and it no longer held the same weight for me as it did for you and Nicu." I gave a small one-shouldered shrug. "In any event, I was content with the knowledge that I'd live out my life alone."

That wasn't completely true. I was resigned to it. I thought it was the only choice left to me. Never thinking I'd couple up, I'd accepted my fate.

But Cat changed that. I had no idea who she was when I first laid eyes on her, but something shifted inside me that day.

He rubbed his chin thoughtfully. "Okay, you won. I believe you. Still, though. Why do you always have to make things difficult?" he retraced his steps back to the same argument. "For once, we have the Popescus at a disadvantage. You used the blood bond to circumvent the rules, but you didn't handle the situation properly. Especially for a Lupu son like you. There are standards to uphold, Luca."

"Lupu son?" I scoffed with a laugh but sobered at Alex's steady gaze on me. He saw me as equally Lupu as him. Sure, I was, but I wasn't as good at upholding those precious ideals as he was.

Shaking my head, I said, "I didn't think I had a choice."

"Bullshit, you always have a choice," he growled.

"Then I didn't want to risk someone denying us, whether it was you or Nelu." I spread my hands out in supplication. "Either way, here we are. I understand that this is inconvenient for you, and for that, I am sorry."

"That's the first time you've apologized for anything

you've done," he grumbled. Spotting the coffeepot, he retrieved a cup and poured himself what was left over. I was pretty sure there was only sludge left at the bottom but didn't stop him.

Sitting down heavily, he took a sip and made a grimace. Yup, sludge. "I swear, I have half a mind to join Cristo when he and his thugs beat the shit out of you. If I didn't have to show them a united front, I'd be right there by his side. First time in a fucking lifetime."

"You always were constrained by your position as *şef*," I joked. "You should be used to it by now. Guess I should count myself lucky this time."

Leaning over the table, he gave me a small slap to my cheek. "You owe me big time. Beating you up won't be enough. It might've worked if Cristo was head of the family because he's a hot-headed idiot, but not Nelu. He's a wily motherfucker, and he's going to milk this for all he can. He's going to require serious monetary retribution, and I'm warning you now, it's going to come out of your paycheck." He snorted. "Who am I kidding, your portion won't cover half of what he'll demand. I hope you're ready, asshole, because it would serve you right if I left you to clean up this mess by yourself."

I suppressed a grin. Knowing Alex like I did, that was an empty threat. He wouldn't leave me alone with this mess any more than he could stop breathing. Anyway, he was the best negotiator in the family. There was no way he'd step aside to let me take on a formidable opponent like Nelu. Alex was a competitive prick who could barely stand to lose a game of chess. He'd be chomping at the bit for a showdown with Nelu.

I'd let him pretend for as long as he needed to, but in the end, we both knew he'd never leave me out to dry or allow the Lupu name to get dragged through the mud by the Popescu. That wasn't happening. The fucker might have his faults, but it felt good to know that when it mattered to me, he'd have my back.

Eyeing me curiously over the rim of his cup, he asked, "Seriously though, you trust her? She's a Popescu after all."

He was throwing my main argument for not marrying her in my face. That she would spy on us for Nelu. It was certainly what Nicu and many in our clan thought. For an instant, there was a niggling doubt in the back of my mind, but I shoved it away brusquely. Cat didn't have a duplicitous bone in her body.

"I trust her implicitly," I responded. "I wouldn't blood bond with a woman that I didn't trust with my life." That was a lie. I didn't trust anyone with my life, but I trusted myself and my ability to read people. "She's a young, innocent girl. And it helps that she's lived away from that nest of vipers for the past six years. Truth be told, they treat her like gold. Probably the only nice thing I can say about that family. They sent her away for her mental health, and it was a sacrifice."

"Why did they send her away?"

I shrugged. "Not my story to tell. Once you get to know her, you can ask her yourself. She's an open book. Gotta say, it's pretty refreshing after the intrigue and drama that's routine among our people."

He arched an eyebrow. I had surprised him. Members of a *mafie* family were taught to covet secrets like hoarders. Perhaps because she'd lived away from her family, Cat wasn't like that. I wasn't lying when I said that she was like a breath of fresh air. Unlike so many women in our society, with Cat, what you saw was what you got. It was one of the qualities that I liked most about her.

There was one more issue that needed to be addressed with my şef.

"I'm blood bonded with her, Alex. Under the circumstances, I can't allow her to go home. I won't have them shaming her or stressing her out. You need to contact Nelu ASAP. Explain the situation and set up a meeting. She can only avoid their texts and calls for so long."

"Are you fucking serious? It's ballsy of you to have one more ask after what you did. How did you manage to get her out of the house? Did she climb down her window, or what? Because I haven't gotten any alerts that she's missing, although Nelu might try to keep it from me as long as possible."

"They allowed her to sleep over at her friend Jewel's dorm room last night," I explained with a huff.

Neglectful at best, dangerous at worst.

Alex looked at me with an incredulous expression. "Have they lost their minds? Fuck man, this is half their fault for letting her out of their sight. Do they even care about what happens to her?"

I waved away his arguments. "They'd already had her in a boarding school for the past six years. After that, what's another night?"

He shook his head. "Un-fucking-believable."

"The point is, we need to get this resolved before the day is out. There will be a lot to discuss and negotiate, but it should stay between us, Nelu, and Cristo. I don't want her going back there."

"You're kidding me, right? You want her to stay with you, out of wedlock, for the next two months before the wedding?" he ground out.

I gave a matter-of-fact shrug. "I popped her cherry," I drawled. "What more is there?"

"There's a fucking wedding, Luca," he snapped.

"I know, but it's no longer a wedding to a virgin. There's no point in living apart for the interim. You know blood bonds are a sealed deal. It irrevocably tied her to our clan. Cat is now a Lupu. If you prefer that she live with Mama and *Bunică* in Queens, I'm open to the suggestion and willing to bring it to her. But they're strangers to her. I'm her husband in every way but paper."

He let out a long-exhausted sigh and gripped the sides of his head.

"She's my responsibility now," I continued relentlessly. "I don't want them poisoning her toward me. She's strong but impressionable, and for the safety of the clan, you don't want her living with Nelu. God only knows what he can stir up. If they were true allies, that would be one thing. I don't trust Simu either. He and Cat have a bit of history, so he might take this worse than he took her engagement to Nicu. That, along with our history, and the douche will take any opportunity to make my life difficult, and I don't want Cat caught in the middle of our feud. Anyway, it's in our best interest to take her in as a Lupu right away. The added perk is that it will solidify our reputation for ruthlessness. Stealing a bride, blood bonding her, and not giving her back? A warning to the daddies who fuck with us. We take what we want without fear."

"You make a valid point," he mused, rubbing his lips with his finger.

Pulling out his cell phone, he shot off a few texts. "It's done. Now we wait and see, but you're going to make this up to me. I am not fucking joking. For the foreseeable future, you're my little bitch, understand? If I say jump, you ask how high."

Nodding, I slapped my hands on the table and stood up.

"I'm going to check on Cat and let her know what's happened."

Canting his head to the side, he inquired curiously, "How do you think she'll react to not going home?"

"There are pros and cons, either way. As you might already know, her mom was sick recently, but I imagine she'll be relieved that she won't have to live with their disappointment. She was a naughty girl," I said with a wink.

"You won't be able to protect her completely," he called out after me as I stepped out of the kitchen.

"True, but I can serve as a buffer. I already told her that she can put the blame on me. They'll likely try to assassinate me in retribution, but it's a risk I'm willing to take," I tossed out as I walked into the living room.

15

Cat was on the edge of the bed, fiddling with the belt of my robe and staring down at her phone. It took me aback, seeing her slim, forlorn form on my large unmade bed, framed by the drapes swooping down from the carved wooden posts of the bed.

It felt like someone had karate-chopped me in the chest.

Marriage or not, this was my wife.

She looked so young, so achingly beautiful. Locks of unbrushed hair toppled off her shoulder and her large chocolate-sweet eyes locked on me. She returned the silver glitter-cased phone to the night table. The moment she set it down, it vibrated on the wooden surface. Her eyes darted to the phone and then back to me, asking for permission. It must be her family. I shook my head as I approached her, taking her fluttering hands in mine.

Noting the empty plate near her phone, I teased, "Glad it didn't keep you from eating."

Giving me a shy look beneath her lashes, she shrugged her shoulders. "I'd worked up an appetite."

I huffed out a laugh. The unabashed honesty in her answer shot warmth through my chest.

Taking a seat beside her, I wrapped an arm around her shoulder. She instantly snuggled into my side, her fine blonde hair tickling my chin. I took her lips and was rewarded when she opened for me. We indulged in a long, sweet kiss that tore my concentration to shreds. My hands roamed over her curves, one squeezing her hip, the other strumming her nipple.

Damn, I could lose myself in this woman.

"It must have gone well with Alex," she observed, cocking her head to the side. "You don't seem upset."

Observant. Then again, I shouldn't be surprised. Cat was as smart as a whip.

"It went as well as could be expected. Alex texted your father to set up an emergency meeting." Motioning to her cell, I asked, "Have they been blowing up your phone?"

"Not yet, but that last text was from one of them. If Alex contacted my father, they'll be calling soon."

"About your family...I want you here, Kitty. I don't want you returning to them until the wedding. You're with me now. This is your home."

She pulled back from me, although not enough to break my hold, but enough to get a good look at my face. Eyes roved over me to gauge how genuine I was. *Oh, I'm dead serious, baby girl.* I wasn't used to outing my feelings like this, but I'd work on trusting for Cat. A little jolt of fear fluttered through my chest. *No one can be fully trusted.* I shoved the insidious fear away. That came from my past, and Cat wasn't my father.

"You're serious," she stated.

"Fuck, yes, I'm serious. I don't want to be separated for two whole months. I'd elope today if your mother wasn't deep in wedding planning mode and if it wasn't crucial that we have a statement-making wedding. We need it to be appallingly lavish and over-the-top, so no one dares question whom you belong to. That means our wedding will remain on the date you were supposed to marry Nicu." My jaws clenched at how close she'd come to marrying my brother. Cat was mine now, not Nicu's. Not that she was ever Nicu's. "I don't want to be separated from you when we just got together."

Her brows knotted together. "Are you worried that something will happen?"

"Honestly, yes, I am. What if they turn you against me? Simu, especially. He has a special place in his black heart for me. I'm his enemy number one. And your brother isn't a fan of mine either."

A peal of laughter resembling chimes tumbled out of her parted lips. "Don't worry about my brother. Once they find out about the blood bond, they will have to accept it. They won't have a choice."

"That doesn't mean they can't turn you against me," I repeated.

Her hand covered mine. "They're not like that. I know the Popescus have a harsh reputation, but you make them sound like monsters."

I remained silent because, really, I didn't know what to say to that. I didn't want to insult her family, but I wasn't about to back down either.

She let out a little sigh of frustration. "Being away for so long, sometimes I forget how it is here. They're not going to try to tear us apart. Of course, they'll be disappointed in me—"

"Maybe your mother won't try to undercut me because she's a *mafie* wife," I cut in. "But you don't know your brother, Simu, and your father like I do. What we did"—I shook my head—"was not right in their minds. I don't regret it for a second, but they have every right to be angry. It's fine by me if they sling mud my way. I can handle anything they throw at me directly. The only way they can get to me is through you, Cat. Do you understand that?"

"I'm your weakness," she murmured.

"Hell, yes, you are." I tweaked her nipple, and she let out a little gasp of shock mixed with arousal. "But you're worth it. You'll always be worth it. I trust you, but you're young. Sensitive. This is the big brother and father you love that we're talking about. You may think you're strong, but you haven't been through what I've been through with my father. If there's any time that would induce them to treat you badly, it's now. Being family doesn't guarantee your safety, and I must protect you and what we're building together."

My chest tightened at the thought of anything happening to her. Was I projecting my experiences onto her? Probably, but for the first time in my life, the state of my heart depended on something outside of my control, and I couldn't help but worry. It was bad enough I'd fallen for her, but to throw her to the wolves unprotected? No, that was a nonstarter.

Her hand squeezed mine. "What your father did to you has no relation to my family, but I get it. You don't know them like I do. Anyway, I selfishly want to be with you, too, but... Luca, I won't ever stop seeing them," she said, her tone firming toward the end.

"I'd never ask you to, but I need you with me. It's the only way I can guarantee your safety. You can see them, as long as you're in my bed at the end of the day. If I have that, I can handle anything." Ideally, I wanted her as far from her family as possible, but that's not the woman I fell in love with. *There, I just admitted it. I'm in love with her.* Cat was loving and loyal. There was no way she'd turn her back on them. She was right; her childhood was nothing like mine. Even after witnessing her father choke someone out in front of her eyes, she still loved and respected him. It had fucked with her head, given her nightmares that plagued her to this day, but she hadn't turned her back on him.

She pursed her pouty lips, nodding thoughtfully. Raking her eyes down the length of my frame, she replied, "I can do that. I trust you'll find a way to make it up to me." The little minx loved to tease me, and my body was responding in kind. My finger slid down her chest and parted the slit of her robe. It gaped open enough to give me a splendid view of her tits, upturned nipples begging for my mouth.

Flashing me a smile, she declared, "I think this was our first compromise. I'm so proud of us!"

I pressed my lips against hers with a groan, plucking a beaded nipple between my fingers. "I'm impressed with *you*, and don't you worry, I'll make it up to you. I'll have my tongue on your sugar pussy. Every. Single. Night. That's a promise, beautiful."

Letting out a little moan, she kissed me again, tasting like caramel and sticky cotton candy on my tongue. The sultry, sweet taste of her, so erotic in its innocence, seeped into my veins. One taste would never be enough. Grateful we were in bed, I leaned into our kiss. Alex, wherever he was, could handle himself because I wasn't going anywhere.

Breaking our kiss, I pulled off my sweats and leaned back against the headboard, dragging her with me.

"I want you on my cock," I rasped out. Her chest rose and fell in quick succession, her lids hooded low over those wide melted-chocolate eyes of hers. She shrugged off my robe, her tits bouncing in my face. Goddamn, was she sexy. Her opening was slick as she rested above the crown of my shaft. Hands on my shoulders, she circled her hips, working herself on my cock.

"You're wet, but you're still so damn tight," I murmured, eyes riveted on the spread of her cunt as she shimmied down an inch and lifted up, giving me a view of my shaft slick with her juices.

"Come on, "I urged her, "take what you need, Kitty. Take it. Use it. *Ride it.*"

A little whimper came out as she struggled to take more, but she set her jaw and doubled down. Such a good girl, working hard to make my cock fit. And what a tight fit it was. A little notch of frustration between her brows, her struggle to take me was hot as fuck. With my size, gravity could only do so much. I placed my hands behind my head, watching as she fought the natural resistance of her body, writhing above me, her tight hole stretching a little more each time.

"God, you're huge, Luca," she whined.

Slapping me on the chest, she snapped, "Help me. I need help."

Her plea gutted me. Maybe it was too soon to play games with her. She was so desirable that it hadn't crossed my mind that she might feel insecure, but she was new to all this.

Taking over, I buried my face in her throat and licked my way down, over her collarbone to her nipple. Lapping it between my lips, I sucked it hard into my mouth. She let out a sigh of relief. One hand went to the beautiful curve of her hip while the other played with her clit, toying with her little button until she was so slippery that my shaft glided in.

After some work, I was planted inside her, my balls nestled between her ass cheeks.

Her gasp told me how she felt, impaled on my cock. Dipping her head back, she released a garbled *fuck* as she shuddered above me. A pent-up breath left my lungs. I suckled her other breast while moving inside her. Little fingers fisted my shoulders as she got into it and fucked me slowly, her eyes clenched tight and brows drawn together in concentrated pleasure.

"You need this cock, don't you?" I intoned.

"Yes," she cried out. "You don't know how many times I wanted to straddle your lap in the car every time you drove me to class."

"Oh, I remember how you teased me, bending over as you got out, flashing me. Reminding me of the forbidden, untouched treasure beneath your innocent white panties."

"I liked your eyes on me," she confessed.

I knew she would've never taken the first step, but I said, "What would you have done if I lifted the hem of your short summer dress? If I had slid my finger inside those pristine panties?"

Her breathing hitched, but her movements got faster. She slammed down harder, her tight cunt choking my cock in the best of ways.

"I-I don't know," she breathed out. On a downstroke, she said, "Maybe I would've spread my thighs a little and pretended to ignore you while you played with me. Or I would've given in and fondled your cock, like I was dying to do. Pull the zipper down slooowly and slip my hand inside." She batted her eyes at me. "Would I find you wearing briefs or going commando?"

I let out a growl as I pulled her off me and flipped her on her hands and knees. My little girl wanted to play with the fantasy. I could do that.

"Dirty girl, if you'd done that, you would've ended up

with a pussy bleeding all over my leather seats." My mouth found the curve of her ear. "I would've fucked you so hard."

My hand on her nape, I knocked her knees wide and pushed myself in deep. We both moaned simultaneously. "That's how you wanted it, right? You wanted me to fuck you when I shouldn't. Your fiancé's big brother. Off-limits in every way."

"Yes, I did," she hissed. "You wanted it, too. The way you eye fucked me every chance you got. The way you bent your head to get an eyeful each time my skirt rode up my thighs in the car."

"Damn fucking straight, I did." My pace got faster, more brutal. My hips pumped hard. My fingers found her clit, and I teased that slippery pearl until she matched my pace. "I didn't know who you were when I first met you. Turned out, I'd clocked you as mine from the get-go. By the time I found out you were with Nicu, it was already too late." I slammed into her hard, pushing her up a few inches. "I was a goner."

My grip on her hips was rough, likely leaving marks. That should've slowed me down, but it didn't. My hand cupped her pussy, making a V with my fingers on either side of my cock, feeling the friction as my shaft moved in and out of her.

"Tell me, who does this pussy belong to?"

"You," she whispered.

I gave her mound a sharp slap. "I can't hear you," I mocked.

Louder, she said, "You. It's yours."

"Who's is it?" I demanded.

"Luca's. It's Luca's pussy," she screamed.

My lips came to the side of her throat. "That's right, baby. This kitten is all mine." And then I bit down on the side of her throat. I'd been working her good, thrusting into her from behind while tickling her clit with my hand, but the bite triggered a climax. She came on my cock, strangling the shit out of it, and I was helpless to hold back.

Bucking into her, I went wild. Lost my mind. Dragged under, my soul linked with hers. We were two entities joined as one, moving and writhing in tandem, cresting in unison. Her inner walls milked me. My cock jerked, and I unloaded inside her.

After a time, our movements slowed down. I leaned over and we shared a long kiss. Softening, I pulled out and collapsed on my side. Catching my breath, I brought her into my chest. She was snuggling into my chest as a knock sounded against the bedroom door. Shooting a glare at the interruption, I threw a sheet over her bare body.

"Fuck," I muttered, dropping a brief kiss on the crown of her head.

"We have to go. Now," Alex's rumbling voice came through. My body rebelled, my mind screaming at me to stay with her. But, if my şef was interrupting us, then it was important. Nelu had probably gotten back to Alex. As if confirming my suspicion, Cat's phone went off. She scrambled off my lap and lunged for the phone.

Glancing at me, she said, "It's my mother. I just got a text from my brother. They know."

I leaned over to place a gentle kiss on her lips. "Pick it up. Do you want me to stay with you?"

She shook her head. "You should go. It won't help to keep them waiting any longer than necessary. I can handle this."

With a little slap to her tight ass cheek, I vaulted off the bed and marched to the door. Opening it just enough, I listened as Alex spoke in a low voice. Nicu would join us to provide a united front. Stegan would be there as well, which

I thought was a good idea. Stegan was one of our most loyal soldiers and had discovered the Popescu plot to try to manipulate Alex into marrying Cat. Stegan's presence would remind that cocksucking bastard, Cristo, what a sniveling snake he was. We had to use every weapon in our arsenal because this was going to be painful. I was going to have to deal with the repercussions agreed upon by both families. Once that was done, I was going to have to face Nicu.

And those were the things I had a bit of control over. It didn't include whatever Cat would have to face. With the blood bond intact, at least I was confident that she couldn't back out of our arrangement, but who the fuck knew what her family would do to her. Undermine our bond? Try turning her against me? The possibilities were endless with that trio of assholes, Nelu, Cristo, and Simu. The anxiety ratcheted up inside me.

It was going to be one long-ass day.

With a tight nod, I suggested he get Tatum over here to watch Cat while we were gone.

Shutting the door, I found my kitten back to the edge of my bed, phone gripped tightly to her ear. The panicked tone of her mother rattling off in Romanian emanated from her phone. She glanced up at me and gave me a tired smile.

"You okay?" I asked again, cupping the cheek that didn't have a phone attached to it.

She nodded curtly before returning her attention to her conversation.

"Yes, Mama," she murmured. "You're right, Mama."

She traced the outline of my hip bone before gliding her palm around and grabbing my buttock, gripping hard with her slim fingers. I fought hard not to groan out loud and risk being overheard by her mother, but I liked her bold, possessive touch too much. It was her way of telling me that she'd touch me exactly the way she wanted. Her hand moved back to the front and cupped my balls. *Fuck, damn, fuck.* Fondling me while managing her hysterical mother told me that she could handle herself.

If I didn't have to deal with her father, I would've waited until she was done to finish what she'd started. But there would be time for that later.

16

D ressed to the nines in a pin-striped suit with a sharp blue-and-gray tie, I waltzed into the French restaurant in Tribeca where we frequently met with Nelu. It was owned by a Romanian Frenchman who was not partial to either clan. It wasn't open yet, but employees flittered about getting the place ready.

Nodding to the owner, my brothers, Stegan, and I made our way to his office near the kitchen. Opening the door, we were confronted by Nelu, sitting at a large ornate white antique desk with Simu at his shoulder and Cristo pacing the length of the room. My gaze narrowed in on Simu, remembering that he'd once dared touch what was mine. A third man leaned against the wall with his arms crossed over his chest. There was no bottle of *țuică* and shot glasses, which was traditionally served at meetings. A little dig at us, a reminder that we were in the doghouse in the latest episode of the decades-long struggle between our clans.

The men's eyes snapped to us, narrowing in on Stegan.

Nelu's upper lip curled in a sneer.

"What the fuck is he doing here?" Cristo snarled, lifting

his chin toward Stegan. Cristo despised him, which wasn't surprising since Stegan beat him to a pulp and discovered the ruse they'd played on Alex to force him into an engagement with Cat.

The man leaning against the wall came to standing, glaring at Stegan with murderous intent. I recognized him now. He was the brother of the bodyguard Stegan had killed when he'd rescued Una, Cristo's girlfriend, from being beaten half to death. Never understood what a fine-looking woman like Una saw in Cristo. Sure, he had that easygoing, frat boy look, with his floppy brown hair and brown eyes, but the man was a menace with a nasty temper.

"A little reminder that you aren't as pure as the driven snow," Alex drawled, strolling in with utter confidence.

Just as relaxed, I walked in beside him. Nicu flanked his other side. Cristo stumbled back a step, flustered. He'd been ready to gloat, expecting Nicu to be angry, humiliated. Instead, we showed a unified front. The three of us made quite an impression. We stood tall and dressed to kill, from our styled hair to the gleam of our wingtip shoes. Regardless of anything that went down behind the scenes, nothing would shatter our unity, and we represented that.

Alex leisurely took a seat, as if he weren't surrounded by four men who were at this moment plotting our deaths in excruciating detail.

"Nelu," he greeted with a nod of his head.

"What the fuck, Alex?" started Nelu. "First, this *putoi* rejects my beautiful daughter. Then he adds insult to injury by taking her virginity behind our backs. His brother's fiancée no less. What is the meaning of this?" His voice was a bellow by the time he finished, the veins on his neck popping out.

Alex raised his hand. "I've told you once, and I'll tell you again, there's no need for profanity. When you played that little trick on me, cornered me like a hog in a pen, I didn't revert to gutter language."

We cursed as much as the next man amongst ourselves, but this was Alex reminding them of their humble origins. Going toe to toe against a Popescu required using any means to get on top because they were the first to play dirty.

Nelu made a disgusted noise and leaned forward, teeth gritted. Simu pressed closer to Nelu's shoulder at Alex's subtle insult of the Popescu coarseness. I curled my upper lip at him in a snarl. His very presence irritated me, and he was going to do what he could to make my life difficult. Only, it wasn't my life anymore. Cat was involved, and that narrowed down my options.

Alex placed his elbows on the desk and steepled his fingers. "You're upset because you've been caught unawares, but if you looked at the signs, you would've seen what was in front of your eyes. Instead, you were blind, Nelu." He tsked. "Did you not think it strange that Nicu never once asked to visit or spend time with Cat? Or that he chose Luca to personally escort Cat around? Nicu was aware of what was going on at every stage," he finished with a shrug. "They've had his blessing from the beginning."

This was why Alex was *şef*. He was always one step ahead. He had the brilliant ability to twist and manipulate any situation to serve his interest. And he was a consummate liar when he needed to be. This moment was a prime example. If I didn't know better, I would've believed him because of his blasé tone alone.

Alex shrugged his shoulders. "What can I say? My brother caught sight of Cat at the engagement party. She is a beauty; you were right about that. Wanting to see if she was worthy of his attention, he asked Nicu's permission to pursue her. He's a cautious one, that Luca. He wanted to get to know her, so he asked if he could drive her. During those rides, he discovered that the feeling was mutual. He then approached me with the idea of the blood bond. Figuring it was the easiest solution to the matter, I gave him permission, and now, here we are. I understand what a shock this is to you, but we've been in on it from the beginning. He saw, he came, he conquered." Not looking at me, he snapped his fingers as he asked, "Luca, help me out here. Who said that again?"

"*Veni, vidi, vici.* It was Caesar, *şef*," I replied smugly.

Cristo threw his hands up and roared, "Are you out of your goddamn minds? That's not how this works. You don't go behind the family you contracted with. She's not an object you can toss around from man to man."

I jerked, about to grab for him and pummel him into the ground, when Nicu's hand landed on my chest. Clenching my fists tight, I forced myself to remain in place.

"An object like Una, you mean? You certainly batted her around like she was an object instead of the woman you supposedly loved. The woman who'd once carried your baby."

"That's different," he snapped.

Stegan growled behind us.

"Is it?" Alex tossed back. "Pray tell, illuminate us exactly as to how? They're both women."

"Cat is a *princess*," snarled Cristo. "And my baby *sister*. An innocent."

"Oh, so the fact that Una isn't a princess and chose to have sex with you meant you had the right to beat her up. I struggle to understand the thread of logic in your argument, Cristo."

Turning to Nelu, he continued, "I'd think you'd be

impressed. This is, after all, a play out of your playbook. You see, we're learning from the Popescus."

"Fuck!" thundered Cristo. Nelu raised a hand to silence his son. Eyeing Alex, he said, "Well played. So, this was revenge?"

Alex spread his hands, palms out. "God forbid. This is about love, Nelu. This is a love story, and who doesn't adore a love story?"

By pivoting this as a star-crossed love story, the only part of this farce that was true, Alex was minimizing it. If he admitted to revenge, then retaliation could be expected. But it was not uncommon to hear about couples creating a blood bond against the wishes of their families for love. It was an age-old fairy tale that existed since the inception of the blood bond.

"No harm, no foul," Alex went on. "At one point, you preferred Luca. Nicu was always your last choice." He motioned toward me. "Well, now you have him. You're welcome."

By controlling the narrative, and making it seem as if my brothers were aware of my intentions and had given their blessing, all in the name of love, our șef corroded the platform on which Nelu could demand restitution. Nelu would try anyway, but it would be far less than he had hoped to get out of us.

"Why didn't you approach us the honorable way instead of sneaking around and stealing what wasn't yours to take?" Nelu asked, tilting his head to face me.

"Do you not know me, Nelu? Since when do I follow the rule book? I've never pretended to be honorable. I'm a gangster and I take what I want when I want it. End of story," I said, keeping my gaze locked on him. His cheek twitched with irritation, but he held his anger in check remarkably well. Then again, he wasn't the one with the temper. That would be Cristo.

As if on cue, Cristo butted in, "I've never liked you, and I like you even less now. Should've known you'd do something underhanded like this. I was fucking glad when Nicu was chosen, even if he's a cold bastard. Better him than you, in my opinion."

"Let's not pretend any one of us has clean hands, shall we," suggested Alex.

I jabbed my finger toward Cristo. "See, right there is why I didn't come forward. With Nicu on the hook, you wouldn't have allowed me to marry Cat, even if it made her happy. No, you'd spite her to spite me. Don't deny it, Cristo. You might love your sister, but you're as vindictive as they come."

His face turned a mottled purple with rage. "Fuck you! Don't you dare question my love for my sister. You have no idea who I am to my family. And if I didn't let her marry you, it's because I know what's best for her, and it sure as hell is not you!"

"Yeah? Like you knew what was best for Una? Because you declared your undying love to her at one point. Is that how you treat the people you love? If so, then thankfully, I've gotten Cat out of your hands."

Gripping the air as if it were my throat, he warned, "I'm going to kill you."

"*Suficient*," snarled Nelu to his son. *Enough.* That seemed to set him back a step. Chest heaving, he stumbled back against the wall, his spine slamming against the plaster.

When I said he'd never accept me as an alternative, I wasn't lying. Even if I had told my own family, even if every one of Alex's lies had been true, I wouldn't have approached the Popescus.

Unbothered by Cristo's outburst, Alex continued, "I say

we keep the wedding date the same. Considering the animosity Cristo has displayed over this union, I think it's best if Cat stays with us until the wedding. I don't trust him not to hurt her."

Cristo made a choking noise and propelled himself off the wall, but Simu shoved him back.

Pulling up the sleeve of his jacket, Alex checked his watch and came to standing. "Well, I'd say we're done here, Nelu."

Nelu put a staying hand on Alex's forearm and replied, "Not so fast."

Alex heaved a dramatic sigh and returned to his seat. Looking thoroughly bored, he asked, "Yes, what is it?"

"There's the matter of the blood bond."

"What of it?" Alex replied with a hint of impatience.

"He took Cat's virginity. There needs to be restitution."

"Oh." He arched an eyebrow. "What do you suggest?"

"Monetary restitution."

"That's not happening," Alex replied coldly. "The issue has been resolved between the brothers. Nicu will not accept Cat. Luca has. If you want to withdraw from the marriage contract, that's your prerogative, but I can assure you, that will not be acceptable to us."

The suggestion was a low blow, but he'd preempted a strike with one of his own and hobbled Nelu's advantage. Nelu wouldn't consider withdrawing from the contract; it was too lucrative for him. Not only that, but he genuinely loved his daughter, and a broken marriage contract would leave her reputation in tatters.

"Then blood for blood."

"Such as?"

"There's an alley in the back of the restaurant. After we finish up here, each man takes a turn at Luca."

I rolled my eyes. I expected such a suggestion from these fucking barbarians. At least my father's training made me invulnerable to hits from people I despised.

Alex took his time staring at each man for a long moment. Pointing to the silent man leaning against the wall, he said, "Not him. I don't even know who the hell he is, and he has nothing to do with this."

"Fine," Nelu replied.

"As for the three of you, you each get two hits. I don't need lasting damage on the groom's pretty face. If you can't make him bleed after two times, that's on you."

"Three. We each get three hits or kicks," burst out Simu.

I gritted my teeth at his demand. *Little fuck, he's enjoying this.* I threw him an unrepentant grin to get under his skin. He could kiss my ass. I'd take any hit he threw my way, but I'd keep count, and, one day, I'd get even with the prick. Not only for the hits, but also for every single time he'd kissed Cat.

Alex eyed Simu with disdain. "I don't even know why he gets a go at Luca. He's not blood."

"But he's family," replied Nelu.

Gaze zeroing back on Nelu, Alex said, "You and Cristo get three. Simu only gets two."

"Accepted," Nelu muttered, reaching out to shake hands. Alex clasped Nelu's hand and they shook on it.

"Now, as for Cat living with you until the wedding, that's not happening."

Alex let out a chuckle. "Do I need to remind you what a blood bond is exactly? The wedding is a symbol of respect toward the woman as the newest member of our family. Luca here is sweet on her and wants to give her whatever her little heart desires." He leaned over the desk. "But make no mistake, the second he breached her, she was his. His to do with as he wants. Considering the way Cristo spoke to my brother, I don't see why he'd let her return to your family for any reason. Ever."

Damn, *fratele*. It had been a while since I'd seen him in action. Nelu was known as a supreme negotiator, but Alex had done his homework and hit back with an argument to every one of his demands.

Nelu's eyes narrowed on Alex. "We want proof that there's a blood bond."

"For your sake, I will not take insult at your request. What do you want? Bloody sheets or an examination by a doctor? What are we talking about here?"

"Meeting her and speaking to her will be enough. Alone. We want to make sure she hasn't been coerced in any way."

I saw red. Rising to my feet, I bellowed out, "And what, Nelu? Even if she's been coerced, blood has been shed. There's no changing the facts. You want to test the semen on her? Should I have made sure she didn't shower before I left her in my bed? Let me save you the effort. I breached her. Talk to her, and you'll find out I took her virginity. Check the sheets, and you'll see I took her virginity. Test her, and the result will still be that I took her virginity."

Nicu took my hand and guided me back to my seat with a calming hand. The gall of these people. They were the worst sort of *mafie*. They played dirty and smeared anyone in their vicinity. It was a sheer miracle that Cat came out of this environment intact.

Coolly, Nelu ignored me and repeated, "Seeing and speaking to her alone will suffice."

I let out a snort of disgust.

"Very well, it will be arranged," Alex agreed.

Nelu motioned to an antique bar cart crafted of white-washed wood and burnished metal near the door. The silent bodyguard procured a bottle of țuică and shot glasses. Banging them down on the ornate desk, he poured the shot glasses.

"*Noroc*," saluted Nelu, raising his glass.

"*Noroc*," we responded in staggered intervals.

"Drink up," Nicu muttered. "You're going to need it."

We threw the shots back, not one of us flinching from the harsh burn of alcohol.

And it was done. Now, I only had to make it through getting beaten up and Cat would be mine. Simu would make sure to hit me extra hard. On my end, I'd provoke him by reminding him exactly who Cat belonged to. *Me.*

17

The men filed out of the office, down the white-tiled hallway, and out through the back of the restaurant. The narrow alley was surrounded on three sides by tenement buildings, the gnarled black wrought-iron fire escapes rising above us, blocking out half the light coming from the periwinkle-colored sky. Graffiti decorated the walls. A dumpster was lined up against the wall of the restaurant, the ground below it marked with grease stains and other grime. The place stank of garbage and urine. I needed to make sure I stayed on my feet because I didn't want to get close and personal with the filth on the ground.

The men formed a semicircle around me. Nelu's body-guard stood by the exit to make sure no one inadvertently stumbled upon us. I scoped out the area, but there weren't any cameras situated outside the restaurant or the other buildings. Standing shoulder width apart, I shook out my hands and stretched my neck from side to side, garnering a popping sound when my neck cracked. It was imperative to remain loose and relaxed. If my muscles tightened, it would only cause me more pain. The goal was to take the hits and let them roll through me.

As the patriarch, Nelu stepped up first. With his paunch protruding over his tight belt, he wasn't in the best of shape, unlike our father who saw physical fitness as a reflection of the strength of his clan and family. I sighed with gratitude at his one-two punch to my chin. It was jarring and hurt like a bitch, but his punches were straightforward. He threw another to my shoulder and it was over. His heart wasn't in it. Money was Nelu's primary motivator. If it didn't line his pockets, he wasn't interested. Having finished his perfunctory hits, he stepped out of the circle and gave way to Cristo.

Cristo was another story altogether. Not only did his blood run hot, but he loathed me. He may not hate me as much as he hated Nicu, but he harbored enough resentment to make sure his hits would count. I had a trick up my sleeve that would help me come out unscathed. I'd taught myself to mentally disengage from pain during those mindless hours that I was bound and gagged, or during my so-called "punishments." The goal was to focus on the oncoming punches while detaching from the pain.

Cristo stepped forward, punching his fist to the palm of his hand with a smirk on his face. This was going to hurt. He pivoted to the side, fists raised in front of him. Stable, he threw a double punch to the stomach. Hard.

"Fuck," I wheezed out as I doubled over, the wind punched right out of me. My stomach muscles throbbed. It felt like a foreign object was trying to force its way out of my throat.

Righting myself, I turned to my side and shifted a little on my feet. When Cristo swung out with a serious right hook, I swiveled backward just a tad, enough to lessen the impact of his punch. The tangy taste of blood exploded in my mouth. Goddamn, that hurt! Red edged around my vision. One more blow like that and I'd have to get my jaw wired shut. I breathed in, reaching deep in search of that detachment. Turned out, after decades of lack of use, I was rusty. Spitting out blood and saliva, I glared up at Cristo.

"You stepped back," he accused.

"I didn't move my fucking feet," I countered, swiping at the blood trickling out the corner of my mouth.

"You moved, though," he asserted.

"Fuck. You," I snarled.

"Alright, you got your chance, Cristo. Step back," interjected Alex.

Grumbling, Cristo turned on his heel and stomped away, murmuring something to Simu as he passed him.

Simu was the one with the biggest grudge. In addition to our feud, he was driven by the trinity of wounded pride, envy, and spite.

"I made her mine before you got your hands on her," he swore as he stepped up to me. "And I promise, you won't have her forever."

He was spewing lies but taunted me with the kisses and touches he'd snatched from her.

I laughed in his face. "Maybe you don't understand how the blood bond works, bro. Hate to break it to you, but I've already had her, so I'm the lifer in this situation."

Getting smacked around might not rile me up but the thought of him touching Cat, much less taking her from me, got to me. Fury rolled over me in waves. My vision tunneled, turning dark at the edges.

Control snapping, I jeered, "And I will again right after I leave here. You didn't pop that sweet cherry. I did, and oh, did I make it *bleed*."

Charging, Simu roared, "You cradle-robbing fucker. I will fucking end you!"

Gripping my shirt and tie, he threw me against the side of the dumpster. A loud bang echoed off the facade of the buildings. This wasn't about payback for the blood bond. This was a brawl, and I welcomed it. My pride smarted from Nelu and Cristo's hits, but Simu pushed me over the edge. Clutching my shirt, he threw a hard punch. I dodged it. His knuckles slammed against the metal of the dumpster with an echo.

"Mother*fucker*," Simu swore, shaking his hand before curling it into a fist.

Before he could swing again, I ripped out of his grip and got into a defensive position. Swerving around, he stalked me, throwing punches in the air. He made a quick swipe of my feet that I didn't anticipate. Stepping back, I slipped on slime and toppled to the ground. Simu straddled me, his stale breath washing over me.

He attacked. Rounding my shoulders, I blocked his blows while bucking up to dislodge him. I might be tall and broad, but he outweighed me enough that I couldn't throw him off. Risking a flurry of punches to my face, I planted my hand on the ground. Twisting hard and fast, I tossed the beast off me. He fell to his side. I swung my leg out and jumped up into a fighting pose and backed away.

Simu rolled up to standing. Around and around, we circled each other, the sounds of heavy breathing broken up by a car alarm down the street. The Popescus and my brothers had moved back to give us more room. Keeping far from Simu, I kicked his legs to rile him up. Kick, slide, kick, slide. He swung at me, but I ducked and gave him another hard strike. He buckled to the ground with a hiss.

Sliding from side to side, I taunted, "Come on, get up!

You were too much of a pussy to take her when you had a chance. Don't be jealous 'cause I was man enough to do it."

Roaring at the top of his lungs, he hopped up and barreled toward me. I stepped to my power side, further luring him toward me. Loading my back foot, I drove through my hips and struck my arm out. His momentum propelled him into my fist. Down he went. His skull bounced off the ground with an ugly crunch. Laid out on his back, he went limp.

Turning to the men, I pounded my chest and let out a roar of triumph. *Fuck, yeah.* That felt good. Cristo rushed to Simu, fury written on his face. A bemused smile played on Nicu's lips while Alex raised an indulgent eyebrow at me. Flexing my shoulders, I fixed my tie, buttoned up my jacket, and adjusted the cuffs of my sleeves. Cristo helped Simu roll to his side and sit up. Simu shook his head, flapping his lips like a horse.

Nelu came forward. With a staying hand on my chest, he stretched out his other hand for Simu to take. With that, the fight was over.

Nicu and Alex approached me, laughing and clapping me on my back. Those good-natured slaps made my ears ring from the hits I took to the head, but whatever. My jaw ached like a motherfucker. I touched my cheekbone gingerly. I'd soon be sporting a few rainbow-colored bruises.

Simu glowered at me as he rubbed his temples.

I smirked back at him because he knew what I knew.

I'd won.

Whatever dreams he'd harbored of Cat were officially dead. Topping Simu certainly hadn't factored into my decision to take Cat, but I'd glory in it anyway. Without a backward glance at the Popescus, I took my time exiting the alley. As I rounded the corner, I took a moment to shake off the spinning in my head and made my way to the car, where Stegan was waiting.

"They worked you over good," he observed.

"If you think I look bad, you should see what I did to Simu," I countered.

"Yeah?"

"The fucker rushed me. It was no holds barred after that. I clocked him, and he went down like a fucking pussy."

"Good," he grunted as he opened the back door. "Hate that smug asshole."

I shot off a text to Cat, but she didn't respond. A couple of hours had passed since I left her in my apartment, and I expected her to be waiting by her phone. Worry settled in my chest.

Moments later, Alex slipped into the passenger seat up front, and Nicu came in beside me.

Alex said, "I told Nelu you'd bring Cat by their house tonight so we can get that shit over with. While she's there, she should pack a few bags. Where are you going to be, the penthouse or in Westchester?"

"I figure it's best to stay at the penthouse until we settle everything with her family and bring her around to Mama. Then, I have to put a ring on her finger and show her off in public so everyone will know that I've claimed her."

"Sounds like a plan," Alex approved, turning to face forward as Stegan pulled out into the street.

Nicu and I hadn't talked on the ride to meet the Popescus, but it was now time to fix this. Although he didn't care for Cat, Nicu had a healthy dose of pride, like all the Lupu men. My main worry was to make sure he came out of this with his reputation intact. Alex had already done a lot to protect his image. I wasn't too worried about Nicu's feelings.

On a scale of one to ten, Nicu's sentimentality hovered near zero.

"You seem more than okay with this," I began.

As he turned to meet my gaze, I said, "I didn't expect this to happen, Nicu. I never meant to hurt you and the last thing I want is for you to feel humiliated."

"Hurt me? Humiliated?" he sputtered out, followed by a laugh. "I'm fucking relieved that I'm off the hook. You've saved me from a loveless marriage. Christ, it's not like I ever hid the fact that I thought you should be with her. She was always yours, but you were too much of a stubborn ass to see that. When I caught the way you looked at her at the engagement party, I started plotting how to get out of this marriage."

My eyebrows shot up.

"Yeah," he went on without skipping a beat. "That's why I gave her the cold shoulder and insisted that you drive her to her classes. Luca, do you seriously believe I would've passed that task on to anyone if I intended to fuck her, much less make her my wife?" He shook his head like I amused him. "Come now, I'm no idiot."

"The fuck..." I muttered under my breath.

Nicu clamped a hand on my shoulder and said, "Not everyone is as oblivious as you are. The two of you were meant to be together. You would've seen that earlier if you hadn't been so busy fighting everything and everyone. If I had tried to step in, you would've resisted, so I stepped back and let you find your own way. For once, you finally did the right thing."

I was so relieved that I chose to ignore that last jab. Nicu was right. I'm not sure how I would've reacted if he'd been straight with me. Either way, he didn't feel betrayed, and that was the most important thing.

"So, everything worked out for the best," I said.

"Damn straight it did," he retorted.

With the air cleared between us, I checked my phone for a text from Cat. Still nothing. I shifted in my seat, antsy to get back to her. Her lack of response was a worrying sign.

18

"You *what?*" my mother screeched during our video chat, her hand flying to her throat. I cringed. This outburst wasn't good for her health, post-chemo, but considering Luca was out there getting beaten up by my family, I was in no position to complain. My phone beeped with an incoming text, but I was too focused on my mother to look at it.

It was going about as well as could be expected, considering I just told her I lost my virginity to a man who was not my husband. Oh, and the fact that he also happened to be my fiancé's brother, although the "not married" part was the real sticking point.

"You heard me," I replied. It was never a good day when you broke your mother's heart.

"*O, Doamne,*" she bemoaned. *Oh my God* was as close as she got to a curse. "What was the one thing I always told you, Cat? Stay a virgin until you're married. The rule you swore on your *bunică*'s life that you would abide by. The rule that finally convinced me to let you go to boarding school. The one and only rule, Cat. The one and only!"

"Okay, calm down, Mama. I know you're disappointed, but Nicu didn't love me—"

"What does love have to do with anything?" she screeched out incredulously. "Since when have I ever told you that love had anything to do with marriage?"

"You and Tata love—"

"Yes, but I wasn't born into a *mafie* family. Your father was a nobody when we got together. He built this family, this clan, from the gutters of Bucharest. You can't compare my life to yours. I did my part. I supported him. I had two children. A boy to lead after we're gone and a girl to bring honor to us through her marriage. You had one duty to this family and you've failed. You failed us and the Popescu name."

Her words hit me like a blow to the chest. My breath rattled out. Wow, she was hitting below the belt. I knew how our world worked, but to hear her baldly lay out like that was devastating. I was so much more than a vessel for their stupid honor. Anger flared inside me. I expected her to be upset, but she was being unnecessarily cruel. The irony of it was that I was still marrying into the Lupu clan, and she was still getting her big wedding.

"I'm still going to be a Lupu. I'll just end up marrying Luca instead of Nicu. And, while you say that love doesn't matter, I'll get the same love you have with Tata. Everyone wins."

"God, how naïve can you be? I don't even recognize you anymore. Have you been gone so long that you don't know how things work around here anymore? We're considered low-class, low-level criminals that somehow, by sheer luck, rose to the top. By marrying *royalty* like the Lupu, we had a chance to clean up our image. Now, you've dragged us down to the gutter once again. No blood bond or lavish wedding is going to stop the whispers, Cat. Whispers calling you a whore and a slut."

Her voice turned nasally as she mimicked the women, young and old alike, who would gossip. "Look at him, such a fine young man, marrying that whore who opened her legs for him before her marriage. The Jezebel who stole her fiancé's brother."

I inhaled a sharp breath, my cheeks flushing with humiliation.

"Enough, Mama," I snapped.

Ignoring me, she forged onward. "I'm being honest with you, Cat. That's what everyone will say behind your back. Including every single Lupu you meet."

"That's not fair," I rasped out. "I love him." My admission triggered a flare of ownership. Luca was mine. He was my man, and I was proud of him.

She barked out a harsh laugh. "Life is not fair. Since when did I *ever* teach you that life was fair? Was it fair that your father and brother had to become killers to protect what was ours and pull us out of poverty? You speak of love? *Pfft.* You think a man like that can love *you*? If he loved you, he would've left you alone and insisted you marry his brother as contracted between the families. I've heard of this Luca and his reputation. He's known to be stubborn and selfish."

Good God. She had a way of tearing me down, of infiltrating my soul and ripping my heart to shreds. For the most part, my mother was loving and supportive, but she had a ruthless side to her. She could assassinate with words.

This happened once before, after I had witnessed my father murdering a man. She was so infuriated that she lashed out, blaming me for having gone downstairs, accusing that I should have known better. *You know what*

your father does, so why were you creeping around downstairs at
night? What did you think you were going to see, hmm, Cat?

It was only after months of nightmares, *Bunică* sleeping
on a cot beside my bed, and Tata talking to her, that she
finally came around and forgave me for my gaffe.

"You don't know what Luca is like. You don't know Alex
or how he thinks. He's accepted this," I tried to argue.

Unable to hold back any longer, my lip trembled and
tears gathered in my eyes.

At that moment, the bedroom door flew open, and Luca
stalked in like an avenging berserker. His beautiful silver
eyes were ringed in red and lavender. A third bruise blos-
somed along his jaw. My heart lurched at the sight of the
proof of what he'd gone through for me.

He loomed above me, radiating strength and prowess.
And anger. "What the hell is going on?"

My stomach did a little flip at the indignation in his
tone.

His eyes flicked to my phone. Swiping it out of my hand,
he registered who it was and hung up on my mother.

Tossing the phone on the floor, he yanked off his jacket
and threw it on the bed. Then he swept me into his strong
arms and cooed softly as I wept into his shoulder. Pulling
away, I gingerly touched his bruises as tears coursed down
my face. I was crying for him, for me, for my mother. With a
shushing sound, he pressed my head back into him and
rocked me. In the strength of his embrace, I let go and cried
until there was only the occasional hiccup.

"What did she say?" he asked in a voice I'd never heard
him use before. So soothing and gentle. It would've lulled
me into a trance if it didn't prove my mother's warning that I
didn't know this man. Despite the hours we'd spent
together, I didn't *really* know him.

Moaning into his shirt, I mumbled out, "She said you were selfish and that you didn't love me. If you *really* loved me, you wouldn't have touched me. You would've forced me to marry Nicu. She said that I dishonored the family because I'm not a virgin. None of the Lupu will respect me. They'll think I'm a whore, and nothing will ever change that."

He made a low growl, the sound vibrating through his chest.

"First of all, your mother doesn't know me or the Lupu clan. Even though you won't be going into our marriage as a virgin, we have the blood bond. I don't know what dishonor she's talking about. Since when is a blood bond *not* a supreme form of honor? And I'm a better choice than a third son like Nicu."

Adjusting me on his lap, he continued, "As for the Lupu clan, they will look to my behavior, not yours. They will respect the fact that I took what I wanted. As long as I give them a big-ass wedding where they can drink themselves under the table, they'll be satisfied. Lastly, she called me selfish. Okay, that part is true. It was selfish of me to snap you up, but too bad for her, I don't give two fucks. I'll wear that judgment like a badge of honor if it keeps us together."

"But we don't know each other that well," I said, flinching at the whiny tinge of my voice. God, I was out of my element. I always thought of myself as strong, but I had never rebelled on this level before. Never challenged my family like this before. It was much harder than I had expected. I was intimidated, and I didn't like this feeling.

"Please, woman. You know me a hell of a lot better than you knew my brother, and you were engaged to him. We knew enough to know that this was it for us. Granted, we didn't follow the typical path. We didn't meet on a dating app, date for a year, then move in together and get a puppy to see if we had compatible parenting styles, but we're *mafie*. Sure, we'll have to adjust to each other. We might discover traits we're not as crazy about, but that's how real love works. It's understandable that your mother's upset, but right now, she's throwing spaghetti at the wall and seeing what sticks. If she says something that upsets you, trust your gut or come to me. I'll lead you back to the promised land, baby."

I snorted. "The promised land? Are you referring to yourself?"

"No, I'm referring to us," he responded seriously.

My heart did a funny pitter-pat as I turned over what he'd said in my mind. His arms tightened around me, his spicy cedar scent calming me. He hadn't shaved, and the scruff of his jaw grazed against my temple. I traced the line of his biceps, following a protruding vein along his arm as I snuggled into his broad chest. Luca personified power, strength, and oddly enough, stability. I was used to depending on myself and didn't expect to draw so much comfort from him.

We stayed quiet for a little while.

"She say anything else?" he queried gently.

I pursed my lips together. "Alex won't support us. She didn't say that last one outright, but she thinks it. She said that everyone sees the Popescus as low class and I solidified our reputation. There's no way I'll live it down, especially with Alex. She really looks up to him, what with that aristocratic air of his."

He let out a half-laugh, half-snuffle. "She has no clue who Alex is and what makes him tic. This is the same man who twisted himself like a contortionist to get out from under his engagement with you so he could marry the outsider he loves. Alex is a romantic. And he blood bonded with Nina, so he can't cast any stones. Once I showed him how damn serious I am about you, he accepted it whole-heartedly."

He snorted softly. "I didn't accidentally take a princess's virginity. I don't go around purposely binding myself to women *for life*. This wasn't a mistake. This was a well-executed plan. We wanted this."

After a pause, he suggested, "Just blame me for this mess. Your mother will give you a pass if she thinks I seduced you—the young, innocent virgin. Hell, she already thinks I'm the big, bad, selfish wolf, so she's halfway there already."

"I guess..." I replied, although I wasn't comfortable with the idea. I didn't want to hide behind him. I may have been a virgin, but I had boldly pursued him. Granted, I hadn't anticipated how hard it would be to face my family, but I was proud of myself. If anything, I wanted to show him off. Strut around Little Bucharest on Luca's arm, shouting to the world that here was *my* man.

Carefully, Luca said, "Alex told your father and brother that he knew about this from the beginning. That I had received his permission and Nicu's blessing to pursue you and for the blood bond." After a long, weighty pause, he continued, "You're a Lupu now. Your allegiance is to us, Cat. You understand that, no?"

He was saying that as a Lupu, it was my duty to perpetuate the lie to protect their reputation. "That was brilliant of him. Of course, I understand."

"You will need to stick with that narrative when you see your family," he clarified.

My eyes shot to his. "I'm going to see them?"

"It was decided on at the meeting. Apparently, your

brother's convinced that you've been coerced or brain-washed, and he wants to hear it directly from you that you weren't taken advantage of."

I huffed out a laugh. "My mother certainly doesn't think that. When am I going to see them?"

"I will drive you over there this evening. If you want me with you, I'm more than happy to do it."

The glint in his eye hinted that there'd be another fight if anyone said anything unpleasant. His defense on my behalf was adorable, but this was for the Popescus to hash out. We spoke bluntly in my family, especially Cristo. There was no doubt that he'd lose his temper and say something crude, which would only cause a fight. That would help no one. In any case, they were my family, and I would handle them.

"I can manage them by myself. Truthfully, they need the space to vent their frustration."

"That doesn't give them the right to mistreat you," he stated.

"True, but they deserve some leeway. This was a shock for them and shouting is one of the ways we work through things. You know how Romanians can be," I explained with a shrug. Didn't mean it would be pleasant, but after the conversation with my mother, I knew what to expect. I'd be better prepared this evening. "Anyway, you'll be there to comfort me afterward, right?" I teased.

"It's my job to take care of you, and you know how seriously I take that." He bent down to kiss me, his hand cupping me between the legs. Pulling back, he continued, "After you're done dealing with your family, brace yourself to handle mine. And I'm not talking about them judging you. It's when they accept you that you'll have your work cut out for you."

"I've been well trained, believe me," I quipped. "I'm not afraid of yours. But one thing at a time. I have to get through this first."

I only hoped that Cristo was calmer by the time I showed up tonight.

19

Luca dropped me off at the stoop of my house after I reassured him again that I'd be fine. *I can do this*, I reminded myself as I stared up at the redbrick row house I'd called home for so long. Soon, I'd be free to start my new life with Luca. Nerves mingled with excitement. It felt surreal, like I'd been thrown into a wormhole, but there was no denying how lucky I was to be marrying him instead of Nicu.

A face popped up from the bay window, and I saw my grandmother wave at me to come inside. Nodding, I took the steps up, mumbling to myself that I could handle anything. Luca had parked down the street, ready to rescue me at any moment.

The front door swung open. *Bunică* stood in the middle of the doorway, a kerchief wrapped around her head, arms wide open. I threw myself at her, bending over to bury my face into the padding of her shoulder.

"There, there, everything will be fine. That Nicu wasn't good enough for my girl, was he? Bah! Too wet behind the ears, the young pup. You were right to find yourself a grown man. As it should be."

I puffed out a laugh of surprise. Always my biggest champion, *Bunică* spun anything I did into a positive. Like when I was eight years old and my mother forced me to join a local gymnastics club. I cried every day because I hated the cliquey girls and wasn't interested in the sport. After almost a year of cajoling, my grandmother finally convinced her to let me stop.

I dragged my feet as she propelled me into the living room, where my father, mother, and brother somberly waited for me. My mother and brother sat on the reupholstered couch, piled high with cushions, while my father sat in one of the comfy, mismatched armchairs. A votive candle flickered low behind him, on the shelf displaying my grandmother's favorite icon.

Again, I was struck by the fact that this was no longer my home. I'd gone to boarding school, but I always felt a distinct moment of homecoming when I stepped into the living room after a long absence. This would be the last time, I thought nostalgically. My home would be a huge mansion in Westchester or a sleek, impersonal penthouse in midtown. At least I was looking forward to Westchester, with its gorgeous garden and pool. The penthouse, not so much, but Luca didn't seem attached to it, so hopefully, I could bring my own style to it.

My father was the first to rise. He lifted heavily out of his favorite armchair, the stuffing of the arms dipping in the center, the material faded and worn. Suddenly, he seemed old, the crow's feet and bags under his eyes were accentuated.

Wrapping me in his thick arms, he murmured, "I'm not

angry, but I wish you had come to me. To hear it from Alex was humiliating."

He was a proud man, and it was a blow to his ego to have heard the news from his rival. It certainly added to the shock. A stab of remorse slashed through me. Unfortunately, I wouldn't have taken the risk of him denying me and closing my one chance at happiness with Luca.

"I'm sorry, Tata."

Not rising from the couch, my mother acknowledged me, "Cat."

Cristo cracked his knuckles, a nervous habit of his, as he glowered up at me. I looked up to my older brother. We'd always had a supportive, loving relationship, and this was the first test of our easy camaraderie.

Blowing out a long breath, I went to my mother and kissed her on both cheeks. As I moved to kiss my brother, he flung his head aside, rejecting me. Pressing my lips into a thin line, I pulled back and took a seat across from them.

"Congratulations are in order, Cat," began my father, returning to his armchair. "I'm glad that you're with Luca. He's a better match for you. He may be hardheaded, but Nicu's a loose cannon. Immature. Which shows in his ruthless behavior."

Turning to my mother and brother, I said, "I'm sorry that you're unhappy. I started having feelings for Luca, and once I sensed that he shared them...well, I couldn't go through with marrying Nicu. I didn't plan for any of this to happen."

Shaking her head, my mother lamented, "Everyone will say it's my fault for letting you sleep over at an outsider's place. They'll accuse me of neglect for letting you go off to boarding school. You ran wild up there and lost touch with our traditions."

"Doina, don't let those gossiping vipers get to you. We

know how we brought up our children. We know that we did the best thing for her by letting her go away," my father said, attempting to comfort her.

His words only made me feel worse. If I hadn't messed up the night I caught my father murdering a man, my parents wouldn't have had to send me away. If I'd been home, I would've been able to help Cristo take care of my mother. The brunt of caring for her fell on him because my father was busy, especially with our recent financial problems. He was the one who drove her back and forth to doctor and chemo appointments. He had to clean up after her when she was sick from the meds. I tried catching his eye, but my brother refused to look at me. Guilt sloshed around in my gut like a bottled-up tidal wave.

My grandmother spoke up, "You're exaggerating, Doina. The girl did the right thing. Instead of settling for the young one, she found herself a mature man. What is he, twenty-six?"

"Twenty-seven," grumped out Cristo.

"There you go! Twenty-seven. A man ready to settle down and have a family. Have children. Not like the youngest. Choosing him has been an insult. The girl took what was owed to her as the Popescu princess. You say people will look down on you, but who needs to know that you didn't plan it yourself? Tell everyone, *hush-hush*, that you had been working behind the scenes, pushing Cat to do this because you couldn't stand Nicu."

Cristo chuckled. "Clever, *Bunică*."

Turning his head slightly toward me, he lobbed an accusatory stare my way. "You might as well do everything you can to salvage this situation. Pretend you did it as revenge because the *Lupul* forced Nicu on us when Luca was available. No one can prove you didn't do it. Tell your *closest friends*," he sneered the last two words, "and swear them to secrecy, which of course, they won't keep. Cat here won't deny it. Will you, Cat?"

My brother sent me a scathing glare. While he was helping me manage my mother, the waves of anger rolling off him were undeniable. His temper was hanging by a thread, and I was dreading the moment it snapped.

"No," I quickly replied. "Of course not. I'll play coy. Won't outright deny or admit to anything and let them come to their own conclusions."

"That's right. Keep them guessing. The seed will be planted that you pushed Cat to use the blood bond to our advantage. If they think you were behind it, you'll look like the cunning one," he finished to my mother, ignoring me completely.

My mother thoughtfully stroked her bottom lip. "While I would've preferred Cat had simply done what she was supposed to do, I suppose this is a better alternative to the scandal we have on our hands."

Bunică sent me a covert wink. I mouthed thank you back to her.

I sagged into my chair with relief until Cristo turned his attention sharply to me. His brown eyes were flinty hard, narrowed in anger. I stiffened under his hostile gaze.

"You owe us," he threatened, in a brittle tone he'd never used on me before. *And...there it is.* I understood that he was upset, but his words still hit me like a spray of bullets.

"W-what do you mean?" I stammered out, half rising from my seat.

"I mean that we are making the best out of a bad situation, but don't be fooled by what you just saw," he said, indicating to my mother.

"Cristo—" my grandmother began.

"Silence, *Bunică*," Cristo cut her off with a slash of his hand. "You spoil her too much, and look where it's gotten us. She went away to school to pursue whatever bullshit she wanted and see what it led to? While we busted our asses, day in day out, she's turned into a silly girl with ridiculous notions of love."

His eyes flashed as he spat out, "There is nothing more important than serving the family. I loved Una, but I did what I had to do to protect the family. Your only goal in life should've been to marry right and not bring shame down on us. You failed. Even if we cover it up, the Lupu brothers won't be fooled by the gossip. That might've tricked stupider people, but not Alex or Luca. And especially not Nicu. He's going to use any chance he gets to dig into me with an insult. God, I hate that fucker."

I glanced over at my father for reassurance, but his face was a mask of stoicism, a sign that he agreed with my brother.

"But we've got bigger problems," he went on. "Marrying Luca may just be our ticket out. You know the financial strain we're under, with the partners in Afghanistan we lost with the American withdrawal. We're scrambling to create new allegiances, but the Taliban are not making it easy. Then there's the half million we spent for Mama's treatment on top of the steep discount we gave Alex to compensate him for our failed trick with Una. We had to borrow from the Hagi clan to keep afloat."

Cristo paused, his eyes darting away from mine. "There's been a complication and the debt has to be paid back right away. I mean, *right away*." His gaze met mine. "And you're going to help us."

I blinked at him, gulping down the acid rocketing up from my gut. "W-what did you do, Cristo?"

"I—" He cleared his throat. "During a meeting, the Hagi's youngest son—the fucking spoiled prick—insulted me. I lost my temper." His tone dropped. "I attacked him. It took Simu and his uncle to pull me off him, but...the damage was done. He won't be a pretty boy no more."

My eyes flew to my father, who gave me a nonchalant shrug as if to say, *you know your brother.*

"What the hell, Cristo? That temper of yours will get you killed one day. When are you going to do something about it?"

"Shut up, Cat," he growled. Flinging out his hand, he snarled, "You've been gone for the past six fucking years. *Six. Years.* You were nowhere to be found when I was lifting Mama off the toilet bowl and cleaning vomit off the floor." He jabbed his finger at me. "While you were traipsing around with your head in the sky, falling in love and embarrassing your family, I was holding down the fort. You have no idea what it takes to lead this clan, what kind of pressure I'm under. And I will *not* be insulted by a little douche like the Hagi boy."

I didn't tell him that I would've dropped my senior year and moved back to help, but that our parents insisted I graduate from my boarding school. He already knew that. Nor did I lecture him that the pressures he endured did not justify his behavior. I refrained from shouting that he was going to get himself killed if he continued in this way. Instead, I swallowed down my barrage of retorts.

Only one thing mattered: Cristo was my brother and he was in trouble. I was a Popescu and we stuck together, no matter what. I could easily guess what happened when you provoked a *șef* that you owed money to. Cristo was in deep trouble, and I couldn't abandon him in his time of need. It wasn't just loyalty because he'd been the best of older brothers (for the most part). It was because I loved that son of a bitch. As awful as his temper was, he was *my* brother. *Mine*.

"How bad is it?" I asked.

"Bad," he replied instantly. "We have to pay it back. Like right now, or else they will hurt me."

He didn't have to get into the details. The ruling principle in our world was an eye for an eye. Revenge for beating up the Hagi boy was in order.

"Is it what I think it is? The Hagi şef is demanding full repayment, plus interest, due immediately. And if we don't pay..."

"Then, I'm living on borrowed time," he finished for me.

One misstep could be fixed. But two? And back to back? Not so much. Sure, he was being set up but being a şef's heir wouldn't save Cristo with the kind of money involved.

What choice did I have? *None.* We Popescus had fought tooth and nail to get where we were. For so long, it had been us against the world. As upstarts, we were constantly looked down upon, and that had spawned a deep loyalty within us. Within me. More than that, Cristo was my brother and I couldn't abandon him to his fate, even if he'd brought it on himself.

Swallowing, I stared at Cristo. I could tell from his expression that he already had a plan.

Bracing myself, I asked, "What do you need from me?"

"Luca wants you to live with him before the marriage. That's a fucking insult, but Tata and I agreed because it will give you free rein to search his apartment, which I happen to know he uses as his office. I want you to dig around, find something useful, and report back. Look through his files, his computer, his phone. Whatever you have to do, you do it," he gritted out.

As Cristo talked, my finger curled into the upholstery of the chair, nails digging in. I didn't want this. To see him this anxious, this stressed out, only proved how desperate he was, but it meant betraying Luca, and that thought tore through me like a knife. I was petrified of losing him.

"I'm sure his computer is password protected and he uses facial recognition for his phone," I hedged. "Isn't there another way?"

"We've thought through every way, Cat. And for the love of God, don't you dare tell Luca. You need to find something. Find anything. He's a computer genius and he's in charge of the Lupu financial schemes. They're legendary moneymakers. I've heard rumors that they were involved in the most recent ransomware attack on that oil pipeline. He's a supreme hacker, stalking them online and making it seem as if they're based in Eastern Europe. Received ten million in bitcoin, which is near impossible to trace."

Reading my face, he gave me a pleading look, his eyes blazing with desperation. "Cat, they're loaded. They have a fucking empire. They can afford to share. And if you can find out something that hurts them? Even better."

I recoiled. No way was I going to hurt Luca or his brothers. An image of Luca shimmered in my mind, his passion when he looked at me like I was his, his gentleness when he took my virginity, his vulnerability in the car when he shared about his father. I loved his independence and his principles, clearly something I lacked in comparison.

Here I thought I was a bit of a rebel, not buying into the bullshit of arranged marriages and forging my own path with the blood bond. Turned out, I wasn't half as strong as he was because the moment my big brother was in trouble, I jumped in to save him. *Luca has been good to you, and this is how you repay him?* I paused, indecision racking my system.

I glanced at my father. He was slumped back in his armchair, arms hanging over the sides in exhaustion. The lines around his eyes and dark bags spoke of worry and sleepless nights. Cristo was his heir, and I was only a girl, one who was now part of another clan. Not only would it gut him if anything happened to Cristo, but it would mark the end of the Popescus. I turned to my mother, who was still rail thin from the months of not being able to keep down any food. No, I couldn't desert them.

Taking a huge breath of air, I blurted out, "One time. I'll help you one time, but that's it, Cristo. After that, I've paid my moral debt for being away and for ruining my engagement with Nicu. I swear, you better do whatever you have to do to change, because next time, you're on your own."

"Yes," he replied eagerly, his head snapping toward my father for confirmation. My father nodded gratefully. Cristo cracked that notorious easygoing grin of his for the first time today.

My stomach lurched in revolt. What I was about to do was wrong, but I would make that sacrifice for them this one time. It was a crazy risk, but I'd do it once and never again.

"Cristo, swear to me that if I do this, you will never use it against me or ask me again."

His smile slipped and his eyes grew sober. "I swear on my honor," he promised.

I didn't know how much honor he held in that tainted soul of his anymore, but I had already agreed. Silently, I made an oath as well. I would only turn over information that helped my family but did not directly harm Luca or the Lupu clan.

For a moment, I thought of going behind Cristo and telling Luca, but I immediately shut it down. The last six years of self-dependence made the decision easy for me. I mean, I had busted my butt for years to become valedictorian and didn't even tell my parents, much less invite them to my graduation. At school, no one outside of Jewel knew anything about my family. I was used to living a double life and handling my problems on my own. But underneath it was fear. The Lupus, like the Popescus, were a prideful clan. There was no reason for Luca to help Cristo.

With Cristo's life on the line, I couldn't afford to trust Luca. There was no love lost between the two of them. Luca couldn't pay off another clan's debt, and he had no leverage with the Hagi family, which was located on the other coast. It was best to be cautious. As long as I protected Luca, I would help Cristo. As for the guilt that would come from my betrayal, I'd figure out how to live with that once the deed was done.

20

Cat settled into the passenger seat of my car. I instantly noticed a shift in her. She'd changed into a cerulean-blue silk dress that hugged her curves, but her shoulders were bunched up. Her beautiful face was strained, eyes creased with worry. They must've done a real number on her, and it pissed me off. That was family for you. Rarely supportive. I was surprised by how well Alex had taken what we'd done.

Grabbing her balled hand, I loosened her fist and pressed a kiss in the center of her palm.

"You okay, Kitty?" I asked.

Her downcast gaze finally lifted and met mine. Trouble shadowed her chocolate eyes.

"Yeah." She blew out a breath. "It was tough."

"What did they say? Tell me everything so I can blow their arguments out of the water."

"More of the same," she muttered. "I wronged them, my mother will get blamed for my bad behavior, and they've lost face in front of Alex and our own clan. My father said that I should have told him so that he wouldn't have been taken for a loop."

"Christ, I'm sick of how they try to brainwash us with this infernal duty to the family." She flinched and I softened my tone. "It's okay, baby girl. You have the right to make the best choice about *your* future. As for your mother, she should be used to the gossip. That's one of the tough breaks of being part of *mafie* society. I swear, sometimes it's like we're in a cult."

I released Cat's hand and pulled out into the street. I felt her eyes on me and the heat in them singed me.

"What?"

"You're so good to me. So strong. I have to warn you that my grandmother gave my mom the bright idea to tell everyone that she put me up to seducing you. In that way, the Popescus were able to right the wrong of forcing me to wed Nicu," she confessed.

I slanted a glance her way and chuckled. "Wily old woman, your *bunică*. No worries, sweet girl. Neither Alex nor I care what people say. We know the truth and that's all that matters."

"Cristo said something to that affect."

"And how was he? I know you two are tight," I prodded gently.

Staring outside the window, she blew out a breath and shrugged despondently. "He had some harsh things to say. Between our age difference and living apart for six years, we don't bicker or squabble. Until now. He resents this. Especially on top of almost single-handedly taking care of my mom this past year. It's been rough, to say the least."

I took hold of her hand and squeezed. "The worst is over. I have an overbearing older brother as well, and although I'm used to pissing him off, he eventually calms down and we get back to it. Alex and I have had many ups and downs. This is the first you and your brother have faced, but believe me, it will pass."

I had taken my jacket off and rolled up my sleeves while waiting for her in the car. Her eyes kept returning to my hand and forearm, desire flickering in them. She liked what she saw, and damn if it didn't make my chest puff up with pride. If she needed a distraction from all of this, I was more than happy to oblige. Glancing away, she bit down on her plump bottom lip. The tip of her tongue darted out. Fuck, that was sexy.

Her parents' house wasn't far from the Queensboro Bridge, and this late in the evening, we flew high above the East River. The shoreline of midtown Manhattan, lit up with towering buildings, was spread out before us. Another ten minutes and we'd be at the penthouse.

But I couldn't wait that long to taste her.

At the first stoplight, I demanded, "Give me your mouth."

Without waiting, I dragged my lips across her cheek and took her mouth with brutal force. She was tooth-achingly sweet. I sipped from whatever wine she had drunk from. A beep from behind alerted me that the light had changed, and I broke off with a groan and put the car into gear.

I grinned smugly when a hot shiver passed through her. I spied her nipples jutting out from the thin silk of her bra and shirt. Only I knew the color and taste of those plump berries. My hand slipped down to her thigh, rubbing the soft material of her dress.

"You don't know how many times we were in the car together that I wanted to reach out and touch you like this," I admitted.

Her chest began to rise and fall like bellows.

"Oh yeah?" she croaked out.

I nodded. "Wasn't the only thing I wanted to do."

She cleared her throat and asked in a husky tone, "What else did you want to do?"

A taxi swerved in front of me, but I pressed on the brake gently enough to not disrupt our conversation, our foreplay. I began massaging her thigh.

"I wanted to slide my hand under those sexy little skirts you constantly wore. Admit it, you wore them to drive me insane."

"I may have noticed your eyes on my legs once or twice," she replied coyly.

My hand slipped beneath the hem of her skirt, my wrist pushing one side up high and exposing the smooth skin of her thigh. She squirmed in her seat, spreading her thighs a little open for me.

"Such a good girl," I murmured as my fingers traveled up the seam of her thighs. "Kitty, I can feel the heat of your pussy from here."

I grazed my fingers up her inner thigh and down the other. Each pass prompted her to open a little wider. When I was satisfied by her silent begging, I dipped my fingers to the gusset of her panties and rubbed over the seam of her lower lips. The material over her cunt was drenched. *Drenched.*

Her thighs quivered in anticipation and she let out a low keen when I cupped her entire pussy. My palm practically burned from the wet heat. My cock stiffened like a steel pipe in my pants, my balls pulsing with pressure. I was ready to blow just from touching her. Unbelievable. My fingers pushed her panties aside and plunged inside. Soft and wet, her flesh wrapped around my fingers, sucking them in.

We'd arrived at my building, and I had to pull my

desperate fingers out of her pussy. Fumbling around, I clicked the fob to open the door to the underground parking. I tore through it to get to my space. After parking, I unclipped our seat belts, pulled my seat back and swooped her onto my lap. The instant her hot pussy pressed down on my shaft, I moaned out loud. Our mouths crashed together, her whimpering into our kiss as we devoured each other.

My hips lifted off my seat, bouncing her on my lap. With the sexual tension we'd experienced in the car, it was no surprise that we'd end up fucking here.

"I need inside you," I murmured against her mouth. "I can't wait to get into the apartment. I need you *now*."

"Yes, yes," she moaned, her fingers roaming over my chest like she couldn't get enough of me.

I tugged at the tiny buttons running down the length of her dress to get better access. Frustrated, I yanked a little too hard and tore the silk, but we were both too far gone to care. My hands traveled over her lacy bra and dragged the cups down to get to her luscious tits. Then there they were, their perfect weight cupped in the palms of my hands. The light coming through the tinted windows illuminated her cherry-colored nipples as her chest heaved in the tight space of the car. I laved and doted on them like it was my last supper. I was never hungry for a woman before, but with Cat, I was voracious.

Her dress was already halfway off her, so it wasn't hard to divest her of the rest of it. I tossed her panties over my shoulder. A notch formed between her brows as she concentrated on opening my shirt. Bottom lip snagged between her teeth, her trembling fingers fumbled with the buttons of my shirt.

"The Lupu," she breathed out, tracing the tattoo of the

wolf baring its teeth that every clan member had inked on their bodies.

"You'll have one soon," I promised her.

Her eyes were riveted on my ink; she swallowed audibly. *Oh, it's real, baby girl.* I had to get an appointment with our tattoo artist scheduled right away because I wanted my ink on her. For a Lupu, this was as important as the wedding ceremony.

Lifting on her knees, she gave me space to unbuckle my belt, unzip, and chuck my trousers and boxer briefs down into the footwell. My cock slapped against my abs, thanking me for its freedom. Goddamn, when her sweet, juicy slit hovered right above the crown, a drop of arousal beaded and rolled down my shaft. That had to be one of the most erotic visions I'd ever seen. I needed in, in, *in.*

"You dripped on me," I muttered, my gaze zeroed in on the contact of her pussy with my cock. "You have no idea how damn hot that is."

Taking her curvy ass in my hands, I drew her down, and fuck! Every inch she swallowed with her tight, *tight* cunt wrapped around my dick brought me a step closer to heaven.

Fingers tangled in my hair; one hand slapped my chest hard. I stared down at her bouncing tits and the shifting, flexing muscles of her belly as her wet pussy moved up and down my cock, swallowing it so good each time she moved farther down my shaft.

"It's a snug fit, but I busted through this virgin hole once before and made it mine. This tight pussy is mine, only —*gasp*—mine," I breathed out, shuddering.

"Yours," she confirmed.

"Damn straight it is," I growled.

I shoved her down hard, her slickness paving the way,

until I was balls deep in the most gorgeous woman I've ever had. The ripple of her tits each time I slammed home from below added to the delirium, and I fought to keep control. Christ, she was a fucking sight. Head tilted to the side, jaw dropped open, eyes screwed tight in ecstasy.

I was the one pounding hard into her, but I felt so weak. She had me all twisted up inside. Stripped bare like I was bones and sinew, but no muscle. Every one of my secrets was there for the picking. Thank Christ her eyes hadn't popped open and turned on me because I couldn't have her seeing me so exposed. If she did, who the hell knew if she would stay. It was humbling and fucking terrifying at the same time, but that's what fucking Cat was like. It went far beyond the physical.

This was only her third time, and not knowing any better, she rolled with it. But I knew how rare this was. It was a once-in-a-lifetime communion of body and soul. This woman was a power to be reckoned with. So help me God, if it was like this *now*, she'd slay me once she had a little experience under her belt.

MY STROKES GOT ROUGHER, more demanding, but she was right there with me, riding me like a surfer catching a wave. I pumped from below and she dropped from above, the sound of our smacking flesh reverberating through the cramped quarters of my car. My balls slapped against her ass as sparks shot behind my eyelids.

On instinct, I gripped her throat. Her eyes shot wide for a moment and then dropped and hooded over.

"You like it. You like my dominance," I murmured. Never was a woman created to fit me, piece by piece, so perfectly.

We lined up together in every way. Anything I tried, she took to like a fish in water.

"Yes, Luca," she moaned.

Stroking in and out of her tight, clenching pussy, I pressed my fingers deeper into the slim column of her throat. Her eyelids batted wildly as I controlled her breathing, constricting it slightly and then letting go. I switched up the angle and hit a spot that had her shuddering above me. Her nails scraped along the tight skin of my skull, drawing blood.

"Yeah, there you go, baby. Come on, come for daddy. Come hard for me," I coaxed. Her hips worked me. She started cursing. Never heard anything dirty ever come out of her mouth before, but here she was whispering *fuck, fuck, fuck* on repeat. She was so far gone that she didn't realize what she was saying.

Her eyes went blind. It was a gorgeous sight to witness her completely unravel. She threw her head back, baring her throat to me. She jerked and twitched, forming an erotic vision for me as her climax ricocheted through her lithe body. Caught up in her orgasm, she was unaware as she released my hair and her nails raked down the side of my face, probably leaving bright red claw marks.

I fucking loved it.

"That's right. What a good girl. So dirty for daddy. So goddamn goo—"

I was cut off by a snap of her hips. She may have barely peaked, but she was suddenly in control. Staring me down, she gripped my shoulders and slammed down on me, rising and descending with total command. Eyes riveted on mine, they demanded I come.

Sweat rolled down both our torsos. Holy fuck, I wanted to keep pounding into her, making my claim, but she felt too good milking me. The inner muscles of her already tight-as-fuck pussy ruthlessly worked my cock. Her taking command was too much. She left me no choice but to let go.

My body jerked. Once. Twice. I blacked out as come shot out with an intensity that took my breath away. I wanted her pussy overflowing with my come, and...I wanted it to count. As my hips twisted and ground up into her, as ropes of seed lashed her womb, I desperately imagined that I was breeding her.

Her pussy squeezed of its own accord, drawing every drop out of me. Once it was done, she collapsed on top of me like a rag doll. She'd used up her last bit of energy. My arms went around and crossed over her back, pressing her in close. I felt her pounding heart against mine.

In that moment, whatever walls remained had crumbled to dust. I was all hers.

21

After spending the morning luxuriating in bed together, Luca left me to go to work while I put away the clothes and items I'd brought from home. My body ached in the most delicious manner. I was sure there would be bruises along my hips, the exact shape of his fingers, from when he took me from behind this morning. That position had seemed degrading from the little bit of porn I'd watched. Turned out, it was so not demeaning. In fact, it was my favorite to date. He could get in so deep. I felt like I had been thoroughly *taken*.

This was a perfect time to go through the apartment for Cristo, but I was crippled by guilt and had been battling myself for the past couple of hours. At my parents' house, the guilt had been overshadowed by worry for my brother's safety. But after the incredible time I had with Luca, it came roaring back a hundred times stronger.

Pacing up and down the living room, I wrung my hands as I sifted through any alternatives. Hours later, I came to the realization that there were none. If I didn't at least try to help my brother, he could legitimately end up dead.

Procrastinating, I went into the bedroom and focused on putting my clothes away. How could I survive Cristo's death? That was easy. I couldn't. Then again, how could I live with myself if I betrayed Luca? Crushing a shirt to my mouth, I screeched into the material.

Pushing past the guilt plaguing me, I hurled the shirt across the walk-in closet and stormed out, leaving clothing tumbling out of my suitcases and hanging off every available space.

Barefoot, I crept around the apartment, quickly snooping through every room of the apartment before pausing in front of Luca's office. I'd already found a collection of guns and knives littered throughout the house, in random places like his underwear drawer. I supposed the idea was that he'd have easy access to a weapon if there was a surprise attack.

The man was prepared for every contingency, but he hadn't seen me and my shady family coming.

God, the idea made me want to run to the bathroom and vomit, but I gave myself a mental slap. *Get it together! You do this one thing and it's over.*

Facing his office door, I pressed my forefinger into the center of the door and pushed. With a tiny *creeeak*, it swept open the rest of the way. I hovered at the threshold, listening for any sounds. The only sound breaking the eerie silence was my own heavy panting. God, this was so nerve-racking I wanted to scream.

Taking a huge breath of air, I stepped into the quiet room. Shimmering from the windows, sunlight bathed the room and bounced off the monochrome white-on-white furniture. Like the rest of his place, Luca's office was tidy. On a sleek white lacquer desk, there was a wireless keyboard, two monitors propped up on stands, an aluminum desk lamp, and a small leather notebook with a pen lying across it. One wall was made of recessed shelving, holding a large aquarium and custom-made drawers, which most likely held files.

Not bothering with his computer, which I figured was impenetrable, I decided to start with his desk. First, I rifled through the drawers of the desk. Nothing. I opened the leather notebook and read through his calendar and a smattering of private notes that made no sense to me.

So far, so good.

Taking a bracing breath, I walked to the shelves and pulled open the first drawer. I flipped through the different files and halted at a little tab labeled "L.A.- Hagi."

Hagi? As in the Romanian *mafie* family out West that my father owed money to? If I had any idea that the Lupu clan was involved with them, I might have told Luca. I shook the thought from my head. It was too late now.

Pulling out the first file folder, I flipped it open. There were bills, each one of them had a circled "Paid" in red ink. There was a sheet with a list of names and numbers beside them. That might prove useful.

Putting that one aside, I pulled out another file. Taxes. Flinging that aside, I grabbed another and opened it. This one had colored brochures of Soviet-style weapons. I should've known it wouldn't be as easy as this. A man like Luca wasn't going to have incriminating evidence lying around. The only thing interesting so far was that the Lupu family was in deep with the Hagi clan. Checking to see how far back their relationship went, I snagged the file with paid notices and noted that they only went back two years.

I leaned over to pick out another file when I heard a scuffling noise.

Before I had time to move an inch, a low, gruff voice demanded, "What the hell are you doing with my files?"

I froze in place, crumpling the file folder in my hands.

Oh, God.

Oh no, no, no.

My head swung over my shoulder as I slowly pulled away from the cabinet. Luca stood across the threshold, feet apart, arms crossed over his chest. He was fuming. *Fuming.* He looked like he'd instantaneously combust, with flames licking the outline of his body, right about now. This looked bad. This *was* bad. My stomach dropped to the floor. A whoosh of tingling covered my skin, like one might feel before free-falling from a plane. *Busted.* My tongue was glued to the top of my mouth. Shaking my head numbly, I remained mute.

"Answer me," he snarled. "I leave you alone in my home to go to work, rushing through my errands so I can return to my fiancée. Instead of finding her on her hands and knees, naked in my bed, ready for my cock, I find her on the floor of my fucking office, going through my files. Are you spying on me for your family, Cat? Is that what you're doing here? Is that what you've been doing here all along?"

"No! I-I was looking for something..."

Stupid, stupid, stupid.

His eyes narrowed on me.

"Answer me, and try the truth this time," he spat out.

I averted my eyes, unable to watch the disappointment and indignation in his eyes.

"Only one time," I murmured. "I had to find something to help my family. They're going bankrupt a-and they owe a *mafie* family a lot of money. Cristo beat up their prince. Now we have to pay them back or they'll kill him. But I never meant to hurt you," I rambled.

He recoiled as if I'd slapped him. "You mean you never meant to get caught. In what world would betraying me not hurt me, Cat?"

"I wouldn't have given them anything that could be used against you or your family. Only something to help them. The Lupu clan is so rich. They can afford it."

He barked out a bitter laugh. "*They* can afford it, you say? The Lupu family, you mean. That's supposed to be *you*. As my fucking wife, you're supposed to be a Lupu. But you don't see yourself as one. You could've come to me and told me. I would've helped you. Nicu was right. I should've known better, you being a Popescu."

I flinched at his accusation. He was right. I saw it in his eyes. He would've helped me. But I didn't know that until now. I was so used to looking after myself that I automatically went into self-reliant mode. If it was me alone, if my brother's life wasn't on the line, I would've risked it. But I'd been too afraid to come to him.

I rose to my knees, my hands coming together in supplication as I argued the only thing I had on my side, "My brother's in serious trouble, but I wouldn't have hurt you, Luca—"

His palm came up. "Don't. Stop trying to defend yourself. You know better than anyone how important trust is in a family. It's the difference between life and death. Do you know, this whole time, Nicu hated you because he believed you were a spy? That your father insisted on a marriage to plant you in the bosom of our family? I believed it as well, until I met you. Then I thought, *there's no way*. I thought that boarding school must have saved you from the worst of the Popescu tribe poison, but you've proved me wrong. Do you even care for me?"

"Of cour—"

His hand slashed through the air. "Don't answer that. I can't stand hearing another lie come out of that pretty, treacherous mouth of yours. Of course, you don't."

I flew to my feet. "But I do! I do, Luca. God, I do."

"Stop," he thundered, his voice thundering through the air, bouncing off the walls and ringing in my ears. My nostrils burned. My eyes stung with pain, tears spilling out in a fast and steady stream.

My head and shoulders dropped. Swallowing over the lump in my constricted throat, I mumbled, "I'm sorry. I would have made sure not to hurt you. You have to believe me."

"Too late for sorry," he clipped out. "I don't believe a damn thing you say to me."

"Don't," I whimpered, my bottom lip trembling.

"I want you out." He pointed a trembling finger to the open doorway. "I want you fucking out of my house. Out of my life."

The tremor that had started in my hands radiated up my arms and my shoulders began shaking.

He jabbed his forefinger again. "Go. Get the hell out, Cat. Go!" he thundered.

I jerked as if smacked across the face. It was what I deserved. Fuck, fuck, *fuck*. He was right. I had betrayed him. The pain of losing him seared through me, and I tried again, "Luca, can I explain—"

"No," he declared hoarsely. "I need you to leave before I say something regrettable. I need you gone. *Now.*"

My chest heaved with agony. I'd lost him. Stupid me, I thought I'd get away with it, that I could have my cake and eat it, too. Instead, I'd thrown away the best thing in my life.

Reeling, I staggered past him like a drunkard. Grabbing my purse, I shoved my feet into my shoes, threw the door open, and fled. My skin was clammy and cold, doused by waves of shame and hopelessness. The way my heart was palpitating, I knew I couldn't stay on this floor and wait. Stabbing the elevator button, I snapped my head from side to side, searching for a fast escape route. There was a door at the end of the corridor. I lurched toward it and yanked on the doorknob. Thank God, thank *God*, it flew open.

Propelling myself forward, I caught the banister in time before flying headfirst down a flight of stairs. Stumbling down a couple of steps, I righted myself and took the rest of the stairs two by two as fast as I could without cracking my head open. Tormented by what I'd done, the idea crossed my mind to fling myself down the stairs and take my chances on anyone finding my splattered brains this far up a building of seventy-seven floors.

My blubbering cries and gasps for breath ricocheted off the walls of the narrow stairway, making me feel stupid, but I couldn't help myself. I'd ruined everything. In the end, I did the one thing I'd tried to avoid—hurting Luca. Somewhere around the fiftieth floor, I paused to pull out my cell phone. Raising my face to the ceiling, I sent out a silent prayer that there were enough bars on my Wi-Fi to make a call. I'd normally text, but it was hard enough finding Cristo's number through my tears.

Pressing the call button, I continued to make my way down as I waited for him to pick up.

"What?" he answered irritably.

"Cristo?" I croaked out.

His tone changed from annoyed to alarmed in an instant. "What is it, Cat? What's wrong?"

"He caught me. He threw me out," I blubbered out,

followed by a sharp cry before I shoved my fist into my mouth to stop myself.

"Fuck. Where are you?"

"I'm i-in the stairway, going down the stairs. I can't stay here. What sh-should I do, Cristo?"

He moved into big brother mode. "Fuck, sweetie. You can't walk the streets alone."

"I'm not staying down there," I replied in growing panic. "I'm a mess—"

"No, you can't wait there. Who knows what will happen once he talks to Alex? They could take this chance to take you out. You need to hide until Simu can get there to pick you up. You've got to get out of the building right away."

"Not Simu," I mumbled.

"Pull it together, Cat. I can't come get you. I'm in the middle of something. I'm going to text you a safe place to hide until he can get to you."

He covered the mic with his hand because suddenly his voice was muffled. Then he was back on, "Simu's leaving now. Get off the phone and get out of there. Take the service exit and check your phone right before you step outside so you know where to go. Once you're on the street, make yourself as inconspicuous as possible, and follow the directions to the meeting spot."

"Okay," I muttered and hung up. Thrusting the cell phone in my purse, I lopped it across my chest and quickly took the stairs down. Did I agree with Cristo that I was in danger? In a heartbeat. This wasn't simply about upsetting or hurting Luca's feelings, this was about betraying a *mafie* clan, and not just any *mafie* clan, either. The most powerful *mafie* this side of the Atlantic.

Mafie was *mafie* was *mafie*. There were a few hard-line rules, and betrayal was as black and white as they came.

There was no room for gray, for shading. Even if Luca was willing to spare me, there was little chance that Alex would. And Nicu? He'd insist on disposing of me in case I'd found something incriminating.

Skidding to a halt when I heard a noise, I snapped my mouth shut and breathed through my nostrils. I waited a few moments but didn't hear another sound, so I resumed my descent until I hit the ground level. Peeking out into the hallway, I found myself near the mail room, off the main foyer. *Shit.*

I sifted through my muddled brain to remember which direction the service entrance might be. Did it even matter? I deserved whatever they did to me. Then the image of my father choking that man in our basement flashed in front of my eyes. *Yikes.* I wasn't sure I was worthy of living, but I wasn't going to let someone torture me to death. It would break my mother's and *Bunică*'s hearts. Although, dying by my own hand was still up for debate. After what I had done, I wasn't sure I'd be able to live with myself.

Sneaking out of the stairway, I flattened myself against the wall and followed the hallway until I passed the service elevators. Spotting a "Service" sign on a door, I sprinted the rest of the way and slipped into another stairway. The walls of this staircase were bare concrete and scuffed-up. I dashed down to the lower level. Halfway across a dark, gray-colored corridor, I saw a crack in a pair of double doors.

The service entrance.

I checked my phone and opened Cristo's text. It was the address of a movie theater a few blocks away on Broadway. He directed me to buy a ticket and hide in a stall of the women's bathroom until I got a text from Simu. My spine slammed against the wall as a building maintenance worker came whistling down the hall and turned a corner without noticing me.

The moment he disappeared, I raced to the opening and slipped out onto the street. Stooping forward in an attempt to make myself smaller, I ducked my head and hugged the storefronts as I fled to my meeting point.

22

I didn't run after her. Thinking back, I probably should have. I didn't know where she was or if she was okay, and that...bothered me. The look of devastation on her face was seared in my mind's eye. The one time I thought I could be happy had been a fucking illusion. This proved a sneaking suspicion I'd buried down deep; I didn't deserve to have what everyone else had.

Instead of going after her, I did the next best thing. I trashed my place. Wireless keyboard, books, files, vases, overturned furniture. I started in the office and methodically made my way to the living room, leaving holes in the wall in my wake.

Nicu flew into my apartment, door slapping against the wall, gun propped in both hands. Swinging it left and right, he scanned the area until he saw me.

"No one's broken in. It's only me, ruining my own apartment," I declared. By this time, I'd collapsed on the floor, legs splayed open as I stared down at my bloody knuckles.

"What in the ever-loving fuck happened?" he asked, looking around in bafflement.

I might get angry and snarky. I might give a dressing-down or a verbal lashing, but I didn't do destruction. That was more his thing. Even as a kid, if we'd both been given gifts, he'd have obliterated his toy car before dusk had fallen while I kept mine pristine in its box, taking it out on occasion to play and then safely returning it to its rightful place.

Until today.

I was so furious and hurt, that the violence exploded out of me, unimpeded. My control snapped, and I didn't want her to see me lose my shit. That was the primary reason for making her leave.

I told Nicu that I caught Cat digging into my files and had thrown her out. She didn't know they were dummy files, placed there in case we ever got searched by the Feds. Please, I wasn't stupid enough to leave a paper trail of our activities. Every single transaction was encrypted and untraceable, holed up in a server farm in a converted Weimar bunker in Germany.

But that didn't stop me from hating her betrayal. Had she played me for a fool from the beginning? I shook my head adamantly. Before finding her sprawled over my folder files, I would've sworn on my mother's life that she'd never do something like that. A prickling on my nape scolded me for not listening, for not digging deeper, but I was so consumed with the need to get rid of her before I wrecked the place, I couldn't think clearly. Fuck, I was conflicted, and I didn't like it one bit. I should have nothing to do with her, *want* nothing to do with her. Instead, I felt like I'd made a mistake. Maybe I should've listened to her stumbling excuses. Sifted through her reasoning. For the first time, I was willing to give someone the benefit of the doubt.

I turned to Nicu, who was praising me, "Good riddance,

brother. She's a Popescu, for Christ's sake. I could never trust another *mafie* female outside our family. Never."

"That's because you're a suspicious motherfucker," I grumbled.

"You can't live in this life, even vicariously as our women do, without it tainting you. Not fucking possible. And a Popescu is as dirty as they come."

"Stop saying that," I snapped. I had no idea why his words were pissing me off, but they were. No, I did know. I was still protective of her. God only knows why, considering what I'd caught her doing, but there it was again. That feeling of having missed something.

"It's true, Luca. That's why I never allowed myself to get close to her. She's poison. I didn't fall for that little innocent act. Impossible for a Popescu to be innocent. It's not in their DNA. Are you sure she was a virgin, because I had my doubts."

"She was a virgin. I can vouch for that," I growled as I got to my feet. Damn, his matter-of-fact acceptance of her deceit infuriated me. Lack of shock was one thing, but his lack of surprise was getting on my nerves.

"Sure about that?" he challenged, as he took a seat and lounged across my couch. "They already used fake blood to make it seem like Una had a miscarriage. Who says they wouldn't do it for a hymen."

"It wasn't fake," I ground out, pacing. Swear to God, if he kept up this line of questioning, I was going to clock him.

Nicu bent over his phone, tapping out a text. Pressing send with a flourish, he righted the upended coffee table and tossed his cell phone on top. "I just texted Alex and Tatum. They're coming over."

I buried my head in my hands and groaned before falling onto the couch beside Nicu. "Fucking thanks, bro.

Just what I needed is those two assholes in here. Can't catch a break."

"Seriously? You caught her ransacking your files. This needs to be dealt with. And why did you kick her out? You should've locked her in a room and called us to figure out what to do with her," he said.

"To do with her?" I pulled back and blinked at him. "What were you thinking of doing to her? You couldn't hurt her."

He waved his hand dismissively, even though there were strict rules of engagement. No touching women or children was one of those bright-line rules. I snorted. With Nicu, you never knew.

"Of course, I wasn't going to hurt her." His voice dropped to a dangerous tone. "I don't hurt women."

"Good to know," I muttered.

"But that doesn't mean you should've let her waltz out of here. We could have used her. Exchanged her for something. How long has she been gone? I could run her down."

He made to get up, but I slapped a hand on his chest and shoved him back into the depths of the leather couch. "Stay there. She's long gone."

Fuck that. He wasn't touching my woman. Christ, she was no longer my woman, but there was no way in hell Nicu was laying a hand on her. A vision of her kneeling at my feet, haunted eyes staring up at me, bleeding remorse and desperation, reared up. I scrubbed my eyes with the heels of my palms.

I bet her family put her up to this, those godless jackals, but it had been her choice to go with their plan. That was what hurt most. Although, she'd gone about it like she wanted to get caught. Thinking back, I realized they must have gotten to her when she'd visited them. It explained her quietness and withdrawal when I picked her up. Fuck, guilt percolated inside me. She was young and impressionable. I should have been there to protect her. Then again, she was her own woman. She should've chosen better. She should've chosen me. I gripped my forehead; a migraine was coming on.

Alex and Tatum sauntered through the door, left open by Nicu. Tatum locked it and turned to survey the damage. His razor-sharp gaze ended its voyage on me, sizing me up for a long moment. Whatever he saw made him avert his eyes. Tatum was my closest friend. I wasn't his closest friend, because, until Cat, I was unwilling to reciprocate the intimacy required for a mutually intimate friendship, but he knew me. He knew my heart was bleeding out.

Alex, on the other hand, was deep in fixing mode. Lifting an armchair, he placed it upright only to have it crash over as the leg splintered off. Undaunted, he cleaned as Nicu and I watched mutely.

"What happened?" Alex asked, as he came back from the kitchen holding a broom.

"Jesus, what happened to *you*?" Nicu choked as he stifled a laugh. "Look how domesticated you've become since Nina moved in."

"Yeah, she's tamed him," threw in Tatum.

"Hardy-har-har," muttered Alex as he swept up the shards of a broken crystal vase scattered across the parquet. He zeroed in on me and prompted, "Luca?"

"I caught her snooping through my files. She admitted that her family put her up to it," I explained tersely.

Nicu barked out a sharp laugh. "Last time I checked, she was an adult."

"I'm aware, Nicu," I bit out.

"Where is she?" Tatum asked as he came from my office.

"I cut her loose."

"Come again?" Alex said.

"I. Cut. Her. Loose," I gritted out between clenched teeth. "What the fuck did you expect me to do?"

"Regardless of whatever she's done, she's still yours," Alex explained.

"*What?*" I bellowed, jumping to my feet.

With a raised brow, he clarified, "She's yours. She's *mafie,* and you fucked her. You fucked her *knowing* she was a *mafie* princess. There's no going back from that. I don't care what the fuck happened or what the fuck she did to us. You bonded with her, so now you'll marry her. If not, I will punish you."

I sputtered out sounds, incapable of speaking through my rising fury.

"Consequences," he persisted. "You won't be going anywhere. Not to Cali, not to Chicago, not to Westchester. I'll fucking skin you alive until you do right by this family."

My mind went blank and I saw red.

"I may have fucked her, but I clearly didn't know she was a lying snake. Since when have you known me to be self-sacrificing? Not since I got out from under that fucking bastard, our beloved *pater.* Do you remember the last time he hit me, Alex?"

My head snapped to my youngest brother. "Nicu?"

I choked back a bellow of tormented rage. "No, you don't. The answer is when I hit him back. He stopped when he realized that I wouldn't stand for it anymore. When I was ready to leave it all, leave *you* all. Walk away from every-thing. My clan, my family, my fucking blood bond." I smacked the clan tattoo on my chest. "If I was ready to do that, then walking away from Cat is nothing for me. *Nothing,* do you hear me?"

If there was a chance that I would take her back, it vanished the instant Alex opened his big fucking mouth and spewed out his ultimatum.

My brothers blinked up at me in shock. I'd gone further into the past than ever before. Getting my heart ripped out of my chest cracked the invisible wall of silence that I had maintained for so long. Frozen in place, I let out a gust of shocked breath. What I had done was unprecedented. I swallowed around my cinched throat.

Taking a seat, Tatum's eyes darted from me to each of my brothers, trying to read the situation. He cleared his throat and said, "This has been festering for years. It's time we deal with it."

Alex's eyes flickered to him, then Nicu.

Nicu's blinking had gotten faster until he shook himself out of his daze. "Why, Luca? He was so good to us. Why did he treat you differently?"

"Honestly, I don't know," I croaked, my throat twisting tighter.

Rapping his fingers on his knee, Tatum said, "Something happened. It—my mother once let something slip after you slept over one night, when we were still kids."

Alex's eyes returned to Tatum, some sort of realization dawning on his face. His wily brain was always the fastest on the uptake. "What is it, Tatum? You know something."

"I do," he admitted, nodding sagely. "But it's not my story to tell."

"Fuck, what the hell does that even mean, Tatum?" I fumed.

"It means that the three of you are finally ready to face the truth." Addressing me, he said, "You rarely talk about it, even with me, and never to your brothers. Whatever happened today has burst through the invisible line you never cross." He spread his hands out. "Well, here we are. It's time for some truth telling, and if you want to know why you were treated differently, why you *are* different, then it's time to find out." He paused. "From the source."

Heat crawled up my nape. "And who the fuck is the source?"

"Who else? The women in your family," he replied simply.

23

I made it to the movie theater without a problem. I kept checking to see if I was being followed, but Cristo's worries were for nothing. Waiting for a text from Simu, I hid out in a bathroom stall, crouched over the toilet. Fitting, since it felt like my heart was swirling down the drain of said toilet. Luca hadn't bothered to follow me, further proof that he was done with me. I let out a strangled sound of despair and covered my mouth to suppress it. If he had any feelings for me, even hatred, he would've come after me.

But he'd done nothing, which had to be the worst thing he could possibly do. If only he hadn't thrown me out, if only I had a chance to explain myself. I would've taken his shouts over his dismissal any day. I was so enraged with myself that I wanted to scratch my eyes out. I should've ignored my family's wishes and told Luca everything.

"Oh, God," I gasped out, staring up at the white ceiling as tears tracked down my cheeks. "It's over."

My phone vibrated. Simu was outside. Rushing out of the theater, I found his car idling at the curb and flung myself into it. It was midday traffic, but he casually ignored the blaring horns of cars turning sharply around his car and streaking past. The instant I slammed the door closed, he pressed on the gas and merged into the rushing traffic on Broadway.

His hand landed on my knee and squeezed, his anxious eyes roving over my face and body for an instant before returning to the street. "You okay, baby?"

I cringed at his touch coupled with the endearment. Bile rose up my gullet.

"Yeah," I murmured, dropping my purse into the footwell and slipping on my seat belt. The back of my head hit the headrest. I closed my eyes, releasing a long breath of defeat.

"I'm going to fucking kill him. I'm going to fuck with him and torture him for an entire week. Keep him hanging from the ceiling on a steel hook until he bleeds out like a gutted hog. Then I'm going to dismember him, piece by piece, and scatter his body parts over the entire city. No one disrespects you or the Popescus like that. *No one.*"

My heart banged against my chest. There was no way I'd allow him to touch a hair on Luca's head. It was bad enough that I had hurt Luca and ruined his love for me. I wasn't going to see him get harmed by a Popescu. We'd done enough damage, thank you very much.

Crushing his hand in mine, I released it quickly and dug my fingers into my eyelids. "Simu, please stop. I can't deal with this right now. Promise me you won't touch him."

"Why the fuck not?" he growled.

My eyes popped open. "Um, maybe because I betrayed him? Because I screwed him over? He did nothing wrong. And then he released me, Simu. He could've tortured and dismembered me. Think about that. It was in his rights to make me pay for my disloyalty."

"Fuck that," he grumbled, eyes narrowed and laser focused as he zipped between cars and whipped around a corner turning east toward Queens.

"No," I replied tightly. "After what I did, he had every right to make me pay. Instead, he let me go without a scratch," I finished in a cracked voice. *Let me go and broke my heart.* "I don't know if Cristo told you—"

"Of course, he told me. I'm the *consilier*. Who do you think thought of trying to steal something from Luca in the first place? Regardless of what you did, Cat, you're a woman and the daughter of one of the most powerful *şefs* in the country. Luca has no right to touch you."

You bastard, I should've known you were involved.

"Oh, please, as if retribution doesn't come to women who betray their clans. What don't you get, Simu? I blood bonded with him. I was a Lupu." I swallowed back the tears threatening to fall. "And then I deceived him. He had the right to hurt me. At the very least, he had the power to turn me over to Alex, who could've used me as ransom to extract something from Tata. He had any number of options at his disposal, but he let me go. So no, we won't be hurting him," I said with finality. My lips flattened as I gave him a hard stare.

"I can't believe you're protecting him," he argued. "You're giving him far more credit than he deserves. Regardless of what you did, you're still a Popescu princess."

"You mean, puppet," I snapped. I had stupidly followed my family's plan, which turned out to be Simu's, instead of turning to my husband-to-be for help. Another wave of shame crashed over me. God, I was such an idiot to trust my family to fix this. This wasn't the first time they'd messed things up. Despite their attempts at outwitting the Lupu men, their plans often turned bad. We were either cursed or just plain stupid. If I hadn't panicked about Cristo and kept my head, I would've realized that my best chance of saving him was to turn to Luca. He and the Lupu men were diabolically clever, with a healthy dose of luck on their side. They'd always seen through every Popescu trick.

Instead, I spectacularly failed the first test between Luca and me. Now I was going to be a spinster. I sniffed and wiped my nose with the back of my hand. After having sex only a few times, I could kiss those moments of bliss goodbye. Knowing that I would never be touched again wasn't even the worst of it. The worst part was seeing the stark pain in Luca's eyes.

I was supposed to have his back. He was my partner, and I should've accepted that my future was with him. His love was unconditional, unlike my parents and brother. Their conditions wouldn't have stopped me from helping Cristo, but it was the truth. Tears sprang to my eyes, my throat tight and clogged with remorse. I'd thrown away the best thing that ever happened to me. God, I was such an idiot. Now I would have to live with the consequences, but at the very least, I would make sure that they left Luca alone.

"Bullshit. You were taking care of your family," Simu countered.

I threw my hands up in exasperation. "Oh my God, are you delusional? I was going to marry into the Lupu family. They were my family. My loyalty should've been toward them. My common sense was clouded by Cristo, but what I did was wrong. On top of everything, I now realize that Luca would've helped me." Simu made a sound of derision. "I deserve whatever punishment is coming to me," I ended miserably.

"Baby, you're killing me here. Cristo needed your help. And I have no idea what makes you think Luca would've helped. They hate the Popescus. Hell, I doubt he would've even gone through with the marriage. He was using you."

I looked at him, horrified. "Are you for real? If there's one thing I know, it's that Luca grasps the meaning of honor. He would've *never* used me like that. Why would he have taken a beating from you, my father, *and* Cristo if he planned on tossing me aside? You're grabbing at straws, Simu. A move like that would've gotten him killed."

"Oh, it's *going* to get him killed," he muttered under his breath, but I heard him in the quiet of the car. We were on the Queensboro Bridge at this point, and the play of shadow and light flickered over us as we passed under the criss-crossing steel bars of the cantilever bridge.

"Simu!" I chastised. "I'm not joking. You cannot, I mean can*not* hurt him. Do not touch a hair on his head."

"Come on, Cat. He humiliated you and shamed the Popescu name. He had no right to toss you out like yesterday's trash. At the very least, a real man would have approached Nelu and negotiated a way to make up for your faux pas."

"*Faux pas?*" I stuttered. This guy was driving me crazy. I was emotionally exhausted, but Simu's persistence made me want to throttle him. Yet, I had no choice but to try to convince him because he was a loose cannon when his feathers got ruffled. My fingers curled into tight balls, the urge to punch him was looming over me. I wasn't having it. No one was going to hurt my Luca.

"Oh, what I did was far worse than a little faux pas. If I were anyone else, I'd be the one strung up on a hook in some abandoned warehouse somewhere. I don't want any bloodshed in the name of my honor. I don't know how many times I have to say this, but the man did nothing wrong. He's the wronged party here."

He blew out a long breath and muttered, "I shouldn't be surprised you'd stick up for him. It's who you are. Sweet and innocent. Those are only two of the many things I love about you."

Oh, God. *Ewww.* I couldn't hear a declaration of love right now, especially from him. I grimaced and shuddered inwardly. The idea of Simu wanting me was gross, but I had to keep on his good side to convince him to leave Luca alone.

"Ugh, don't say that. I don't deserve your love. I don't deserve love, period. And I'm not going to get another chance at love, either. I'm damaged goods now. No one's going to want me."

"I want you," he pronounced, his eyes sliding to me for an instant before returning to the road.

"What?" I gasped out of surprise more than anything else. *No, no, no. Please shut up, Simu. Don't keep talking.*

"Did you really expect anything else?"

"Of course, I did. I'm not a virgin anymore."

"I'm aware," he replied. "And I don't care."

This was insane. The idea of him touching me made my skin crawl. Sex? Out of the question. I complained about being a spinster moments before, but that was a thousand times better than being with him.

"Don't be silly, Simu. Of course, you do. I don't need a knight in shining armor. Just because my father saved you doesn't mean you have to return the favor. I don't want to owe anything to anyone. I'd rather live out the rest of my life alone. At least I can go to college now that my hopes for marriage are forever ruined."

The last sentence popped out of my mouth without

thinking. I didn't want to be with anyone else. Ever. Maybe I would go to medical school and become a psychologist. Help other people. That would give my life meaning. I had to do something with my life after tossing away my one chance at happiness.

"I'm serious, Cat," he insisted. "I didn't stop wanting you when you were engaged to Nicu or with Luca. I didn't stop when you lost your virginity. I never stopped. And before you say it and piss me off, no, this isn't a pity move on my part."

My head whipped to the side. I was speechless, but inside I was screeching *nooo*. I had just betrayed the only man I ever loved. My heart was Luca's, even if it resembled the splintered windshield of a car after a head-on collision. The very idea of being touched by another man sickened me, so the idea of *marriage*...

No, just no.

He glanced at me again and repeated, "I'm dead serious."

My brows shot up. The only move I'd made since his declaration.

"Think about it," he finished.

I didn't need to think about it. I already knew that it was out of the question.

My brows dropped low and I shook my head. "I can't. Since I won't have a family, maybe I'll go into a helping profession. Become a shrink or a nun or something. Maybe I'll be the next Mother Theresa."

"For fuck's sake, this isn't a joke," he snapped.

"I'm not joking," I cried out. "You think you're saving me, but I can't do this again. I can't be with someone else. I. Am. Done."

I was breathing hard. He was going too far, and as much as I wanted to protect Luca, I couldn't lead Simu on.

"You can and you will," he replied, his jaw clenched tight in stubbornness.

My eyes flared wide. *What?* I recognized that glint in his eyes. *Uh-oh.* When he got something in his head, he was like a dog with a bone. Relentless.

His voice turned hard as he declared, "If you want me off Luca's back, then you'll marry me. Otherwise, consider him as good as dead. Not only that, Cat. I won't help Cristo with the Hagi family. Now that you've failed, I'm the only thing standing between him and a Hagi gun pressed to his temple. I won't use my clout with my uncle unless you first swear you'll marry me."

My body jerked.

"What?!"

"You heard me."

"Jesus, what the hell? Have you lost your mind?"

First, he threatened Luca, and now Cristo? It was a low blow, even for him.

His eyes flashed with an unholy look, borderline crazy if you asked me. For the first time, I was scared of him. This wasn't about love. This was the furthest thing from love.

"I get what I want, and God fucking knows I've wanted you for years. You were mine from the beginning."

"I'm not an object," I retorted.

"Like hell you aren't." My head snapped back like I'd been slapped in the face. "You represent the heart of the Popescus, and if I marry you, I will finally be seen as an equal in the eyes of your father and the entire family. As an equal, I have a chance at being șef once your father retires."

"And Cristo? Cristo is heir," I whispered, cringing. I already knew his answer before he spoke.

"Fuck, Cristo. With you by my side, I'm equally capable of taking the crown." He turned to me, crazy-eyed. "I will get your total cooperation, Cat, or you can kiss your brother and Luca goodbye forever."

My jaw dropped open. His declaration of love had always been a lie, an unadulterated lie. What he was in love with was the power he'd get from marrying me.

Snapping my mouth shut, I crossed my arms over my chest and fumed while he rambled on, "I know you think you're in love with him, but you're not." *Oh, I am, you fucker. The gall to think you know how I feel. Unbelievable.*

"You're young and inexperienced. Not only is Luca handsome, dressed to the nines, and charming as fuck, but he seduced you." *Ha! Shows how much you know. I seduced him first.*

"Yet, you don't really know him. Not like you know me. You've known me your entire life. I'm giving you a chance to have a full life. Even if you graduated college and became a professional, you'd never have a normal life. You'd live with your parents until they died, and then you'd move in with Cristo and his family." *Better than you, you manipulative little prick.*

"Or your father takes pity on you and marries you off to a low-level soldier. You will have no power to deny him. Instead, you can marry me," he finished smugly. *Gag, I'd rather do anything but that.*

Ugh, I could vomit from disgust.

"I won't let you ruin your good name for me," I argued, grasping for any reason to dissuade him while clenching my shirt to stop from choking him. The man was a callous, power-hungry asshole. He'd go to any lengths to get what he wanted, the rat bastard. I had to stop him, but first, I had to get him to save Cristo. I had no choice but to marry him. I wanted to scream at the top of my lungs and cut his black heart out of his chest.

"Don't worry about me. I can handle anything thrown my way. I've wanted you since before you were legal. You've known that. I didn't think I'd have to convince you, much less blackmail you to marry me, but whatever," he claimed.

After the debacle with Luca, the only reason a proud aristocrat like him would put up with the whispers, sly comments, and insinuations that would dog me for years, maybe decades, was a power grab.

God, this was exhausting. Not only did I lose the only man I ever loved, not only would I beat myself up for eternity for breaking his trust, but I couldn't even be left alone to lick my wounds. I was being bullied into a marriage with a selfish, heartless man, and I couldn't do anything about it. But I was going to at least extract an oath from him. He wanted it bad enough that it was worth a try.

Simu was a Cantacuzino, an aristocratic family that could trace their line back to Byzantine imperial families. They were no joke. I'd never heard Simu's story, other than that my father pulled him out of the street and gave him a place with our clan, but I knew his oath was serious.

"If you want me, then swear that you will leave Luca alone. You won't touch him. Not you yourself, not through someone else. Not now, not later, not ever," I intoned. "And you will help Cristo. If you don't, all of this goes to hell."

His eye twitched and he slammed the heel of his hand against the steering wheel, but he spat out, "Fine, I swear on the name of my family, the Cantacuzino. I don't know why you feel the need to protect him, but if you marry me, I will let him live. As for Cristo, that's without saying."

My back teeth ground together. Pretending he cared about Cristo was too much. *Grrr. What an asshole.*

"Fine, I accept it. I will marry you." I had no intention of ever having this discussion again. "From here on out, I don't want to hear his name again. Understood?"

"Understood, baby," he crooned. A satisfied grin spread across his lips.

My spine hit the back of the seat. There, it was done. I'd sacrificed myself for Cristo's life and Luca's safety. Hopefully, I'd redeemed myself, at least a little. Luca would never know, and I was fine with that. It was small compensation after what I had done, but now that a whole part of my life —love, passion...delicious sex—had been hacked away, I'd better get used to lowering my expectations on all fronts.

His hand landed on my knee. My gut churned, and I gritted my teeth to stop myself from ripping it off me. Now that I was his, his hand on my knee took on a completely different meaning. It felt heavier. Weightier. Horrible. My back stooped forward as his grip clamped around my knee. I had exhausted what little leverage I had making sure he wouldn't take Luca out, so I had to grin and bear it.

"I want to go to college, Simu. I'm going to be shunned from society and need to get my mind off everything that happened."

"No one will hurt you if they know what's good for them," he threatened.

"Oh, please. I'm not talking about the men. I'm talking about the women. What I did violated a primal rule, and they're going to get their pound of flesh. You can threaten their fathers and husbands all you want, but that will only drive them underground. They'll do it behind the men's backs and make sure they never get caught. I won't have you fighting a battle that you can't win. It will undermine your authority," I reasoned.

His fingertips dug into my knee, but then he eased up

and patted it condescendingly. It took everything in my power not to hiss at him.

"Let me think about it," he said.

"Please," I bit out.

"I said I'd think about it, but in the meantime, I better not catch you doing anything stupid," he warned as we pulled up on my street.

"I swear, I'll be good, Simu," I promised.

PEERING UP at my family's house, I braced myself. I'd failed them, and my stomach cramped at the thought of what would happen to Cristo. Now the only thing I had up my sleeve was the lying son of a bitch beside me.

Gazing out at my family's home, I'd never felt lonelier. These had once been my people. What happened today changed that forever. I could no longer put my faith in them and my broken heart was tethered to another. Even knowing he hated me didn't stop the excruciating ache in my chest. How was I going to survive my constant scratchy, tight throat, my burning eyes, and the gaping hole in my heart? *How?*

I sucked in a rattling breath and let out a cry. Pressing my lips together, I flew out of the car and ran up the flight of stairs. Once inside, I fled up to my room, locked the door, and threw myself on my bed. Sobs racked my body as I buried my face and wailed into the pillow. Fully dressed, I crawled under the blanket and curled into the fetal position. Agonizing pain slashed through me like a rampaging beast.

Everything was so unfair.

So wrong.

And I had no one to blame but myself.

24

Tatum's cryptic comment pricked up the hairs on the back of my neck. My brain was like a flood breaking through a dam. First, Cat's betrayal. Now this. Whatever "this" was remained to be seen, but I already had an ugly premonition. It was about my father, so it couldn't be good. The last secret surprise about him ended with a new pair of half siblings.

I burst out of my apartment like a madman, tore through the streets in my car, and double-parked in front of our family home in Queens. Taking the steps three at a time, I powered through the house, searching for my mother. I found her in the backyard, gardening.

One look at my face and Mama gently put down her watering can, eyes wide.

"What the fuck, Mama? Tatum said you've been holding out on me about a secret. What is it?"

Bursting into tears, she covered her face as she made her way to the nearest stone bench. Sitting down heavily, she patted the seat beside her.

"I always knew this day would come," she confessed,

pulling her hands away. "I thought I would be ready for it, but I'm not. I've been so scared, Luca. So scared for many years."

I took the seat she offered and grabbed her hands.

"Whatever it is, just know that I love you no matter what. You will always be my mother," I insisted. I meant it. I might not be a mama's boy like Nicu, but Mama and I had a special bond. Unbreakable. She worshipped my father, but she loved me. It was one of the reasons I strove so hard to hide his abuse.

She pulled away from me, hurried into the house, and came back minutes later with a small photo in her hand. Returning to her seat, she placed it face down on the bench and took my hands again.

"It's quite a story," she started with a nervous chuckle. "You know of my sister, Clara, no?"

I frowned. "The one who died?"

"Yes, the one who died." She gave me an odd look, picked up the photo, and handed it to me. "The one who had six children."

I grabbed it and looked down briefly. Recognition jolted through me as I asked, "Six? I have five cousins on your side of the family."

I had a sinking feeling in my stomach.

"Six," she repeated firmly, squeezing my hands tighter. "She died giving birth to her last one. A beautiful son with blond hair and gray eyes, just like her. Your father and I had trouble conceiving. This was before we considered IVF, which is how we had the twins. The moment I saw you, I knew I was staring into the eyes of my son. You may have looked exactly like my beloved sister, but you were mine. All mine."

Blond hair. Gray eyes.

My birth mother.

I'd never seen a photo of her dead sister. There weren't any on the mantle of the fireplace in the living room, the bookshelves of the family room, or the myriad walls layered with framed photos scattered throughout the house. I had heard about the death of Mama's sister, but not that she'd died giving birth to *me*. This new discovery sifted through my soul. It felt strange. More than that, I didn't know how I felt about it.

"Why?" I whispered out.

"You uncle was overwhelmed and in deep mourning. Like I told you, your father and I had been trying to have another child without any success. I had gone to Romania to help my sister toward the end of her pregnancy. I was in the delivery room while your uncle stayed home to tend to the children. Later, she got an infection. As she fought for her life, I held you. I couldn't seem to put you down, not even to place you in your crib in the hospital. When she didn't make it, I spoke to your uncle and he agreed to my suggestion. I took you home, and I've never let you go since."

"Do you not have any photos of her because you didn't want to be reminded that I wasn't yours?" I asked bitterly.

"You are *mine*," she replied viciously. I was taken aback by her tone. Mama was normally soft-spoken. She had a spine of steel, but rarely showed it. Before my father's death, she followed every one of his commands. Or so I thought. Clearly, in this matter, she'd unilaterally gotten her way because he would've never claimed another man's child as his own. Whatever she did or did not know about the way he'd treated me, I never doubted that she loved me. It was written on her face, and I was humbled by it, by the fierceness of her love for me.

"I loved you from the moment I set eyes on you. Not only

because you reminded me of my sister, but because we were meant for each other. Do you have any idea what it's like to meet your destiny? Because that's what it was like when I saw you. I was meant to be your mother. I hid her photos but only because I didn't want to confuse you. I didn't want anyone to question the unquestionable. People can be silly and...petty. You deserved better than that. It wasn't for my benefit; you are undoubtedly mine. You simply came from the womb of my sister, a woman I loved and grieved deeply. It's an honor to be your mother, Luca."

"That's why he treated me the way he did," I stated. Those years I suffered, believing there was something wrong with me. He resented me because I wasn't his. My father was a prideful man, and I assumed that he would've viewed his inability to have more children as a failure. As the *Lupul*, he wouldn't be able to tolerate such blatant weakness, especially with respect to his manhood. I reminded him of this, time and time again.

Needing a confirmation, I asked, "Was he unable to have children?"

"Yes, that's right. Alex was a one-off. Every other child, the twins, Sebastian and Emma from that other woman, came with IVF. Part of the reason he went with that hippie American was that he thought she was particularly fertile. In the end, she had to use artificial means. It was his greatest shame, which is why I forgave him his indiscretion," she verified.

My head spun, almost like I was having an out-of-body experience. Everything had an eerily crisp clarity to it. The slight breeze that brushed against the hot skin of my cheeks. The spicy sweet perfume of the white jasmine blossoms along the fence near us. The hard roughness of the stone bench beneath my hands. My mother's labored breaths beside me.

Did she know what he had done to me? How he had punished me because I wasn't a product of his loins. Our society could be so narrow-minded. Defective loins for a *Lupul* was an intolerable flaw. Basically, any time he felt a prick of self-disgust, he took it out on me. It certainly put my childhood in perspective. It was the answer to a question that I had been subconsciously searching for my entire life. Why only me? Why not any of my brothers?

It was hard wrapping my head around the fact that the man I thought of as an uncle was my biological father. My cousins were my siblings and my siblings were really my cousins. *No.* That wasn't right. I may have fought with Alex and Nicu relentlessly, but nothing could undo the bond we had.

A tumult of emotions tumbled through me, shame and anger and relief vying for dominance. I didn't know if this new truth would change anything. I knew what it didn't change. It didn't change my past. It didn't change what I felt for Alex and the twins. I already knew that it would change nothing for Alex. We'd survived attempts on our lives together. We'd hunted and killed together. For Nicu and Tasa, I didn't think it would make a difference, either. Nor for the Lupu clan. I'd proven my loyalty and worth too many times to count.

Still...unease clawed at my throat. Cat had ripped my heart into shreds with her betrayal. Now, here was another lie. Both upended my life. Feeling dizzy, I brought a shaky hand to my forehead. My chest caved in like I'd been body dropped to the ground.

Tearing off my jacket, I yanked my tie off and unbuttoned my collar. I crushed the photo in my palm and said, "I have to go. I have to think, and I can't do that here."

Hands wringing together, she rose to her feet. Her worried eyes were glued to me.

"I know this is difficult for you, but please don't do anything foolish," she urged.

I kissed her cheek to ease her fears.

"I won't, Mama, but I need space," I reiterated and turned to go.

Discarding my jacket, tie, and phone on the ornate sofa of the living room, I stalked out the front door of my childhood home.

I WALKED the streets of Queens, heading north into Astoria. I roamed blindly for hours, long after the sun had set. I didn't realize where I was until I found myself staring at the back fence of Cat's home. I flattened myself against the brick wall of the house across the alleyway, hidden in the shadows of the balcony above me. Honestly, I didn't know how I ended up here. It was the last place I would've consciously chosen, but Mama's revelation had left me unhinged.

I could say that I didn't know why I remained, spying on her house, except that I did. Anger gnawed at my heart, but also a yawning ache that I couldn't shake off. As if attached to her by an invisible tether, our bond strengthened each moment I was rooted to the ground.

Under the balcony I stayed, watching as the lights went off one by one, except for the basement, where Nelu had his office.

Making my decision, I slipped away and retraced my steps to a drugstore I'd passed down the street. I bought

petroleum jelly and a baseball cap to hide my face. Back at
her house, I surveyed the area. Nelu had a few cameras
installed around the periphery of his property. *That's it?* The
man probably thought no one would dare attack his home. I
knew for a fact that every member of the family was handy
with guns. Even Cat. If there were a breach, the intruder
probably wouldn't get very far before getting shot. One
could only hope. It still left me uneasy about her safety.

Grabbing hold of a branch from a large chestnut tree, I
jumped over the fence with little effort. Face hidden, I
hugged the fence and cut between the trees of the narrow
backyard. Advancing on the camera, I smeared jelly around
the entire lens. Any image coming into their feed would be
blurry. I took care of the other cameras before circling
around until I was below her bedroom.

Gripping the rough stones protruding from the wall, I
scaled the side of the townhouse and tried her window.
Not only was it unlocked, but the thing was open. *The fuck
is she thinking...* In fact, both windows were open to the
balmy summer air, curtains fluttering from the breeze.
Jesus. Did she have a death wish or something? Her
parents were unbelievably irresponsible. Sheer luck and
the fact that they had such a good girl were the only
things that had saved her from some god-awful
misfortune.

I stepped in through the window and remained still as I
gauged whether she took notice of my presence. Turned
away from the window, Cat's sleeping form didn't shift in the
least. I took a look around.

Her room was...unexpected. I didn't know how I thought
an eighteen-year-old girl would decorate her room, but it
wasn't this. Among the heavy, dark wood furniture were
bookshelves stuffed to the gills with books. There were

books and discarded clothing covering almost every surface of her messy room.

I squinted at one of the posters on her wall, reading a quote by Susan Sontag in the dusky moonlight sifting through the window. *Attention is vitality. It connects you with others. It makes you eager. Stay eager.* Something about that tugged at my heart. There were two other posters, with quotes from Nietzsche and the feminist trailblazer, bell hooks. Sure, I knew she was taking a class on anthropology, but I wasn't aware the extent to which my little fiancée was an academic.

Fierce pride seared in my heart. After perusing her eclectic collection of books, with topics ranging from Chicago Theory of Economics and philosophy to Anaïs Nin erotica, I snooped through her large ornate secretary desk. I figured it was only fair since she'd done the same to me. Two drawers were filled with journals. I pulled out the top one and flipped it open. Scrawling cursive covered the pages without break. From the ink smudges, it looked like she'd used a fountain pen.

I scanned over the last few pages and snapped it shut. Christ, she was ripping herself to shreds over what happened. Turned out Cristo's life was on the line. I hadn't been sure whether to believe her when she'd said that his life was at risk. People will say anything under duress. Okay, she was speaking the truth, but still, she should've come directly to me instead of sneaking behind my back. She didn't think I'd help her brother, which wasn't an unreasonable assumption. I would have, but I didn't blame her for not trusting me with that. I wouldn't have automatically trusted someone like me if a beloved sibling was on the line. Cat was different, but she didn't know that. I closed my eyes, shaking my head. I was weakening.

A little keening sound came from the bed. My gaze shot over to her sleeping form. Her beautiful face, so young, was pinched in pain. I had the insane urge to caress her creased brow and scrunched nose until they smoothed back into peaceful slumber. Today's events had triggered her nightmares, and that thought did not settle well with me.

My resolve was cracking, and I shored it up by telling myself that betrayal and lies dogged me everywhere I turned today. But in the overall scheme of things, there were greater betrayals than trying to find something in my office to save one's only brother. In the end, it didn't matter, because even if I could forgive her, I had to resist Alex's demands. But was that a good enough reason? The idea of fighting Alex for the sake of fighting abruptly lost its appeal.

Suddenly exhausted, I dropped into the oversize velvet armchair across from her bed. Sinking into the cozy down-filled chair, I realized that it didn't fit with the rest of the room. This must be where she spent most of her time, reading her precious books. I took off my baseball cap and placed it beside a half-empty glass of red wine and an open book lying face-down on a small round table. I peered at the title. *Romance?* I grinned as I read the back cover. My little academic was also a filthy little girl.

My eyes were drawn back to her. A pang of longing rippled through me.

Shaking it off, I tilted my head back and closed my eyes; my nostrils flared. I caught faint traces of nectarines and peaches, with those beguiling accents of fresh, green notes. I glanced down at my lap. Fucking fantastic. I was hard knowing her sweet, pliant body was lying underneath a sheet a mere foot or two away from me.

Cat shifted in her sleep, turning onto her back. Her arm flung out. Her foot kicked out and drew the sheet covering her halfway down her torso. Ironically, she was wearing a virginal white nightie. Her high tits pushed up against the thin material, her nipples beaded tight. My mouth salivated as I imaged those ripe raspberry nipples between my lips. The light from the streetlamp outside her window cast a hallowed glow over her face. Her pursed lips popped open, and she let out a poignant moan of pain.

Her nightmare was here, present. It had barely started, and already I couldn't stand it. Moving to her bed, I sat on the edge and bent over, murmuring in her ear, "Kitty, wake up."

She moaned, turning toward me like a creature seeking comfort. I urged her to wake up. *Beautiful, sweetness,* and other endearments effortlessly fell from my lips. She needed comfort, and so did I. I shouldn't have allowed this indulgence, but after my mother's revelation, here I was.

Eventually, her long eyelashes fluttered open. Half asleep, she moved toward me, hand reaching out. Her fingers tangled with the hair on my nape, urging my head down. I let her drag me down until our lips touched. Her tongue ventured out and swiped once, twice. Her grip tightened, urging me on. Our mouths crashed into each other. Her peach fragrance wrapped around me like a cloud of everything that was good and clean in this world. A lie, I knew, but I didn't care. Plunging deeper, I took her mouth harder.

She jerked. Tearing away from me, her breaths came out hard and fast. She rasped out, "W-what is— What are you doing here?"

Ah, now she was fully awake.

25

I had a dream. An amazing, beautiful dream. It started out as the usual nightmare that plagued my nights when I was anxious or upset. My father's fingers wrapped around a man's throat, his face turning red and then redder, sputtering out curses and pleas and choked breathes. His fingernails broke as he tore at my father's hands.

Abruptly, the images shifted and morphed into something else. Into someone else.

The fingers of the dying man transformed into Luca's strong fingers. They caressed the side of my face, leaving behind tingles. His fingertips ran down my throat, gentle yet teasing. Seeking, my hand reached up and I felt the silky glide of his locks as I coiled them between my fingers.

It was remarkable, the vividness of my dream. I even smelled his cologne. That unique mixture of cedar and spice was like the crisp air of a pine forest after a snowstorm, stillness surrounding you on all sides. It was imprinted in my brain like a tattoo.

God, I missed that scent. My hips worked beneath the

sheet, twisting it between my legs, feeding the building pressure.

Alongside his tantalizing scent, I sensed a wall of warmth. Another phantom memory of Luca. I licked my dry lips. Hmmm, I shouldn't have had that last glass of wine before I went to sleep. I was parched, craving more, but only one person could quench this scorching need.

My eyes pried themselves open, my vision fuzzy. I frowned at the wrinkly dark-blue tailored shirt dominating my vision. That shirt was familiar. My brows bunched together. What was this? Before I could follow my line of thought, warm, firm lips pressed against mine, distracting me. My tongue peeked out to taste. Luca's flavor exploded on my tongue. I arched up, seeking more.

A hot, moist mouth covered mine. A tongue invaded. A moan broke free. I inhaled more of the spicy, woodsy scent. My body hummed, nerve endings snapping like live wires. The tongue came in again, thrusting harder and— Like the screech of a needle tearing up an LP record, my brain snapped into place.

I jolted awake.

Luca.

Ripping my mouth from his, I sucked in a much-needed breath as my gaze bounced around, taking in my surroundings.

This was no dream.

Luca was in my bedroom.

In my bed.

Kissing me.

I stammered, stumbling over my words as my mind tried playing catch-up. "W-what is— What are you doing here?"

His burning cold gray eyes pierced me.

"Does it matter?" he replied, leaning down to kiss me again.

I placed a hand on his chest, warding him off. "Of course, it does."

I peered over his shoulder at my open windows. In the summer, when the city heat died down, I liked to sleep with the windows open. It had its potential dangers, but I figured no one would dare break into this house. We had cameras around the property. Although, clearly, they were useless in keeping Luca away.

My eyes returned to him, greedily drinking him in. There were shadows around his eyes. Tension at the corners of his gorgeous, sculpted lips. I let out a pained sigh. I had done this to him. I'd inflicted this agony on him. I peered closer. A profound sadness radiated from him. It didn't match the righteous anger from the morning.

"What happened, Luca? Something must have happened for you to come here, to me of all people."

His hand caressed my hair. "You're so fucking smart, you know that? I watched as you took me in and processed everything until you came to that conclusion. You're so damn perceptive it's almost frightening."

My heart stuttered in my chest. Of course, his praise had me preening with pride, even though I had no right to it. I was struck by an intense longing to touch him, to forget everything and snuggle into him, but I forced myself back. He was suffering and I wanted to comfort him. I *yearned* to reach for him, but something made me hesitate. I may have felt guilty but that didn't mean I'd let him use my body willy-nilly. My heart was on the line and any touch between us had consequences for me.

His eyes cast down, he said, "I-I can't talk about it."

My heart cracked at the defeat in his posture and the

despair in his voice. I placed a finger beneath his chin and lifted it until his eyes were on me. "Hey, don't you dare. You better keep your head up around me."

Staring deep into his eyes, I suggested, "Can we suspend time for a moment? Put aside what happened between us for tonight? I swear that whatever you tell me will stay between us. I don't deserve your forgiveness, but it doesn't change the fact that I love you, Luca. I can't change the past, but I'd do anything to make it up to you."

He made a choked sound, his eyes averted for an instant before returning to mine and holding. I pleaded with him with my eyes, begging him to believe that I would never betray him again.

After a few long moments of tension, he took my hand and pressed a kiss to each knuckle. "I can't. It's not only my secret to tell."

"Then tell me something. Tell me enough," I begged. Enough so that I could help.

"After you left, I had it out with my brothers about my father. I found out something unbelievable." He gave a mirthless laugh. "Today, yours wasn't the only betrayal. But in the end, I found out the truth." His eyes got a faraway look. "It explains so much," he replied cryptically. "In that way, I guess it's good."

"Okaaay," I said, squeezing his hand to continue.

"That's all I can say."

It had to do with his father. Nothing else could get him this much off his game, not even our breakup.

"Our fathers are not good people. It's a shock when we find out exactly what their true nature is," I said, leaning more on guesswork than anything.

"Yeah," he breathed out. "That's for fucking sure. I had to

get away from them. I roamed around half the night until I found myself here."

The cinched feeling in my chest tightened further, and tears pricked the corners of my eyes. The fact that he made his way to me, despite what happened, was humbling and broke my heart all over again. I'd lost this beautiful, imperfect man.

I discreetly swiped at my eyes and cleared my throat. "Do they know where you are?"

He shook his head. "I dumped my phone. Each of our phones have trackers in case something happens to us. I didn't want to talk to anyone, and I knew they'd blow it up."

"Not even Tatum?"

"Not even him," he replied with a heavy sigh. "I needed space away from them to think."

I glanced at my digital clock. It was past one o'clock in the morning. Luca was in a bad way if he'd purposely abandoned his phone and avoided everyone for hours. I bet his family was beside themselves with worry.

His fingers trailed down the front of my chest to cup me between the legs. "I need you. I need to taste you, Kitty."

His eyes were stark. Desperate. He couldn't tell me his secret, fearing that I'd use it against him. It had been thoughtless to assume that I could convince him otherwise. I swallowed around the lump in my throat. If this had happened last night, he would've told me, whether the secret was his or not. But we were not yesterday anymore.

I was faced with a choice.

Do I comfort him?

If Luca was hurting, I'd always be there to comfort him. It was selfish on my part because it comforted me as well. With my marriage to Simu, this would likely be the last time I'd be touched like this again.

Heart banging against my chest, I stroked his cheek down along his angled jaw.

I inched closer until our chests brushed and our breaths mingled.

Caressing my lips against his, I whispered, "Yes."

He ran his knuckles over my stiff nipple, catching it between two knuckles. I gasped and he took control of my mouth. From there, it was a whirlwind of rash, brusque movements. I ripped at the buttons of his shirt until it gaped open, while he tore at my nightie until it was puddled at my feet. He licked his way down my throat, murmuring about how good I tasted, how creamy my skin was, until his mouth was too occupied with one of my breasts to continue.

My hands landed on his head, holding him in place as he suckled one nipple while plucking the other one. Biting down, the edge of his teeth dragged off my nipple with a hard pop that had me crying out over his head.

He growled, "Fucking delicious. I'm going to fuck you till you're sweaty, sore, and begging me to stop."

His eyes snapped with cold blue-gray flames. Determined. Dominant. Possessive. Everything I loved about this man. He gripped my silk panties, twisted, and tore them right off me with a loud *riiip*. Pressing my thighs open for his perusal, he explored, teased my clit, and spread my slickness everywhere.

Standing up, he took his fingers off my pussy just long enough to tear off his wrinkled shirt, sporting streaks of dirt from rock climbing the side of my house. My eyes raked his naked form, from his broad shoulders down his washboard abs to the hard beast between his legs. A large patch over the opposite shoulder of his Lupu tat distracted me from the main attraction.

"What's that?" I asked.

"I got another tat," he muttered.

Another tat? It was a well-known fact that the Lupu men only sported one tat on their chests, a green-eyed wolf head. Anywhere else was open season, but the chest was sacred, and the new tat was a big one at that.

Oh boy. A break in protocol like that was a scream for help.

"Come here," I coaxed, crooking my finger at him.

His eyes blazed as they scoured down my body. Feeling shy, I bent my legs and tucked them into my chest.

Stepping to me, he placed a hand on my knee and splayed my thighs open.

"Don't hide from me," he warned, as he settled in between my legs. Eyes locked on mine, he shimmied down my torso until his mouth hovered right above my spread pussy. Like a snake, his tongue flicked out and tapped my clit. My lower torso bucked off the bed, banging into him. Eyes on me, he opened those beautiful, sculpted lips and mouthed my mound. *Holy shit.* His tongue came out to play and every nerve ending was thrumming with high-voltage energy.

I fisted the sheets as he gorged himself on me. With a firm hold on my thighs, he held me down as he licked and sucked. Completely attuned to my reactions, his tongue moved with me, pulling back when he sensed it was too much, going deeper when he knew I could handle it. He played me like an instrument, bringing me to the edge again and again. I was hit with a pang of jealousy at the thought of how many times it took him to become such an expert.

As he fucked me with his mouth, he began humming. Vibrations undulated through my pussy. Lifting myself onto my elbows, I stared over the expanse of his broad back down the length of his spine. His back muscles shifted like water rippling over sand as it retreated to sea. I fixated on the dimples in his perfect, tight ass, moving as he humped the mattress. Two fingers pumped inside me to partner with his tongue circling my clit.

Oh, God. So good.

I released the sheet bunched in my fists and clawed at his shoulders. Panting, I licked the salt from my lips. But something was missing...I needed more of him.

"I need more," I croaked.

His head shot up, eyes on fire. "What do you need?"

"I-I don't know...I need to taste you." I threw caution to the wind and admitted, "I want your cock. In my mouth."

His lips spread and tilted upward in a wicked feline grin. Hands on my hips, he dragged me down and positioned us on our sides until his long cock waved in my face, his testicles bumping beneath my chin.

"Open wide," he ordered, and the instant I did, he pushed between my parted lips. My eyes fluttered shut, and I moaned at the musky taste of him. Enveloped by that drugging spice-and-wood fragrance, his hot flesh thrust between my lips. Then I felt his moist breath back on my pussy.

This was it. This was what was missing. I loved the taste of him, the sensation of silky, smooth skin gliding over hard, uncompromising steel.

I gave him a little bit of teeth, the way I knew he liked it, and was gratified to hear his hiss of pleasure.

"You've got some dirty in you, don't you, girlie?" he murmured. His fingers returned to my pussy, sinking into my sopping wetness in a commanding thrust. Arching my back, I bucked as he pushed his cock further inside my mouth, his thick girth lying against the flat of my tongue.

My throat stuffed full, I switched to breathing through

my nostrils. Just in time, because his next thrust breached the back of my throat, and I gagged. He pulled free long enough for me to catch my breath, and then he was back. The rhythm of his fingers in my pussy sped up along with the thrusts of his cock, until it was one relentless, endless loop of building pleasure.

Eventually, he did something with his tongue—not sure what because I was too busy focusing on his shaft—that took me by surprise. Abruptly, I was thrown over the edge and came hard. I screamed around his cock. Rubbing his face into my pussy, I was tossed in a riptide so intense the muscles of my abdomen clenched. Whatever tension coiled inside me exploded into mind-blowing rapture.

I must have been struggling to breathe because he pulled out. I heaved in deep breaths, staring as he sat up, his face coated in my essence, and pumped his shaft until semen sprayed across my face, throat, and chest.

I licked around my mouth, catching his seed and humming. He prowled up my body, giving me a brutal kiss, before lying beside me and tucking me into his body. Sweaty and sore, just as he'd promised, I felt myself dozing off. I was addicted to the feel of his body covering mine during the night. I woke up only once to him spoon fucking me, but the rest of the time, I luxuriated in his encompassing embrace.

By the time I woke up, the bright sunlight streaming over my bed revealed that he was gone. A baseball cap on the round side table by my reading spot was the only proof that it hadn't all been a dream.

26

Things were tense. After the lapse in sanity that sent me scaling up the side of Cat's home, I returned home to find Alex, Nicu, and Tatum sleeping on my couch and floor. Considering I had two spare bedrooms, I surmised by the empty bottles of liquor strewn across the living room that they had passed out where they'd been drinking at some point during the night, most likely waiting for me to return.

I wanted to howl in rage. It had nothing to do with my family and everything to do with Cat's broken eyes last night when I wouldn't tell her the reason that drove me to her. They haunted me with their remorse, which I was closer to forgiving than was healthy. She'd done everything in her power to comfort me, from sucking my cock to cuddling in my arms. It took herculean willpower to sneak out of her bedroom before the crack of dawn. At least her family was none the wiser.

Walking up to the men splayed out on my furniture, I smacked at their heads. One by one, they woke up, alternating between cursing and groaning as they clutched their heads. My mother had called Alex to tell him what had gone down. My brothers had a speech prepared, a bumbling declaration of love and fealty toward me as their true brother.

Uneasy with the emotions at play, I grumbled about how if they really loved me, they'd stop sobbing and get back to normal. To accelerate their exit from my living space, I shot off a text to Nina, Alex's wife, to come over and pick him up. I bit my nails waiting for her arrival, and together, we got Alex onto his swaying feet and into the elevator.

One down, two to go. Unfortunately, it wasn't quite as easy to get rid of the remaining pains in my ass.

Tatum and Nicu decided that it was best to stay and get hydrated while urging me to make something to eat. Since I was the only sober one, I cooked and nursed them back to health. They returned the favor by lounging around my apartment for the rest of the day, covertly monitoring me. They thought they were so smart, but their ruse was absurdly transparent.

They worried that I'd fall apart, but it was a relief to learn the truth from Mama. It explained why I was so different from my brothers, not only in my blond hair and pale eyes, but in my personality. *Did my birth mother also prefer her own company?*

By evening, I was long over their oppressive worrying and finally kicked them out.

I had to hand it to them, they were persistent in their determination to prove how much I meant to them. It had brought us closer, chipping away at the distance created by my father's abuse and my continual silence. A code of silence I had no intention of breaking any further. Maybe one day, but for now, I was satisfied that we'd landed safely on the other side of the big revelation. As per Alex and my mother's decision, we'd maintain the secret about my birth, even to Sebastian and Emma.

As for my mother, I visited her that evening, and we talked more about it. With her, I did break the code. Why? Because she was my mother, and she'd done right by me. Her love was unwavering. A true constant in my life, she deserved to know my truth after revealing hers. Plus, seeing this other side of her, I felt that she could handle it. Needless to say, there was a barrage of tears. I was a little surprised to see her indignation on my behalf, and I think it shook her worship of my father, something even discovering he had another family hadn't succeeded in doing.

On the topic of forgiveness, Mama tried to get me to discuss Cat. *If you can forgive me, then why not her? Everyone makes mistakes. You may make one. In fact, I'm fairly certain you're making one now.* She had a point, but I argued that her so-called "mistake" had been a form of protection. Misguided, but concern over my happiness was at the heart of her decision. The same could not be said of Cat.

No one was perfect, she countered. Cat was protecting her brother and should be given a second chance. I couldn't admit how close I was to caving after last night. Cat had accepted my limits and comforted me without pressuring me to tell her what had happened. Her care had unmanned me, but fear kept me away. Complicated didn't begin to describe my feelings. I was paralyzed by the struggle between my need for her and my fear of getting hurt again.

I should've been pleased, a few days later, when Nicu's deference toward me crumbled, signaling that everything was back to normal. His tone had thankfully reverted to its usual tone, but our conversation wrecked what little oasis of peace I'd managed to carve out for myself in the gloomy depression I felt over Cat.

We were in my apartment, nursing a beer together over a soccer game, AC Milan playing against their archrivals, Inter Milan, in a quarter-final clash of the Coppa Italia.

It started with him chastising me over not marrying Cat. "Not sure what you expected, Luca. It was a fucked-up thing to do, taking her virginity. And I'm not saying that because I was her fiancé. I'm saying it 'cause it's the truth."

"You act like I forced her or something. Trust me," I drawled. "It was entirely consensual."

"I don't doubt it, but she's young and a woman."

"So what? If she's old enough to get married and lose her virginity to her husband, then she's old enough to choose who she wants to give it up to. Cat has her own agency, regardless of her gender."

"A blood bond is a blood bond. That supersedes a little snooping behind your back," he refuted.

My jaw clenched so hard, swear to God, it was going to crack. "Fuck no, it doesn't," I snapped. I was being obstinate, but Nicu butting into my business made me argue with him.

"You're talking like an idiot, like you don't know the rules of our world."

"She betrayed me."

"So did Mama, but you forgave her. I don't get you, I really don't. You're into her. Despite what some of the busy-body mamas go around saying, this wasn't about hurting me. We both know I don't give a shit. You sure as hell didn't hit that for your ego. So that leaves one reason. You care for her. Are you really going to let another man touch what's yours? Especially *him*?"

My spine snapped straight up. "What other man? Who the hell is *him*?"

"Slimy Simu," Nicu replied with the pithy nickname he'd given the Popescu *consilier*.

"What?" The blood drained from my face. "What the fuck are you talking about?"

"You didn't hear?" he replied with a sly smirk. "Simu asked for her hand. He doesn't care that she's not a virgin. Apparently, he doesn't care that she's still in love with you, either. My spies told me that he refused to help her brother if she didn't marry him. Get this, his uncle is the Hagi *consilier*. Simu's influence is their last hope, so she has no choice but to accept him. She's his now."

"She's not," I denied.

Pity was written over my little brother's face as he shook his head. "Believe me, it's true. The point is, are you going to allow another man, *the enemy*, to clean up your mess? It's not a good look for you, brother."

I stood up, towering over him. My head was about to explode. *Explode.* "What in the fuck are you talking about?"

Casually draping his arm over the top of the couch, he raised a brow at me. "What, the part about other people cleaning up your mess? First, you refused to marry her, so I picked up the slack. Then, you fucking bond with her and refuse to marry her, leaving Slimy Simu to take the damaged goods off her father's hands."

"Don't. Fucking. Call her that," I spat out. God, I hated how obsessed our society was with women and sexual purity, like they were only as good as their hymen. Such fucking bullshit.

He rolled his eyes. "Okay, whatever."

"I'm not a fucking puppet that you can pull by the strings. I didn't marry her the first time around because I'm not Alex's little fuck toy, unlike you."

His eyes narrowed. "And what's your excuse for not marrying her now? Don't try to use the excuse that she rifled through your shit because that's nowhere near a good enough reason to turn your back on a blood bond."

That pulled me up short. My eyes shot away from his incisive glare. I swallowed and said, "I can't marry her."

He leaned forward, muscles coiled to pounce. "Why the fuck not?"

"There are too many reasons," I grumbled.

I fucking ached for her. I was close to forgiving her, vacillating back and forth, back and forth. Hell, I hadn't made it through one night without sneaking over to her house, arguing with myself as I paced beneath her bedroom window, only to creep away hours later. It was a miracle that I hadn't already ended up in her bed, but I doubted I'd win the battle tonight.

I couldn't admit to Nicu that I was fucking shaking in my boots from fear. I'd given my heart to her, and she'd hurt me. She'd made a bad mistake, and I believed she learned from it. Problem was, Cat left me exposed. Loving her had made me vulnerable to getting hurt again. After my father, I made an oath to myself that I'd never put myself in a position to get hurt again.

"Well, humor me. Since there are so many, why not name a few."

I shook my head.

"Alright, let me come up with a few. You don't want to marry. You don't want to marry a *mafie* girl. You don't respect our rules, even though you know the blood bond is as close to a sacrament as they come. You don't want to make your family happy. You don't want to make yourself happy. She snooped around on you because she's young and stupid and easily manipulated by her sick fuck of a father and brother. But the real reason has little to do with any of that, does it?

No, it goes much deeper. Something like you don't feel worthy of love. Of happiness. Am I getting warm?"

Pow! And there it went. My head exploded. Fuck, since when was my little brother so fucking perceptive? I had dug in my heels, weaponizing my stubbornness and my fury at Alex to help me stay away. But the fever had broken with Simu back on the scene. That fucker was dangerous. Not only was there no doubt that she still loved me, but his motivations for wanting to marry her were highly suspect.

Yes, she could theoretically hurt me again, but instead of focusing on the potential damage, what if I focused on how she shielded me the other night? The remorse I read in her journal was real, and Cat was too intelligent to make the same mistake twice. The core issue was that I didn't think I deserved love. It came back to my father. Knowing he was the source of that fear empowered me to fight it. I wouldn't let my daddy-dearest fear win. Cat was in danger, and I wasn't letting her go. I could resolve the Cristo problem. Cat might not know this, but Simu wasn't the only one with clout with the Hagi clan.

My head whipped around, my glare boring into my brother. He gave me a nonchalant shrug as he persisted, "After what you pulled, I don't think you're wrong. You sure as hell don't deserve her, even if she's a Popescu. Hell, if I found a girl I wanted and I'd popped her cherry, especially if she was *mafie*, I'd run her to the ground and lock her down. I swear, I don't understand you."

"And you never will," I thundered. "Now get the fuck out of my apartment."

He gave a light shrug. Bracing his hands on the couch, he placed his beer bottle on the coffee table, got to his feet, and sauntered to the front door, leaving it open as he left. He knew that annoyed the shit out of me, but he did it anyway, the little punk.

Stalking to the entrance, I slammed the door hard, letting it shudder in its frame. A wave of guilt gripped me by the throat so tightly I struggled to breathe. I pushed her to this by throwing her out and leaving her to take care of the Cristo situation alone. By not taking care of her, I allowed Simu this entry point back into her life. And now he had power over her.

If Simu touched a hair on Cat's head, I'd take a knife to his throat. *Has he already touched her?* Just the thought made me want to track him down and kick him to death. He didn't deserve to breathe next to her, much less touch her or fuck her or, God forbid, marry her. My hands curled into fists at my side.

The image of him lying beside her in bed, lying on top of her—*fuck!* I couldn't go there. If I did, I'd go hunting. Murderous intent pounded through my bloodstream, but I reined it back. Killing Simu would definitely make me feel better, but it wouldn't solve the root of my problem. Getting Cat back would.

And with that, I knew what to do.

She was mine and I was going after her.

27

I was in my comfy chair, laptop propped on my knees, going over the courses I was hoping to convince Simu to let me audit in the fall. He'd already visited me, and to call it horrible was an understatement. Now that I knew what he was really about, I felt nothing but disgust for him. When he bent down to exchange kisses, I had to force myself not to pull back in revulsion.

Thoughts of Simu led me to Luca, where my mind routinely escaped to avoid the very real scariness of marrying Simu. There was a hole in my heart, especially after the night we spent together. Almost a week had passed since Luca was in my bedroom. I spent my nights in bed, eyes wide open, praying, bargaining, and begging the universe for him to come back, even for one last stolen night, but to no avail.

I gazed out my window. At this time of night, the neighborhood was quiet for once. Other than the swaying branches of trees in the backyard and the occasional passing car blasting music, it was as close to silent as it got in the city. I rubbed my tired eyes. My nightmares had returned and I slept poorly, so my plan was to stay up for as long as I could. Hopefully, I'd be so exhausted, I'd fall into bed and collapse.

Eyes burning with fatigue and sadness, I was staring out into the inky black sky when I heard a scraping noise against the side of the house. *What the...?* I stilled, my ears perking up. There it was again! Gently putting the laptop down, I crept to the open window. I didn't have a gun in my room, but I had my lungs and I was ready to use them.

Two hands smacked down on the windowsill. Jumping back, I let out a little screech and covered my mouth. Luca's face popped up into the frame of the window. Eyes bulging, I stared as he hoisted himself through the narrow opening, crouched on the windowsill, and hopped into my room. Rising to his full height, he loomed over me, a baseball cap casting a shadow over the top half of his face. His black T-shirt fitted over his broad chest, black basketball shorts hugging his thick quads. This time he'd come prepared. My heart fluttered with hope.

"W-why...what are you doing here?" I stammered.

Legs braced shoulder-width apart, he folded his arms across his broad chest and intoned, "You're not marrying him, Cat. Over my dead fucking body."

Annoyance flared in my chest. He was here because he was *jealous*. Was he serious? Mimicking his stance, I crossed my arms over my chest and raised my chin high. "Um...I'm pretty sure you don't have a say in whom I marry anymore."

His brows slashed down.

"Like hell I don't," he growled. He actually growled. Grabbing my upper arms, he hauled me up against his big warm chest. Normally, I wouldn't object, but guilty or not, I wasn't going to let yet another person trample on my life choices. It was one thing to come to me for comfort. It was even understandable if he'd scampered up the side of my house for a booty call. But he had no right to tell me how to live my life. It was mine, and I was just trying to make it through the day.

I had to tip my head far back to lock in on his eyes, but lock on them I did, because he was veering out of his lane, and I was going to be the one to put him in his place. "Honestly, Luca, it's not like you're gunning for the position. You threw me out, so you have zero say on how I choose to live my life."

"Fuck that, I have every right. I blood bonded you, and I don't see a wedding ring on your finger," his eyes dipped down to my scantily clad figure, "Hell, I don't even see an engagement ring. I've got dibs. You're mine."

I threw my hands up, broke his hold, and stalked away before I gave in to the urge to slap him.

Twisting around, I hissed, "Listen to me and listen closely. I'm sick of being treated like an object that can be tossed around from man to man."

I jabbed my finger toward the window. "If I had any choice, any choice at all, I'd leave and never return. But since I can't escape *mafie* society, I'm trying to do the best I can with the options I have left. I get that I screwed you over. I get that you're still upset about that, but so help me God, I will not become another toy for you and Simu to fight over. You made it clear you didn't want me. Now that I'm engaged to him, you want to resurrect a blood bond that meant nothing to you a day ago?"

"Who said it meant nothing to me?" He stormed up to me until we were standing toe to toe. "If you only knew what it means—"

"If that were true, then you wouldn't have turned your back on it. On me. I understand that I wronged you, but you can't walk all over me. I'm not going to marry a man who doesn't want me. That's a recipe for disaster. I've done enough damage, and I'm not looking to add to it."

It was too painful to watch the various tortured emotions flittering over his face. Tearing my gaze away from him, I begged, "Just go, Luca."

"No," he ground out. His finger tucked under my chin, and he turned my head around to face him. "I'm fighting for this. For us. Yes, I admit that when I heard about Simu, I was jealous. Murderously jealous. But that was the least of it. I never stopped loving you, I'm just a stubborn, grudge-bearing asshole. Then Alex gave me an ultimatum that I had to marry you, and that made me retreat even further. I know why you did what you did. I hate lies, but I recently learned that lies can sometimes be forgiven if there's a foundation of trust. Outside of my family, I've never trusted anyone like I have you. Before you, I didn't think it was possible to care for someone as much, no—even more—than my clan."

Tears sprang to my eyes. Oh, how desperate I was to hear those words, but I shook my head. "I don't believe you."

"Cat, when have I ever lied to you? I'm not saying this simply because you're engaged to him. Yes, I hate him, and yes, the idea of you with him makes me want to tear him to pieces, but he's a dangerous motherfucker."

So noble, my Luca. He felt responsible for me.

I swallowed the lump in my throat and said, "I absolve you of all responsibility, Luca. You don't have to save me from Simu."

"Christ, woman, of course I won't let that fucker touch you, but it's so much more than that. I've been downstairs every night since I last saw you." My eyes went wide. "I pace under your window, fighting with myself not to climb up and crawl on my hands and knees, begging you to take me back."

I placed a hand over my heart to stop it from pounding out of my chest. "What stopped you?"

"Fear. Fucking fear that you could hurt me again." He shook his head. "No, that's not right. It goes even deeper. I knew you wouldn't hurt me again. Not on purpose, at least. It's fear of happiness. When I found you, I found my purpose in life, and when it was snatched away from me, I freaked out. I feared that I didn't deserve it. When I heard about your engagement, I finally snapped out of this vicious circle of self-pity."

Whipping his shirt off, he gave me a show of his carved torso. A trail of coarse dusty-blond hair divided his rock-hard abs and vanished into his shorts. He smacked lightly on the tattoo that was covered the other night. I peered closer. It was a portrait of a...woman? I squinted. With gray eyes?

"This is the reason. I'm my mother's nephew, not her biological son. This woman is my birth mother, but she died after giving birth to me. My so-called father had trouble making babies. My mother took me in, and he hated me for it. All that abuse, Cat? It made me feel like I didn't deserve what everyone else had. And your betrayal reinforced that belief."

He cupped my cheek, and his touch zapped me with a charge.

His tone dripped with remorse, his cool gray eyes on fire. "But I would've found my way back to you. I didn't tell you the other night because I let my pride and fear get in the way, but I'd already forgiven you."

His forgiveness meant so much. So did the fact that he'd been downstairs every night battling his demons. Although I wasn't totally convinced that Simu wasn't a big part of his reasonings, my chest cracked open with sorrow because this changed nothing. It was too late. I had already promised Simu, and with Cristo's and Luca's lives on the line, I was powerless.

Fighting down the sobs, I pushed his hand away. "Hearing that means a lot, but even if I wanted to, it's not possible to get out of the marriage."

His eyes darkened like a brewing storm. "Why the fuck not?"

"Because I gave him my vow, Luca, and I won't let anything happen to you."

Shit, I didn't mean to let that slip out.

His brows gathered ominously. "What does your promise have to do with anything happening to me?"

"Never mind, just forget I said anything," I hurried to answer.

No good would come of him knowing about my pact with Simu. Luca would only get offended. And I didn't want to stir anything up, what with the high level of animosity brewing between them.

"Tell me."

The low rasp of his demand sent a shiver down my spine, but I pursed my lips and held strong.

Frustrated, he dragged me to the bed and forced me down. I struggled to shove him off, but he easily maneuvered me onto my back. Straddling me, he pinned me by the throat and demanded, "Fucking tell me. I'm not leaving here until you do."

Dammit, he knew what that commanding move did to me. I shimmied to distribute the bulk of his weight between my hips, but it did nothing to relieve the tension building between my thighs.

I huffed and puffed and snapped my teeth, but he didn't rise to my bait.

"Out with it," he ordered.

"God, you're so bossy, you know that?" I sniffed.

"Yes, I'm aware." He hardened his tone. "Now talk."

I breathed out heavily and replied, "I extracted a promise from Simu that I'd marry him if he didn't kill you and if he'd help fix things for Cristo with his uncle. Although his reason for marrying me is to become the Popescu şef, I'll deal with that problem once I cross that bridge. So, you see, blood bond or not, we can't be together and there's nothing you can do about it."

A strange look came over his face, and then he threw his head back and laughed.

I bucked my hips to throw him off, but he didn't budge an inch. Once he was done laughing, he looked down at me with a soft twinkle in the cool silver of his eyes. I scowled at him in return.

"I don't see how this is a laughing matter," I snapped indignantly.

His forehead creased as if he was pondering something important. One of his hands dropped on my breast and swiped at my nipple until I was squirming beneath him.

"Stop it," I breathed out, although the protest died on my lips when he tweaked it. Dammit, his power over my body was ungodly.

"Jesus, I thought it was something serious. Simu and I have been at each other's throats for ages. I appreciate the gesture, but I can take care of myself. As for Cristo, Simu's not the only one with influence. As you know from the files you found, we have a relationship with the Hagi clan, and I will use the Lupu name when I negotiate with them.

Honestly, though, it's a bit naïve of you to think you could hold him to a promise of not hurting me."

My scowl turned deeper.

"I'll have you know that Simu and I have history. If he touched you...well, let's just say that it's not something I would forgive," I bluffed. I held little power over Simu, but Luca's argument irritated me.

"And once you were married to him, how much weight do you think your lack of forgiveness would hold, especially if it pitted him against a direct order from his *şef*? If your father ordered the kill, you couldn't stop him. You wouldn't be able to leave him for it, either," he stated nonchalantly.

"Okay, fine, you're probably right," I replied, throwing up my hands. I gave up disputing him and trying to defend the indefensible. It's not like I didn't know what Simu was really like. The man's ambitions resided in darkness. No, the real reason behind my snippiness was that I didn't trust Luca's motives for returning.

He'd turned to me for comfort, but afterward, he'd stayed away for days, only showing up once he'd heard about my engagement. Sure, he *said* he'd forgiven me, that he'd struggled and wanted to take me back, but what broke him was my engagement to Simu. That wasn't the behavior of a man who really wanted me.

I gritted my teeth. I was no better than a fuck doll being fought over by two snot-nosed boys, and I was done with it. Done with being volleyed back and forth between men like a disposable toy. First Alex, next Luca, and then Nicu. Luca again. Now Simu and maybe Luca yet again? They were impossible, and I'd had it.

Pressing my hands to his chest, I declared, "You don't really want me, Luca. Admit it, you only came here tonight because of Simu."

His expression darkened. His eyes morphed from silver to a stormy gray.

Burying his fingers in my hair, he crushed his mouth to mine. A ferocious, claiming kiss. My core clenched, growing wet and needy. Damn the man. He knew what he did to me.

This time, I refused to be so easily swayed.

Grinding down against my mound so that I felt his hard cock, he spat out, "Does that feel like I don't want you?"

I shoved at his broad shoulders. "You know that this is about more than sex."

"You're damn right it is," he growled. "Why are you rejecting me?"

I slapped my hand hard across his chest, catching his nipple with my nails. He inhaled sharply, lust flaring in his eyes. I had to douse his lust fast. Otherwise, we'd end up fucking, and that would be the end of my resistance.

"Because I've been treated like a-a-a *thing* that can be tossed from man to man without any say. You're no better than any of them—my father, Cristo, Simu—barging in here and bossing me around. Your main motivation for coming here wasn't that you loved me, that you couldn't live without me. The only reason you're here is because of the engagement." I glared up at him, putting as much grit as I could in my tone. "Nothing you've done makes me believe that you're here for *me*, so yes, I am rejecting you."

He jerked back in surprise.

Sheesh. Finally.

Shadows crossed over his eyes. "I'm Romanian, and you know what we're like. Jealousy runs hot in our veins."

"Oh, I know," I griped.

"But I also love you, Cat. I want you as my own. If I walked away from the blood bond, do you really think I only came back because of Simu?"

My eyes narrowed into slits. He sounded suspiciously sincere, but I wasn't buying it. Actions spoke louder than words. I loved him, and the stakes were too high for me to risk binding myself to him under these circumstances. He'd only come to me when he was upset, and even then, he held back on his secret. I didn't begrudge him that, but he had yet to make a move that signaled he loved me. And that's what it would take for me to choose him.

"Oh, please. Stop it, just stop it." I pushed and shoved, wiggling until he moved off just enough for me to slip out from underneath him. Scrambling away, I tucked my knees into my chest, and glared at him.

He got to his feet and paced the length of my room. "God, this is such a clusterfuck." Whirling around, he stopped at my bedside, pointed at me, and accused incredulously, "You don't believe me."

I snorted and tightened my hold on my knees. "No. I don't."

"What will it take to prove it to you?" he asked. He was about to say more but thought better of it and sealed his lips shut.

Prowling closer, he slapped his hands on either side of my head and leaned in.

"Tell me," he commanded.

"You really want to know?" I snapped back defiantly. "Save Cristo so I don't have to marry Simu and don't ask anything in return. Not the fulfillment of the blood bond, not marriage, not my love, nothing."

His reply was instant.

"Done."

Gaze burning into my face, it glided down to my nose, my mouth and then snapped back up to my eyes.

"You want your freedom? Then I free you of any obligation under the blood bond. I don't need a bond, a marriage certificate, or any-fucking-thing else. I just need you and I'm going to win you back, Cat. It wasn't over after you betrayed me, and it isn't over now. Don't for a goddamn second think it will ever be over."

"That's exactly what I think will happen," I retorted.

Enough with the pretty words, I wanted action. But my demands were excessive. Save Cristo and not demand anything in return? That wasn't how *mafie* men worked, and I didn't think Luca could do it.

"Just go," I pleaded.

His lips swept over mine in a heartbreakingly tender kiss. Then he threw on his shirt and slipped out of my window.

I flopped down on my bed, staring up at the ceiling. Now that he was gone, I let go of my bravado, and the tears flowed, dripping down the sides of my cheeks. In my heart, I wanted to believe in fairy tales. I wanted to believe that Luca would go out and slay the dragons, bringing back the prize of Cristo's safety and his heart to lay it at my feet. But what I had asked for was insane, and I'd learned at the ripe old age of twelve that in the underworld of the *mafie*, there were no heroes. Only monsters.

28

"It's about time," Nicu piped up when I laid out my plan of how to win Cat back. "Finally, you're manning up."

I threw daggers at him with my eyes. My little brother existed to annoy me. Glimpsing over at Alex, who was sitting beside Tatum on one of the couches in my living room, I figured that was most likely how he felt about me. Good, annoying the hell out of each other was proof that everything was right in our world.

My nocturnal visit to Cat yesterday had been a revelation on several fronts. First off, I had no idea Cat could be so stubborn. In my hubris, it hadn't crossed my mind that she would be anything but thrilled at my declaration. Considering the alternative was a lifelong marriage to Simu, I assumed she would fall on her knees with gratitude. Turned out, I was an idiot.

Her refusal revealed her integrity, which confirmed that her snooping had been an aberration of character. That she was willing to defy the blood bond and accept a life sentence with Simu was remarkable. And irritating as hell. I was hoping that she believed in me enough to know that I would protect her brother and set her free from Simu.

Cat was a sheltered teenage girl, and yet she stood up to the challenge, making a decision that carried a high toll of sacrifice. I was touched that she was partly motivated to protect me from Simu. I chuckled to myself. As if she could hold sway over a monster like him. The man had no soul. That, and the very idea that the fucker could get to me, were ludicrous.

After listening to her, I realized that I had come off as unfeeling and relentlessly focused on Simu. Since it was clear that nothing I said would change her mind, I decided on a tactical retreat. But I wasn't giving up. It was obvious that she loved me, but she was scared. I could relate to that, so I'd prove myself to her. Not only would I fulfill her demand, but I'd raise her one. There was only one thing Cat cared about, outside of her family and me, and I was going to get it for her.

But first, we needed to set up a meeting with Nelu.

"He's going to gut us," Tatum predicted, rapping his fingers on his knee as he calculated the potential cost of my plan.

"Isn't that the point," I retorted.

We were going to ask Nelu to side with us and break the engagement with Simu. Since we'd be giving him enough money to satisfy most of his debt with the Hagi clan, there was no doubt it would work. After Nelu paid off what he could, Alex and I would fly out to Cali to negotiate with the Hagi boss for Cristo's life. To pull this off, my brothers and the Popescus needed to believe that I was ready to go through with marrying Cat, which I was. Once Cristo was safe and I killed Simu (because that fucker was living on borrowed time), she and I would decide what was best for us. If she still wanted her freedom, I'd give it to her.

Alex side-eyed him. "Money's not an object. It's worth it, if only because it's the first time Luca capitulated to one of my demands," he said slyly.

"And we'll do right by our custom of the blood bond," Nicu added. "You can't put a price on that."

"You're obsessed with this," I complained.

"Hey, I'm not the one who fucked a *mafie* virgin. That was you," he launched back at me.

"Alright already, let's do this before something comes out of your mouth that makes me change my mind," I snapped. "Or beat you to a pulp."

"Ha, you wish," he replied.

"I'll set up the meeting," Alex stated. "Simu is going to be furious. Our offer will satisfy Nelu, but no amount of money is going to placate Simu. This will be the second time you'll have taken Cat from him. Only blood will satisfy him. Specifically, you bleeding to death."

Tatum nodded in agreement. "Simu will leave us no choice. We'll have to take him out."

"If we do that, we'll start a war. He's like a son to Nelu," Nicu argued.

Having thought about this long and hard through half the night, I proposed, "What if we set him up to come after me? Then, when I'm forced to kill him, it will be self-defense."

Alex stroked his chin, thinking. "That might work, but he could also kill you in the process. Mama would never forgive us if you got offed, even if it was unintentional," he teased.

"Ha ha, you're a riot today. Nina must've been extra

giving last night to put you in such a damn humorous mood," I taunted.

A smug smile spread over his face. "Nina's the most generous woman in the world. No one can top her, and yes, last night was particularly...enjoyable. I will never be accused of leaving my woman unsatisfied."

"Yeah, were you fucking her against the front door or what? I could hear you in the hallway on my way home," Tatum griped.

Alex guffawed and slapped his knee. "A gentleman never tells."

"Christ," muttered Nicu, clutching his head. "Stop already."

"Wait until you find the right woman," Alex challenged. "You'll be more obsessed than the two of us combined."

"Never happening," he grumbled. "I will not end up neutered like you and Luca."

"Famous last words, brother," murmured Alex with a grin.

Returning to business, Tatum asked me, "How are you thinking of getting Simu to attack you?"

"I'll set up a meeting with him. Only the two of us in an isolated location. Taunt him about having won her back. He'll go rabid because he's a brute with half a brain. We fight and I kill him," I responded easily.

"That's problematic. There's a risk he could kill you. Of course, you can handle yourself, but the man's a menace. This isn't the time to get cocky and underestimate him," Alex counseled.

"I think you underestimate *me*," I said, with a curl of my lip.

Did he think I'd let Simu walk out alive? Never going to happen.

"I want Nicu present, but at a distance," Alex concluded. "He's got the best sniping skills so, worst-case scenario, he'll be there to shoot him down."

I sent Nicu a scowl. "I don't need help."

"Too bad, you're getting it anyway."

"Fucking fine, then," I grumbled.

"I will contact Nelu to set up a meeting to hash out our differences so that the marriage goes forward. I will argue that Simu is too biased to be involved in the negotiations, and that you and he need to meet on neutral ground to squash this feud, once and for all. Whether he tells Simu or not, it will work to our advantage. If he doesn't say anything, you'll have the element of surprise. If Nelu does, Simu will be seething over the burn of losing her. By the time you two meet, he'll be easy to provoke."

Nicu turned to me and asked with mild curiosity, "How are you going to handle her? When she finds out that we've negotiated the marriage to go forward, she'll be furious with you. She won't come willingly to the marriage bed."

A stab of guilt sliced through me. I hated lying to my brothers, but I had no other choice. She would be coming willingly or not at all. Unable to say the truth, I mislead him by saying, "She wants me to prove myself, so I'm going to give her the one thing she covets."

"What could that be? So help me God, don't answer with 'me,'" he said.

"Of course not. I know what makes her tick. What will make her feel seen," I answered enigmatically.

My little brother had no patience and no finesse, and he hated surprises. Not telling him served my daily goal of pissing him off. Nicu waved his hand in a gesture of *tell me more*.

"You'll just have to wait and see," I goaded him as I waggled my eyebrows at him.

"Fuck you," he rumbled out.

"Enough," cut in Alex as he grabbed his cell off the coffee table. "Let me call Nelu and set it up."

I WALKED under the scaffolding of a deserted warehouse in Rockaway Beach until I found the paint-chipped, rusted double doors. Rattling the doorknob, I yanked hard on one of the doors. It scraped over the sidewalk as I shoved it open enough for me to slip through.

"Christ," I breathed out, shielding my eyes from the shafts of light streaming in through the broken windows, glinting off the corroded steel beams of the roof. The scent of decay and dust hung in the air. Between rows of concrete columns, the cement floor was littered with debris from teenage parties: dozens of bottles, an old, urine-stained mattress with the stuffing coming out, and an abandoned shopping cart, of all things. Near a stack of empty metal barrels, I kicked at a lone cleaver with a jagged edge. I could only imagine what role that makeshift weapon had played in someone's life...or death.

I waited, scanning the building across the street, making out the small bump on the roof that was Nicu's prone form. He was well camouflaged. The only reason I spotted him was because I knew to look for him. The August heat in the stuffy warehouse was sweltering. I cursed Simu. Of course, the fucker would make me wait.

The familiar scraping of the front entrance alerted me to his presence. He stepped into the warehouse and stilled when he saw me. Eyeing him critically, I noted his height and the breadth of his shoulders. With brown hair and blue eyes, he wasn't ugly, although his face was a little too narrow and his nose a little too long. Unlike the Lupu men, he wore a pair of loose jeans and a black short-sleeve shirt, unbuttoned down the front to show off the gold chain with a cross swinging from his thick neck.

"Your brother managed to bribe Nelu into giving up his daughter once again. The man has no morals. You already rejected her twice. And the second time..." He shook his head. "So public. So humiliating. If you cared for the girl at all, you'd leave her alone."

I snorted. "Leave her alone for you? I think not," I replied dryly. "That's the beauty of being a Lupu. We have infinite resources, connections, and wealth. We always get what we want. Whereas you're a two-bit player hanging onto the coattails of a family that's going down the drain."

"Cat will hate you for forcing a marriage on her," he threatened.

I made a scoffing sound. "Don't worry about me, worry about yourself. I do whatever the fuck I want to do, in spite of my brother and my clan. You're the one who isn't man enough to keep her," I jeered.

"Typical arrogance from a Lupu, thinking you're entitled to anything you want regardless of who you destroy along the way," he spat out.

I pulled back. "What the hell are you talking about? Unlike you, we didn't grow up with a silver spoon in our mouths. We fought for every bit of power we have, unlike you, you *Cantacuzino*," I derided. "You're the one who came from an aristocratic family. The famous Byzantine family, with the Cantacuzino Palace on Victoriei Avenue in Bucharest. Yet, didn't your last prince abandon the homeland during the Second World War and take off for Sweden?

Hmm, wasn't that a convenient escape, right before the pro-Soviet government was installed."

He shot me an eviscerating glare. "Oh, my side of the family was not so lucky. We stayed and suffered through decades of misery, like everyone else. It didn't help that your father partnered with mine only to cut him off at the knees. As revenge, my father attacked yours on the road back from your grandmother's village and was slaughtered in a nearby birch forest. His body left to rot like a mongrel dog instead of the *şef* of a prestigious family with a legacy that goes back a thousand years. And me, his son? Without protection, I resorted to common thievery in the streets with the riffraff, until Nelu saved me."

"What the fuck are you talking about, you madman? Me, my brother, and father were attacked by a rogue Roma clan," I blurted out. There was only one attack he could be referring to, and it was the one where my father was shot and sent us into the forest to hunt down the perpetrators.

"That was to cover his tracks, you ignorant fool. Your father recognized mine that day. How could he not, having personally stabbed him in the back. The selfish bastard cheated him on a big job they'd partnered on, raked up the money, and fled the country. How do you think your father had the funds to establish himself in America?"

Fuck, that explained so much about Simu's unrelenting hatred toward us. He didn't know that Alex and I killed his father. Even now, I had no idea who pulled the trigger. Not that it mattered. Whether Cantacuzino or Roma, his father's life was forfeited the moment he attacked us on that empty road. A shiver coursed down my spine at the spray of bullets that rained down on us that day.

"He attacked us, Simu. It was kill or be killed. We had no

choice. You know that, and yet you've been holding this over our heads all this time," I said, incredulous.

Lunging at me, he grabbed my shirt. "Yes, goddammit. Your clan's success rests on the destruction of mine. Now, after all these years, the time for retribution has come, and you're going to pay for it."

With his strong hold, he had the leverage to swing me around, but before he could do anything, I popped my hand over his and caught his baby finger, the weakest part of his grip. Nice and quick, I twisted my shoulder and thrust his hand away. Shoving him off me, I tossed him to the ground and got into a defensive stance.

Simu leapt to his feet, dirt tracking down the side of his face, and rammed his shoulder into my gut, shouting, "You little pussy, you are so dead. Get ready for the pain."

My back slammed against a concrete column, but I threw him off and put distance between us. Circling around each other, we bobbed and dodged each other's punches. I miscalculated and my shoulder hit a column as I moved out of his swing. Simu's hand shot out and grabbed my throat. His choke hold tightened fast.

I had a short window of time before I blacked out, so I jammed my forearm in the crook of his elbow. Throwing all my weight forward, I snapped down hard. The instant his hold broke, I grabbed his nape and spiked my knee into his gut.

Stunned, he toppled to the ground. But he recuperated quickly and swiped his leg at me from below. I jumped over it, but his hand shot out and grabbed my leg. I crashed to the concrete floor with an *oomph*. He pounced on me, this time with a double grip around my throat. Shit was getting hectic now. His grip tightened, halfway crushing my trachea.

Bucking with my hips, I slapped my palm on the filth of the floor. Nails scraping the grit, my fingers touched the handle of the discarded cleaver. Stretching to get a good hold of it, I used my other arm to punch up between his arms but couldn't dislodge him. He squeezed and black spots blotted my vision.

At the last instant, my fingers curved around the cleaver. I swung hard. There was a swooshing sound as metal sliced the air.

"*Gaaah!*" Simu choked out as the cleaver struck his shoulder blade. The impact made an awful sound.

Blood sprayed into my eyes.

His agonized scream pierced my eardrums.

Nicu busted through the double doors as I rolled Simu off me. Groaning, Simu planted his hand on the ground and swayed to his feet. He bent over, the cleaver sticking out of his shoulder. Blood dripped to the ground.

"*Pula mea*, you sliced me, motherfucker."

Nicu stalked him from behind.

"We're going to do more than that," I warned. Nodding to Nicu, I said, "Remember that ambush on the road to Bucharest when Alex and I were on vacation as kids? We killed his father."

Nicu's face turned to stone, his blue eyes morphed into dark, soulless pits of coal. I recognized that look. He was mentally gunning for a kill.

"You wanna do it or should I?" he asked, but we both knew the question was perfunctory.

Getting up to my feet, I riffled my hands through my hair, showering blood on myself. I swiped it off my face. "Nah, you go for it."

I had to give Simu kudos for not acting like a pussy. He didn't run or cry or beg for his life. Then again, he knew this was a mercy killing. We could've tortured him for days for trying to murder me.

Simu bowed his head. Nicu lowered his sniper rifle, pulled out his favorite black and gray Kimber Rapide, and let off a single shot to the back of the head. The loud popping sound reverberated through the cavernous warehouse.

Simu crashed to the ground with a hard thump. I winced as his body hit the floor.

It was done.

Putting away his gun, Nicu stared down at the prone body and asked with mild curiosity, "What do you think Cat's going to say when she finds out we killed him?"

"We tell everyone it was self-defense."

He raised a brow at me. "Is she getting the same story?"

I shook my head. "She gets the truth. I'm not starting our life together with a lie. Fucker was a ticking time bomb. After finding out that either Alex or I ended his father, he would've never stopped until we were dead. She understands our ways, so she'll see the necessity of our action."

Staring down thoughtfully at the pool of blood spreading beneath Simu, he said, "I'd love to be a fly on the wall and see how that plays out between the two of you. He's Cristo's best friend and tight with the family. It's going to be one hell of a fight."

Extracting a plastic bag from his suit pocket, he shook it out and bent down to wrap Simu's head to avoid leaving a conspicuous trail of blood behind when we moved the body. We had to transport his body to the cellar of the café for Nelu to pick up. Normally, we'd have gotten rid of him but, closed casket or not, Nelu would want a proper burial.

"I can already tell you how it will end up," I retorted,

hooking my hands beneath Simu's armpits, and pulling his torso up with a grunt as Nicu grabbed his legs.

"Oh yeah? And how is that?" he asked as he heaved up Simu's lower body.

"With her beneath me and screaming my name," I crowed as I shuffled forward. "Fuck, he's heavy."

"Dead men always are," he supplied helpfully.

We got his body into the back of an unmarked truck and cracked jokes as we made our way back to our family-owned café in Sunnyside. Nothing like a fight and a kill to bring brothers together. A glimmer of hope passed through me as we drove along the tranquil residential streets, the body bouncing around in the back of the truck as we bumped over potholes.

Phase one was done with. Now, on to phase two. Hopefully, the second part of my elaborate plan would compensate for what I had done to Cat's beau.

29

I glared at Luca across the living room of my parents' home, eyes slitted in fury. *The man has lost his mind if he thinks he can bulldoze his way back into my life.* The waning sunlight filtered in through the windows, accentuating the vivid golden highlights of his hair. I ground down on my back teeth in simmering rage. Lounging back in the armchair like a king on his throne, he returned my glare with a smirk. God, I wanted to smack that smug grin right off his gorgeous face. It was one of the rare times I'd seen him without a tie. With a couple of buttons undone, I caught a glimpse of smooth skin. Why did the bastard have to look so good without even trying?

The coffee table was covered in drinks and food. *Bunică* was making a statement, showing Luca respect with her bounty of traditional dishes. She really pulled out all the stops. Besides the different plum brandies, *țuică* and *palinca*, she had made her famous stuffed cabbage leaves, *sarmale*. The scent wafting off the *mici*—grilled minced meat rolls— made my stomach grumble, but I refused to partake. Instead, I lifted my nose at the food, showing my displeasure at my grandmother, who I knew was lurking around the outskirts, peeking in to eavesdrop. I might be acting like a spoiled child, but I refused to be bribed with my favorite food.

Slapping his knees with both hands, my father stood up and gestured to my mother to follow him. "Let's leave the lovebirds alone to get reacquainted."

Rising to her feet, my mother smoothed her skirt and gave me a narrow-eyed look, her message loud and clear. I should be nice and *make this work*. Those were her exact words to me earlier, right before Luca showed up at our doorstep. Despite my father's anger and grief over Simu's death, he resigned himself to the loss when he found out the details surrounding Simu's death. There were rules, and this had been a clear-cut case of kill or be killed. I was grateful that I wouldn't have to marry him, but that didn't mean I was going to fall into Luca's lap.

Like I'd predicted, he failed my test. My eyes narrowed on him again. *Asshole.*

My mother was relieved that our family name would be restored, and my father got a chunk of change to pay back enough of his debt to hold off the Hagi. More than anything, they were grateful that Luca and Alex had stepped in to save Cristo. This new appreciation for Luca only served to irritate me further. My parents assumed that his visit meant the marriage was back on. If he thought I was going to marry him, he'd lost touch with reality.

With one last warning glance my way, my mother slipped out of the room, leaving us alone. *Bunică* popped her head in, nodding encouragingly before retreating.

Silence descended.

The tension was thick, but I refused to break first. Crossing my legs and folding my hands over my knee, I waited. He could try to pressure me as much as he wanted, but it would be nothing more than a sham marriage. I didn't even have to have sex with him again, since everyone and their brother knew he'd already taken my virginity.

Luca broke the silence. "Are you done pouting?"

I averted my eyes because the urge to claw his beautiful cold ones rode me hard. *Bastard.*

He picked off nonexistent lint from the linen of his pants and let out a tired sigh. "I see. I'm getting the silent treatment."

I rolled my eyes condescendingly. "I'm sure we covered all the bases. What more is there to say?"

Placing his hands on the armrests, he raised himself up slowly, almost as if he was in pain. I watched him indignantly as he crossed the room and took a seat beside me. Stretching his neck a little, he absently massaged it. Close up, I saw the outline of bruises in the shape of fingers around his throat.

I bit down on my gasp. God, Luca had been in real danger if Simu had choked him hard enough to leave marks. Luca's thick neck looked unbreakable, and yet those faint bluish shadows spoke to how close he had been to losing his life. I gulped around my suddenly tight throat. Unlike most *mafie* women, I'd witnessed a man getting choked to death. Luca's face was superimposed on the image branded in my mind. The back of my eyes burned. My anger burned off, and I could feel my resolve was about to follow.

I asked, "Are you okay?"

It came out husky. I cleared my throat and wet my lips. That last movement brought Luca's gaze to my mouth. The flames in his eyes burned right through me, like fire.

"Yeah, I'm good. It was touch and go for a few moments, but I managed to beat him off me."

"God, I don't even know what to say, Luca." My voice dropped. "What if you had died?"

He waved me off. Of course, he did. "Nicu flew through the door like an avenging angel. I wouldn't have died." His perceptive eyes sharpened on me. He leaned in and asked, "Why, Kitty? Would you have missed me?"

I threw up my hands. "Of course, I didn't want you to die. Isn't that why I made my pact with Simu?"

"That wasn't my question."

I dropped my hands and fidgeted with my skirt. Giving him a bland look, I said, "Sorry, what was the question?"

He returned my look with a baleful one. Embarrassment crawled up my throat and I clasped it to try to hide my emotions. Having fair skin was the worst in moments like these.

Gently, he pulled my hand off. "I like seeing the pink. Gives me a glimpse of what your ass will look like when I give you a punishment."

I jerked in my seat. *A punishment?* The center of my chest went up in flames. My core, on the other hand, got wet in anticipation.

"Oh, I love how dirty you are. I can't wait to have you back underneath me," he drawled, his eyelids dropping to half-mast.

"Is that all you want from me?" I snapped.

"Don't be ridiculous. I'm not hard up for partners, and I don't risk my life for just any woman. We have chemistry. I was only stating the obvious. Now, back to my question, and in case you want to pretend you don't remember, let me remind you. Would you miss me, beautiful?"

I toyed with my hair and then checked my earrings, anything to avoid his question.

His hand snaked underneath my hair, gripped hard, and

pulled my head back. His lips grazed across my cheek. In the shell of my ear, he growled, "So much pride. You won't admit it."

I quickly suppressed the moan trying to claw its way out of my throat.

"No," I hissed. "You don't deserve it."

"I could slip my fingers between your luscious thighs and find out for myself just how much you missed me," he threatened. Instantly, my thighs clamped shut.

He yanked at my hair.

"Yield," he demanded.

"Never!" I sneered back at him. "You may have saved Cristo, but I'm still forced to marry you, and I resent it."

He brought my face closer to his and snarled, "Who's forcing you to marry me? Your parents?"

Shoving my face closer, I gritted out, "You. My parents are acting like it's a done deal."

"Oh, baby, I had to tell Alex that I'd marry you to give Nelu the money to pay off his debt for Cristo, but I gave you my word. I won't marry you until you beg me to."

I stopped breathing. He'd completed every one of the tasks I'd set out for him and given me complete power over my future. No one had ever done that for me.

"You lied to your brother for me? He'll be furious," I observed.

He shrugged. "It's nothing I can't handle. Anyway, I have one more thing for you..."

He released my hair. Leaning back, I eyed him speculatively and asked, "Oh, and what is that?"

"I got you into Barnard for the fall," he stated succinctly.

My pulse pounded hard. "I'm sorry, I thought I heard you say you got me into Barnard."

"That's right. I have an associate who knows someone

who knows someone..." He waved his hand. "You'd be surprised what money can buy. Long story short, I got you on the top of the waiting list when, lo and behold, a student withdrew and now you're in."

I shook my head slightly. "I-I didn't even apply," I stammered out.

"I got your SAT scores, which were impressive by the way, and your grades. The rest...well, I may have written your essays and completed the application for you. Oh, and you have an interview next week. It's a requirement for your attendance, but I'm confident you'll pass with flying colors. I've received the list of questions the interviewer uses off her computer."

My jaw dropped as he nonchalantly pulled out his phone and poked at it.

"You hacked into the school computers?"

Without responding to my question, he replied, "I emailed them to you."

My brain was reeling, trying to process everything. He'd given me everything I asked for and then some. It didn't have to do with my family or our marriage or our relationship. It was solely for me and my happiness.

Stunned, I blinked my eyes.

I licked my dry lips. His eyes snapped to them again.

"How much money?" I croaked out.

"That's none of your concern. You're not indebted to me. Consider it a wedding gift, if you like," he teased with a wink. "You wanted me to prove that I love you, that I see you, that I know what makes you tick, that I'll go to any length for you? There it is. I want you to be happy, with or without me." He lifted his index finger. "That was by no means an admission of defeat. I'll do anything for you, kitten. I'll lavish you with my love. Oh, and I also have this," he pulled out a black velvet box. "To request your hand the right way."

I was already shaking my head in denial when he dropped to one knee and propped it open. It was a gorgeous, and huge, solitaire in a delicate four-prong setting with a tapered platinum band.

"I thought you said you'd wait until I begged you."

"That was posturing. I'm not letting you go without a fight. Now, be quiet so I can do this right." He cleared his throat and gazed into my eyes, which even on his knees, were just above mine. I felt the white-hot love pouring out of what others thought of as cold silver eyes.

"Cătălina Popescu, I love you. Would you do me the honor of spending the rest of your life with me?"

Between the look in his eyes and the sincerity in his voice, but especially in his actions, I believed him. He wanted me. More than paying for school, a man didn't take the time to forge boring college essays unless he was serious.

Taking the ring out, he held it up to me with a question in his expression. He swallowed audibly. That had to be the first and only time I had seen Luca almost...flustered.

My tummy fluttered and I shivered with pleasure. Stifling a wild laugh, I gave a dramatic sigh, wiggled my fingers in front of him, and said breathlessly, "After all the effort you've gone to, I suppose I could give it a try."

Taking my hand, he placed the ring on my finger and kissed my knuckles. Then, he swept me off the couch and onto his lap and wrapped his arms around me tightly. "You won't regret it." He peppered kisses over my face. "I won't ever let a day pass when I don't prove myself to you, sweet girl."

Hooking my arms around his neck, I nuzzled into the

crook of his throat, inhaling his delicious scent. I went limp with relief. For the first time since Cristo convinced me to spy on Luca, I stretched my lungs and took in a full breath of relief. I tightened my hold around him and let out a little squeal of joy.

"We're going to get married! Oh my God, I have to tell Jewel," I said, pulling away to grab the cell beside me.

Tensing his hold on me, he said, "Hold up, take a minute and breathe before you run away to do something else, and...tell me you'll move in with me." His voice dropped a few octaves. "I missed you, baby."

I cast my eyes down. "We shouldn't tempt fate. The first time around, we did things in the wrong order and look where it got us. Like opening an umbrella inside, it triggers bad luck."

He huffed out an exasperated laugh. "That's a trivial Romanian superstition, it's not real. The blood bond is a legitimate union."

"Not as legitimate as a wedding," I countered.

"Still, it's been hell. I *won't* live without you," he growled, dropping kisses down the side of my face and nipping at my earlobe. "It's too long to wait for the big wedding over a *month* away." He gave a dramatic sigh.

"You're getting bossy again," I scolded.

"You like me bossy," he retorted.

"Sure about that?"

He captured my lips, trapping me in a hedonistic kiss that had me moaning into his mouth.

Pulling away, he replied, "I'm sure."

Playing with the button of his shirt, I smoothed my hand down his hard chest. "It would be safer if I didn't."

"Fuck safe, baby. I need you with me. Promise me that you'll come home now. We can order takeout and eat in bed and go over the course catalog," he cajoled, burrowing his nose into my hair. "The first year has general requirements you'll need to fulfill."

My heart melted. "You already know that there's a required curriculum?"

"Yeah, for first-years," he confirmed.

I caught the glint of the diamond ring on my finger and my eyes stung. My dream of going to college was coming true, and it had everything to do with this stubborn, sexy man. This man who loved me enough to let me go and gave me every reason to come back to him. My gaze returned to his, and I said, "Yes, Luca, I'll come with you."

EPILOGUE

I n the end, we eloped.

At her parents' house, I somehow managed to convince Cat to come home with me. Considering I didn't deserve it, it felt like a walking miracle when we stepped down the stoop of their house, carrying a suitcase in each hand. And home we went to Westchester. We needed to reconnect and recharge our relationship. I wouldn't stand for the inevitable interruption from one of my brothers or Tatum, so I spirited us away to the place where we'd first met.

I did everything in my power to make her happy, but one little problem cropped up. Cat was bothered that we weren't married. It took a while for me to pick up on it, since it hadn't been an issue the first time around. She received a nasty tongue-lashing from the *mafie* gossip mill. There was some vicious talk on a private group chat. Screenshots were made and sent to Cat. It had put her on edge, which, amid her excitement at starting school, was saying something. I was both livid and helpless since I couldn't intervene on her behalf. Whatever shit went on between the women was generally out of our hands.

One night, I woke up to her sniffling in the dark. I wasn't about to have my woman crying in our bed and decided, right then and there, that we would have *our* wedding. *Our* ceremony. One that was free from petty negativity. Afterward, we'd have the big wedding everyone was itching for, but I wanted us to have a moment that was only for *us*, without the bullshit that was typical of weddings. Well, at least big *mafie* weddings.

The next morning, I declared my intentions to a red-eyed Cat, and the smile that broke out on her face brought me to my knees. I ate her out and then fucked her on her hands and knees before we got dressed and went down to City Hall to fill out an application. With marriage license in hand, we walked out together, and I drove her to school. We had to wait a mandatory twenty-four-hour period.

Afterward, I called my brothers, Tatum, and Sebastian to let them know that we'd meet at City Hall the following day. Alex would bring Nina, and Sebastian would bring Emma, my half sister. After discussing it, Cat decided not to tell her family. She texted Jewel, whose response was practically hysterical. She was a good friend, and thank fuck, because I wanted Cat to have someone by her side. Although, I shouldn't have worried, because Nicu texted Tasa, who came down from upstate New York with her husband.

Friday morning, we got up bright and early. She wore a white summer dress with Romanian red embroidery on the front and the cuffs, her hair falling in long waves. I wore a dark suit, as I did most days, and added a red pocket square to match her outfit.

We skipped up the steps of City Hall to the bronze door with the words "New York State Building" emblazoned on top and made our way to the marriage bureau. Everyone was already waiting outside. My brothers and Tatum slapped me on the back. Tasa gave me a pat on the cheek, which was patronizing considering I was older than she was.

Cat and I went inside to present our identification and take a ticket. When we returned outside, the women surrounded Cat while the men encircled me.

Nina stepped away for a moment, came up to me, and kissed me on both cheeks. "We didn't bring crowns. That's for the religious ceremony, but I did bring this." From behind her back, she brought forth a delicate crown of small flowers with ribbons flowing down, like they would've had at a wedding in my grandmother's village. "I wanted to ask you first before presenting it to Cat."

My eyes sought out Alex's, and I gave him a nod of gratitude. My voice came out scratchy when I replied, "Thanks for checking with me. She'll love it."

She gave me a bright smile and bounded off to Cat, who let out a little shriek when she saw the crown of flowers.

"You did good marrying her," I said to Alex, knowing what a hard road it had been for him to shake off the burden of family tradition and marry an outsider. Not that Nina ever felt that way, having lived next door to us and been my sister's best friend since she was a toddler. Until Nina came into his life, I hadn't realized how heavily the mantle of power sat on his shoulders.

"Thanks, *fratele*," he said gruffly. Throughout my life, I saw Alex as an impenetrable, unmovable force that I had to fight or differentiate myself from, but he was simply a man in love. Like me.

Nicu, my bratty little brother, smacked me lightly on the

chest. "You did it. It's a goddamn miracle, but you finally did something right."

"Shut up," I grumbled good-naturedly. Not that we would ever stop arguing but revealing to him the cracks in our father's character and killing Simu together had solidified our relationship.

"Can't wait till it's your turn to fuck up with a woman," I joked.

His eyes slid over to Jewel, standing beside Cat. They returned to me as he swore, "That's never going to happen."

His eyes gravitated back to Jewel.

"Good luck with that," I said.

Tatum held out his arm and we gave each other a man hug, slapping each other heartily on the back.

"I could never have done what you did," he stated gruffly, referring to the blood bond.

"That's only because you don't know how to draw outside the lines," I replied with a smirk.

"I'm proud of you and how far you've come," he declared.

Sebastian came and congratulated me. Shaking his hand, I stared at him and Tatum, and said, "It's good to have all my brothers here."

The clerk called out our number, and we entered as a family unit. Greeted by light-blue walls with pink molding and a modern-style chandelier, we approached the marriage officiant waiting for us at the podium. Our family and friends fanned out around Cat and me like a protective band as she started the ceremony.

I took Cat's hands in mine, letting every ounce of everything I felt for her pour out of me.

From the office windows, beams of crisp sanctified sunlight sparkled in the air. Hushed silence descended.

Staring into each other's eyes, it was time to exchange our vows.

The officiant asked, "Is there a witness?"

Alex stepped up confidently. "That would be me."

Nodding, she turned to me and began, "Will you take this woman as your wedded wife, to have and—"

"Yes," I growled, cutting her off. Facing Cat, I said the words I'd memorized. "I, Luca Lupu, take you, Cătălina Popescu, to be my lawfully wedded wife, to have and to hold, from this day forward, for better, for worse, for richer, for poorer, in sickness and in health." Then, eyes blazing into her, I veered off script. "I will protect you and love you until my last breath. I fucking love you, Cat. I'd die for you. I'd burn and kill for you, and I'll be by your side till death pulls me from your arms."

I heard Nicu choke behind me, but my gaze remained on her face.

Her velvety, warm eyes anchored me with adoration as she replied, "I, Cătălina Popescu take you, Luca Lupu, to be my lawfully wedded husband, to have and to hold, from this day forward, for better, for worse, for richer, for poorer, in sickness and in health, until death do us part. And I'm crazy in love with you, too. You have my heart forever."

My head swam, my ears buzzing so loud I didn't hear another thing the officiant said until, "... and you may now kiss the bride."

No need to be told twice, my fingers fisted the back of her head to hold her steady as I buried my tongue in her wet, hot mouth. One long kiss was not enough. I wanted more. So much more. I let out a frustrated growl, and Cat responded with a soft whine of need.

"Mine," I swore on her lips before pulling back.

If no one was present, I'd have pushed her into the green

banquette seats lining one wall and claimed her, because now, she was mine completely. There were no barriers left. Nothing to keep us apart. We had it all. The blood bond. The wedding. Sure, we'd have another one for our families and to shut up the mean old ladies, but this was for us.

From here on out, our fates were sealed. She was mine and I was hers. Forever.

EPILOGUE TWO
NICU

I slapped my hand on the flimsy door beside Jewel's head. The clap shook the wood in its frame, the sound reverberating in her dorm room. That wasn't the only thing that'd be shaking by the time I was done here.

"I don't fuck gentle, and I have no intention of starting now. I'm going to fuck you till you're screaming my name like it's God's."

Bright hazel eyes flashed up to me.

"Is that supposed to scare me, Nicu?" she taunted. "Because I'm not one of your little *mafie* virgins. I know how to fuck."

Curling my shoulders inward, I bent over her and barked out a laugh. "Wait till you meet my demon cock, little girl. You *think* you've been fucked right, but you've never been fucked by the likes of someone like me."

Stepping closer, she eliminated the couple of inches between us and bared her teeth at me. "You arrogant prick. Bring it, then, because from what I've seen, the men who brag the most, fuck the worst."

"What do you know about *men*?" I scoffed before fisting

her hair in my grip. I yanked it back hard, banging her head against the door. My lips smashed down on hers, devouring her red lips like I'd wanted to from the instant I saw them.

She pressed them together tightly, denying me access.

That was a no-go.

She wanted to test me? Fucking go for it. I wasn't backing down a motherfucking inch. Gripping her jaw, I pried it open for my invasion. This was why I never wanted a virgin or a staid *mafie* wife. Because I fucked dirty and I fucked hard. The moment I spotted the wicked curves of her tits in my club, I knew that sexy body could handle anything I threw its way. And when she tossed her head and shot me a look of challenge, I knew *she* could handle anything I threw her way. Her body may have piqued my interest, but her haughty look had sealed her fate.

"Make sure you're ready," I warned against her lips, "because we may be in a building full of women, but I'm not subbing you out."

Jewel pulled against my tight hold on her hair.

"Let's see if you even know what to do with that precious dick of yours," she taunted just before flicking my lips with her tongue.

Her comment almost made me laugh. Almost. The time for words was over, so instead of answering, it was best to go ahead and start domesticating this wildcat.

I attacked her mouth. Teeth clanged together, catching skin. The tang of iron flooded our mouths, but neither of us stopped. She gave as good as she got, because her nails came out, raking down the side of my neck, eliciting a deep groan from me. Little kitty was coming out to play. Who knew what else was buried in that devastating body? She tangled her fingers in the longer strands at my nape and dragged me closer, crushing my mouth deeper.

My hand raked up her bare thigh, dragging her dress up and cupping her pussy roughly. Fuck, that's wet silk. Mother of God, she was ripe for me. I couldn't wait till I got my fingers between those slick, plump lips. Griping the gusset of her panties, I ripped them down her legs and thrust two fingers past the knuckles. Tight and wet, just the way I liked it.

She jerked in my hold, taking in a sharp inhale of breath. Maybe I should've paused, but I didn't. Her supple, moist flesh clamped down on my digits and she started riding the heel of my hand. Mother*fucker*—she was as filthy as I was. Her nails scraped down my buttoned shirt, ripping at them until the shirt was half torn open. Then she fumbled with my buckle.

Tearing my mouth from hers, I threw a glance over my shoulder.

Bed.

Batting her hands out of the way, I caught the back of her thighs and lifted her up. Stalking to her bed, I threw her down. She bounced a few times before catching herself.

With a scathing look and a growl, she got to her knees. Spread wide, chest heaving, eyes flashing, she looked glorious.

"I'm not a fucking doll," she snapped.

"No, you're right," I said, pausing as I stripped off my tie. Eyeing her narrow single mattress, I found nothing to tie her to. "You're my new fuck toy. My dirty little whore. Are you going to be a well-behaved slut for me, Jewel?" Her eyes flared wide with lust. I took a step closer. Then another. Clutching the back of her neck, I pressed her face into my chest as I leaned down to whisper in her ear, "Or am I going to have to tie you up to keep you still while I suck on your clit? It's your choice. I'll always give you a choice, 'cause I'm magnanimous like that."

I felt the muscles of her slim throat shift as she swallowed hard. I pulled back to watch her, gazing down into her expressive eyes. "Baby girl, you have to trust me to know what you need. I'm rough, but my endgame will always be to make you come. Either by my hand, my tongue, or my cock, but you *will* come."

When she tipped her head back, I saw a bit of the lust fading from her eyes, reality streaming back in. Damn, did I regret it. I liked this girl wild for me. I thumbed her plump bottom lip, opening it slightly and slipping two fingers into her mouth.

I pumped in and out a few times before pulling them out and gripping her chin with my wet fingers.

"What is it?" I demanded with a little shake.

Remaining silent, she averted her eyes.

"Use your words, Jewel."

"We shouldn't be doing this..." she trailed off. "Cat would be hurt."

My fingers slid down her throat and cradled the delicate column in my palm. I tilted her head up until her eyes met mine. There was guilt, but there was desperation as well. She wanted this there was no doubt of that. We wouldn't have ended up here otherwise. She knew I was her best friend's fiancé the instant she met me, and yet, here we were.

"If everything goes to plan, Luca will be feeding Cat his dick right about now."

"Ugh, you're so crass," she griped.

I chuckled, "Yeah, I am, but don't pretend you don't like my nasty mouth. Stop overthinking it. As of now, you turn your will over to me. I'll decide what we do, when and how we do it. Understand?"

Her eyes returned to mine and searched them. The light coming from the streetlight outside her window streamed in, basking her in a dusky glow. The hazel irises of her eyes stood out like a riot of meadow wildflowers. I held my breath, waiting for her. My fingers instinctually tightened around her throat the longer she remained silent. The humidity from the hot city night seeping in through the window exhaled a sultry breath. The noise of cars driving along Broadway intermingled with her erratic pulse beneath my finger pad. A deep, heavy beat throbbed between us.

I pushed the strap of her dress off her shoulder, exposing the beautiful slope of her full breast. My palm caressed it, cupped it. Weighed it. I tweaked her nipple, causing her lush body to jolt against mine. That was enough for me. Guilt was making her hesitate, but we both knew I was in control. Just to prove my point, I gave the tip of her tit a sharp smack. She inhaled harshly, her mouth hanging open. Pants escaped, the rough and low needy sounds exciting me.

"What'll it be, Jewel? I don't have all fucking night to wait before I push my cock into your tight paradise. And I will be inside you, have no doubt of that."

Canting my head to the side, I continued, "Want to know my plans for you? First, I'm going to lick that pussy. Play with your little pearl between my lips. Then, I'm going to slurp down the come you smear on my face when you lose control and ride my mouth. I'm going to consume you so many times, you'll collapse on the bed limp. And you? You…"

I gripped the thin material of her dress and tore it in half down to her navel. A ripping sound slashed through the air. "You're going to have to earn my cock with orgasms before I allow you to take a single inch of it. You think you can do that for me, pretty doll?"

Chest heaving, she stared down in shock as the dress slinked down the sides of her body and pooled at her hips.

Her eyes snapped to me, blazing a kaleidoscope of colors.

Then she did something so goddamn beautiful, I almost faltered in my resolve to make her wait.

She threw her shoulders back, pushed her chest out, and intoned the one and only word I ever wanted to hear come out of her mouth. "Yes."

And there it was.

The consent I was looking for.

Game. Fucking. On.

Thank you for reading THE RECLUSE HEIR! I hope you loved meeting Luca and Cat. The next book in the Lupu Chronicles dark mafia series is The Savage Heir.

I am Nicu, **the savage heir of the Romanian *mafie* Lupu clan.**

I love rules: following them, imposing them, *enforcing* them.

CLICK HERE TO READ THE SAVAGE HEIR >>

Sign up to my newsletter to find out more about what I'm up to or when I have new books!

A war is brewing between love and duty...which shall triumph?

CLICK THE CHOSEN HEIR, Book One of The Lupu Chronicles.

"Sexy Mafia read! Monique Moreau knocks this one out the park. Alex is what dreams are made of. He command's the room and doesn't back down from anyone but her." – 5 Star Review

Here's a taste...

"Fucking hell," I gritted out as I read the text over my grandmother's shoulder. Tasa was safe and she begged us not to look for her. *Really, Tasa?* As if I'd leave my baby sister to hang out to dry, regardless of whether she'd run away from home or not. Oh, and had she conveniently forgotten about her fiancé, Cristo? And what part of the term "dangerous enemies" had not penetrated her thick skull, despite my relentless repetition of that threat?

Bunică gave a nonchalant shrug of her skinny shoulders and a grin that showed off her gold tooth. That woman could get her teeth fixed a thousand times over, but she wasn't one to put on airs. As she always said, "I was born a peasant girl, and I'll die a peasant girl."

Peasant girl, my ass. She was as sharp as they came, and while she loved to ham it up with her country ways, she'd graduated from Romania's finest medical school. No lie, she could dig out a bullet and sew up the wound in under half an hour. It had come in handy on more than one occasion, when the doctor on our payroll didn't arrive quickly enough.

"What is she thinking?" I spat out. "She's roaming the country doing God knows what. No protection, no body-guard, no—"

"Oh, hush, you act as if Tasa's an invalid instead of a smart young woman who can take on the world with one hand tied behind her back. She'll be fine. And you best leave her alone," she warned, poking at my chest with her bony finger.

I stared down at her, incredulous. Leave my sister to roam the country unprotected? *Is she insane?*

"Christ, *Bunică*, she's a female. Alone."

My eyes rolled up to the kitchen ceiling, seeking patience, as I took a seat on one of the stools scattered around the island in the kitchen of our family home. This was where *Bunică* practically lived so this was where family members came to talk to her. Was I the only rational one in this conversation? It wasn't like she didn't know who we were. It's not like she wasn't acutely aware that our enemies would start crawling out of the woodwork to kidnap Tasa.

"A *lone* female," I reiterated, emphasizing the word "lone" in hopes of getting through to my grandmother. "Of the *Lupu* clan." My gaze passed over the midnight-blue double oven range my father had imported directly from Italy when he busted out the back wall and extended the kitchen to please his mother and wife. The chrome from the state-of-the-art appliances gleamed under the bronze farmhouse lights.

We are the Lupus, the Romanian upstarts who quickly rose to the top of the New York City mafias. The speed of our rise was a point of embarrassment for the Bratva, the Russian mafia, and the main reason why they're so intent on destroying us. As for the Italians, they were a shadow of what they were before the takedowns and trials of the '90s. Which had left a vacuum for my father to fill when he arrived in New York, solidifying our foothold in Sunnyside, Queens. Better known now as "Little Bucharest."

Returning my attention to *Bunică*, I reminded her, "Enemies? Remember them? Why do I need to mention this? It's not like you don't know what I'm talking about. She's in real danger."

She let out a cackle as she whipped out a bottle of *palincă*, a traditional Romanian spirit from the region she came from. Plunking down two small glasses, she poured two shots and pushed one over the kitchen island to me. The other, she threw back like a pro.

"What's obvious to everyone but you and your mother is that Tasa is her own woman. She's smart, and she's not going to get caught by some two-bit *mafie* idiot. She'll be fine."

I narrowed my eyes at her. She was too relaxed by far, considering her youngest grandchild had just run off to god-knows-where.

"What do you know?" I demanded.

Fluttering her wrinkled hand weakly in front of her chest, she lied without a shred of remorse, "Who? Little old me? Why, nothing!"

"You're as deceitful as the day is long," I snapped, my patience finally fraying.

"Back off," she warned, her innocent features turning dark. *Ah, there's the real* Bunică. "I don't happen to know anything, but if I did, you bet your last dollar I wouldn't tell you. I won't help you drag her back here and keep her prisoner until she marries that worthless *tâmpit*, Cristo. *Uck.* He's barely a man. And he has a little two-bit hussy of a side piece. Each of you must marry in the *familie*, but why him? *Bah!*"

"You're unbelievable, you know that, right? Come on, out with it," I insisted, flicking the fingers of my open hand at her.

"Like I said, my lips are sealed." She made a gesture as if locking her lips together and flinging away an imaginary key.

My jaw clenched. Women. The bane of my existence. And those two stuck together like super glue. It was hopeless on my part to try to sever the unbreakable.

"Fine, then," I replied, releasing a long, exhausted breath. "You're not the only person I can press for information."

Her hand nabbed the sleeve of my jacket, crushing the fine wool between her bony fingers. "Leave that poor girl alone. You know she's in love with you. Don't you dare take advantage of her."

My grandmother was talking about Tasa's little best friend, the beautiful, supple Nina, of course.

Nina.

Damn, that girl. Smelled like jasmine and a hard fuck waiting to happen. Just the thought of her brought crackling heat to my skin and a stiffness to my cock. That woman was my Achilles' heel, if ever there was one. Sweet as could be, with large brown eyes and a chest I could face-plant in and suck on for days on end. Annnd...

And she's also like a sister to you, asshole.

Not.

There wasn't a shred of brotherly feelings toward that little minx. Unless one included the taboo kind.

Laying my forearms heavily on the smooth wood of the kitchen island, I warned, "*Bunică*, it's Tasa we're talking about here. My little *sister*. For some insane reason, you don't think she's in jeopardy, but I happen to know exactly what our enemies are capable of. I know exactly what they do during a torture session. Once it's out that she's gone, finding her and using her to get to us will be at the top of their list. This is like a nuclear arms race, during the Cold War." I tapped the watch around my wrist. "Time is ticking, and I can assure you that this won't finish well. Least of all for Tasa. Who's going to want to marry her if she's tarnished? Think about that and come talk to me when you've regained your common sense."

"*Băiețel*, don't speak to your *Bunică* like that. I wiped your bottom when you couldn't even feed yourself. Any man should be grateful for the chance to marry my little girl."

I snorted out an exasperated sigh. I hated it when she called me *little boy*. Deciding it was in my best interest to pretend I didn't hear her last comment, I bent down low and dropped a kiss on the crown of her head. "Do you think I enjoy this? Do you think I enjoy having to lay down the law and act like an enforcer with the people I love?"

"You *do* enjoy it," she shot back. "You always think you're right. In that way, you take after your father. Regardless of what everyone in this family thinks, he wasn't a saint, you know. He was human, and he made his fair share of mistakes."

Yeah, right. She always said that, but it was never quite believable. The man was a brilliant businessman and strategist. He loved his family and was the paradigm of how to behave in our twisted world. He was honorable to his core. If I could live up to half of the man he'd been, I'd die content. Which brought me back to the issue at hand: Tasa's marriage.

"I've been negotiating with Nelu on this marriage contract between Tasa and Cristo for *years*. It's more than a simple wedding, as you well know. What's going to happen when he finds out his future daughter-in-law ran away? It will be perceived as a stain on his honor. It could legitimately lead to war when we've only just begun our truce.

Not only is business booming, but Tata would be disappointed in me. I gave him my oath that I would do everything in my power to make this happen. There's too much on the line," I finished with a frown.

The responsibility of taking care of my family fell heavily on my shoulders, but on days like today, the weight was crushing. Although *Bunică* was whip smart, the truth was she couldn't relate. She'd always been taken care of. First by my grandfather, then my father, and now me. She could afford to focus solely on the personal, not the big picture. No, that fell on me.

"Pfft. And so you had to sell Tasa to do this? Of all people, you chose to sacrifice your little sister?" Reproval shimmered in her eyes at me.

"*Tata* would've commended me for it. *He* would've thought it was a brilliant move. With the Popescus, Tasa will be taken care of. She'll be protected. And it would solidify a peace that's eluded our families for decades."

Bunică stared at me like she was about to spit on the ground. "Don't make it seem like you're doing this for Tasa, Alex. It's beneath you to lie."

"I *am* doing it for her," I ground out, fists balling at my sides. Christ, this old woman was never satisfied. She was spoiling the girl with notions of love. Our life was based on duty and, for women, that included the duty to marry a man chosen by her family. As the boss or *șef* of this family, I might be given a leeway regarding this rule. But for a princess of marriageable age like Tasa, it was unthinkable.

"She's the baby of the family. The Popescus, curse their name, are worthless mongrels. Animals. Unlike the Lupu clan, they didn't gain power until the fall of Communism. That's a blink of an eye in the span of history, and you sold your precious sister to those heathens?"

I snorted. "They're powerful enough now; I can tell you that much. We can look down on the Popescu clan all we want, but only a fool would underestimate their potential to do damage. They're *vicious*. Ruthless. You know this as well as anyone." It was also common knowledge that their tempers were like hair triggers. One wrong move and *kapow*. I made a dismissive wave. "In any case, it's done. My hands are tied. There's nothing I can do but retrieve her and make sure her marriage goes off without a hitch."

She stalked up to me. Barely five feet tall, she went toe to toe with me and spat out, "Then, you will get no help from me. I will do everything in my power to thwart you. The marriage be damned."

"You're impossible," I heaved out, throwing up my hands. "You know the situation."

When Tata was bleeding out in the ambulance roaring through the quiet streets, his dying wish had been for me to take care of the family. I'd already failed on that promise, with Tasa stranded somewhere out there, alone and vulnerable. Possibly hurt. My back teeth ground together at that last possibility.

The second oath had been to reconcile our family with the lowbred Popescus. I didn't disagree with *Bunică* that every one of them was a bottom-feeder. No education, no class, no nothing. Violence was their greatest attribute. The two families had been at each other's throats for generations, clawing their way to the top by throat-punching the other. We may be at the pinnacle, but they came in at a close second.

Nelu, their *şef*, and Tata were always vying to be the top dog. Tata often said that it was too late for their generation, that there was too much bad blood. But at his death bed, he declared, "There needs to be a marriage. It's the only way." Those last words were the proverbial nails in my coffin.

"Go back to your fancy apartment in Columbus Circle, Alex. I don't want you under my roof until you come to your senses."

Goddamn, this woman was impossible. She refused to acknowledge the possibility of a looming war. Instead, she was banishing me to the penthouse floors of the two towers of the Time Warner Center building in Manhattan, where my brothers and I lived.

Tasa had moved in with Nina a few avenues over, in a nice high-rise building overlooking the Hudson. Of course, Tasa, always with the rebellious streak, couldn't share an apartment with her twin, Nicu. Oh no, our building was too snooty and fancy for her. And Tasa was as opinionated as the day was long. Thank Christ, she had her little best friend living with her.

My back teeth ground down harder, my fists flexing by my sides, but there was nothing I could say when *Bunică* got into one of her fits. Turning on my heel, I marched out of the kitchen, grabbed my coat from the hallway closet, and stalked out of the house. What in the ever-loving fuck?

Tasa gone.

Contract in ruins.

Potential war on the horizon.

Everything I'd worked for gone.

Gone.

I was an abject failure. No, I refused to let that stand. I didn't care what it took to make this right. I'd fulfill Tata's oath. I'd drag Tasa back by her hair to marry the Popescu if need be. I'd make my father proud if it fucking killed me.

If you loved THE RECLUSE HEIR, you'll love my steamy, bad boy biker series, the Demon Squad MC. Start this new series now with Kingdom's Reign.

Or read about Alex's little sister, Tasa, in Whistle's War, a biker-mafia romance novel.

A Mafia princess on the run. A Bratva prince turned biker. Will their love start a war?

Here's a glimpse of Tasa and Whistle's story...

Tasa checked the cell phone in her clenched hand for the hundredth time. Her excruciating audience with Alex in his upstairs office was over. *Finally.* Once again, her eldest brother had overreacted. Simply because he was the head of the family, he assumed he could rule over every single aspect of her life. *The nerve of him, giving me an order like I'm a child.*

Tasa fidgeted as she once again glanced out of the bay window of the Dacia Café, the center of her family's world. She couldn't wait for Nikki to pull up to the curb so she could get out of there before she stomped back up the stairs and wrung Alex's neck. Leaning forward, she spotted the ubiquitous black Mercedes pulling up on the quiet 43rd Street. Quiet in comparison to Queens Boulevard, the bustling commercial center of Sunnyside, Queens.

From behind, she heard a scuffling sound. Her mother moved forward, giving her a quick last hug from behind. Twisting around in her seat, Tasa returned her embrace and lifted her left cheek for a quick peck. "See you later, Mama."

A stern frown descended on her face as she gently

chided her mother, "I'm not happy that you didn't stick up for me once with Alex. He's such a brute."

Her mother caressed her hair. "Darling, you have to settle down. You're too energetic, and you'll be graduating in the spring. It'd be one thing if you wanted to pursue a career in opera, but we know that's not your desire. What better way to move on to the next phase of your life but with a husband? Because with a husband, soon comes children."

That last part was the crux of her mother's never-ending argument.

Tasa rolled her eyes. "Always with the children."

"Children give meaning to a woman's life," her mother crooned.

"Not every woman," she grumbled under her breath, but the Mercedes was pulling up to the curb, and really, she had zero energy to continue this endless discussion. It's not as if her mother ever budged an inch from her notions of femininity and womanhood, all of which circled around being a wife and mother. Rather, she cudgeled her only daughter with them. Sure, that had worked out fine for her mother. She'd married the love of her life. Growing up in a small village in the valley of the Carpathian Mountains, she'd been utterly fulfilled by her role, but that wasn't Tasa. Not that anyone in her family seemed to care. She could've escaped those expectations with the opera. While she was a decent alto, she wasn't any more interested in pursuing an intensive career in the opera than she was in shackling herself to a man at the age of twenty.

Hitching her Dolce & Gabbana handbag over her shoulder, Tasa slipped out of the café, leaving behind the clinking of porcelain coffee cups on small saucers, and took in a deep breath of brisk, cold winter air.

Yanking the Mercedes passenger door open, she slid onto the leather seat with a sigh of relief.

"Tasa, are you trying to get me in trouble?" griped Nikki, giving her a side-glance with a small scowl.

"Oh, hush, and just drive if you don't want him catching you," she replied. Her control freak of a brother believed a princess like her shouldn't be seen in the front seat, beside her chauffeur-slash-bodyguard. There was a certain level of decorum to maintain. For Nikki's sake, she usually took the back seat when she came home to visit, but she was holding on to her temper by the thinnest of threads as it was.

"*Dragă mea*—"

Oh, sweetheart. Nikki always resorted to his mother tongue when he was upset.

"Don't *dragă mea*," she snapped as she dragged the seat belt over her chest and clipped it in. She didn't need his pity, the primary sentiment coming off his endearment. "Hit the accelerator already so we can get out of this godforsaken neighborhood. Then he won't see you."

He squeezed her knee briefly. His hand didn't linger, but Tasa was well aware of Nikki's feelings. It was only natural he should crush on her. After all, they spent so much time together, and she'd finally grown into her figure.

But he'd never cross *the* line. He might be family, but she was a princess. A princess was supposed to marry a prince. *Gag.* The thought of Cristo made her stomach turn. He was a good enough guy, if you were into the clean-cut bro type. Well, as close a version to that as a *mafie* prince could get. She'd known him since they were in diapers. Being only a few years older than her, they hung out in the same scene. The idea of kissing him was about as appealing as kissing her twin brother, Nicu. And Cristo was half in love with his little side piece, a cute girl named Una. There was no way she was marrying a guy who was already in love with another woman. She didn't expect him to give up on Una, and Tasa wasn't the sharing type. Of course, she couldn't divulge any of this to Alex. If he found out, Cristo would be in trouble with his old man. More importantly, she was afraid of her own reaction if her brother responded the way she predicted. *What, Tasa? You think men are loyal. You think Tata never cheated on Mama?*

Grrr.

Seriously, the less she knew about the way *mafie* men lived their lives, the better. A second family was probably out there somewhere, with kids who sported the same deep-brown eyes as she and her beloved father. She shook her head. Again, not something she wanted to know. With three overbearing brothers, she didn't need additional stepsiblings creeping out of the woodwork. She could barely breathe as it was, with the ones surrounding her.

Nicu was her other half in many ways, but he was far from perfect. And he got to live a normal life because he was a male and he was Alex's good little soldier boy. Luca, her middle brother, might be the black sheep, but he had all the liberties he could possibly want. Pressing her lips together, she focused her gaze outside the window at the passing brick townhouses. Her eyes began to burn. Luca. She sighed, as she often did when she thought of him. Such a tortured soul, with everything so bottled up inside.

That one, she was going to miss.

"What's wrong, babe?" Nikki asked. "What happened in there?"

She let out a weary sigh.

"What do you think happened?"

She'd gotten her marching orders.

"Be a good little girl and fall in line like everyone else.

The Lupu family are a bunch of empty-headed dunces, all walking to the tune of their pied piper, Alexandru Lupu," she grumbled.

The *Lupul*, or the Wolf, as people called him, was the puppet master, pulling the strings of the mafia family from America to Paris, Milan, Bucharest, and beyond.

Blood was blood.

Duty was duty.

Orders were orders.

Blah, blah, blah. She felt like gagging after the number of times she'd heard that litany throughout her life.

"Sorry, babe. When he gets an idea into his head, he won't let it go."

"You can say that again," she conceded as she swiped at a rogue tear. "I'm impressed you even went that far." It was unusual for Nikki to say *any*thing against Alex. Suggesting stubbornness, while completely accurate, was borderline betrayal in a secret society where loyalty was the be-all and end-all. Another reason Nikki had never so much as tried to kiss her. It wasn't even the idea that he might be murdered for such an infraction. He'd simply never cross that line. Lupu allegiance was implacable.

He may not have been born a Lupu, but she knew there was some sort of ancient, secret blood ceremony that made him as good as blood. Fucking her would be the equivalent of incest, regardless of what the tenting in his pants told her. Considering she wasn't in love with Nikki any more than she was with Cristo, she didn't push it.

That, and she didn't want to get Nikki killed.

"He catches me at one club and comes down like a dictator," she grumbled.

"Babe ... it was the kind of club. And the fact that you

escaped from me. You could've gotten killed ... or worse. What were you thinking?"

Nikki was talking about the sex club she's gone to with her best friend, Nina. So sue them; they were curious little virgins. Unfortunately, Alex had found the selfie Nina posted, sitting at the iconic bar. A selfie that included part of Tasa's shoulder, which bared her Lupu tat of a wolf. In the darkness and the strobe lights, Nina hadn't noticed and posted the pic. A pic Alex happened to view on her Instagram feed.

Oh, boy, did all hell break loose that night. And so began the lockdown. Other than attending her classes at Juilliard, she could go to the apartment she shared with Nina and home in Sunnyside. That was it. Now, she couldn't even shake Nikki off her tale.

But if everything went according to plan, things would be irrevocably changed in a few short days. She wasn't a Lupu for nothing, and as her *tata* had always said, "You have to fight for what you want in this life."

Damn straight.

He wasn't the only relentless person in her family. For instance, it took her for-ev-er to get any action between the sheets, but she'd managed in the end. It had taken seducing one of her vocal instructors to finally learn her way around the male body.

At the end of the day, she'd kept her virginity intact, something she was coming to regret. Her verdict, after her little adventure, was that sex was *way* overrated.

Which is why she'd ended up in Tribeca at the infamous sex club NSFW with Nina. Her curiosity had been piqued by the idea of something beyond vanilla. She'd already done every vanilla thing on her non-intercourse sex bucket list during her brief affair and had walked away with little enthusiasm. A few hours at the sex club, on the other hand, and she'd seen things that made her toes curl.

Nikki dropped her off at the lobby of the high-rise on 68th Street overlooking the Hudson and went to park the car in the underground parking. Entering the apartment she shared with Nina, she dropped her keys in the little crystal-cut bowl on the small Louis XVI wooden table in the vestibule. Part of the deal of getting the apartment near Juilliard, instead of commuting from Queens every day, was to have Nina come live with her and to have her mother decorate their apartment. Of course, she'd decorated it like a Prussian aristocrat from the mid-nineteenth century. Hence the old-people's furniture scattered around their apartment like at an auction house instead of posters of Degas dancers or Callas like in the Juilliard student dorms.

The apartment's best feature was the wall of windows overlooking an unimpeded view of the Hudson and the Jersey coast beyond. Throwing her coat over another atrociously overwrought sofa, Tasa kicked off her high heels and threw herself down beside Nina.

"How was it?" asked Nina without bothering with a greeting. A little furrow dug between her dark, fine winged brows.

"Jellie, are you?"

"Over Alex? Hardly," she scoffed. "I'd never be jealous of you."

"Mm-hmm," replied Tasa noncommittedly, tossing waves of her long brown hair over her shoulder. Nina was head-over-heels in love with Alex, although she felt the need to deny it in deference to their friendship. They'd been best friends since the day Nina tottered across the broken sidewalk from her house to Tasa as a toddler. While Tasa had the ability to get Nina out of her shell and Nina was her number-one partner in crime, her friend was really a gentle soul inside.

"He's like a brother to me," muttered Nina.

Double lie.

"Just because we joke that we must've been switched at birth in no way means there's a shred of sibling-like feelings between the two of you," Tasa fired back.

God knows both of them would've had easier child-hoods if they'd been brought up by the other's household. Nina's mother was a badass who prodded Nina to take life by the balls, while Tasa's mother continually bemoaned her daughter's lack of ladylike manners. At least Tasa had *Bunica*, her grandmother, to serve as a buffer between her and her mother and Alex.

"It was disastrous. I swear the man thinks he's my father, and he acts worse than a tyrant. Besides the boring lecture about my reputation, which I truly think he actually believed, he gave me an ultimatum. Either the opera or marriage ... to Cristo."

While this was no huge surprise, Nina's eyes squeezed together in commiseration.

"No," she breathed out. Nina's loyalty was solidly behind Tasa, but she always believed the best in Alex, no matter how irrational he acted. Which was why Tasa had to keep every detail of her upcoming jailbreak from Nina. It hurt to lie, but realistically, the woman would crumble in under five minutes in Alex's presence.

The theoretical scene played out in her mind. Alex would wrap his arm around Nina's shoulder, bringing her in tight to his side to woo her into feeling safe with him. Nina, a softie to her core, would instantly melt against him. She'd look up at him, batting those absurdly long lashes of hers. He'd grace her with one of his beatific angel-slash-devilish smiles, and she'd turn into a puddle of goo. Game over. She'd gush like a bad oil spill in the Gulf of Mexico.

Tasa clenched her fists. *Pathetic.* Her oldest brother got everything he wanted, anytime he wanted.

But not this time.

If she had any hope of escaping her predicament, she had to play it smart. And Tasa could pride herself on that much at least. She may not be respectful or obedient, but she was nothing if not conniving. She'd been fantasizing about this for years and plotting its execution for months.

"You always expect him to act decently," she reprimanded Nina, laying her arm over the intricately carved, gilded wood curling up from the top of the couch. Her eyes drifted toward the windows, sunlight splashing through the panes and highlighting the jewel-like colors of the Persian rug across the floor. That was another thing about Romanians. Rugs everywhere. Almost every inch of their apartment was covered in intricate silk rugs.

"He's a decent guy inside. Granted, you have to dig *deep* sometimes, but he disappoints me when he acts like this. I expect better from him."

Tasa let out a little snort. "Good luck with that. He's such a hypocrite. The bedroom in his apartment is a revolving door of women, but he expects me to remain chaste and turn my virginity and life over to my husband at his command. As if."

"Well, there's the other option."

"Yes, be part of the bastion of high culture. What about giving me a chance to figure out what *I* want to do? I'm only twenty years old. You'd think I'd be given a few years to *live*. To travel the world and explore. Who knows, maybe I want to be a fashion designer."

Nina tipped her head to the side, her lips pressed

together to suppress a laugh. Nina wouldn't dare laugh in her face. She was too polite and kind for that. "Do you?"

"No." Tasa huffed. "What about an organic-apple farmer in Upstate New York? Does it matter? The point is that because he has the imagination of a flea, he's only come up with two options, and I'm forced to follow one of those. It's arbitrary and absurd and ... and ... insane! Like him!"

Another thing she'd never told Nina. That she'd changed her major to experimental dance. Her family would have conniptions if she turned away from a refined career singing opera to experimental performance art, or what they'd mockingly describe as twisting and flopping around like a dying fish on the floor.

"It's because he was so young when he was thrust into his position as head of your family and of that business empire," defended Nina. "It doesn't help that your brothers immediately knew they wanted to follow in his footsteps."

"It's not like we don't live in the twenty-first century," she threw out.

"You know he doesn't think that way. Your parents instilled in him the same idea every immigrant has. Come here and make something of yourself. You can't just have a random job. No, you have to be a doctor, a lawyer, or something crazy impressive like alto for the Metropolitan Opera."

Fiddling with the two tassels dangling from her silk blouse, Tasa muttered, "Whatever."

Nina peered into her face, watching her with a concerned expression. "So, what are you going to do?"

"I have no idea. I have one more semester at Juilliard. That gives me a little more time of freedom."

Liar.

Tasa knew exactly what she was going to do. She'd checked with the bursar's office, and after three weeks of school, she could get fifty percent of her $30,000 tuition refunded to her bank account if she withdrew. And that was exactly what she was going to do. Then she'd disappear and make her way to the source of cutting-edge experimental dance, Madame Pierrette's dance company in Montreal, Canada. Everyone who knew anything knew of the notoriously exclusive workshop she hosted every spring. A workshop Tasa got accepted to. It was close to a miracle and she wasn't going to pass up the opportunity of a lifetime. Alex be damned.

MORE BY MONIQUE MOREAU

The Lupu Chronicles

The Savage Heir (Book 3)

I am Nicu, the savage heir of the Romanian *mafie* Lupu clan.
I love rules: following them, imposing them, *enforcing* them.

Nicu

As the last son of the Lupu clan, I would never dishonor our
name or tarnish our reputation. But Jewel is neither *mafie*,
nor a virgin.

With no rules to temper my savage nature, it's no hold's bar
when it comes to her.

And the fact that she's my fiancée's best friend?
Means absolutely *nothing* to me.

Jewel

I made a terrible mistake, hooking up with my best friend's
fiancé. Those frosty blue eyes and dominant nature were a
deadly combination I couldn't resist.

Not only do I loathe the traditional *mafie* culture he comes from, but guilt over my mistake is eating me up inside.
I threw him out, swearing to myself that it would never happen again.
There's just one problem...he won't leave me alone.
I have a stalker on my hands, only I'm not sure I hate it.

The Perfect Heir (Book 4)
The Bastard Heir (Book 5)
The Princess Heir (Book 6)

Fans of sizzling hot, alpha bikers will love...

The Demon Squad MC Series

Kingdom's Reign
Cutter's Claim
Loki's Luck
Stanton's Sins
Puck's Property
Whistle's War
Her Hidden Valentine,
a Demon Squad Novella